PRAISE FOR ZANE LOVITT AND *THE*

WINNER, NED KELLY AWARD FOR BEST
SYDNEY MORNING HERALD **BEST YOUNG AUSTRALIAN** NO...
LONGLISTED, COMMONWEALTH BOOK PRIZE FOR BEST FIRST BOOK, 2013

'Beautifully written, elegantly crafted tales that not only demonstrate a command of the short story as a form, but also dark humour and biting wit...There's poetry in the formal structure of its various moves, as well as a precise attention to the rhythm of the prose. There's also a striking rendition of people and place...*The Midnight Promise* is a superb debut and may just be the best Australian crime fiction of last year.' Sue Turnbull, *Sydney Morning Herald*

'What makes Dorn such a compelling narrator is that for all his decrepitude he has a reflective spirit and an insightful eye...An often brutal, yet brutally reflective, examination of the human condition.' *Australian*

'Crashes straight into Temple, Corris and Chandler territory... You can recommend *The Midnight Promise* by the back cover— Text has it nailed.' *Australian Bookseller & Publisher*

'Stylistically reminiscent of Quentin Tarantino's *Pulp Fiction* or *Kill Bill*...The writing is sharp, the scenarios are well conceived, suitably violent, stupid or pointless and very funny...*The Midnight Promise* is an exciting and original debut.' *The Hoopla*

'Flat-out one of the most enjoyable crime books out there. Australian noir with a nod to Raymond Carver...You'll put the book down wishing for more.' *Readings Monthly*

'Lovitt's on-the-brink-of-self-destruction antihero, acute talent for low-life scenarios and convincing desperado dialogue has him treading Temple turf. A writer on the rise.' *Qantas Magazine*

'If you like hard-edged fiction, then *The Midnight Promise* is for you...A fine book. Read it with the light on and the lock on the door.' *Weekly Times*

'A notable, confident first novel. Intelligent, never ponderous, *The Midnight Promise* wears the battered fedora of the crime genre with stylish ease and moves at a brisk pace.' *Australian Book Review*

'Whip-smart...Delivered in short, snappy chapters, each detailing a different case, and the ending is so good it will feel like a lesson in breakneck speed reading. An extraordinary debut.' *Mx*

Zane Lovitt lives in Melbourne. *Black Teeth* is his second book.

BLACK TEETH
ZANE LOVITT

TEXT PUBLISHING MELBOURNE AUSTRALIA

textpublishing.com.au

The Text Publishing Company
Swann House
22 William Street
Melbourne Victoria 3000
Australia

First published in 2016 by The Text Publishing Company

Cover design by W. H. Chong
Page design by Jessica Horrocks
Typeset in Bembo 11.3/15 by J & M Typesetting

Printed in Australia by Griffin Press, an Accredited ISO AS/NZS 14001:2004 Environmental Management System printer.

National Library of Australia Cataloguing-in-Publication entry
Creator: Lovitt, Zane, author.
Title: Black teeth / by Zane Lovitt.
ISBN: 9781925355147 (paperback)
9781922253736 (ebook)
Dewey Number: A823.4

BLACK TEETH

For Tunko

PART I

AFFIDAVIT

The doorbell. It ground out a weak metallic chime but it was loud enough. A raw breeze cut against his neck, alien weeds slithered beneath his feet. They grew across the porch unchallenged, up from the cracks in the tiles but mostly from a small yard that hadn't felt the love for a decade, a cartoon of neglect. Beyond the iron paling ran a footpath hemmed with itchy-bomb trees; further beyond ran the afternoon traffic that didn't judge the now-woeful state of a once-resplendent two-storey terrace. He tugged his tie with a gloved hand, glanced again at the precariousness of his footing, flinched at a sound from within: a creak, maybe a footfall. The man straightened, on parade.

The door fell back just inches to reveal a tiny, dispassionate eye. An unseen mouth said nothing.

'Hello. Mister Alamein? Rudy Alamein?'

No response. Just the eye.

'Mister Alamein, I'm with Fortunate Insurance. My name is Anthony Halloway.'

Still nothing. It was not clear that the man inside had heard. The eye merely blinked. Beyond it was darkness.

'I believe you contacted our office this morning for a quote on our Prime Life cover. I've brought you a copy of the policy and I'm here to answer any questions you may have.'

Anthony Halloway sucked his lips and raised his eyebrows: his politest method of demanding a response. The tiny eye blinked more, blinked faster. Then the door opened.

Rudy Alamein was perhaps the same age as Anthony Halloway, perhaps in his later twenties. He wore a woollen jumper too short in the sleeves and tracksuit pants too big at the waist, held them up with a fist on his hip and they were stained with something purple, maybe beetroot. A few tufts of red hair sprouted from a smooth, enormous cranium. The tiny eyes in there continued to blink against the daylight.

Anthony smiled with relief. 'Good afternoon.'

'I already spoke to…somebody called me.'

Rudy's voice was weak, like that of a much smaller man sitting inside his mouth.

'Somebody called you today?'

'Like…before.'

'And if I may ask, what was the upshot of that conversation?'

'Ummm…'

'Did you purchase a policy with us?'

'I said I'd think. Think about it.'

Anthony performed a pantomime face of disappointment and a short bow.

'In that case, Mister Alamein, I seem to be wasting your time. Unless you have any further questions?'

The big head shook, but with a confusion, as if Rudy didn't quite know why it was shaking.

'Well, thank you,' Anthony said. 'And we hope to be hearing from you soon.' He turned to assess the return journey to the sidewalk. Whatever path had once existed could no longer be seen through the wooden tangle of foliage. He'd taken three long steps in retreat before he heard again that high voice, just barely above the urban ambience.

'Ummm…'

He stopped, rotated awkwardly.

Rudy said, 'Did you say…have you got it with you?'

Anthony raised his right hand. It held a briefcase. 'Sure do. Would you like to read it over?'

'Is it long?'

The honest answer was, 'Yes.' He said: 'It's our standard contract.'

Rudy snorted and murmured something, then beckoned with a flap of his hand. Anthony made the return strides to the porch, over-came his gracelessness with a brush of his lapels and smiled his way inside.

The door closed, engulfing them in black. He was about to holler in protest or even panic but the lights came on: only Rudy and a swarm of old furniture scattered mindlessly around a reception room, what had once been a formal dining room. The bay windows hid behind heavy brown curtains and the air was thick with dust you could taste. Rudy led the way along the hall, holding up his pants.

'There's one thing that you need to be aware of,' Anthony said as he passed an armoire, a credenza; other European words. 'The benefit is capped at one-point-five million. While your premium will continue to rise with inflation, the benefit will not. That needs to be clear.'

No response from Rudy. They passed a set of carpeted stairs that steeply climbed the south wall then curved out of sight. Anthony's gaze lingered but there was nothing more to see.

The kitchen plumed with the scent of decay, vaguely rancid, plainly organic. Anthony's stomach sent up a distress signal and he poked at it, stifled a belch, while Rudy continued wordlessly past a large benchtop above which grey saucepans hung from a cast iron gallery. The grey colouring wasn't by design, was a dust veneer undisturbed for an age.

A heating duct in the corner administered no heat; the insurance man gave thanks for his gloves and jacket.

Rudy sat into a cane chair over a circular table where a half-eaten bowl of cereal awaited him. Tripping on a loose floor tile, Anthony regained his balance with a nervous laugh, checked the room for further hazards.

'What I want to know…' said Rudy, swallowing and bringing to his lips another spoonload, '…is how soon it will come to…like, be enactive.'

'Let's take a look at the contract, shall we?'

Anthony lowered his briefcase onto the tablecloth. Strewn across the dull blue cotton were tiny shavings like crumbs of parmesan cheese and it took a moment to determine that they were in fact nail clippings, hundreds of them, chewed off and left to mingle. Some had already attached themselves to Anthony's jacket but he thought better of openly brushing them away.

The contract was a colourful document of at least nine pages, more like a brochure, bejewelled with yellow SIGN HERE stickers and labelled in block letters: PRODUCT DISCLOSURE. Followed by: *Fortunate Insurance—There Is More to Life*. It appeared to intimidate Rudy, who cowered to his bowl, tipped it forwards and dug into the remains of his meal.

'Now,' said Anthony. 'Has anyone explained to you the difference between a level and a stepped premium?'

Rudy ducked further.

'I don't care about any of that.'

'I know this sort of thing can be tedious, Mister Alamein. But you've requested the maximum possible cover, so it's important you understand the—'

'What about suicide?'

Anthony felt his neck go rigid.

'I'm sorry?'

'Like, if I commit suicide, is that…is there, like…'

The insurance man allowed himself to appear thoughtful. He turned his head.

The end of the kitchen was the end of the house. Through eight or nine cobwebbed windowpanes, three of which constituted a door, he could see out to an overgrown courtyard, festooned with upturned plastic furniture into which an ambitious, strangling vine had laced itself. At the far end of the 'garden' was a freestanding two-storey structure, a studio or granny flat. Unlike the front yard there was a trampled pathway and visible brickwork beneath the creeping greenery that was otherwise rampant on the fences, on the trellises, on all of the space out there.

It was a cloudy grey day, deep in a Melbourne winter, but even on the sunniest First Day of Spring, Anthony thought, this house would still feel doomed.

He spoke slowly.

'You're asking if the payment will be made in circumstances where you take your own life?'

'Yeah.'

He flicked through the contract, frowning, then read aloud:

'*No benefit is payable where the claim arises out of or in connection with any deliberately self-inflicted injury for the initial thirteen months of cover.*'

'Right...' said Rudy, struggling. 'So...I'd have to wait...after thirteen months?'

'In theory, yes. But...may I sit down?'

Rudy nodded, scraped out his bowl.

'Mister Alamein...' Anthony lowered himself into a cane chair. 'If it is your intention to apply for cover in an effort to profit your beneficiary in the immediate future—'

'It's not the immediate future. It's thirteen months. You said it.' His mouth was full.

'Yes, but if your plan is to take your own life, I would have to recommend against Fortunate Insurance accepting your application.'

Rudy licked his spoon and flung it into the empty bowl.

'Why? It's the rules. I'm following the rules. You said it.'

'Yeah, no...' Anthony shifted in his seat, felt the nail clippings prickle his buttocks through his trousers. 'Not really. The purpose of life insurance is protection against...the hand of fate, as it were. Not to profit, or for your beneficiary to profit, from any given technicality.'

'But...' Rudy said, and had nothing to go on with. His eyes shut tight, hard at thought.

'So, I think the best thing for us to do is if I recommend for you another provider, or better yet an insurance broker, and you—'

It was a long moment before Rudy opened his eyes. When he did he saw Anthony's, fixed into a face of astonishment.

He knew what the salesman was staring at. It was in his voice when he said, 'What?'

'On your hand,' Anthony's voice quavered. 'What is that?'

Rudy lowered his right hand to consider the marking there, on the webbing between his thumb and forefinger.

'Tattoo.'

The intensity of Anthony's reaction must have appeared to Rudy as mere curiosity. He explained without a skerrick of humiliation.

'They give it to people sometimes in…at the Severington prison. Branded like horses get. It means, like, you're someone's…you belong to them. And they can do whatever they want.' He held it out to better contemplate it.

'It's meant to be teeth.' His mouth bent into a sick sneer. 'But I kind of reckon it looks like a crown. Like, a dodgy crown.'

He cradled the marking in his lap.

'You were in Severington?' Anthony asked, his throat sounding dry.

'I wasn't. My father was. He died there.'

'Your father had that?'

'Yes.'

'So why do you?'

'Because I'm his *son*,' Rudy spat. 'Why do you *think*?'

His indignation was hot in his eyes and in his breath. He crushed his right hand against his thigh and glared at the wall past his guest, who picked at the fingers of his glove.

'I get it,' Anthony said. 'Like a sympathy tattoo.'

'I don't know.' A big shrug. 'It's just—'

Now it was Rudy who went abruptly silent.

Anthony's glove had come away. He'd turned his wrist to display the same mark in the same place on his right hand.

Rudy grabbed at it in a sudden lurch, knocked the spoon from his bowl and wailed a half-word. Anthony yanked his arm out of reach and pulled the glove quickly back into place.

'Sorry,' he said. 'I don't like to be ogled.'

'Sorry sorry,' Rudy's eyes bulged. 'I'm just…never met anyone else who had it before.'

He settled back in his chair, shot glances at Anthony's hand.

'What was the…like, what did you do?'

'To get sent up?'

'I mean, why did they put you in jail?'

'Fucking parking tickets, mate.'

Rudy cocked his head, one eye shut tight. 'You went to

Severington…because…with parking tickets?'

'Yeah. Well, because I didn't pay them. Cops made an example of me.'

He looked into Rudy's boggle-eyes and said, 'That's why I hate cops.'

Rudy only gazed back.

Anthony said, 'You're the first bloke on the outside I've seen with the teeth, too.'

With a meaningless hum, Rudy's attention switched back to his own hand. He stared down at it. Down into it. Anthony shook off the drama and raised his tone.

'As I was saying, I can put you in touch with a broker and they can take it from there, okay? But you may want to think about exactly what you tell them up front.'

There was no indication that Rudy had heard. Dreamily he was somewhere else, punching his thigh with a vacant agitation.

'Oh *wait*,' cried Anthony, boggle-eyed himself. 'Shit, was your father Piers Alamein?'

Those tiny eyes snapped to meet his. The response was breathless. 'Yeah.'

'I knew Piers. On the sixth floor.'

Rudy nodded, urgent, gripped the tablecloth. Anthony laughed.

'I was on the sixth floor!' He clapped his hands. 'In D-Wing. He and I always used to talk. He was a jeweller!'

'Yes!' Rudy cackled in awe. He clapped too.

'He talked about you. Only child. You slept in a bungalow at the back of the house!' Anthony fingered out the window to the red-brick studio.

'*Yeah!*'

'He was a great bloke. A really good guy. I remember he told me about the underwriting for the shop. He had a shop in the city, right?'

Rudy didn't answer now, just leaned slightly as if to check that Anthony was three-dimensional.

'Dude, I've seen some big policies. But those numbers had so many zeroes, I didn't know how to pronounce them!'

Anthony guffawed and so did Rudy. Their rowdy laughter fed on each other's, peaking and receding, shaking the copper saucepans hung from the gallery.

'I remember the day they put this on me.' Anthony flexed his glove. The leather squeaked. 'Two of them held me down in the rec room and then that Russian arsehole fired up the needle and...I mean, I couldn't stop it. Piers was in his bunk when I came back. He gave me his toilet paper because I was bleeding so much, all down my wrist. In Severington, that's like giving someone a kidney.'

Something glistened in Rudy's eye. He absently tugged on the tablecloth, setting nail clippings to dance like gnats.

Anthony's voice was grave: 'Did you say he died?'

'Just, like, a month ago.'

'How?'

'They said he bled out.' Rudy blinked up at the roof. 'He did it to himself.'

'Shit. I'm sorry, mate. I only did two years and I almost went batshit. It's taken all this time for me to get my head right. He was tough. He lasted ten.'

'Eleven years.' Rudy looked at him now, eyes bloody. 'Almost eleven and a third.'

He jerked to his feet, gripped his pants in place and whirled away from the table with his cereal bowl. It clattered into the kitchen sink. A modern sculpture of used cereal bowls teetered there, probably the source of the incredible odour. Rudy sidled out of view, behind a pillar that held up the second floor.

His voice asked, 'Did he tell you why he was there?'

'Yeah, but...everyone knew about Piers Alamein.'

Attached to the pillar was a landline with TELECOM etched onto it, covered with dust and fading to yellow. Half of Rudy's face peeked around, chewing on the inside of his lip.

Anthony said, 'Was it your mum that he...?'

'He *didn't*. It wasn't him. He wasn't even *here*.'

Anthony looked around himself with a sudden shock.

'*This* is where it...?'

'Yeah. Upstairs. She was...died in the bedroom.'

Anthony couldn't help a glance at the ceiling. Sick paint peeled in strips and hung down like a disgusting chandelier, laid bare rotten plaster and the hump of an electrical cable.

Rudy followed his gaze.

'I don't go up there anymore. I don't...I mean.' He turned to the windows. 'I always sleep down there. Like you said.'

He pointed at the bungalow. Then he murmured, almost whispered:

'It's so funny. It's so funny that you came...just showed up. Like, now. Out of the woodwork.'

'I'll say.'

'No.' Rudy rushed to his seat, perched on the edge. 'I mean it's *really* funny.'

For the first time Anthony noticed Rudy's actual teeth, like claws in his slack mouth.

'Because my dad's dead,' Rudy whispered, eyes shiny. 'But the man who got him put in jail, who *lied*...' A snarl formed on his face, one of someone consciously turning pain into anger. 'The man who lied to the newspaper...*he's* still alive.'

Rudy glowered, baring his determination.

'Do you understand what I'm...I mean?'

'I don't know. You're saying—'

'He's going to bleed out. In his bed. Like Dad did.'

Anthony had to stop himself from recoiling, maintained their proximity. In the green tyranny of the garden a wind rose up. Every branch and leaf trembled.

He said, softly:

'You're going to go to this man's house?'

'Yeah. While he's sleeping. Tonight.'

'*Tonight?*'

'Yep. With the insurance, there's not anything to...no reason to not.'

'Look, Rudy, I loved your dad. Really. But even if...You can't...' His shoulders hunched tight. 'They'll put *you* in Severington.'

'I know.'

'So *then* what?'

For Rudy, the answer was obvious.

'So then I wait thirteen months.'

Now Anthony did recoil. He slumped back in the chair and it protested, sharp, like the cane was snapping into pieces.

'Wow.' He shifted. 'You really hatched a plot, didn't you.'

'I thought about it for a long time. I've thought about it for…it's thirteen years.'

'Who's the beneficiary?'

'What?'

'Who gets the money?'

'Oh.' He shook his head. 'That's just a friend.'

'What's his name?'

'It's a girl.'

'Right. A girl…friend?'

'Not a girlfriend. Not like that.'

'What's her name?'

'Um, Elizabeth. Elizabeth Cannon. She just started, like, this furniture company. Or shop.'

'You must like her a lot.'

'I don't know if it's a shop. It's furniture…'

'What's she done to deserve one-point-five million dollars?'

'Because she's, like, the only friend I've got.'

'Well…' Anthony managed to hold Rudy's eyes this time. 'Let's say you've got one more as of today.'

An embarrassed smirk spread across Rudy's face, then cooled.

'She doesn't know, if that's what you think.'

'Doesn't know she gets the money?'

A hand sliced through the air. 'Doesn't know that. Doesn't know I'm going to do it. Doesn't know anything. She doesn't have to know anything, does she?'

'I guess not.'

'Good. Good. I want it to be a surprise.'

'Have you told anybody else?'

'No. Nup.'

'You sure?'

'Yep.'

'Okay. *Don't tell anybody else*. You shouldn't have even told me. And don't tell *me* anything else. I don't want to know who this bloke is. What he did. Or anything. Nothing, okay?'

'Okay.' Rudy grinned and rocked in his seat, a big overbite grin. 'I knew you'd understand. After what you…with the teeth.'

There was a twinge behind Anthony's eyes and before he could stop himself he was stretching, fists in the air; a yawn popped his ears.

'You know, coming here today, I thought this would be a waste of time. Especially on a Friday afternoon. I can never sell a policy on a Friday afternoon.'

His customer sniggered at the irony. The two smiled.

'But Rudy,' he got serious. 'You can't do this thing tonight.'

'Why not?'

Anthony pushed a thumb and forefinger into the bridge of his nose. The brown leather scratched. He wasn't accustomed to wearing gloves.

'Because if you're arrested, some stickybeak at the office could hold up your application, stamp you as an unnecessary risk. And no one will underwrite you once you're in prison. But you see, once you're covered, you're covered. They can't withdraw it.'

'So…'

'So you've got to wait.'

'Until when?'

'Until the policy is active.'

'How long does that take?'

'It depends. But also…'

'What?'

'I need to think about this. Over the weekend.'

'Think about what?'

'About *this*. Now that you've told me, *I* could go to jail. And I didn't like it so much that I'm pining to go back. Maybe I *shouldn't* arrange this policy for you. Maybe I should just go and forget all about it.'

'But…you loved him. You said…You said—'

'I said I need to think about it. I'll call you Monday.'

Anthony stood, snapped the case shut and hauled it off the table, willing now to brush at the chewed fingernails adhering to its base.

'I promise,' he said.

'No.'

The tightness of Rudy's voice was obvious to Anthony, who moved purposefully to the kitchen entrance and into the hallway.

'*No*,' he heard again, tighter.

Anthony's speed picked up past the stairwell.

'I'll call you on Monday!'

Bounding footsteps. Rudy was agile, despite his flaccid frame and the need to hold up his pants. He slipped between Anthony and the wall and halted Anthony's march to the door.

'*Please*,' he gripped the deadbolt. 'My dad...I've done the waiting.'

'I know, dude. I get it. Really. But—'

'He *didn't*!' Rudy's mouth seemed to rupture with these words. 'My dad *didn't do it*. They *told* me he didn't.'

This surprised the insurance man.

'Someone told you that? Who?'

The outburst faltered.

'A...A man.'

'What man?'

'A tall man.'

'Who was he?'

Rudy's eyes rolled up like he was trying to find the information in his brain.

'Lawyer.'

'Your father's *lawyer*? Of course *he* said—'

'*No*,' Rudy growled to shout him down. He took a threatening step forward, Anthony a flinching step back. '*Not* him. Someone else. Someone else came. He came here and told me.'

'Who?'

'I don't *know*. A *lawyer*. He got for me this...power...power...'

'Power-of-attorney?'

'Yeah. Power-of-attorney. I got the house. He didn't want me to pay him or *anything*. He *said* that dad didn't do it.'

'How would he know?'

A choking sound. Rudy was trying to speak but couldn't.

'Dude…' Anthony adopted a soothing tone, inhaled long and deep, hoped Rudy would do likewise. 'Even if we signed the papers today, you'd have to wait until the policy is active.'

'*When*? How long is that?'

Anthony looked at his watch, calculating…

'A week.'

'*A week?*'

'It's a big policy. It takes time. I'll call you next—'

'Let me do it now,' he said, that incessant blinking. 'You can think about it or whatever, but let's get the papers done and like…done.'

'Ummm…'

Rudy smelled weakness.

'You *have* to. I can't wait *more* than a week.' He twisted his body like he needed permission to use the toilet. 'You have to.'

'All right.' Anthony raised his arms in surrender. 'You want to do it, we can do it.'

The front room was still random unused tables and chairs, like an estate waiting to be executed. Half a dining table was buried beneath an upturned writing desk. Anthony placed his briefcase on the other half. Dust rose and dissipated.

Not daring to hesitate, Rudy dropped quickly into a settee that coughed up another cloud of dust. He swiped at the air, quizzically, but at the sight of the contract he sat on his hands.

Anthony reclined in a swivel chair, pulled a ballpoint from his pocket.

'Is Rudy short for something?'

'What?'

'What's your full name?'

'Rudyard. Rudyard Christopher Alamein.'

Anthony wrote this into the contract. It occurred to him that he should ask how to spell it, but before he could, Rudy said:

'It really has to be a week? I've got to wait till Friday?'

'Friday is the fastest it can be. That's with me pulling all the strings I can. But the good news is that in special circumstances I'm empowered to waive the initial premium. How does that sound?'

A petulant shrug. 'Great.'

'Rudy…' Anthony planted a fist on his knee and looked him in the eye. 'You've waited eleven years. You're going to have to wait another seven days.'

They did the remaining work in silence, but for Anthony reading out questions from the application—'Have you ever been diagnosed with a malignant growth?'—and Rudy's stilted responses, which were invariably 'no', except where something needed explanation—'What's a malignant growth?'—after which the answer was invariably 'no'. He appeared to have no medical history whatsoever. By the time they were finished, night had fallen.

'Geez,' said Rudy. 'Lots of questions.'

'It's a lot of money. You've got to do more than just raise your hand.'

'I know…I know.'

He initialled each page without reading back, signed three times on the last, went on chewing his fingernails. Anthony signed too, above *Fortunate Australia representative*. Then he stood and filed the document gently into his briefcase.

'I have to hurry back to the office, get this into the system.'

Disappointment tugged at Rudy's face.

'All right…'

'The sooner this gets done, the better for you.'

'I know. I know.'

'If there are any problems, I'll be in touch.'

It was disappointment, Anthony realised, at his departure. For all the impatient talk, Rudy didn't want his new friend to leave. He flicked the door lock with contempt, like it was the only thing in the world over which he held power and he had to make it count.

'That's really nice of you,' he said, another tear in his eye. The streetlights caught it as the door opened.

'It's the least I can do.'

'Right. And, like, the least *I* can do is go ahead with…with…' He waved his tattooed hand. 'On Friday. Like, as soon as this is ready. Friday night.'

'Rudy, your dad knew you loved him. You don't need to hurt somebody to prove that.'

'No,' he said, swaying. He seemed to be expecting this line of argument. 'No. He didn't know it. I didn't say it. I mean...yes, I did say it. But that's not anything. You can't just say it. You have to do it.'

'I'll call you.'

With a final clap on Rudy's shoulder, Anthony moved directly across the untended garden to the gate and the footpath and kept walking, felt Rudy's gaze on him as he reached his car. When the motor turned over he looked and Rudy was there on his porch.

He followed Grand Street to Kings Way, past the casino and over the river and through the west end of the CBD, peak hour easing its chokehold. At Flagstaff Gardens he turned right, saying back to himself some of the things he'd said to Rudy. What Rudy had said there at the end.

Then he realised that he'd pulled over. He was in Carlton. Anthony stared through the windscreen, through the early evening air and the brittle city wind to a dying tree near the intersection, just twenty metres ahead. The engine was running. It was a quiet street, idyllic at any time of year. There were no moving cars or headlights that Anthony could see. But he wasn't looking.

He took off both gloves and gazed at the marking on his hand, thoughts of Rudy Alamein washing over him.

There was the black ink in the pores of his skin. Two or three skinny blond hairs poking through. He licked his finger and rubbed.

It didn't give way at first, then it did: the teeth swirled into a storm cloud, then a deep green bruise, then black clots of skin that rolled across his webbing. Then nothing.

Anthony didn't stop until all the black was gone. As much a memory as anything Rudy Alamein had said.

PART II

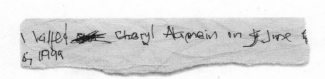

I killed ~~~~ Cheryl Aumann in June of 1999

2

Something happens first.

This is in the pimped and plushy halls of the County Court, epic and glassy so you at least feel like you can breathe. Half the stooges that come here are verging on a meltdown, so all this light and space is meant to keep you based, keep you breathing. Meltdowns can wait for the tram ride home.

The actual courts have been running for an hour so the morning bottleneck is done, leaving only the whir of the escalator and the occasional dork like me waiting for my cue. I'm sat on a bench of chairs all attached and facing the court doors and I'm on my phone, trolling random e-celebs for keks and such, when I see them. Way down the way, a man and a woman and a child and the child is not quite a baby now. They're waiting too, outside their respective court, but they're not waiting like I'm waiting. They don't have the vibe of people who sometimes give evidence for a living. Everything about Dad, the red in his eyes, how he's dressed, everything, the hair on his face, it all scans like he's here for sentencing. That his right to just *walk around* like the rest of us is about to be abruptly, absolutely withdrawn. Or maybe I've reverse-engineered that, the obviousness of that, because of what happens.

The boy is trying to stand up. Dad's got him by the hands, is gently raising him off the carpet and this kid seems to understand what he's supposed to do, seems to be right there mentally, but his fat fleshy legs aren't voting with the majority. They don't take weight like they're supposed to, instead squish into the floor and this frustrated boy, sitting there on his nappied arse, he starts to cry. Dad smiles and Mum strokes his head.

How I know it's a little boy is: I just know.

I go back to noodling on my phone but when I glance up Mum and Dad are speaking with sad faces and the little stooge is pushing himself off the ground with his hands. Mum and Dad aren't even looking when he swings back, stands awkwardly like a drunk gymnast. Without thinking I yell, 'Oi!' They don't hear, but then the kid wails with his own surprise, prompts both adults to whirl around and see him take three tiny steps, teetering all the way, then collapse four victorious inches back down to the carpet.

What happens next is, Dad makes a sound like I've never heard before. Something wholly new, a musical note undiscovered until now. He reaches with his giant hands and clutches the boy and pulls him into a hug, tight and strong and he might be hurting him but of course he isn't. Big dad tears on a hairy face are all I can see and those teeth and then Mum's crying too and that's when I stop watching because I can't anymore, just stare at the ground and listen to that man cry and thank god a greybeard in a green uniform comes out of the court and calls my name, loud and roaring like I'm not right there in front of him.

'*Jason Ginaff.*'

3

It's not paranoia—everybody stares at you when you enter a court-room. The judge and her associate, throbbing with objectivity; the barrister who called you as a witness, standing now at the bar table and smiling his thin lips, no longer the laconic chadwick you met last week, now a man *appearing*; the instructing solicitor who wordlessly communicates his support; the opposing nest of hostiles who word-lessly communicate their whatever; and a plaintiff who deep down knows all the things you've come to say, seated right there in the first row of the gallery, ring binders piled either side of him like a fort he's built against the truth.

If this was a jury trial there'd be six randoms on the far side of the room, staring harder than anyone because that's kind of what the judge would have told them to do. So at least they're not here doing that.

We reach the witness box and the tipstaff blurts fast, words he's blurted a thousand times before. I've been in enough courts to know there's a script taped to the wall of the box, one that only he can see, but this craggy old Anzac doesn't need it.

'Would you like to swear on the bible or make an affirmation?'

'An affirmation.'

'Do you solemnly and sincerely declare and affirm that the evidence you shall give will be the truth, the whole truth, and nothing but the truth?'

'I do.'

He turns away and sits at his station beneath the judge. She smiles, reassuring.

'You may sit or stand, Mister Ginaff. Whichever you prefer.'

I sit. Perry clears his throat, shuffles at the lectern, reads from his notes there and says, 'If you would, Mister Ginaff, please direct your answers to Her Honour.'

Barristers always ask you to speak directly to the judge, but I can't ever seem to manage it. Something about it turns your evidence into a weird kind of performance. Mind you, I hate being here enough that it's going to be a weird kind of performance anyway. Perry knows—I told him last week how uncomfortable I get in the witness box and he said there was nothing to be nervous about.

I told him I would not be nervous. I told him I'd be taking a couple of beta-blockers to make sure I wasn't nervous.

He looked at me, perplexed. 'So what's the problem?'

'It's court. I have to use my real name.'

'So?'

'So…I guess I don't know how to act.'

Now, with his robes and his grave voice, knowing himself exactly how to act, Perry says, 'Would you please state your full name and occupation for the court record?'

'Jason John Ginaff. Researcher. Self-employed.'

'And when you say researcher…what kind of research do you do?'

A week ago in his chambers, with what appeared to be a thousand copies of the same book lining his shelves, Perry laughed.

'Just be yourself!'

But that, of course, was just another way of stating the problem.

So I demanded Perry tell me exactly what he was going to ask me today. Like, word-for-word. I've been practising my answers all week.

'It's limited almost entirely to internet research. Clients engage me to collate what information exists online in relation to a particular subject. A company or a person. Most of the time it's a person.'

What's not helping is that the person on this particular occasion, he's right here in the room. The creepiness of researching the crap out of someone is only bearable so long as you don't then have to look at their real-life face. Knowing this, and uncomfortable as I am, my stupid eyes skip over for the splittest of seconds and there he is:

David Wallis Chapman, born five November 1959, plaintiff in the matter of *Chapman v Revue Technologies Pty Ltd*. Glaring back with all the butthurt he can muster.

Perry nods, making it clear he wasn't listening. He knows these lines as well as I do.

'That's an unusual type of work. Would you give the court an example of the kind of research you're engaged to do?'

'It's not that unusual.' To keep from glancing back at Chapman I peer up at the judge. If she looked carefully she'd see my eyes moving left to right, a side effect of memorising these words off a page. 'Ninety per cent of it is vetting. Like, when a business is looking to fill a position and they've compiled a shortlist, I'll research the candidates. Prospective employers don't like surprises down the track.'

'To put it simply, your job is cyber-vetting.'

I bite down on a smile, like I did in Perry's office the first time he said 'cyber-vetting'.

'That's correct.'

'Mostly by way of standard internet search engines.'

'Yes.'

Perry flinches. Something has occurred to him and, just like that, with no idea of the consequences, he's off-script.

'When you say that your work typically involves vetting job applicants, to be clear, you were *not* engaged by Revue Technologies to vet Mister Chapman prior to his engagement as Senior Financial Consultant, is that correct?'

First comes a thud of blood against my ears and prickles along my hairline, the initial spark of the perspiration that's going to be a deluge because it always is. The blood floods behind my eyes and I'm effectively blind and there's pressure in my throat and I have to get my answer out before it reaches my larynx.

'Um, no. Businesses don't often vet an external contract.'

Perry isn't even looking at me, just around at the room like he's bored.

'In that case, when *was* your first contact with Revue Technologies?'

'My…my first meeting…was on the seventh of April…' My voice falters and the sound of it prompts Perry to look at me and he sees what's happening. I hear the judge's shoulders tighten. My shoes and socks are off now. I tell myself not to pass out.

'The seventh of April,' Perry repeats. Slowly, like he's trying to remind *me* of *my* lines. 'This year? Last year?'

'This year,' I rasp.

'Twenty twelve?'

'Yeah...'

'And who was that meeting with?'

Here comes the sweat. A grand torrent like all the taps have been turned on at once. This is despite how, outside, it's the coldest day in Melbourne since, like, ever.

'Mister Singh. The Chief...' I take in a long breath. '...Chief Financial Officer.'

'Was that after Revue Technologies had repudiated the contract with Mister Chapman?'

'Yes...'

'In fact, that was after Mister Chapman had been locked out of the seventh floor, wasn't it?'

'Yes...'

'Would you like a glass of water?'

'I'm okay.'

I force a dumb smile while inside I'm hating him for abandoning what we'd arranged. Perry smiles back and I'm holding my breath. This is usually the point where I promise myself I'll never give evidence again. This is also the point where I pray to the God of Long Questions that he send down a doozy right this second.

'Given your talent for cyber-vetting, is it fair to say that Revue Technologies would have saved themselves considerable grief if they'd come to you prior to contracting with Mister Chapman?'

Chapman's barrister stands up. God bless you, sir. He too is robed and self-important like a skeksi.

'My friend knows full well that it is *not* fair to say—'

The judge: 'We won't ask the witness to speculate, Mister Perry.'

I take the chance to suck in air.

'The question is withdrawn, Your Honour.'

But remembering to breathe is only half the game; the other half is remembering what breathing is. How much is too much? Too little? On my wrist is a lacker band I keep there for just this situation. It's a method I read about online: flicking it against your skin can keep you in the present, stop you goosing out. I'm flicking it hard now, sending a telegram in Morse code. So hard the tipstaff scowls, wondering what that noise is.

'Mister Ginaff.' Somehow Perry has received my telepathic all-caps to slow down. 'If you were not engaged to vet Mister Chapman prior to his engagement as financial consultant, what was it that Revue Technologies asked you to do?'

He's back to the script. The thumping in my brain tapers. I start to notice my surroundings again: the sparse public gallery, the mouth-pink walls, the array of flat-screen televisions that they use for, I don't know, watching the cricket.

'Um…My job was to interrogate the claims…claims made by Mister Chapman at the time he came on as…financial consultant.'

'Were you told *why* they wanted you to do that?'

I remember the answer to this one and the adrenaline is dropping off, leaving a familiar thrill in my blood. It's the same feeling I had after a big crying jag during my mother's illness. A hollowing out, like nothing even matters.

'They said they were surprised at the poor standard of Mister Chapman's performance and this had led them to doubt the veracity of representations made by him at the time of contracting.'

'All right,' says Perry. He nods, supportive. 'This is still the conversation of the seventh of April, to which you've alluded?'

'Yes.'

'Do you recall anything else from that conversation?'

I make myself comfortable in the court's spongy office chair. The sweat's still coming but slowing. My body language is no longer signalling to the court that I'd rather be dead.

'They told me there was a time factor. They suspected Mister Chapman would commence proceedings like these.'

'So…' Perry actually hooks his thumbs into the collar of his robes. 'You were commissioned to determine whether there had been any false or misleading statements made by Mister Chapman at the time of his engagement as senior financial consultant. In broad compass, how does one go about that?'

'Mostly I look at the documentation.'

'By documentation, you mean...'

'His résumé, primarily.'

'Right. So your job was to scrutinise his CV.'

'That's correct.'

'I see. And when you're scrutinising a CV, and there is a time factor that you're very much aware of, where do you begin?'

'It's different every time.'

'How about in this case?'

'In this case?'

'Yes.'

'In this case,' I say, 'He'd misspelled Rhodes Scholar.'

4

I push out the revolving doors, welcome the cool air, but the wind goes straight for my ears like they're the most delicious part. Cold needles my face and I drive my hands into my pockets, remember what a dickhole I was for not bringing gloves or a beanie or a scarf. I feel the cold more than most people because, according to my mum, I am 'traumatically skinny'. She used to say I look like someone starved Keira Knightley to death. Combine that with my statu

A long walk down sterile corridors. Another
Sunday visit to the familiar pastel walls and
pungency of whatever chemicals they use to clean
up after the dying. I'd received no warning that
her left lung was giving out, that each breath was
such an effort. I didn't know this was the last time
I'd ever take that long walk down sterile corridors.

d my complexion—powdery, pimply, more than my share of eczema—and I look like the kind of stooge who *would* tell a group of norps what's what about computers then freeze to death simply by walking outdoors. I almost wish I needed glasses, just to round off the cliché.

Only a few steps from the courthouse someone calls my name.

'Jason.'

It's Perry, beaming through his sharp white features. While the rest of us are Siberian exiles cowering against the day, scurrying to overcrowded cafés or enduring the wind for the sake of a sad cigarette, Perry is fluid, even bouncing.

'We've adjourned until Monday. Apparently Chapman and his team are going into talks after lunch. I think they're going to settle.'

And I'm like, 'Great.'

'You got pretty nervous on the stand, didn't you.'

And he *fucking* smiles at me.

'It's not nerves.' I peer down to Spencer Street for a tram. If we're adjourned then I can go home.

'Didn't I say you needn't worry?'

'No likelihood I'll be called back?'

'I'll wager these proceedings are done. I'm surprised we've come this far. Poor old Chapman got his bubble burst with everything you had—'

He pulls from his robe a mobile phone, flashing silent yellow.

'I've got to answer this. Look, Gary and the whole Revue cabal want to shout us out to lunch. I've suggested Nick's. You'll come, won't you?'

'Umm...'

Perry answers the phone.

'Hello, Sarah? Just a tick.' He lowers it to his chest. 'Come on. This is all thanks to you, especially after such a wobbly start yesterday. They're only going to shine your shoes for an hour while we eat.'

I picture it: a well-heated hugbox of posh food and warm red wine, the flattery and the back-slapping and the pride at carrying out the most crushing own of my career. Admiring fathers huddled and smiling, jockeying to bask in my genius and me the vital centre of it all...

'I can't. I've got a lunch meeting.'

In a flash his interest is gone. I am of no further use, and he and I will never meet again.

'Right. See you.' He turns and brings the phone back to his ear.

Moments later I'm still longing for a tram and the black-clad Melbourne lawyers are still bustling to their lunch spots when I see the mother and her boy come through the doors. He's in his stroller now, blanketed in cotton; she moves as if obeying the instructions of some unseen hypnotist, tense with cold, wheeling the boy back to their ordinary life, partnerless and fatherless respectively.

I change trams at Swanston Street, take the 57 to Racecourse Road, get chips from the place near my flat, clutch them tight for their warmth and chew on a few as I hike up the driveway, bathe in the hikikomori relief of coming home for the last time today.

5

Marnie hears me as I approach, the way she always does. It's not like she sits and listens for me to come home, but I'm saying she might as well do that. The door to her flat swings open, the one across the stairs from mine, and she steps out with her tallness and her hair coloured deep red and the usual quizzical smile like it's weird how I even exist.

'Hiya, Stevey.'

'Hey, want a chip?'

Marnie waits tables for a living. At first I was only friends with Marnie because scorning your neighbour is like scorning your waiter: it's gruesome to imagine the ways they might exact their revenge. Also, I thought more eyes on my flat would be added security for the hardware I've got inside. But over time we've become friends. Even good friends. Whenever she says 'Stevey' I feel a flutter in my stomach. And it's not even my real name.

Steven Jones is the name on my phone bill, but not the one on my lease. Which is different again from the one on my electricity account. I once considered telling her all about my John Doe life, how my work makes me security-conscious with a hint of paranoia, how my real name is Jason and I'd like to kiss her on the mouth. But the moment passed. And it would only have made her smile that baffled smile.

'Where'd you get them?'

'The Chippery.'

'Ummm...' She considers it. 'No, thanks. They use the wrong

potatoes for their chips. They should use colibans but they use desirees.'

Raindrops spatter on the exposed side of the gallery. Marnie doesn't seem to register the bergschrund misery out here; that long mop of hair might keep her neck warm but the rest of her is loosely draped in thin cotton pyjamas and she's barefoot. Then again, if today is like any other day then she's got the heating cranked up like a boss and it's the nuclear dawn inside her flat, so right now that long body must be revelling in this cool air, even when this cool air is a frigid Melbourne winter.

'Hey, ummm…' she says, 'I had something I wanted to ask you… Oh yeah, what are you doing for dinner?'

'Nothing. You want to go out?'

'Can't. I have to work.'

'What about tomorrow?'

'Working.'

Her eyes fill with pity and I bite my lip. Always I'm making this mistake—thinking she wants me to ask her out but when I do she turns me down. At first it left me red-faced and sleepless, but I've gathered over time that she only wants me to work a little harder.

'Um…Wednesday?'

And she looks at the roof in hectic thought.

'I think that's okay. I'll let you know.'

'Great.'

She makes a face at the rain.

'How rude is this?'

'Yeah,' I say. 'I'm freezing. I've got to get inside.'

'Fine then. See ya.'

And bang, she's gone. Like she can take a hint. I knew as I said the words that they would have that effect but they were out before I could stop. Now I'm the one filled with pity as I unlock my front door. Marnie's had a lot of friends abandon her in her life and I suppose you can see why—she's as defensive as the Battlestar Galactica and I'm just as bad. We're two weirdos staring at the business end of our twenties and we communicate in tortured allusions: she sends up smoke signals, I answer in semaphore. And our respective hints that we want to be vulnerable, that we want more than to merely catch each other coming home to our separate flats, they're like tiny planets in a big solar system: they only align every one hundred and fifty-seven years.

We'll go out on Wednesday, to the pizza place across the street where no matter how often we go the owner never seems to recognise us. Where he puts too much garlic into everything and his two teenage kids don't want to work there but they do. I'll order the bolognese pizza because I love all that garlic and Marnie the capricciosa because she long ago dispensed with being dainty around me. Then we'll come back to her place and talk and dance the Fear of Rejection until I realise it's not going to happen tonight, and I'll hug her and come home. And this is all to say: I'm looking forward to it.

6

I fasten my two deadlocks and the deadbolt and switch on the heater and hang up my coat which is damp from having borne the brunt of the outside world. Now it can bear the brunt of this miracle heating unit that gets up to speed in seconds and which prompted me to rent this flat a year ago, during the coldest month in Melbourne since they bothered keeping records. Of course, records topple so often now they can probably go back to not bothering.

When the property agent demonstrated this wall-mounted godsend I thought the landlords had made a mistake. Who spends this kind of money on a rental? In her skirt and high heels, the agent seemed to have left home wholly unprepared for the bitterness outside, and while she claimed to be from Dunedin and therefore immune to the kind of cold you git un Milbun she was more than happy to hover and feel that giant engine summon heat from thin air and blast it in our faces like a merciful and life-affirming car exhaust.

Which meant that, for five minutes, I had to make small talk as Robert Lavigne, trainee engineer at Jetstar Australia.

There wasn't much else to attract to me to this block, where all the common areas are outdoors, built of sparse concrete and decorated with little more than council bins. Where the body corporate exists in name only and the residents walk around with that look on their face like they *know* this is a halfway house for singles and migrants. After Mum died, I had the money for a classier flat. I had the money for a house. But I'm in this place with this heater and this heater makes this place a womb.

The display comes to life at the first breeze of warmth like a chipmunk waking in the spring. It requests access to the serve

It was a red bandana around her head today, lurid against
the pallor of her skin. Every inhale required a lurching
movement with her elbows, propping her up from the bed,
dropping her back. Over and over like a pop-up book.
The placards she'd made when she first had difficulty
breathing still lay either side of her. One said 'Thank
you!' and the other said, 'Strewth, Cobber!'
and she held them up at opportune moments like Wile
E. Coyote, part-communication, part-entertainment for
the staff and fellow patients. I could see now, before she
even opened her eyes, that 'Strewth, Cobber!' had been
crossed out with angry black texta and replaced with
the most humourless word there is: 'No'.

hich then sends my phone the response code. I log in, delete the message, return to the kitchen for a handful of chips.

When I glance across the room at the terminal, I don't see what's happened. Despite how this is what I'm looking *for*, I don't see it. Clueless, I fill the kettle and rinse a mug.

Already my mind has switched from Wednesday's pizza with Marnie to what's occupied it every day for months: the true purpose of Thruware.

'Thruware' is a working title. I'm considering a catchier name like 'Bloodhound' or 'Aardvark'. It's a new script designed to expedite brute force attacks and rainbow tables and it automates the doxing process to Swedish levels of standardisation. Only certain applications are vulnerable, but if they are then I can raid the datacentre without leaving so much as a timestamp.

Writing and installing this kind of program isn't illegal. People all over the world have programs installed, like say the late great Low Orbital Ion Cannon, because it makes them feel like edgelords and true life genuine AnRkists, but they'd never actually launch it. It's once you *launch* it, once it leaps the node and merges with the traffic that you officially become a criminal. Chalk it up as one more mark against my name when the party van knocks on the door.

Why I'm not worried about the party van is: no one knows about

Thruware. I've never sold it or uploaded it. It has no online status whatsoever, and the Federal Cyber-Crime Department can't scan for what they don't know about.

Also, that they call themselves the Cyber-Crime Department is another reason I'm not worried.

Right now Thruware exists only in this room, is known only to me, and only operates through a secure server and a host of skeletons. I've disguised it with enough nonsense script that even I wouldn't know it if I stumbled on it. But I've left traces of the source code here and there when it hasn't been too risky, tweaked to be rendered useless, and probably the single greatest achievement of my life is that these traces were identified and labelled Ducnet on rollerbrain.com and entered into Wikipedia as 'most likely malware developed by the US military to interrupt the timing systems used in rogue nuclear programs'. That's seriously what it says. The moment I read that, it was like a nerd orgasm.

Ironically, Ducnet, otherwise known as Thruware, otherwise known as Bloodhound or Aardvark, has only ever been used to track down photographs of job candidates doing bucket bongs on Instagram accounts they thought they'd deleted.

But in fact Thruware was written with another project in mind, one it began weeks ago, which is wholly separate from my *job* job and which it completed today. And here's me, I didn't even notice when I looked at the displays.

Rain pummels the window, harmonises with the escalating kettle. I'm about to wash a second mug, an activity I call 'cleaning up', when all of a sudden I feel compelled to check the terminals again. This is not a sixth sense, merely the unease I get when I'm not at my desk.

The kettle in the kitchen is screaming. I don't hear it because of what's onscreen:

1 result(s) found

Below it, in green text against the black of the Thruware interface, in a living room blasted by heat, in a block of flats where all of the residents live alone, in what must be the coldest, bitterest suburb of all of Melbourne, shine eight green numerals:

0398734378

They settle in my brain and I look to my phone, feel the urge to dial the number, as strong as the urge to answer when it rings.

But I don't.

The kettle clicks off. The chair sighs slowly as I sit.

The mad thing I do next is write the number down on a post-it note, in case a power surge wipes it out somehow, or I lose my connection *and* the back-up connection *and* the script corrupts. Then I check I've written it down correctly. Then I look back through the query fields to be sure I didn't error there, that this is what it claims to be. But of course it is. I spent months curating the fields for just this reason—so I would know the number was right if it ever showed up all coy and unassuming in the bottom left corner of my display.

From the home screen it's clear that the target application was Roadside Samaritan, one of eighty-seven granddaddy datacentres that Thruware can exploit because some IT guys don't get paid enough to salt their hashes. To find out more I have to launch the botlog.

```
20120713 10:24:37:59 L2TP traffic for gy7, interface: 9, protocol: 0, privateRoute: 9 :)
20120713 10:24:37:59 Connect: iii/ <-> address added. Destination: 19.24.78.92 :)
20120713 10:24:37:71 traffic hold. Exploit commenced. DNS address. 45.990.00 :)
20120713 10:24:37:88 traffic clearing for gy8, interface: 9, protocol: 0, privateRoute 9 :)
20120713 10:24:38:06 traffic filter cancelled, exploit resolved, retrieval p07::%lo07, link#1 :)
```

I know it's kind of douchey to generate a smiley face at the end of every active line of response code, but the log is UTC divided into milliseconds, which means millions of entries, and I don't have to sort them if I can just search for the smileys.

Reviewing the botlog is, usually, my favourite part of Thruware: watching the magic unfurl in slowmotion. Electronic pulses over the course of, in this case, forty-seven one-hundredths of a second, spanned out for me in prose poetry. It's like time travel, watching past events at the speed of brain.

But the first fantasy crashes over me like a wave of valium. I hadn't expected it so soon. I wanted more time. To consider things, to cost-benefit the crap out of the decision before I made it. Have I made it? Am I really about to call this number?

I tip back in my chair, can't prevent what happens next. Also, I can't deny that, actually, this is my favourite part. The fantasy. The mental holodeck.

By the time I remember I'm hungry, my chips have gone cold.

7

The view from the conference room is grey and low, looming cloud. In summer you can sit in rooms like this and gawp at the tennis courts on the roofs of the CBD, wonder what happens to the errant balls that make it over the chain-link walls and down to the unsuspecting proles below. This time of year you wonder why Melbourne doesn't have those pedways that join all the buildings together like they have in Canada—hermetic, corporatised, dehumidified; relieving us of the need to *interact*.

Stuart says, 'What else does the vetting interview consist of? Apart from inquiries into the person's background?'

Madison takes a third macaroon and bites it.

This should have been a standard meeting, just me and Madison, where she handed over the candidate files and the two of us talked through the schedule for tomorrow's interviews. Which is what we've done every year for the past whatever-years since the firm of Albert Kane and Roach first contracted with me to consult on their internship program. But today we were followed into the conference room by an overweight stooge wearing the kind of colourful braces that lawyers describe as fun. Madison introduced him as Stuart, a partner. He said he wanted to 'shoot a couple of questions'.

'Don't get me wrong,' Stuart says, not waiting for a response. 'We need our candidates vetted. We don't question your ability to do that. But our harvesting process includes half-a-dozen interviews, cocktail parties. Christ, last year we took them ice skating. Why can't your interview be conducted instead by us, at one of those junctures?'

'Yeah, no, they can,' I say, amplifying my geeky professionalism. 'And I promise that all I do in the interview is ask about the subject's background, how much of it is accessible online. It's just preparation for the research phase. You *could* ask the questions yourselves. But then, some people aren't comfortable with…like, digging into a person's…like, online dating history. Or whatever. I mean, to their face. But I'm used to it.'

Madison is the HR boss and she's never so much as coughed suspiciously in the direction of my work. Too, it's her nature to be as direct as a robot overlord: she wouldn't dream of going easy on a third-party actor like me, not out of mere courtesy. But instead of offering even facial support—on her home ground at the edge of the troposphere, in the shmick lawyer's conference room that was *designed* to intimidate me, flanked by an array of sweet biscuits and a crystal water jug paid for by the tears of failed litigants—she looks back with that mannequin bassface and slowly chews her macaroon. Like all these years she's been wondering the exact same thing.

Stuart smiles the way you do when a joke isn't funny, furrows his brow, holds open his mouth and licks his lips.

'That with which we are or are not comfortable needn't be a concern of yours.'

I can't help a nervous smile, a shuffle in my seat. My nipple twitches. It is there, in my breast pocket, where the post-it burns hot and itchy like a mosquito bite. I tap at my suit jacket and scratch, not too hard in case I somehow smudge the number.

'Also,' I say, 'to be honest, I was under the impression my time was cheaper than yours.'

I strafe them with a grin.

'Obviously…' Madison says, her tongue sifting biscuit-mush from her teeth. 'This isn't a question of money.'

Last night, in the warmth of my flat, I wasn't able to make the call. Despite the exhilaration of having found the number, my dialling finger couldn't man up and dial it. I knew what I was going to say, had the pretext all figured out. But last night, at the moment of truth, I got stage fright. Something more than stage fright. Stagefuckingterror.

So coming here on the bus I made a deal with himself: if Madison said 'obviously' eleven times or more, I'd call that number today. If not, the post-it could sit in my pocket another twenty-four hours, let tomorrow wring its hands about it.

It's a word she's fond of, repeats it like there's a glitch in her voice chip. Eleven times was possible, while being in the outer realm of possibility.

But then Stuart walked in and presumed to run the meeting, because he's a partner or because he's a man or both, and I knew in the first five seconds that I wasn't going to get my quota.

Therefore: I have altered the terms of the deal.

'Let me put this another way,' Stuart says, adjusting the tension of his braces. 'It's come to my attention that you don't use your real name in these interviews. I'm sure you have your reasons. But I'm also sure you can understand that, from our point of view, it seems odd. I'm wondering if it doesn't scare off our best candidates. Can you explain that practice to me?'

Madison bends forward as far as her tummy will allow and stares down another biscuit. She does not pick one up.

'You come to embrace certain work practices,' I say, breathe in hard. '…when a crazy person attacks you in your home.'

Stuart licks his lips. He always seems to be preparing to speak, but now he stays quiet. They watch me blink down at the boardroom table to properly dredge up the memory.

'You may have seen it. It was on the news. Do you know the name Paul Heaney?'

Stuart, not a man to let on when he doesn't know something, doesn't respond.

What else I knew in the first five seconds of this meeting was that Madison de Silva is pregnant, evidenced by the baby bump as much as by the macaroons she's had three of. This is someone I've only ever known to nibble at a rice cake, to wear a thick layer of make-up and do aerobics in the park at lunch. My theory is that Madison is not one of those thin people who do not *get* food, for whom eating is as uninspiring an act of replenishment as a visit to the petrol station. My theory is that Madison has fought hunger every day of her life: circled her trouble spots in the mirror; sniffed at a hamburger while she devoured a stick of celery; flirted with eating disorders and maybe even taken one home. But now that she's With Child, something has triggered: she's lurched for cover behind the big-tummy branding of Mother-To-Be.

My decision, therefore, is this: if Madison eats four macaroons or more, I'll make the call. Today. Like, before I go home. As it stands, one more macaroon and it's *ring-a-ding-ding*.

For now, Madison shakes her head, waits for me to explain, doesn't so much as bat her eyes at the biscuits.

'Paul Heaney was a candidate at SoSecure. This is a while ago, before they went public. I used my real name back then and I inter-viewed him and he told me he was a blank slate. He said there was nothing I would find on him.'

Madison just listens. So does Stuart.

'I wound up with a photo of him at the Jabiluka protests. Remember those? Students in the Northern Territory? Big placards, bongos. The photo was a police officer dragging Heaney out of a picket line. He had long hair and a different wardrobe to the one I'd seen, but it was him. So I passed that on to SoSecure and they cut him from the harvest. For obvious reasons. They didn't want an employee who'd once picketed their clients.'

Still nothing. She's had enough. What kind of glutton did I take her for? The alternating current of relief and disappointment surges through me.

'Then one night, I'm at home and there's a knock at my door. And I think it's the pizza guy so I open up. And it's Heaney. And he's got a broken bottle in his hand. And he's drunk. And he demands an explanation from me, for why I doctored that photo. He said he'd never been to Jabiluka, it never happened. So I must have shopped him into the pic. I tried to shut the door, he swiped at me. Cut me pretty deep along here. They call this a defensive wound.'

It's an effort, but I pull up my shirt sleeve to display the four-inch scar below my elbow.

'Oooooh,' Stuart says. Madison sighs in sympathy.

'I got the door closed but he cut up the security screen. Cops showed up and that was it.'

Stuart says, 'Christ.'

'You know the *scariest* thing...' I lower my voice, talk directly to Stuart now. 'I spoke to half-a-dozen people who were up there with him. I saw video footage of Heaney at the site. I saw the bus ticket with his name on it. But he was convinced. I mean, I looked him in the eye. He was *convinced* he'd been the victim of a fraud. He'd made himself believe, without a doubt, that this thing which had happened had never happened. That was the scariest bit.'

Stuart nods, his glower weakening.

'Well...' he says. 'Getting stabbed by a disgruntled job seeker might have been a bit scary too.'

'People can freak out when you dig into their past. So I take precautions.'

And he smiles, looks at his watch with an air of conclusion. I've brought him round.

It's a lie, that story. The scar on my arm came from a tower PC that fell on me at Mum's place. There is no Paul Heaney. He never went to Jabiluka.

I'm just more comfortable being someone else. I don't get panic attacks when I'm being someone else.

It's the same with Madison de Silva, finally bingeing on the biscuits she's been bringing to meetings for years. She had to become someone else before she could be herself.

She swipes another macaroon from the plate, a pink one. I try not to let her see me notice, but she does. She disarms me with a coo:

'Don't look at me like that, Andrew. I'm eating for two here. Obviously.'

•

8

It rings for an age before someone answers. Like, for a minute. No
message bank or answering machine. The ringtone is the weird kind
of analogue one that landlines have. I hug my coat tighter, am about
to hang up when I hear a cough and a man's voice:

'Hello?'

An old man. But not a very old man.

'Hello, is that Mister Glen Tyan?'

'Who is this?'

I'm in a paved alcove skewered between Albert Kane and Roach
and a sheer brick wall, the pedestrians of La Trobe Street just far
enough away for me to believe I've found privacy. But through an
invisible glass door emerges now a hunched and grim-faced woman
and before she does anything I realise this grey nook is the official
smoking yard for her and her fellow office dwellers. A black enamel
ashtray clings to the wall, overflowing with butts and black ash and a
sign beneath it says *Smokers Please*, like it's asking for more smokers.
The ground below is strewn with orange stubs. She lights up and I
turn my back to her and the traffic and the wind and jam a finger in
my ear.

'My name is Alan Harper, I'm a journalist with the *Daily Sun*.
Your name was suggested to me by the Police Association as someone
who may be interested in discussing a piece I'm working on about
the lives of retired police officers.'

'How did you get this number?'

Glen Tyan draws on a cigarette, inhales deep, but the smoke I can smell comes from behind. To keep this conversation private I huddle into the glass wall, an icepack against my forehead.

'Um, the Police Association—'

'The Police Association does not have my home phone number.'

I glance around, thrown. The woman stands silent, as if waiting to hear what I'm going to say to that.

'Mister Tyan, all I can tell you is that Marjorie Schwitzer at the Police Association gave me the names of three former officers who may be appropriate for the feature I'm writing, one of them was you, and she included the telephone numbers.'

'Who were the other names?'

I flounder.

'Paul Heaney and Madison de Silva.'

'Never heard of them.'

'Well I believe they were based in Geelong.'

Tyan sucks back so hard I hear tobacco burning through the phone. His inhale is a rattlesnake.

'What's this really about?'

'Umm...'

'I haven't heard from the press in nine years. You come out of the blue—'

'The piece will be about how you've adjusted to retirement, what parts of the job still haunt you, what you took away from your experience. It's an attempt to show the human side of the police force, not to embarrass you or...anything.'

'Why didn't they contact me themselves and ask if they could give out my number?'

'I'm not sure, Mister Tyan. But I have a long-standing relationship with the VPA and with Marjorie, and they know that any information passed on to me is kept private and secure.'

At the squeak of the glass door behind me I raise the collar of my jacket, like that will somehow keep this conversation private and secure.

'So you're a journalist.'

'That's right.'

'Is it something we can do over the phone?'

'I was hoping we could meet. Perhaps I could buy you a drink.'

The smell of cigarettes becomes a stench. I glance back. Seven or eight people are crowded into this small grey space, breathing and wheezing in silence. I'm the strange-o facing the wall and talking to it. At first my head spins with humiliation and I'm about to make for the street, but Tyan's voice comes back suddenly brightened, as if some new personality has snatched the phone from Old Man Crotchety and it wants to make amends.

'Okay,' he says. 'Let's meet tonight.'

The rasp is gone. The voice is lighter, more friendly. I grind my brow into the glass to hear properly.

'Tonight is perfect.'

'Where?'

'Wherever you want. Somewhere easy for you.'

'Do you know the Good Times in Mitcham?'

'I'll find it.'

'It's on Cemetery Road. Opposite the Caltex.'

'I'll find it. No problem.'

'Yeah. Seven o'clock at Good Times.'

'Great. Let me give you my number, just in case.'

I say it slowly and Tyan at least pretends to write it down, co-operative, even eager. I attribute this to the thrill of being courted by the media.

'What's your name again?'

'Alan Harper.'

'Okay. Bye, Alan.'

'See you.'

Tyan hangs up. I listen to the silence. It must seem like I'm still on the phone. But I'm sniffing at the smoke, warmed by it. The smell of the future.

9

The Good Times on Cemetery Road is so what I expected that I'm literally giggling as I make entrance. A bright green banner in what else but Comic Sans promotes bingo nights and chicken parmigianas, neither of which can be enjoyed anywhere but in this cupboard-cum-bistro overlooking the vista of the staff toilets. The rest is a windowless hellscape of pokies and ebola, norp-tier as fuck, whirls and bleeps sounding out whenever the betacuck autotune pop goes briefly, mercifully silent. A handful of worn gamblers dole out their life-savings one coin at a time, dead-eyed but for a fading belief in *this* turn, in *this* push of the button, while the dining area is desolate: not so much as a staff member slitting their wrists on the lino behind the bar. Then a swarm of pimples finds it within himself to materialise in front of me and he relays that tonight's special is pizza. I order a beer and carry it to a chair and wipe off some yellow paste which itself might be pizza and I sit at a table littered with plastic advertisements for beers, jackpots and tomorrow night's special, which is pizza.

Glen Tyan would have known reporters when he was a police officer, ones that worked a beat, sniffed out stories in back alleys and hotel rooms and the toilets of strip clubs—he'll never believe that I'm one of those. But I can play a touchy-feely dorkoid with a degree in creative non-fiction who talks about the fourth estate and enjoys wine and cheese in the park. I've chosen a pale ale for this reason and it's why my checked shirt is tucked into my jeans and the cuffs are buttoned twice each. It's easier to be someone else when you put on their clothes.

I camp the front door, ignorant of the second door to the carpark at the rear. That's where Tyan comes from, half an hour late and I'm too busy trying to figure out if I'm happy or sad that I've been stood up, don't see him until he's right on me, crotch in my face, and even then he has to speak before I jerk back, ambushed.

'You Alan?'

He's got hair too blond for his age, a polo shirt too tight for his big belly. His eyes are wet and too friendly for the scowl that cuts across his forehead. I never found a DOB when I researched Glen Tyan; the only clue was that he retired nine years ago. From that I expected someone older, even elderly, but this man still has swell in his shoulders, his forearms. One of them comes at me now, catches my hand and shakes it. I refuse to wince—surely he's trying to demonstrate how formidable he still is.

I'm like, 'Yeah.'

The scowl disappears and leaves those wet, friendly eyes.

'I'm a bit late, sorry. Lost track of time.'

'No problem. No problem.'

Whatever he was doing to lose track of time, fapping or sleeping or practising that handshake, he was smoking while he did it. Freshly burnt tobacco roars in my nostrils.

'You right for a drink?'

I nod at the beer I'm halfway through, don't say I'm halfway through my third beer, watch Tyan's slow jaunt to the bar, see the broadness of his shoulders, the pregnant glory of his stomach, and I recognise a man at his home ground. He doesn't seem to know the staff, but he knows soulless vinyl drinking barns like this one, knows they were built for white men with pot bellies and polo shirts. This is their Green Zone, and no amount of immigration or feminism or gay pride out there in the world has yet breached its ramparts.

When he returns with his beer I smile, welcoming. *I'm a white man*, I think. *This should be my home ground too.* But it is not.

'How are you, Mister Tyan?'

'Call me Glen.'

'Okay.' I keep the smile plastered. 'Glen, I hope you don't mind my asking, how old are you?'

With the glass at his mouth his lips spread in a grin. He swallows and wipes his face with the heel of his hand.

'Sixty-one.'

That looks about right, though he may have shaved off a couple of years. Just a garnish of vanity, like the blond hair swept across his scalp.

'And you retired nine years ago?'

'About that.'

It begs a question, one I only pose out of curiosity.

'Why did you retire so young?'

'Hey?'

Something catches in Tyan's throat and he lets loose a hacking cough. Once he recovers, I say:

'You must have left the police force when you were in your early fifties.'

But this brings on another violent surge of coughing. His face flushes and his pores open up like gun turrets. With a series of growls he sips his beer.

'Sorry.' A fresh supply of moisture in his eyeballs. 'I'm still getting over a bit of a cold.'

'That's fine.'

'Alan, don't want to be rude, but I should probably be in bed. Can we get straight to the questions you've got?'

'Absolutely. Mostly I just want to know a bit about you.'

'Don't know if I'm that interesting—'

'Are you married?'

'Nope. Confirmed bachelor. No one would have me.'

He chortles. Politely, so do I.

'No kids?'

'Nah. I'd be a shit dad.'

'How have you spent your retirement?'

He pats his stomach, smiles. 'Meat pies.'

'How old were you when you were recruited?'

'Eighteen or nineteen. I can't remember. Eighteen I think.'

'Do you recall why you wanted to be a policeman?'

'I needed a job.' He performs a shrug. 'That's all it was.'

The bags under his eyes are flabby and wrinkled, but still I can't believe how young this man is compared to how I pictured him. Which means I can't shake the obvious question, tip forward now to ask it again.

'So, if it's all right...Why *did* you leave the police force?'

Tyan grabs his beer, drains it.

'You want another?'

I dig into my pocket for money. 'No. But it's my turn.'

Tyan pushes his chair back in a series of awkward spasms.

'Mate, don't be silly. You run to the loo or whatever, then we'll do the interview proper. I don't want to waste your time.'

He seems to have mistaken my nervousness for the call of nature. Not that I don't need to go—the beers I've drunk are clamouring for release.

It takes Tyan a couple of tries to get out of the chair and then he's up, swaggering off to the bar while I cross to the sanctuary of the men's room, wondering if, while I'm gone, Tyan will consider actually telling me why he retired from the police force.

That is absolutely not what Tyan does while I'm in the men's room.

10

One long toilet trough in here and a machine that vends green condoms. The tiles stick with detergent and all the stall doors hang open, so I'm alone. It seems safe to use the urinal.

Usually I'd cram myself into a stall and lock the door and wallow in self-loathing as I relieved myself but I'm in a hurry so I stand with my back to the door, totally exposed to what's about to happen. I've imagined a million versions of this meeting in my life but never the one where Glen Tyan runs late *on purpose*, obliging me to flood my bladder with watery pale ale and thereby luring me here, to this room, about as private as a public space can be.

The stream comes powerfully and I sigh because pleasure. Also because I've managed it before some stooge can walk in. Then someone *does* walk in and I sigh with pride—I have no trouble in front of people once the stream is underway. I'm as alpha as a prize-winning porn star before I sense that this someone who's walked in, they are not walking. They are rushing.

My brain doesn't have time to process fear before two hands grab at my shoulders, pull me back and slam me down to the urinal sink. My knuckles mash a yellow soap and I holler something high-pitched and throaty and my piss seeps into the flaps of my shirt and the knees of my jeans and I put soiled hands up to cover my face and Tyan's body is one giant fist and he's shouting.

'You *fucking* piece of *shit*. Who's Elizabeth Cannon?'

'*What?*'

Tyan kicks my shin, powerful, driving stirrups into his own

indignation. 'Come near my house again I'll fucking *kill* you.'

'*No!*' The trough seems the safest place and I huddle down, arms balled over my head.

'*Who are you? Who's Elizabeth Cannon?*' Tyan grabs both my wrists with one hand. His strength is a bulldozer.

'*I don't know I don't know!*'

'Is she at my house right now?'

'*Stop no I didn't do anything.*'

'I *saw* you, deadshit. I saw you last *night*.'

'*NO NO NO NO NO—*'

A blow to my shoulder like a gunshot but I do not register pain.

'You'll tell me or I'll break your fucking neck.'

'*Stop stop stop stop! I didn't go to your house! I've never been there! What the fuck!*'

A fist collides with my elbow and I wail, long and terrible through my wet shirtsleeves.

'*Bullshit. What's your real name?*'

'*What?*'

Tyan doesn't miss a beat: an open hand to my ear.

'*Who are you?*'

'*Jason Ginaff! I'm Jason Ginaff! I'm Helen Ginaff's son!*'

Now he does miss a beat. A whole series of them. Not quite enough to lure me out from behind my forearms.

'*How many kids has she got?*'

I flinch again and jerk my head back.

'*No! Just me!*'

Nothing happens. I peek over my defences.

The bags under Tyan's eyes are balloons, as big as the eyeballs that gape at me, his face frozen even as his body slowly straightens, travels the full development from Neanderthal to Homo sapiens.

'Bullshit,' he says.

'She died last year.' I don't know why I say this.

As I do the door opens. Someone in a business shirt and trousers enters, gets as far as showing his flat, oblivious face before Tyan's screech: '*Get the fuck out!*' And he's gone, *whoosh*, without a second look, as if this is the sort of thing you sometimes have to allow for at the Good Times on Cemetery Road.

'Why you following me?' Tyan says.

'I'm not.'

'Who's Elizabeth Cannon? Your girlfriend?'

'I don't know her. I don't...nobody...I don't know anybody named that. I promise. I promise I haven't been following you.'

'*Bullshit.*' He looms again, clenches a fist not to strike this time but to promise that he will. 'How did you get my phone number?'

'*I looked you up online! That's all! That's all I did, I promise!*'

'What do you mean, online?'

'On the internet!'

'*What?*' He doesn't seem to have heard of it.

'The internet!'

'What else does it say?'

'Nothing, it just...That's how I got your phone number. Your Roadside Samaritan account.'

'My *what?*'

'It's *illegal*. It's *totally* illegal. But I wanted to meet you.'

'*How did you know I was a cop?*'

'*Mum told me!*'

'*How did you know I quit?*'

'*The internet,*' I squeal, wondering if I'm about to pass out. Blood isn't getting to my head. 'I mean, online. Just old news reports. Bulletin boards. That's what I do. For a job. I find stuff on the internet.'

Tyan appears to have little understanding of these words.

'Why did you want to know so bad why I retired?'

'I was just interested.'

'Why? What did they tell you at the VPA?'

'Nothing. I never spoke to them. It...You retired young. I was just wondering why.'

He cools. As I pull away from the trough wall I sense my hair is matted, sticky. The odour of my situation overwhelms me and I cough the foulness out of my nostrils.

'You found me on the internet?'

He tries to comprehend and his panting echoes on the tiles. He's a sixtysomething chain-smoker—of course he's out of breath. Of course I am.

'I wrote a whole program to find you. To find your phone number.'

'What do you want?'

I try to spit off my tongue anything that's found its way into my mouth, don't dare try to stand.

'Just thought it would be good. To meet you.'

Tyan's eyes go distant and his head lolls gently, visibly overtaken by a wave of depression. Like he's the victim and I a mere instrument of fate. Then he shuffles a slow rotation, makes it to the door, less swagger now. Turns back.

'Come near my house again you'll meet me all right.'

He moves out and he's gone.

Favouring the arse cheek that doesn't ache I lever myself to a sitting position. This is the level of defiance I can muster: to *not* remain in the urinal after Tyan has left. My arm is okay but the elbow stings numb. The rest of me is numb. My mouth yawns open to get the misery out and for a second I think I might retch. I stand up, wash my hands, make a point of not looking in the mirror. I'm about to leave when I feel a real sob come on and so I don't leave. Instead I push into a toilet stall, lock the door and slump onto the seat.

Just let it come.

Shuddering pressure in my chest that bottlenecks in my throat. Tears hit me like a brick wall, fast rivers in the filth of my face, salty splashes on the nastiness of the cubicle floor. Every bone shakes with an ancient kind of muscle memory. When the world confirms how worthless you are it hollows you out. Like after the panic attack in court yesterday. It hollows you out and if you're hollow then nothing even matters.

11

This one is surprisingly old. At least forty. I've got his CV in front of me and if I'd read it I'd probably have found clues to his age and I wouldn't be surprised. But I didn't so I am.

When I shake his hand I say, 'I'm Stan.'

'Hello. It's really great to meet you, Stan.'

He's the second-last interview and, until this moment, today's internship applicants have been what they always are: handsome millennials so coiffed and straight-toothed that I feel derpy. Derpier than usual. And today I feel even derpier than that because I still haven't shaken off the smell of last night's urine bath, despite three showers and a bucket of shampoo. Maybe what's left is so far up my nose it exists only in my brain.

But this stooge is heavy, with big heavy arms and a heavy head and when he came in he had that vague limp that heavy men have. His teeth are not straight and his long nose droops down to laugh at them and his eyes are keen to be liked. On the floor beside his chair he places a flat leather satchel.

People always bring stuff to these interviews. They never need any of it.

The view through the glass is identical to yesterday: dismal. I sit now where Stuart sat, maybe because unconsciously I consider it the power chair. Consciously I consider it to be directly beneath a heating vent. The air has dried out my nostrils over the course of the day but I've found that relaxing.

'Hugh…' I have to focus on the surname on his CV. 'Bre…tza…nitz.'

'That's right.'

'Congratulations on making it to the last round. Not a lot of people get this far.'

'Thank you very much.' A squeaky voice, like that heavy head is crushing his voice box.

'So…' I press play on my pre-interview speech. 'My name is Stan and I specialise in vetting job candidates. I'm tasked with researching your online history and identifying what, if anything, might compromise the firm in the future should they choose to employ you.'

Hugh Bretzanitz provides a conscientious smile and shuffles in his seat.

'I take the view that, because so much of what a person does online they do anonymously, these activities are the best indication of what kind of employee they'll be, what kind of loyalty they'll show the firm. The reason I'm talking to you now is because if something comes out, and if the firm wants to know why you never owned up, you don't get to say, *Well crikey, mate, you never asked!*'

I like this performance bit. It helps to put the candidate at ease. But Hugh already seems at ease.

'Yes, sir,' he squeaks. 'No problem. I've done ones like this before.'

Now I shuffle in my seat. Not because I'm nervous but because of the bruise on my arse, purple and marbled like a tattoo of Jupiter.

'Then you understand that this is not a job interview. I don't have any say in whether or not you get the position. My opinion doesn't matter. All that matters is what I find. I pass that on to HR and that's it.'

'Yes, mate. I understand.'

One tiny reference to how my opinion doesn't matter and he's demoted me from sir to mate.

'Is there anything you want to tell me at the outset? Anything I'm going to find when I look you up?'

'No,' he shakes his head, innocent. 'No.'

'Have you got a Facebook account?'

'No.'

'What about other online profiles?'

'You mean…'

'Twitter, Lucid, Freeball...'

'No, nothing like that.'

Older candidates don't represent the kind of risk to firms that younger ones do because they have a different approach to privacy, in that they've heard of it. But then, Hugh's disadvantage is that a younger intern is more inclined to be a doormat for the first five years of their career. Firms are wary of older candidates who might have heard of that other thing...what you call it...self-respect.

I'm like, 'What about pornography?'

Hugh smiles and lowers his head to look serious.

'What about it?'

'Have you ever been involved in the production of a pornographic photograph?'

'God, no.'

'A pornographic video.'

'No.'

'Of any kind.'

'No.'

'If you have then I'll find out. If you're straight with me your odds improve in the long run.'

Hugh has a confident smile.

'How would you find out?'

'Well, I think the most likely scenario is that you'll tell me.'

'But what if I said I wanted to keep it private?'

He's still grinning, like he's only testing me out.

'I'd say you were naive. Believe it or not, I'm trying to protect your privacy. Because one day, when you're leading a multi-million dollar lawsuit, there will be people out there who do what I do, and they won't start with a discreet conversation like this. They will drill down, they will go public, and your career will be over. I've seen it happen. Have you ever threatened anyone over social media?'

'No, sir. I don't use the internet for much.'

Hugh's nostrils flare, lips tighten—the first clue that someone would rather be someplace else but has too much at stake to go there. And he's back to calling me sir.

On his CV front page there's a list entitled *Prior Employment*. I'm surprised by what I see.

'You were in the police force?'

'Yes, sir.'

'Where did you work?'

'Drug Squad out of Melbourne.'

'Why did you leave?'

He performs a guilty smile.

'Money.'

'As a cop, shouldn't you have a predilection for criminal law?'

'I thought I would, but at school I didn't.'

'And the real money's in commercial law.'

'That's right.'

'Do you know the name Glen Tyan?'

I'm as surprised by the question as Hugh, who's so ambushed that he chuckles anxiously, with a jiggle of his tummy. But how could I not ask, given the serendipity of it, the fucking timing?

'Yeah. Of course! Detective Glen Tyan?'

He seems incredulous that someone might not have heard of him.

'You know him personally?'

'Well, no, but...'

'You know the name.'

'Yeah, but...' Confusion in his eyes. 'Everybody knows the name Glen Tyan.'

I chuckle along, as if I know why that is.

'Christ,' says Hugh, suddenly bassfaced. 'He doesn't work *here*, does he?'

'No no. I've not met him either. I know him through another client. Just my...Another client.'

'Tell them to watch out.' The chuckling is back but muted. 'The nicest thing you can say about Glen Tyan is that he's unpredictable.'

'Ha! Yes!' This is an entirely honest guffaw.

'They called him the Polygraph. In the Homicide Squad. Did you know that?'

I shake my head, willing Hugh to continue.

'He had a talent...Well, this is what they said. He could tell if someone was lying. I mean, always. Branches all over Victoria used to bring him in for interrogations, he got that famous for it. He was a legend. For a while.'

That pulls the curtain back on last night. Perhaps Tyan knew I was no journalist from the start, from the moment I called him with my face to the glass in the smoking grotto downstairs. He met with me and nodded along to my questions, all the while seeing through my bullshit with a superpower he'd cultivated for years and which is, I can say with confidence, not hereditary.

'Did he ever help you out like that?'

'Not me. People I worked with, yeah. It got to the point where career crims were making deals just so they didn't have to talk to him. But of course, that was before...you know.'

'Sure,' I say.

No idea what he means.

'I guess I don't consider him the laughing stock that other police do. To me it's more sad than anything else. Every bloody year they do a skit about him at the Union Ball too, and that's brutal. I mean, the whole thing happened, what, ten years ago? They're still so brutal. I suppose it is funny. But it's just sad more than anything.'

'Right. Yeah. That's a good way of putting it.'

'He's the cautionary tale, right? The thing every officer is scared of becoming.'

'Can I ask...' I try to seem chatty, 'Do you know *exactly* why he left the police force?'

It's the question that bugged me last night, that seemed to bug Tyan even more.

'Well, I mean, that's...that's what I'm...'

Suspicion comes. I've misstepped. Hugh's face pinches.

'Maybe I shouldn't be discussing this—'

'*No no no,*' I say, too earnest. 'It's *all right*. I'm just *curious*.'

But Hugh can see that that's not true—*his* polygraph kicking in, his brain backpedalling.

'I mean...I don't work there anymore, but VicPol kind of doesn't like it when people talk out of school.'

Somehow my body language or my tone of voice has communicated to Hugh that this interview has gone off the rails because it's gone off the rails, not because 'Stan' is an accomplished interrogator who finds relevance in the most obscure coincidences.

'Hey, man, *I'm* not going to tell anybody. I just know he retired young and I'm wondering why.'

I grin like I only want to be in on the joke, keep my features cool, my body still, wait for Hugh to dive down the rabbit hole in the interest of getting a job.

You often reach the point in an interview when something in the air of the room changes. The subject's eyes and lips and hair, all of their face, their nose, it all kind of slumps, and they come clean and tell you about the article they once wrote for *High Times* magazine, or the anger management course they took to avoid a conviction for assault. You do this job for whatever years, you come to recognise that face. The face that comes right before the confession.

Hugh's got it now. The surrender in his eyes.

Then the door to the conference room swings in and there's Madison. Doesn't even knock. She's eating something and touches her mouth delicately with her painted nails as she speaks, self-consciously hiding the food in there.

'Just to let you know...' She directs this at me. 'Your last interview today has cancelled. Off to work at the UN, believe it or not.'

'Okay.'

'Ummm...' She frowns, swallows, rubs her pregnant belly. 'I'm done for the day. Be in touch soon? We want to announce the harvest next week.'

'Okay.'

And she slips away. The door cruises to a close. Just the two of us again. Hugh's apprehensive face.

But what I think is: fuck Glen Tyan. I'll never see Glen Tyan again. The guy pushed me into a toilet. What do I care about his personal history or his professional history? *It's a victory,* I say to myself, *if I show no interest in him whatsoever.* Let him have his secrets. Nobody cares, least of all me.

At the end of this interview, it's home time.

'All right,' I say. 'Let's talk about online dating.'

12

Spatafina's is one of those pizza joints with red neon in the front window and old Campari ads framed on the walls, plastic tablecloths and stained cutlery. We haven't spotted the owner tonight so maybe he's out playing bocce or concreting his front lawn but his two kids are here, neither of whom has finished high school yet and the girl always seems to avoid us. The boy is the kind of waiter who wants you to know how much he hates his job. Marnie and he have a special kind of spite for each other which she enjoys and which I dread because scorning your waiter is like scorning your neighbour etc. When he brings our drinks I'm telling her about my panic attack on Monday. She interrupts to say:

'I'm sorry. This is a white wine glass. Could I have my red wine in a red wine glass please?'

He rolls his eyes almost imperceptibly, scoops up the beverage and scurries away, leaving behind the phenomenal power of his aftershave.

'It's the pressure of all that court stuff, Stevey. You should meditate. I could teach you.'

Her hair is brown today. I told her once that with all her hair colours she reminded me of Ramona Flowers and she was thrilled with the comparison.

'But I've done evidence in court since forever. This only started a year ago.'

'So what happened a year ago?'

'Um…'

I'm genuinely surprised she has to ask.

'My mother died.'

'Right…' Guilt streaks across her face, pursued by doubt. 'So you get anxious because your mother died?'

'It's more just, like…not having that person in your life…that kind of relationship anymore…'

She nods vaguely, about as unenlightened by my stilted clai

> The room wasn't private. She shared it with an oldie
> who was babbling in French and didn't notice us,
> didn't seem to know where she was. The only words I
> recognised were 'mon dieu' and she was pleading with
> an anguished desperation. Mum grabbed hold of my
> hand and spoke with her eyes shut but I couldn't hear
> over the prattle and I asked the staff if they could
> move the French screamer someplace else and the
> first terrifying thing that happened that day was
> that they did.

my stilted claim warranted. Perhaps I should tell her about the last two days. About Glen Tyan and how I have no explanation for why he's a VicPol punchline.

The problem is: I told her once that my dad was a software designer who died when I was a baby, and my practice is to hold off on revealing to people what a liar I am unless it's absolutely, painfully necessary.

Her eyes silently panic. It's like the eighth awkward pause since we sat down and they wouldn't bother me except that she seems to experience them right in the pit of her stomach. She asks, with an air of desperation:

'Your mum was a cook, right?'

I nod. Her red wine returns in what I assume is a red wine glass because she says nothing to the waiter. I look hard at that glass, try to discern a trace of spittle or botulism.

'You never got the urge to pick up a spatula?'

'Not really.'

'What about, like, football or tennis or something?'

Every couple of dates like this she sniffs around the edges. Usually I sidestep with a broad, meaningless comment before guiding the conversation back to *Game of Thrones*. Maybe tonight I can spare a little more.

'I was the boy who hated sport. Mum said it was because I didn't have a dad. I said it was because I didn't have a backyard. You know that cliché of the kid trolling the internet from his mother's basement? That was me. The original vitamin D deficiency.'

'Right. So the computer thing has been, like, since forever?'

'The first real hobby I ever had was, I used to do a thing on PlayStation where I could dox players with just their gamertag and IP and I could tell them, this is live while we were *playing*, I could tell them their real names, their family members. I called them on their mobile phones. I said I was a psychic and it freaked everybody out. My tag was Mofo the Magnificent.'

When she realises this is a funny anecdote from my past, she chuckles. Marnie is too much in her head to ever respond spontaneously.

I ask, 'What about your parents?'

'What about them?'

'What do they do? Back in Kerang.'

'My mother runs a cleaning business, Dad is...' She sighs. 'I don't want to talk about my parents.'

This is also nothing new. That she's from Kerang is about all she's ever confessed.

I'm like, 'How's work?'

'Fine. Owner's on my case again.'

'Same as before?'

She nods. 'Poor customer service. But, like, I don't suffer fools lightly, Steve. What am I supposed to do?'

'Yeah,' I raise the beer to my lips. 'Working with people. It must be lame sometimes.'

'I wish I had a job like yours. Stay at home all day. Not talk to anyone.'

'Uh-huh...'

'Though it might be nice if you came out from behind your computer every now and then.'

'I come out from there all the time.'

'Only to scurry back as fast as you can.'

'Not always.'

'Well, *I* may not be Mofo the Magnificent,' she looks down into her wine glass. 'But I reckon you will tonight.'

'Maybe,' I say with a pinch of my shoulder, and I understand in that gesture that tonight is the night. Marnie is based, her hair is giving her confidence, while I'm mourning the loss of someone I'd never met before yesterday. The demise of a mere possibility, but one that has occupied so much of my brain for so long. And as it further dissipates with each passing minute, I want that void to be filled with something meaningful, if not also tall, friendly and familiar.

In fact, the resolution comes to me now that tonight I'll tell her everything. It was never that much of a lie to begin with—she knows I never had a dad and she knows how I feel about that. I'll tell her all about the men's room last night and Hugh's story today, and how I've never told anyone before that my father was alive because I never wanted anyone to steal away the daydream that one day I would meet him and then *I'd be a real boy.*

'Look, Marnie,' I say, lowering my voice. She's always had terrific posture, but now she goes rigid, like she's expecting bad news. My lips part, my vocal cords squeeze together to initiate the first word of the first sentence of my confession—

My phone rings.

It doesn't recognise the number, just displays it dumbly onscreen. I recognise it though, gape at it for a few stupefied seconds, then look to Marnie for help. She thinks I'm asking permission to take the call and says, 'Go ahead,' with no idea of the consequences. I have to answer and so I do.

'Hello?'

No coughing this time, just a sharp rasp in my ear.

'Where are you?'

'What?'

'*Where are you?*'

'I'm getting a pizza, Glen. What do you want?'

'*Prove it. Prove you're not outside my house right now.*'

13

Tonight is late closing at Doncaster Shoppingtown so it's weirdly busy, which is good, makes me feel safe. Wrapped in layers of warmth I shiver at the people wearing T-shirts and tank tops, resign myself to the fact that my fear of the common cold is greater than theirs. When I catch my ghost in a store window I think of the little boy at the courthouse on Monday: all bundled up, going home with his mother…

In the food court half the eateries are closed but the other half do a slow trade. I suppose it's the movie crowd that comes hungry, intermittently: young couples feeding soft serve to each other; lonely men scoffing cheap dinners; screaming children hopped up on their own exhaustion.

I drop into a wonky metal seat and remove my beanie.

Marnie must have heard Tyan's bluster from across the table. I'd forgotten he had my number and here he was with more accusation in his voice than even last night. My instinct was to hang up and be done with him. But pride had a point to make. I was no longer the guileless doormat he'd met yesterday.

'I'm sorry?' I said, calm.

'That was you. Just now. Behind my house.'

'No,' I said. 'That was not me.'

'Where are you?'

'In Kensington. A restaurant.'

'Put a waitress on the phone.'

'What?'

'Put a waitress on the bloody phone!'

'Why?'

'Do it or I'll know it was you.'

Suddenly I realise how hungry I am. I trudge across to a Portuguese fast food stand and buy a chicken burger, smear my face with mayonnaise and lettuce and eat and wait. I hadn't so much as *ordered* a pizza before Tyan called. When I held out my phone to the waiter behind me and said, 'Someone needs to talk to you,' Marnie's eyes were two big pizzas, wide and confused.

And the teenage waiter, with his gelled hair and shiny face, he said, 'What?'

'Someone needs to talk to you real quick.' I tried to seem apologetic.

The waiter wiped his hand on his apron and took the phone.

'Hello?'

Silence. Then he said, 'Spatafina's.'

His unibrow formed a deep V on his forehead like a highly inconvenienced Klingon warship. He said, 'Anderson Street. Yeah. 91 Anderson Street, Kensington.'

How I explained this to Marnie is: I didn't look at Marnie.

The boy said, 'Around nine on weekdays. Fridays and Saturdays it's later. Sundays we're closed. Yeah. Sundays we're closed.'

Then Tyan said something that made this kid laugh with his whole body, mouth wide and teeth out like a psychopathic puppet. New information: Glen Tyan can make a person laugh. It flooded me with jealousy.

The waiter said, 'Well I wouldn't know anything about that... All right...Cheers, mate.'

He waved the phone at me and I received it, still emitting apology-vibes, but the boy forgot me instantly and slouched away. I put the phone to my ear.

'Satisfied?'

'Come and see me.'

'What?'

'Look...' His tone had settled. 'Please.'

A word so gapingly unexpected that I couldn't find a response.

Genuine vulnerability. From this guy. I stammered and glanced at Marnie. Her arms raised either side of her like a shruggie. Her face told me to get off the fucking phone.

'When?'

'Right now.'

'I can't right now.'

His voice cracked and he took a moment to swallow. 'I need you to help me, Jason.'

Was that the first time he'd said my name? Gooseflesh prickled my arm. I felt my excitement in the back of my shoulders and fought against that feeling, said, 'Let me call you later.'

'I know you're in a shit about last night. You've got to admit, it's strange this happening the same time you show up. Just show up out of the blue. So of course I'm just...I'm careful.'

'Strange that what has happened?'

'I don't know...' A long, agitated sigh. 'There was someone in my backyard.'

'You should call the police.'

'Come over. I need to talk to you.'

'Why?'

'It's a long fucking story, mate. Just come over. I haven't been able to sleep. I'm going nuts.'

'You understand I'm out? I'm having dinner—'

'Please, matey.' So imploring you'd think he was mocking me. 'If I *am* who you think I am, you can help me just once, can't you?'

I didn't answer.

'*Can't you?*'

Now, in the food court, we spot each other. Tyan's pudgy frame rises on the escalator in exactly the outfit he wore yesterday. He approaches, watching me watch him. How disappointing it must be, to think this weedy dork is his own flesh and blood. Every few steps he shoots a glance to his left or right, analysing the people. I try to relax. I'm not going to speak first. I will wait for Tyan to start speaking.

14

Tyan angles a chair to face the way he came, grunts loud as he sits, murmurs something that might be 'Thanks for coming' with that coconut-husk voice. I don't say 'You're welcome', just shuffle my chair across so that we're not seated side-by-side. I do it noisily. Then Tyan says:

'How did Helen die?'

It is not how I expected him to open. I shift and scratch at my shoulder.

'Umm...It's called pulmonary fibrosis. Her lungs kind of went bad.'

Tyan nods. But like he's got any idea what he's nodding at.

'Did you say it was last year?'

'Yeah.'

'She would have been, what? Fifty-nine?'

'Fifty-two.'

What passes behind his eyes, I don't know if it's Tyan remembering her or just pretending to.

I told Marnie that I had to see a client, that it was an emergency. I waited for her to say something but she just glared, shook her head, offended. On my way out I heard her say, 'Have fun.'

So here we are. Me and Tyan. Having fun.

'I'm sorry,' Tyan says. 'I lost my old man when I was your age. No mum around. No brothers or anything. I know it's...' He frowns, hopeless. '...shithouse.'

This genuine emotion is another surprise.

I don't want to talk about Mum so I ask, 'Are you married?'

Tyan pushes air out of his nose. 'No. I told you last night—'

'Any other kids?'

'*Other* kids? Mate, I'm not...'

He laughs breathily. He doesn't want to finish that denial.

Across from our table a horde of adolescents rounds the corner, lured by pizza slices and dumplings and the kind of chicken burger that's yodelling in my stomach, too many of them to be anything less than a school group and sure enough an adult woman, younger than me and somehow older, speaks with a forced smile to three or four that are lingering, waving them on towards food.

Tyan tries again.

'How do you know...I mean...How do you know I'm the one?'

'Mum told me.'

'My name's not on the birth certificate.'

'I know. She said that was your idea.'

'We didn't know if...if I was responsible.'

'She always seemed pretty sure to me.'

'She shouldn't have been.' Two rows of teeth clack together. His tongue flicks against his cheek. 'You were born long after things had finished between Helen and me.'

'Nine months after, in fact.'

'I'm just saying there's no way for you to be sure. Now, I don't want to blacken the memory of your mother, but she—'

'Do a test.'

He snorts, hates being interrupted.

'What?'

'Do a DNA test.'

'*DNA* test?' He scoffs. 'Do you know how much they cost? *Hundreds* of dollars.'

'Okay, fuck it then. If it costs hundreds of dollars...'

But even as I speak I'm leaning away from Tyan because I don't know how he reacts to sarcasm.

At first that distance comes over him, the same kind he had last night when he realised who I was. Like a wave of sadness he briefly has to withstand. Then, in reluctant surrender, he reaches into his jacket pocket, pulls out a small leather flask, unscrews the lid, thoughtful.

'Even if I was the…' He sighs. 'I wouldn't have been any good to you. I was a pisspot back then. Just like now.'

He drinks a tame slurp. I'm suddenly massively restless.

'What am I doing here…' I look for a word to address him, but I can't call him Dad, won't call him Glen, and Tyan feels like we're at boarding school. And who calls their father 'mate'?

So I finish with nothing and let the question hang.

'Hey,' Tyan puts away the flask. 'You looked me up on the internet, right? *You* came and found *me*.'

'On the phone you begged—'

'Why did you do that? Why did you have to find me so bad?'

I shrug, remove all emotion from my thoughts. All thoughts from my thoughts.

'There's stuff that would be good to know. Like, medical stuff. Like a predisposition to something.'

Tyan shakes his head and arches his mouth. 'Nuh.'

'Prostate issues? Heart problems? Any kind of bug in the system?'

Shakes his head again, not overly vigorous, just not interested, which I take to mean he's not hiding some terminal defect beneath this facade of Overly Manly Man. Then he turns, stares keenly at the escalators, displays for me a bald spot at seventy per cent opacity.

'I'm sorry about last night.'

'Don't worry about it.'

He turns back, uses the palm of his hand to rub his other palm.

'You all right?'

'I'm fine. But you can bet I won't be going for a piss while you're here.'

Tyan nods, doesn't consider this an attempt at humour.

'I'm not myself, you can see. I'm edgy. Can't sleep. The shit that's been…If you've got nothing to do with it, then I'm sorry.'

'What's happened?'

He twitches slightly, tips his head to the side.

'Your job. Finding stuff on the internet…Or was that just bullshit too?'

'It's not bullshit.'

'If I asked you to find out about someone, could you do it? I mean, could you do it without them knowing it?'

'I guess.'

'*Can* you or—'

'Yes. Within limits.'

'What limits?'

'I won't break the law.'

'You broke the law to find me.'

'And then you attacked me and pushed me into a toilet.'

'And then I said I'm sorry. I'll pay you.'

I laugh. 'I don't work for free.'

Tyan stops rubbing his palms but can't stop the fidgeting, seems to grimace at having to ask. 'How much?'

'Three hundred an hour. But it depends what you want done.'

'Three *hundred*?'

'It depends what you want done.'

'I need you to find out about someone.'

'Let me guess,' I say, fucking owning him for just this moment. 'Elizabeth Cannon.'

15

It began last Monday night, after a party at the Darebin RSL. A detective senior sergeant was retiring and a piece ran in the *Daily Sun* that day, Hollywood-taping his career, calling him a legend, previewing the alcoholic circle jerk that awaited him. Tyan's name was written up as one of the likely attendees.

'The point is,' Tyan says, 'Anyone that wanted to know where I'd be that night would know just by picking up the fucking newspaper.'

It's 2012, I want to say. *No one's picked up a newspaper since 1997.* But I let him continue.

He'd drunk more than his share and he shouldn't have driven home. Not that he thought that at the time. At the time he figured it was after midnight and the traffic would be light and he'd motor along on impulse power so he risked it. But he lost focus on the Eastern Freeway, missed the exit and trapped himself on the approach to Mullum Mullum Tunnel. Emboldened by the beer, Tyan U-turned quickly through the centre divider, narrowly avoided a utility vehicle and a motorcyclist.

What was strange was, then a green Volvo did precisely the same thing. He saw it in the rearview. Its break in the oncoming traffic was clearer though; it didn't almost kill someone like Tyan had.

He watched the Volvo in his mirror as he came off the freeway and down onto Springvale Road. Couldn't see the driver. Even at the red lights he tried but couldn't see.

'Did they want you to know they were tailing you? Like, to intimidate you?'

'Nuh. I don't reckon. They were just shit at it.'

He wasn't sure if this was for real or if he was paranoid with booze. Maybe his unconscious was getting nostalgic. After an evening spent carousing with other coppers, maybe he hankered for the old adrenaline, projected this desire onto a vehicle that had coincidentally chosen the exact same moment to U-turn...

It followed him all the way home.

By which time Tyan was halfway to the disturbed ward. He drove past his own house, around the block, all the way around and back again and parked and rushed inside. He thought that had worked. But when he pulled back the curtain on his front window, there it was, stopped on the corner, camping the house. Whoever they were, they'd turned off their lights and slumped down in the seat. But they were there. It wasn't nostalgia.

'Did they see you looking out the window?'

'Nup. It's one-way glass.'

'So he doesn't know you saw him.'

'That's right. But I didn't say it was a *he*. Let me finish.'

Whoever it was, they stayed only a minute, motored slowly around the corner and moved off at speed. They mustn't have realised it was a dead-end because they came back, faster this time, barrelling on towards Maroondah Highway.

'They drove off?'

'Yep.'

'Why would someone follow you home then drive away?'

'That's obvious.' Tyan doesn't hide his disdain for my question. 'To find out where I live.'

He takes another survey of the nearby tables: mostly empty. Way off to the right the chairs are getting stacked, bain-maries wiped, floors mopped, while to our left these high schoolers maintain their petty warfare, far enough away to give us a sense of privacy. He pulls out the hipflask again.

'Something you learn in the police force...' He sips a sip. 'The wackos that send you dead rabbits in the post aren't the wackos you got to worry about. It's the ones trying to sneak up on you that mean business.'

'So do you have any, like, I suppose…enemies?'

'There are a few names that come to mind. A few crims.'

'Did you get the licence plate?'

'Course I did. Mate in the traffic unit traced it for me. Registered to Elizabeth Cannon. An address in Brunswick. Young bird about your age.'

'Does her name mean anything to you?'

'Not fucking remotely.'

'Maybe it wasn't her. Maybe she wasn't driving.'

'I think she was.'

'Why?'

'She gave herself away.'

Tyan lets that hang, so I have to say, 'How?'

But instead of answering he arches back in his seat, distracts himself with the worrisome school teacher who moves slowly past our table. She watches her students the way he watches her—brimming with distrust. As she nears a furtive group of boys, all of them chewing too much food for their tiny mouths, Tyan's glare fades and, after lingering on her a moment longer, his eyes come back to me.

'She reported the car stolen. About six o'clock, earlier that same night. She did that on the *internet*.'

This last point he makes as if we should be surprised.

'But then, the next morning, yesterday morning, she calls up her local copshop and tells them the car's back, right back in her parking space, where it was nicked from. A constable went over and did a report, said the driver's window was smashed and the honey pot was chewed to shit.'

'The honey pot?'

'The key ignition. Someone tore it up with a sharp tool, they said.'

'So it wasn't her. Someone nicked her car and followed you around.'

'But here's the thing…' He puffs his cheeks into a ball and slowly exhales. 'And I swear this on my life. There was no smashed window when I saw that vehicle.'

This puzzles me, but I'm reluctant to reveal that, so I nod gravely.

He says, 'I guarantee it. She drove past my house. I saw *all* the windows. None of them were broken.'

'So…the damage happened after you saw the car?'

'That's right.'

'So she followed you home and the car was nicked *after* that?'

'Maaaaate…' A chuckled slur, like he's amused by how ashamed he is of my stupidity. 'The vehicle wasn't stolen. This Elizabeth character wants to shift focus, in case I clocked the car, which I did, so she gets in first and says it was boosted. Plus, if there's a police report, she can claim the damage on her insurance. Oldest trick in the fucking book.'

'But if it's a ruse, why park it back in her own space? Why not leave it blocks away? Or suburbs away?'

Tyan's amusement evaporates. He fidgets with the lid of his flask.

'Don't know. To make sure it didn't get nicked again. Or pissed on by a dero.'

'So, are they, like, going to arrest her?'

'*Christ*, no.'

'I just thought, you've got friends in the police—'

'This isn't their problem. I just asked someone to trace the plate and even that was pushing it. I didn't tell him what *happened*. Cops have got more important things to worry about than my bullshit.'

The high schoolers are leaving. Their plates and leftovers have magically vanished and they're ambling to the escalators, leaving only Tyan and me and the cleaners to close out the place.

'So what about tonight?

Tyan shrugs, looks away again.

'I don't know. I thought I heard someone in the backyard.'

'No sign of the Volvo?'

'No Volvo. No people. Just me standing out there like a prick in the wind. That's the real problem. I'm not sleeping. I'm seeing shadows. Like with you last night. I need to find out who Elizabeth Cannon is. Can you do that?'

Those big watery eyes look out with something like helplessness.

'How do you spell her name?'

'Normal Elizabeth. Cannon like a ship's cannon.'

I write this into my phone.

'What's the plate number?'

Tyan recalls it without having to think. 'E-L-O, three seven one.'

'And what's your budget?'

More vulnerability. Eyes like teardrops.

'What's your quote?'

I pause, but this isn't shrewd negotiation; Tyan just doesn't know how long it takes to google someone.

'I'll cap it at two-fifty. Call it family rates or whatever. And it gives us a reason to see each other again.'

Tyan seems pleased.

'That's what *I* was thinking. And if I am…the bloke you think, it'd be good to spend more time together, right?'

Then he says, rubbing his satisfied palms down his breasts and without a trace of irony, 'Well, I best be heading home.'

16

It's the next morning and I should be working. I intend to be: my candidate files are out on my desk, mellowing beside my two-day-old, freshly microwaved coffee. I've turned my heater down to keep a crispness in the air, keep me alert. This is how a day starts that usually ends with some light Call of Duty and a fully-compiled dossier; doubly necessary now that Albert Kane and Roach wants to announce its harvest next week.

The thesis here is that Tyan can wait a few days. I don't take well to being pushed into toilets and he has to get the message, at least implicitly, that he has lost his priority status. But of course, there is exactly one problem with that message...

I sip my coffee and tip back in my chair. It's American-style filtered coffee, the kind you can drink all day. Marnie would probably say that this is why I get panic attacks. If she knew how much of it I drank. And if she were still talking to me after last night.

I know why I get the attacks. It's right there in the depths of m

A doctor beckoned me from the hall. He wasn't dressed like a doctor but he was the most senior stooge I'd met and so I left Mum with her glowing white face and sleeping eyes and stepped into the corridor. He told me she'd gone into fibrillation last night, got rushed to the surgery and zapped with a machine and her pulse came back. They put her on an IV and the doc himself found something on the floor of the surgery. Could it be hers? He gave it to me now; a tiny, crumpled piece of card.

...ain if I want to go look, but I won't go looking. These candidate files have to get sorted and the first step is to pick one up and open it.

The thesis here is that Tyan can wait a few days, but who am I kidding? Even if I weren't seeking a distraction from the Albert Kane and Roach job, even if I weren't curious about what happened to Tyan on Monday night, and even if I weren't eternally up for a challenge, there would still be exactly one problem with the notion that Tyan is not a priority for me.

It's like I can feel his blood in my veins. I've felt it all my life. Growing up was like losing an arm and feeling an itch in that arm. And then losing the other arm. And then passing out from panic attacks.

The scrap of card is old, like it's been carried around for years…

But I won't think about that now.

These memories of my mother, these metaphysical phone calls from the past, like Albert Kane and Roach, they can remain on hold for the time being.

I drink more coffee and get started.

She's not listed as married or having kids or changing her name. And no one named Elizabeth Cannon, Lizzy Cannon, Lizzie Cannon, Beth Cannon or Libby Cannon was ever arrested or imprisoned by way of Detective Glen Tyan. The Elizabeth Cannon born in 1987 and living in Brunswick had never been in contact with police until she reported her car stolen last Monday night.

That report includes a scan of her licence. They tell you not to smile in these pictures but she has a beguiling smirk underlining her nose, like she can't help an innate positivity breaking through. Her hair is dark, black or brown, framing the largest blue eyes I've ever seen, like anime come to life. Her cheeks puff with what my mum used to call baby fat. Or maybe she's a woman who eats macaroons just whenever she likes.

My avowal to Tyan's face that I would not break the law was heartfelt at the time, so it's ironic that hacking the VicPol intranet is about as illegal as anything I could do short of spear phishing the attorney-general. Then again, this isn't the first time: I cracked it last year in a drunken attempt to learn something about Glen Tyan. I failed, but not because the app wasn't vulnerable, it just doesn't keep up details on former officers. After fingerprinting this morning I'm pleased to find it's still php script. Even the parameters for the SQL injection are the same. After that, I can't really talk myself out of it. Chalk it up as one more mark against my name when the party van knocks on the door.

The desultory notes of the officer, the stooge dispatched to Elizabeth's flat, are no more detailed than what Tyan told to me. The only surprising aspect is that it notes the 'pistachio green' Volvo is uninsured. Which means Elizabeth will pay for the repairs herself. Which makes Tyan's theory that she false-flagged the car theft gapingly less likely.

All else I find on Elizabeth Cannon is a Twitter account that's protected so only confirmed followers can read her posts. I'm reluctant to crack a Twitter account with Thruware so I set to task a script from chokechan.com that only works on SHA and MD5, and even if that's the encryption, it still could take the rest of the morning.

There's a link in her profile, beneath an equally winsome photograph, to the adoption page of the Northern Lost Dogs' Home, just around the corner from her home address. Pics of dogs who'll be put to sleep if they don't find an owner, looking out at you with those eyes. Also, there are captions:

Minnie is house-broken and loves a cuddle!

Is there a poodle-shaped hole in your life?

Bandit is the PAWfect candidate for obedience training!

It's hard to find a sentence that doesn't end with an exclamation point.

Suddenly the chokechan script throws up her Twitter password: 63m570n3. Leetspeak for *gemstone*. With a password like that it's not surprising a dictionary attack took all of three minutes.

But whatever thrill I get from my high-speed break-in dissolves when I sort through her history. No one tweets at her and the DM file is empty. She follows a handful of news sites, has only twelve followers of her own, all of whom are total randoms waiting for her to follow back. She rarely posts and when she does it's mostly pics taken from her couch of the TV and they have captions like:

Anyone else watching Gilmore Girls?

No one has ever replied. You might as well post in all-caps: *I AM SO LONELY.* The vibe is asinine enough to remind me of the sockpuppet accounts I use to troll SJWs, MRAs, assorted wankers.

After three serves of toast and four hours of digging, I call Tyan to tell him who Elizabeth Cannon is, the answer being: the most boring person I've ever researched. But Tyan doesn't answer, wasn't sitting by the phone, isn't expecting me to call so soon. Throughout our interaction it never occurred to me he doesn't have a mobile. As I listen to the phone ring out, I remember he doesn't have a message bank either. So his position re technology is well and truly established.

My next potential move is to call Elizabeth, put the metaphorical screws on her from the comfort of my flat. But I'd be at the mercy of her mood: her willingness to talk, to be honest. She's not far away, I tell myself. And face-to-face it will be easier to read what's under the surface.

But that's bullshit. In the past I've driven miles out of my way to *avoid* meeting people. What really gets me out the door is a new sense of confidence, my interest in testing it out. Tyan's request for help, his *need* for me, is a rush. Why not ride the wave?

Also, there's the flipside to that confidence: the fear of its evaporation. Disappointing Tyan by finding nothing useful on Elizabeth Cannon would be like a hair dryer on a solitary drop of rain.

On my way to Brunswick I stop at the Smith Street Officeworks. When I return to my car I get my first sense that it is indeed about to rain.

17

Elizabeth Cannon lives in a block of flats in Brunswick, which is like saying she lives in a grain of sand on the beach. A shitty grain of sand, overpriced for its proximity to Sydney Road, built on great brick stilts over its car spaces, all of them oil stained and half of them empty. But the green Volvo is here, its window already repaired, the glass spanking new. I push hand and face against the glass to get a look in the driver's side: the 'honeypot' is scratched and part of it appears cracked and the backseat is a wasteland of water bottles and receipts and strewn clothes: nothing helpful.

For all my research this morning, I never determined what Elizabeth does that she can afford to live here, though according to land.vic.gov she doesn't own the place so she must be renting. When I pass her mailbox I give a tug but it's locked, then I glance up hoping no one saw that. Above the drive a half-dozen east-facing balconies poke out like ashtrays, tiny and useless to the residents unless their hobby is standing still while outdoors. They are unpopulated, probably always are this time of year. At the security door I press the buzzer for flat three as rain starts to fall.

No voice comes to the intercom. I feel these raindrops wash away the confidence that brought me here. The bird life of Brunswick calls to itself, piercing chirrups like the motion detector in *Aliens*. I'm the bad joke the cockatoos are laughing at.

With my finger poised over the button again, I notice the security door isn't shut. Looking closer, it has a spring action that's supposed to close it and lock it but which has failed to do so: it rests gently against its frame, waiting for some conscientious resident to finish the job.

So I forgo the buzzer-pushing and instead enter the small stairwell, return the door to its previous position and climb.

Level one has its predictable unit numbers: one and two. No doormats or decoration, just sad brickwork and the powerful scent of burnt toast. I rise another flight, talking down the butterflies, and here's a white timber door, a number three screwed into it. With a last shake of my hands I knock, gentle.

What I expect is a posse of animals to bark and claw in response. But there's no sound.

'Miz Cannon?' I shout this at the door. 'My name is Timothy Wentworth. I'm here about your car.'

Perhaps a sound now, can't be sure over the patter of rain against the landing windows.

'I'm slipping my card under your door.'

The card says very little: Timothy Wentworth, Investigator, my mobile number. Standing at the print-out station in the Officeworks, I weighed up whether it should be 'Investigator' or 'Private Investigator'. 'Private Investigator' made me feel like a TV show.

Another possible sound. Possibly a hand picking up the card. If so then she's looking out at me now through the peephole and I realise my face is anguished with my effort to listen. So I relax, try to look the way professional people look.

A metal click. The door opens enough to reveal that generous face, more oval than her licence picture, brandishing squarish eyeglasses in sepia frames. Through them she squints at me, blind with curiosity.

My lips dry up and I lick them.

'Elizabeth Cannon?'

'Yes?'

'I've been engaged by the City of Moreland to investigate the incident involving your car last Monday night. May I speak with you?'

'Yeah. Yes.' Her face decompresses, like she's relieved that this is what I've come to talk about. Flattened hair hangs ragged down to her chest, drops of water on her brow and her plump cheeks: she was in the shower. The collar of a fluffy white robe is just visible in the door gap she's allowed. Heat rushes out, flavoursome. Tropical.

'Um, but I already spoke to the police about it, like, a bunch of times.'

Her Aussie inflection makes it sound like a question. *A bunch of times?*

'That's why I'm here. I'm looking into how effectively the police service has done its job. We've had a number of disgruntled car owners claiming that thefts in the Brunswick area are not investigated as thoroughly as they should be.'

Now she shakes her head in an exaggerated denial.

'Okay, but like...*I* never made a complaint like that.'

'Yes, but if you don't mind answering a couple of questions...'

Maybe she thinks I'm too young and scrawny to be an investigator, but she doesn't say it, settles into having this conversation on a freezing concrete landing, hugs her robe, rubs a bare foot against the warmth of her calf and nods with a deeply felt eagerness to help.

'You made an online report to say the vehicle was missing. That was lodged just after eight pm on Monday night, is that correct?'

'Yes,' she says. 'It was just, like, gone.'

'What about the next morning?'

'It was *back*.' She is thrilled with this turn in her story.

'Where were you headed?'

'Ummm...The dog shelter. Where I work sometimes?'

More inflections. So Australian it's almost embarrassing.

'Is that your primary place of employment?'

'Oh, I don't work there. I'm a volunteer.'

'If I may ask you, Miz Cannon, where do you work?'

'Call me Beth. I'm...I suppose I'm between jobs.'

The sides of her mouth pull into her cheeks, reveal a remarkable set of dimples. Then she giggles at herself.

'Listen, I collect donations for the shelter? The Northern Lost Dogs' Home...'

She pushes the door fully open, jams it in place with her foot and has to stretch to reach a cabinet by the door. I appraise the flat. Just two small bedrooms leading off the small living room, brightly lit and unashamedly girly: soft toys line the mantel and a movie poster of smiling happy people is framed on the wall above. To my right there's a kitchenette and a pile of dishes in the sink.

Beth straightens, holding a plastic cash box. At the top is a coin slot and on the side there's an official-looking sticker and a picture of a sad puppy.

'You wouldn't be willing to make a small donation?' She smiles with a gruesome amount of hope.

I dig in my pocket for change, but she says, 'The average contribution is around ten dollars.'

So I draw out my wallet, slip ten dollars into the box. 'No problem. And there was damage to the car when you found it?'

'Actually...' She grimaces, already apologising with her big eyes like adjacent blue planets. 'Winter is the hardest time of year for our puppers. Their numbers increase but there's less reclaims and less adoptions. I wouldn't usually ask but...'

She must have seen the second ten-dollar bill in my wallet. I slide it into the box and she melts with appreciation.

'Thank you *so* much. You should come by the shelter. The pups would like you.'

'The damage to your car...'

'Yeah, no,' she places the box back on the cabinet. 'With the window broken and everything. It was really weird. Like...' She shakes her head, bugs out her eyes, lets her failure to finish her sentence indicate how creepy the events had been.

'Were the police able to give you an explanation?'

'No.' Full of empathy.

'Does the car still run?'

'Oh yeah.'

'Which window was broken?'

'The driver's side.'

'Was there broken glass inside?'

'Yes, all on the seat.'

'So you think the window was smashed to gain access to the

vehicle, whereupon the thief drove the car while sitting in a puddle of broken glass?'

'Um...I didn't...I don't know what I think.'

She cringes and I silently hate myself for my scepticism. It's obvious this girl wouldn't lodge a fraudulent report with Santa Claus let alone the police.

'I'm just saying, it implies that the car was taken, returned, and *then* the damage was done to the window and the ignition.'

'Why would anyone do that?'

'To make it look like it was taken by force.'

'But...why would anyone do *that*?'

'Insurance, usually.'

'I don't have insurance.'

'I know. Which is why I thought I'd visit. It's an unusual case.'

'Are you saying I stole my own car?'

'*No*,' I laugh at the horror in her face. The neck of her robe tugs back to reveal an additional inch of shower-ravaged flesh. I try not to let her see me notice it. 'Do you share this flat with anyone?'

'No.'

'Do you share the car?'

'No.'

'What about a boyfriend or girlfriend.'

She giggles. 'Not at all.'

'Does anyone else have a key to the vehicle?'

'No, but...the man who used to own it...he might still have a key.'

'What's his name?'

'I mean, it's possible. But, like, why would he drive it and then smash it up?'

'Maybe he wanted it to look like a real car theft.'

'But I'm the one who has to pay for it.'

'What's his name?'

'I mean, why would he do that?'

'So you wouldn't think of him as the one who took it. What's his name?'

'Rudy. Rudy Alamein.'

I write this into my phone.

'Rudy short for Rudolph?'

'Rudyard, I think.'

'Rudyard?' My incredulity has no effect on her. 'How did you first make contact with him?'

'He comes to the shelter sometimes. His cocker spaniel ran away, like, years ago. Maybe ten years ago? And he still goes around to all the shelters asking for him.'

'Do you have an address?'

'Not exactly, but he lives on Grand Street in Albert Park. By himself. In, like, the spookiest house you've ever seen.'

'So he's a friend?'

'Yeah.' She says it softly, as if distracted by fond memories of the arsehole who no doubt ripped her off. I've seen that Volvo.

'You should keep your distance for the next few days.'

'Oh.'

'If he stole your car, there's every chance he'll try to get in touch. Don't take his calls, don't agree to meet. Believe me, in my work I've had experience with this. The worst thing a young woman in your situation can do is assume to know what he's capable of.'

It's bullshit—a measure to prevent her from tipping him off. But based on the evidence at hand, it's also not bullshit.

Unconsciously I take a step back. Doing that, I realise I'm leaving. There's nothing left for me here. After speaking with her for two minutes I'm confident she hasn't been tailing people or trashing her own property. But I have to concede, as I take one last breath of the sweet air emanating from within, that she is no longer the most boring query I've ever researched.

A big smile from her. Wholesome. Not remotely flirtatious.

'I'm sorry. I wish I could have been more help.'

'Just keep clear of this Rudy guy, all right?'

'All right.'

'Call me if you remember anything else.'

She picks up my pretend business card from the dining table, holds it up to show that she has it. My voicemail greeting doesn't include my real name. Or any name.

18

Cheryl Watersloe married Piers Alamein in 1984. Their wedding photo has them gawkish and washed-out but grinning in that lipsticked way. On the night of the ceremony they caught a plane to Vanuatu and honeymooned for a week, spent most of it indoors at the whim of Cyclone Hayley. They must have found something NSFW to do in there because nine months later Rudyard Christopher Alamein was born.

The totality of information I return on Rudy Alamein, after hours of searching, using every google dork I know, relates without exception to a killing that took place thirteen years ago. Also during a storm.

With the usual blast of heat in my face and a left hand funnelling fried goods into my mouth, I launched into a brick wall: Rudy Alamein had no online presence. Not any. It took hours to determine this. There was no social media profile linked back to him, no registration of a name change, not even an email address. The chips were finished, the tea brewed and drunk and dry at the bottom of my mug before I found this exchange on Facebook from seven years ago.

> PenAm: u look like Rudy
> Alamein in that pic
>
> > Kath8su94: wut who?
>
> PenAm: u have to remember
> from school his dad went to jail
>
> > Kath8su94: fuk u k?

On Ancestry.com I picked up the names Piers and Cheryl Alamein, didn't need google dorks to search *them*. There was so much commentary on what happened that I resolved to read none of it, flipped off the banshee news sites and made for the eternal mother-lode of crimes and criminals, the all-singing all-dancing electronic database starring every Victorian who ever went to prison: the Adult Parole Board. It stores the sentencing remarks, the court transcript, the prosecution opening at plea, all the written submissions and all the statements-to-police, wrapped up in a bow and left somewhere vulnerable to a cross-site attack. Chalk it up as one more mark against my name when the party van knocks on the door.

The sentencing remarks are the wikiest.

The Alamein family was cashed up in the 1990s. Piers was a jeweller and he rented a workshop opposite the Galleria and the family moved into an Edwardian terrace in Albert Park. No more children popped out but they bought a puppy and Rudy attended a wealthy private school and the three of them returned to Vanuatu more than once to escape the Melbourne winter. It might sound like Disney-tier good times, but within this house of bliss was a fissure. The centre had collapsed.

The murder of Cheryl Alamein by her husband was the climax of animosity and reproach that had bottlenecked since the end of the marriage in 1997. He'd moved out, rented an apartment in South Yarra, saw his family often enough and no one could say that he and Cheryl weren't getting along. Nor could the Crown say that, prior to this separation, Cheryl had suffered so much as a Chinese burn at the hands of her husband.

Piers waived professional privilege and his lawyer gave evidence. She said the process was amicable, mercifully straightforward, that Cheryl and Piers seemed close. They suffered not from irreconcil-able differences but a kind of holistic FOMO, had grown cross-eyed with boredom and pictured for themselves the life of singlehood and liberty wagged in their faces by television and billboards. Over the next two years the divorce was finalised and the parties began to work towards a property settlement; in the interim it was agreed that Piers would contribute a thousand dollars a week in child maintenance and Rudy would spend every second weekend with him in South Yarra.

Exactly how Rudy felt about this, about any of it, about anything at all, is not chronicled. Rudy's existence is a ghost, more a memory to the characters of the story than a living player. Perhaps that's the life of a thirteen-year-old whose parents are circling the wagons. Like I'd know.

On Monday the third of June, 1999, the last ever Monday with Cheryl Alamein alive in it, Piers saw Rudy to the Grand Street house, as arranged, as he had done every second Monday for more than a year. He glimpsed a flash of white in the mailbox and removed the envelope. This was habit, he claimed, having lived there himself for almost a decade. It was a letter to Cheryl from the ATO, obviously a tax statement. At this point, Piers told the police, habit was no longer a factor—he wanted to know Cheryl's income, now that she had returned to teaching and while he continued to fund the entirety of Rudy's upbringing.

Cheryl opened the door to receive Rudy, found Piers tearing at the envelope and Did. Not. Want. She leapt at him. This is how she told it:

> There ensued a brief, physical altercation. I demanded the envelope. He insisted he had the right to read the contents. Piers pushed me down the stairs that led up to our front door and I have a very bad bruise on my thigh.
>
> I was very much in fear for my personal safety and it is possible that Piers would have injured me further if not for the intervention of a local tradesman who appeared on the street and spoke words to the effect of, 'Leave her alone.'
>
> Having wrought the letter from Piers, I insisted that he leave. Which he did, with words to the effect of, 'Go to hell.'

The following day, Cheryl made that statement to police as part of her application for a Family Violence Intervention Order. She said her level of fear, on a scale of one to three, was '3—very fearful', and the likelihood of further violence was '3—very likely'. Piers's lawyers couldn't keep the statement from being entered into evidence at his trial. On the witness stand, Piers claimed he hadn't pushed her, she'd just lost her balance, but by then the mysterious tradesman couldn't be found to break the tie.

Piers also refuted the allegation that he saw his ex-wife again. According to him, words to the effect of 'Go to hell' were the last words he ever spoke to her.

The order was served on Piers that same Monday. It prohibited communication with Cheryl and featured an exclusion condition that he wasn't to come closer to the house than one hundred metres. A court date of June fourteenth was nominated, where he could contest the order if he chose.

His response, according to his friends and to his browser history, was rageface fucking lunacy. He grawlixed at being demonised because his wife had tripped over, was particularly assmad at the discovery that Cheryl would get more in the property settlement if she could prove domestic violence. Piers convinced himself, over the following days, that this had been Cheryl's plan all along.

That Friday, Piers returned to the house to hunt for proof of Cheryl's plot. And her income. If nothing else, he would find that tax statement. The Crown conceded that Piers had no intention of harming Cheryl Alamein when he made entry into the house, using his own key, at 11.45am. Moreover they conceded that, while Cheryl had been sufficiently frightened of Piers to apply for the intervention order he was now in breach of, she had not been so frightened as to change the locks.

This was the Friday of the Queen's Birthday weekend and Cheryl wasn't supposed to be home; she was supposed to be away for three whole nights, at a friend's holiday house in Lorne. The friend, Maria Bonniano, had offered the empty house with a promise to look in on Rudy over the long weekend. It was supposed to be a holiday for Cheryl; arrangements had been made long before the stairs incident and Piers had been apprised. He believed the Grand Street house would be empty until Rudy returned from school.

But with dark clouds moving low and fast, overtaking other, friendlier clouds, combined with her guilt at leaving Rudy and Busby the cocker spaniel to fend for themselves—Busby always freaked his nuts at the sound of thunder—Cheryl sat around in Lorne for all of two hours before she struck out for home again. She called Maria Bonniano to relay as much. According to Bonniano's evidence, there was nothing wackadoo about the call, nothing suspicious or frightening, just Cheryl's regret at not taking advantage of the house and her concentration on the difficult drive, the apocalyptic nightmare of the Great Ocean Road as a storm mustered and broke overhead. What a relief it must have been to make it home safely!

She arrived at 12.17pm.

What the judge wrote next is almost impossible to believe. This is what he pronounced in court, at the conclusion of the plea, as everyone waited to hear the sentence handed down to Piers Alamein, as reporters scratched in their notebooks, as Piers himself stood in the dock and as the door to the whole shitberg creaked shut. What the edgy edgemaster judge said was this:

'Little did she know the terrible fate that awaited her within.'

Lolwut?

Sure, judges get eccentric. But eccentric *and* lame?

19

Scuffing sounds on the concrete landing outside. I'm willing it to be Marnie, mentally urging her to see the glow of my displays under the door. Telepathically I'm pleading with her to chance a visit. To say hi. And I'd tell her everything, just to have someone listen.

That unique jingling of keys that no other keys could replicate, then her door opens. Closes. In the silence I realise there is no storm outside. It's a regular night and I'm the hikikomori dingus swept up in someone else's story, snapped out of it by the sound of footsteps passing me by.

Now is when I first try to call Tyan. To fill him in, to catch him up, to win his fucking approval. But no answer. It's late for him to be out, but dafuq do I know about his habits? Maybe this is normal. I don't think so; my sense is that something is wrong—

No, Jason. Don't catastrophise. You've got work to do...

They knew what time Cheryl had returned home because her neighbour heard the front door. Her name was Lucille Nguyen, a plump retiree whose strategy for sitting out the storm involved rice wine, a calico cat asleep in her lap and a magazine about gardens. This was on the settee in her front room that shared a wall with the Alameins. Their heavy oak door shuddered closed and it woke up the cat and Nguyen checked the time because it was early for Rudy to be home from school.

What else she heard was Cheryl calling her ex-husband's name. The terrace walls were not thin, but Cheryl was shouting to be heard on the next floor, above the roar of the rain.

The Crown claimed Cheryl had spotted Piers's car on Grand Street, the same green Volvo that has a role to play more than a decade later. She clocked that Piers was inside, had gained entry with his own key, was at that moment scrutinising her email. Or her bedsheets.

Whatever he was doing, he was doing it in the master bedroom. That's where Cheryl found him and that's where the angry voices came from. Nguyen thought nothing of this at first and the muffling of the rain prevented her from discerning actual words. But when the cat stirred and carried itself to the back of the house, Lucille Nguyen sighed and did likewise, regrouped in the kitchen, made tea and continued to read about bonsai trees by the light of long windows that sulked with rain.

Had she remained in the sitting room, she would have heard those voices abruptly cease.

It isn't known what Piers had been doing in the house because he never confessed to being there. Obviously Cheryl confronted him, got gaping assmad and so did Piers, still committed to a belief she was defrauding him in the settlement. And amid the heat and ego of the fight, fuelled perhaps by the drama of the lightning outside, Piers picked up a vase from the dressing table.

Within these documents there's a PDF of a xerox of a xerox of a xerox. You can just discern the outline of a thick glass milk bottle. On the base is embossed the word *IKEA* and below that *mouth blown by Lulu Kismet* and one side is blackened with blood because Piers used it to kill his wife.

They didn't find any prints on the vase—not Piers's, not Cheryl's. Instead they found smears of detergent, the same lemon-scented stuff that lived under the kitchen sink. It was concluded that she'd recently cleaned the vase and that Piers had worn gloves when he came to the house that day, though it was unclear why he would.

The pathologist at the trial said the blunt trauma cracked her skull, jolted her temporal lobe and triggered her brain to swell. A damaged skull can't expand like it's supposed to in response to a swelling brain and she haemorrhaged. No one could say how long it was before she died, but she must have been unconscious for several minutes. Then she died.

What was conceded by the Crown was that the cause of death was a single blow to the head. This led the jury to find Piers guilty of manslaughter, not murder. Even so, the judge slotted him for fifteen years. Because of what he did next.

Piers twigged that Cheryl was dying. As much would have been relayed by the blood pooling around her on the bedroom floor. But Piers was based. Didn't panic, clung to the vase, padded downstairs, ignored Busby driven wackadoo by the cracking of thunder and dug a hole in the backyard with a garden trowel, even as the rain kept on and must have soaked him through.

I scroll through colour photos of the ferns and the creepers that hedge the path to a bungalow at the rear of the property—thirteen-year-old Rudy's private fiefdom, including his bedroom. Amid the rows of lush garden is an excavation too small to house a dead body. The Crown argued that Piers had intended to bury the murder weapon.

But something stopped him. Having dug the hole, he left it as it was, water pooling within, dropped the trowel right there and buried nothing. No one knew whether he got spooked or if he chose to keep the vase for a souvenir. What was for sure was that, according to Rudy, this improvised little trench had not been there when he'd left for school that morning.

Piers came back inside, leaving footprints on the kitchen floor that matched his shoe size, though the shoes themselves were never found. He departed by the front door, deep within the deluge, quietly bashing in a small stained-glass plate near enough to the door lock to present as some drug-addled thief's paltry means of entry—an attempt by Piers to set up a 'burglary-gone-wrong'. Man...clichéd much? His grace note was to leave the door ajar like criminals do on TV. Then, behind cooperative curtains of rain, he hightailed it in a green Volvo.

In considering an appropriate jail term, His Honour the Edgy Edgelord declared that a particularly aggravating factor was the decision to allow the murdered woman to be discovered by their thirteen-year-old son upon his return from school.

Rudy did get back earlier than usual because of an altercation at recess: he'd tolchocked another student, one of his regular tormentors, drawn blood with the follow-up swipe of a pen lid. The response of whichever fuck-my-life disciplinarian, unable to raise Rudy's parents on the phone, had been to send him home in the rain at 11.30am.

He didn't get there until after one. By then the storm itself had retreated but the downpour continued and he was drenched when he alighted from the Grand Street tram. The house door was wide open, broken glass across the entryway, and calling Busby's name didn't return a howl or a whine or a shaky pet clumsily thankful for Rudy's homecoming. It was later determined that the animal had run terrified into the street, permitted now by the open door, pursued by thunder overhead. This is the childhood pet, I realise, that Rudy has continued to search for ever since. This is how he met Elizabeth Cannon.

Parked right there on the kerb, his mother's BMW went unseen. He hadn't looked for it since she wouldn't be back until Sunday, so his first move was to call her from the phone in the kitchen to say that the house had been burgled and Busby was missing. He heard her phone ring through the receiver. And he heard it ring upstairs.

Rudy left the phone off the hook, followed the siren. This is what he said in his statement to police:

> I saw no other people in the house until I reached the bedroom. I found my mother on the floor. She was dead. I went downstairs and hung up the telephone. I called triple zero. I went outside to look for Busby.

Rudy didn't take the stand. It was considered sufficient that his statement was entered into evidence without a fight. This scanned document is typewritten, double-spaced beneath a VicPol header. He hadn't exactly gushed—the whole thing is just a page and a half long. At the end Rudy didn't sign his name so much as doodle it.

Beside that, in smaller type and signed by a hand that knows what a signature is, there is this:

Statement procured by: Detective Glen Tyan

I try to call him again. *Still* no answer. Images of the worst possible scenario rain down from the cracks in my ceiling.

20

I'll give Tyan five more minutes. If there's still no answer, should I call triple zero?

It might have happened last night. If Rudy watched as Tyan and I sat in the food court, if he was waiting to get Tyan alone, he could have ambushed him in the carpark of Doncaster Shoppingtown. I doubt I could conceive of a worse place to die.

Maybe Rudy knows who I am. Maybe right now Glen Tyan is dead in the boot of his car and Rudy is lurking outside my door, awaiting the same opportunity...

Calm the fuck down, you gaping wanksock.

I sift the tabloid sites for the murder of a white male in his sixties. Nothing.

Maybe I won't call triple zero. His faith in me will nosedive if the cops have to track him down to the Good Times on Cemetery Road...

I continue reading.

Detective Glen Tyan was clueless as to what had been used to murder Cheryl Alamein. The *who* was less of a mystery—Piers Alamein would have been the prime suspect even if, when a woman is murdered, nine times out of ten it's not her husband who did it. He couldn't account for where he'd been all day other than lying on his couch, listening to the rain.

On the morning of Saturday the eighth of June, detectives searched Piers's apartment and returned nothing.

They interviewed him at the Flinders Street complex, said they were tracking down the killer, not that he *was* the killer, so it was Piers himself who pointed out, poring over photographs of the crime scene, that a clear-lacquer vase in the shape of a milk bottle was missing from his dresser by the fireplace. 'Could this be the murder weapon?' he asked, dripping with Hollywood sincerity.

Eight hours later, Tyan led a group of officers to Piers's workshop—with Piers's permission because in 1999 it was hard to process a search warrant on a Saturday; they even used his key to get in—whereupon the blood-smeared vase was discovered inside an unlocked deed box. This is how a cheap Ikea milk bottle, the one in the grainy xerox of a xerox of a xerox, became the linchpin in the case against Piers Alamein.

What dazzles me is how gapingly analogue this is. What I've seen in the news, what I've seen in *courts*, is that cases are brought using emails and DNA and base-station pings. But track back to 1999 and it's all about what the butler overheard and bloody footprints leading up to the door. It reads like Matlock fanfiction. This case *belongs* in a previous century.

Tyan couldn't explain why there was so much blood on the vase. If Piers had struck her only once, why should there have been any more than a few specks? His theory was that Piers had dropped it at the moment of the killing, whereby it was bloodied by the spreading pool, after which Piers retrieved it upon entering Sinister Plot Mode. But this was just a theory.

Also, why did Piers point to the crime-scene photos and tell the police the vase was missing? Why *hand* them the rope to hang him with, not to mention the keys to his workshop? Tyan was asked that question when he took the stand.

DETECTIVE TYAN (WITNESS): It's clear to me that he wanted us to find it.

LUMIS: To what end?

DETECTIVE TYAN (WITNESS): I'm sorry?

LUMIS: What did you think his objective was in wanting you to find the vase?

DETECTIVE TYAN (WITNESS): To be caught. To end it.

LUMIS: Doesn't that jar with his plea of Not Guilty?

DETECTIVE TYAN (WITNESS): He got a look at a long stretch in prison and said bugger that for a joke.

[*Laughter*]

Piers's defence claimed the vase had been planted by the real murderer. But they couldn't offer a single candidate. And how do you explain the mud tracked in by shoes of exactly his size? The neighbour hearing the fight and the shouting of Piers's name? His failure to prove he was elsewhere?

The case was strong enough that he wasn't bailed prior to the trial. After the trial, the judge ordered him to serve at least another thirteen years.

Throughout the proceedings were a series of interlocutory hearings, ones I don't fully understand but which seemed to hinge on the possibility of a final witness giving evidence. His name was Kenneth Penn, but literally no further information is supplied. Piers's lawyers initially wanted to have him called—it was Piers himself who shouted them down and Penn would remain excluded. The Crown's only argument in these hearings appears to have been that the defence get their shit together.

Attached to all of these records, right there at the bottom of the folder, is a file note. It says that Piers died on June third, 2012. It doesn't list the cause of death, but the fact that June third, 2012 was six weeks ago seems to me to be the last veil in the dance, discarded now to expose the full amplitude of Glen Tyan's predicament.

Back on Google, I skim pictures and find a family portrait from before the fall: Piers, Cheryl and Rudy in 1996. The irony is as powerful as the layout editor hoped: a shiny, buoyant family on the eve of destruction. Cheryl Alamein is patrician, proud, wears a jacket with dramatic shoulder pads like her head is sticking up through a plank of wood. White teeth can just be glimpsed through a peculiar, fetching smile she has mastered.

In front of her there's Rudy, eleven years old, grinning with buck-toothed awkwardness and freckled youth, red hair clippered down to an eighth of an inch like a strange fungus growing across his scalp. He's got the message that he should appear boyishly happy, but his attempts at such an imitation can't conceal the detachment deep within the pupils of his eyes, the void where his love and hate should be. The same eyes as his father, standing above, an arm around Cheryl: a pin-up for white male prosperity, handsome despite his rounded shoulders and ruptured skin. The males' dispassionate faces are strikingly similar and there in my intestines is a quease of jealousy.

I lean away from the image, rub radiation from my eyes. My neck aches from my poor posture, the late hour. Is it really Rudy Alamein tormenting Tyan? Do the children of criminals really grow up to violently resent the coppers who locked up their parents? Why aren't the streets then awash with youths stalking and attacking police officers?

I stare into Rudy's eleven-year-old eyes, try to glimpse the crackpot that lies in wait.

It's that face that makes me pick up my phone. I call Tyan again and this time I let that fucker *ring.*

21

How come Tyan didn't answer his phone is: he was sleeping. Not murdered.

'I heard it ring,' he croaks. 'I was hoping whoever it was would piss off.'

Then he embarks upon the kind of coughing surge you get from being an arsehole too soon after waking up.

'Do you recognise the name Piers Alamein?'

A short silence. Then, 'What?'

'Piers Alamein.'

He swallows twice, clears his throat.

'What about him?'

'The green Volvo you saw belonged to him. Then it went to his son, Rudy. Then Rudy sold it to Elizabeth Cannon.'

'No shit.'

'She reckons Rudy might still have a key. And I believe her when she says she had nothing to do with Monday night.'

'What? You talked to her?'

'Ye—' My voice catches. 'Yeah…I went to her flat.'

'Why the fuck did you do that?'

'Because…' Being grateful was too much to hope for? 'Because I didn't have any luck with my searches. Don't worry, I didn't tell her anything.'

'I didn't ask you to talk to her. You just had to find out who she was.'

'Well…' I consider mounting a defence. 'Okay. Sorry.'

Tyan sighs, grunts as if somehow exerting himself. In a moment of rustling I hear the click of a cigarette lighter, an inhale and a wheeze.

'Rudy Alamein...' He says it slowly, testing the sound. 'What the fuck does *he* want?'

'Perhaps he blames you for what happened to his father. Working up the courage to confront you.'

'I put away plenty of blokes. Plenty of fathers. And it was years ago. Why wait so long?'

'Piers Alamein died last month.'

Silence on the phone.

I'm like, 'Hello?'

'Piers Alamein is dead?'

'Yes.'

'How?'

'Don't know. All I know is his deceased date comes before his parole date. So he must have died in Severington prison.'

I can't tell if Tyan is distracted by that or by some other thought. A memory of thirteen years ago...

'And you reckon Rudy's got it in for me?'

'Obviously, right? He tailed you, found out where you live. He wants payback.'

Tyan sighs.

'The man killed his wife.'

'I know. I read about it.' It wasn't my job to do *that* either, so I skate over just how much reading I've done. 'But if a crazy person is looking for someone to blame, I'm not sure if logic applies. What do you remember about Rudy?'

'Just...He was fucked up with grief.'

'Was he angry at you then, do you remember?'

No answer. A light thud at the end of the line.

'Tyan?' It's possible he's fallen back to sleep. 'Hello?'

Silence. Maybe another grunt, distant.

My spine cramps. Gooseflesh.

'*Tyan!*'

The creak of plastic. Someone handling the receiver.

'Sorry,' Tyan says. 'I thought I heard something.'

'What was it?'

'Nothing.'

My ears instinctively tune to my own outside world: tyres on the wet road, a car door, rain tickling the window.

'Listen,' he says. 'I need a picture.'

'Of what?'

'Him.'

'Rudy?'

'You can get one with your computer.'

'I had a look. The most recent is from 1996. He was, like, eleven.'

'I need a picture.'

'Why?'

'*Because I need to fucking know who I'm looking out for! Why the fuck do you think?*'

Tyan coughs, dredging up sputum from down deep. He takes a moment to base himself, then says, 'I can't remember anything. It was too long back.'

'How am I supposed to get a picture?'

'Do you know where he lives?'

'He's still in the same house in Albert Park.'

'So find him and take a photo. I'll pay you.'

'You're already on the hook for two-fifty.'

'Whatever. We're talking about my life here.'

I shake my head at my empty living room. 'Surely we go to the police now. There's nothing left to find out—'

'Fuck that. There's everything to find out. What's this little prick planning? Is he trying to scare me or what? Why's he picking on me?'

The sound of the lighter again. Chain smoking.

'Get me a picture, then we go to the next level, law enforcement or whatever. All right? So can you get it?'

'I'm just not very comfortable taking pictures of people. I don't even own a camera.'

'Use your phone. I'm not that bloody daft. You've got a phone, I seen it.'

It's late. I feel my vulnerability like you feel a lump in your armpit.

'Okay. I'll get a picture. No extra fee. But you have to do something for me.'

'What?'

'You have to come visit Mum with me. On Sunday.'

22

Rudy Alamein says, 'I'm interested in ummm…How much is that? That…what you just said.'

I'm seated behind him on the number 1 tram. We're back to back, so if I raise my chin our heads will touch and I'm trying to avoid that as we trolley towards Kings Way because I don't want to draw attention. Also because, in the five minutes since I clapped eyes on him, Rudy has presented as the kind of person to unwittingly carry a communicable skin disease.

The two of us are crammed against the window, me with my legs shut tight and Rudy a throbbing presence behind, along with all the other presences. I don't know what's made the tram so crowded today but it's the reason my balls ache. The dreadlocked stooge beside me doesn't have this problem because his legs are entitled to as much space as they need.

Rudy's voice is uninhibited, gratingly nasal. When his phone buzzed and he started speaking, it seemed to me that he lacked any kind of school-tier education. But as I listen it seems more accurate to say that Rudy had once been getting an education and then it stopped, somewhere between learning all the words and learning how to string them together. Somewhere between the death of his mother and the incarceration of his father.

'Yeah…Yeah…' Rudy says. 'The maximum. Whatever is the maximum…The maximum payment or whatever.'

It was so cold outside Rudy's house this morning that twice I started the car engine just to get the heat flowing, the feeling back in my hands. In those warmer moments I was able to properly absorb where I was: a street of snazballs homes with one glaring imperfection—a single bad tooth in a perfect, laser-whitened smile.

Grand Street was wide and run through by a seam of tram tracks, like a zipper holding the bitumen together, that crooked left at Montague Street and continued all the way to the beach. Albert Park was baller country, for all the blandness of its name, thanks mostly to its placement between the CBD and the bay and its wide streets and historical homes. Someone dumped a mess of Commission flats on the east side of Ferrars Street and you could see suicide-prevention bars across each of the windows as they rose twenty storeys high. Because nothing makes poor people want to kill themselves like cars bigger than your home, pets better groomed than your girlfriend, teenagers pushing prams who are not mums but nannies.

From there on it was fifteen blocks of middle-class paradise, beginning with a series of twelve terraces that even had a name written above in proud, concrete lettering: *Montrose Row*. And right in the middle was number 486, where a woman had been murdered thirteen years ago.

Behind me, on the tram, Rudy says, 'No, don't smoke. I never smoke. Never smoked. But could you, like, say that bit again?'

Beth had said the house was spooky and I suppose it was. All the paint was peeled away and nocturnal creatures appeared to have burrowed into the brickwork and made homes of pitch dark. There was a balcony running the width of the house but the ironwork had turned white with decay like a million pigeons all pooped on it at once; above it the drainpipe had come loose and one end was collapsed onto the deck, which surely must then flood at the first splash of rain. There was no door there but two large windows because a hundred years ago the trend had been to build these balconies with no thought of how someone might access them. They looked out from what was probably the master bedroom, where Cheryl had confronted her ex-husband, where they'd had the argument that ended so badly. The blinds were open but I couldn't see inside.

At ground level the front garden, too small for a lawn, had devolved into a single thatch of primeval weeds. From the front door to the street they hadn't been trimmed back but merely trampled in such a way as to indicate that this was indeed how the resident transported himself from the ruin where he lived to the footpath.

If the house had looked like this in 1999, you could believe that someone got murdered here. But you know it didn't. You know that, back then, it was crafted and spruced and maintained.

Just like the homes either side. Thin, protected dwellings where you imagined the children wore spotless school uniforms and the mothers spoke authoritatively to cleaners and gardeners who also wore uniforms. The pots for the pot plants were perfectly coordinated and the ceramic tiles along the porch perfectly uncracked. It was surely only the memory of what had happened at number 486 that kept these people from demanding their neighbour fix the garden, paint the house. Or maybe they did demand it, but he was such a user-interface disaster he never twitched.

Rudy says, 'Prime Life? Is that, like, is that the…Prime Life?'

From my car I watched the sidewalks and the eucalypts and everybody going to work. After two hours it seemed that waiting for Rudy Alamein like this was way ambitious and the true burden of sitting forever turned my mood. When Tyan had assumed, as I had, that Rudy would surely *leave the house* on any given day, it was an assumption based on normal patterns of behaviour. Perhaps Rudy Alamein was not subject to normal patterns of behaviour. It was entirely possible, I thought as I switched to the passenger seat for the legroom, that Rudy hadn't left the house since the last time he'd actively stalked Glen Tyan.

So I noodled at my phone, updated my Steam but mostly I was getting hungry, thinking about slipping off to a bakery when the massive wooden door peeled open and a man scurried out.

Behind me now, that same man says, 'And if that's what I get, what's the…what does it…you know?'

I wasn't able to say at first if this was Rudy Alamein, the eleven-year-old in the only photo of him I'd ever seen. I'd thought the red hair would give him away but there was almost none to speak of, balding in his mid-twenties and what growth there was was cut short. But the roundness of his head and the quick, jerky movements of his body sealed it for me. *This is the demeanour*, I thought, *of a numpty twentysomething wastrel bent on revenge.*

Rudy's hands were buried deep in the pockets of his black jeans and his Goretex jacket was done up to the neck and he approached the street with a kind of stomp. At first the stomping seemed necessary, to navigate that insane front yard, but then Rudy prised open the wrought-iron gate and came onto the sidewalk and it was clear that this was how he rolled, killing bugs with every stride.

I couldn't very well follow leisurely in my car and so I was out, crossing the road, hiding my own hands from the cold. Rudy ran to catch a tram that trundled up from Montague Street and I ran too, hoping to seat myself opposite and to seem as though I was texting a friend when actually I'd be taking a picture, but Rudy moved swiftly to a seat beside an old-timer, forcing her to clear her shopping for him, blind to the inconvenience this was, even accidentally kicking over a bag as he went, prompting her leathery face to pout and search the crowd for someone to validate her disbelief. There was no space in front of him, not even to stand, so I sat behind Rudy against the window. The carriage had barely taken off before his phone rang. Rudy answered it with, 'Yes? Hello?' and followed up with these timorous inquiries about whatever the fuck.

The tram passes Kings Way and frees itself of traffic and picks up speed, really motors so even dreadlocks with his stone face and wide legs shoots an anxious glance out the window.

Then Rudy says, in a voice that's loud enough to demonstrate he doesn't know how loud he is:

'Right, so that's, like…Does it matter if I go to jail?'

23

The words trigger an instinctive turn of my head and I confront Rudy's reflection in the window, the phone held to his ear. A sharp voice warbles within, female perhaps. Then I see a mark on his hand that might be a trick of reflected light...

A tattoo on the webbing. A crown, about an inch across, four stalactites poking up towards the gap between his thumb and forefinger, filled in with a weak black ink like a horizontal triforce. I strain to look closer but the hand pulls away—Rudy is out of his seat.

Plunging down Swanston Street now, past the town hall into the city proper. I have time to casually stand and excuse my way to the front, steal a glance at Rudy who's waiting at the centre doors with the phone still to his ear.

Even from this far away: 'Not now. Not now. Can I, yeah...Just, I don't know, yeah.'

We step into the bustle and throng of the Bourke Street Mall and instantly I regret my choice of the front exit because outside in the dimness and fog, fighting through crowds fighting to get onboard, Rudy has vanished like a magic trick.

I wonder if he sensed a disturbance in the force and made a run for it, but there he is, stomping his way along the tile work, past the shivering buskers that have somehow drawn a crowd. Various hands hold mobile phones aloft to periscope the performance and it would be the perfect cover for photographing Rudy if only he would stop to watch. He doesn't, hands dug into those pockets, his phone conversation finished. I fall in behind, don't feel conspicuous because of all these other strangers. Also because Rudy moves with his head down, scared of other people or just not used to them.

We veer to the Myer department store where Rudy lingers, reading the store guide, a great stone tablet by the entrance. Beside it there's an interactive version; he doesn't want that one. I loiter outside, examine the store windows and their swanky knowing mannequins until Rudy finds what he's looking for and he's off. When I enter a blast of warm air greets me like a shot of nuke to the neck.

Through the make-up and perfume and the pancake faces of the women who work here I'm hoping Rudy won't take the elevator: he'll get a solid look at me if we're its only occupants. But he rides the escalators and with each floor I'm noticing how everything is white and spacious like the whole place wants to be an Apple store. It's different to the last time I came, with Mum about ten years ago, shopping for socks and boxer briefs. I didn't want to be here, was a total shitlord and bitched all afternoon and Mum couldn't wait to get me home. The memory is like an electrocution and I ha

This tiny clump of card the doctor had handed me, it
was old, like Mum had carried it around in her pocket
for years. She was still asleep and the doctor walked
off because he had other random bits of trash to give to
visiting families. It was like a sheet of cotton in my hands
as I unfolded it. This side of the card was blank, but I
turned it over and recognised it, cut out from a birthday
card I'd given her years before. Her fortieth birthday. The
part she'd cut out is this, in my weird teenager writing:

My love for you is as deep as
Ed Harris in The Abyss.

It made me squirm as I read it because it's the kind
of joke you write to your girlfriend, not your mother.
But I was fourteen and we'd watched that movie
together. I thought I was hilarious. And she'd cut it
out and kept it, probably because she thought it was
hilarious how I thought I was hilarious. I dropped
it into her purse, there on the table beside her bed,
and that's when I saw that her eyes were open.

concentrate to hijack my own thoughts, flick the band on my wrist and take off my jacket.

On the top level Rudy arrives at Video and Photography, but I hang back in Home Entertainment Systems and quickly lose sight of him; saunter, casual, to the rows of SLRs and handycams, don't know where he is, can't see another human being until the searching look on my face invites a uniformed stooge with a pink lanyard to ask if I need help. Derpily I decline, drift to the far side of the store and with no glimpse of Rudy I worry again that I've been sprung.

Then a figure passes behind me while I'm focussed on the GoPro accessories and by the hair standing up on my arms I know it's him. I move on towards a great nest of futuristic cameras and circle around.

At the end of the row stands an enormous flat television showing nothing. But then he's on it, his face the size of a weather balloon. Staring down at me like he can see me, like he's God and this is Judgment Day.

I draw back, spooked, look away to the empty clerk's desk and a hundred other screens featuring Rudy's head. Over there, among the cameras on tripods, real-life Rudy is gazing deep into one of the lenses, unaware that it's narrowcasting him all across the store and to this display as big as a billboard.

Without so much as changing my stance, I raise my phone and photograph the image. It's crisp, as good as any I'd have taken if I'd stuck the camera in his face and bolted like a purse snatcher. Rudy's flat nose, his rounded head and lightly freckled face give him the look of an unpeeled potato. What he wants with that camera is not clear—he seems to be picking something off the side of it, affording me a moment of appraisal. The small lips hang slightly ajar, green jacket done up to his chin like a Chinese communist, but it's the depth of fear in those eyes that demonstrates, to anyone who cares to look, the instability of Rudy Alamein. Even here, where no one knows him, where he's oblivious to me and the suspicions of Glen Tyan, where he's entirely self-involved, Rudy's eyeballs tingle and dart, under siege.

That face makes me want to leave.

And I'm right about to. My neurons have already ordered my feet to pivot, to carry me directly to the escalator and back to my car on Grand Street. But in that instant there's a new figure on the giant TV. Rudy is at once startled, then grinning. They hug and release, reveal the smiling, loving face of someone who, just yesterday, promised me she'd steer clear of Rudy Alamein.

24

I'm in a florist taking pictures with my phone when a shop clerk appears beside me.

'We'd prefer you didn't photograph our arrangements.'

'Why not?'

'We'd just prefer you didn't.'

'Because it's a secret? You don't want people to know what flowers look like?'

I don't say that last part but I think it as I leave the store and loiter at a food stand that spruiks the warming powers of soup. I pretend to be choosing between nutmeg-pumpkin and fennel-chickpea when in fact I'm watching Beth and Rudy, seated in a café at the exit onto Little Lonsdale. That's what I was doing in the florist, monitoring them over my shoulder with my phone's selfie lens, so I suppose I should be pleased the cover worked, that actually it looked like industrial espionage.

Beth and Rudy chat and drink juice and despite Rudy's face being permanently terrified they seem to be getting along, not like boyfriend and girlfriend but affectionate and chemically conducive. It reminds me of Marnie, how she and I are sitting around, awaiting the inevitable. Maybe Rudy and Beth have the same dormancy to overcome.

I should call Marnie. We haven't spoken since the pizza incident.

At last they stand, hug again, go their separate ways: Rudy past the florist, past me and back the way we came; Beth across Little Lonsdale and into Melbourne Central.

I stay with Beth.

She bought something in the camera store. In fact she bought a camera. Rudy just hovered, didn't make eye contact with anyone until it came time to pay and he was insistent. There followed a classic nanna fight and she seemed genuinely annoyed, but he waved his credit card so fiercely at the cashier that the transaction was completed almost as an act of self-defence. Beth couldn't hide her embarrassment, resolved it all with a kiss on his cheek and led him here to the café.

Now she leads me deeper into Melbourne Central, stopping to glance in the windows of these chic af clothing stores and I maintain a distance, make sure to keep my reflection out of those windows. Her transformation from yesterday was to be expected but it's still compelling. That bedraggled hair is curly and expansive: Professor River Song's only darker. Instead of a stained bathrobe she wears a blazer with green embroidery and a sort-of-elastic shirt beneath with horizontal stripes. According to the fashion police you're not supposed to wear that kind of shirt if you're large around the tummy but she flouts the rule so majestically that she proves what horseshit it is. All she has in common with yesterday are those glasses, a point of refinement on her rosy, peering face.

More escalators, down down to Melbourne Central station. She knows her way through the turnstiles, past the black and yellow posters that explain how to use escalators and then further under-ground to platform three, the Upfield line—she's going home.

'I'm surprised to see you.'

She turns and there I am, leaning against the glossy cream brick. A James Bond entrance I straightaway regret.

'The last we spoke you said you wouldn't be in contact with Rudy Alamein.'

It's almost as if she doesn't recognise me—the way she hesitates, freezes even, eyebrows questioning.

Then she comes to life, blinks quickly. 'I'm sorry. I'm so sorry...'

Blink blink blink.

'He called me and I just couldn't turn him down...you know...'

'Sure.'

She squirms against the shiny metal pipes that are meant to be seats. The big TV on the tunnel wall shows two young people kissing after sweetening their breath with something like a can of mace.

She says again: 'I'm sorry,' drenched in so much panic that I have to say: 'Don't worry about it.'

'I didn't know what to do...'

'Why did he want to see you?'

'Ummm...' She seems to have forgotten. 'He told me he wants to sell some furniture.'

'Why?'

'He's broke, I think.'

'No, I mean, why tell you?'

'*Oh!*' She cackles at the confusion, overdoes it because she's nervous, even face-palms for what a dunce she is. 'It's my work. Antique furniture. At least, I'm still trying to get it off the ground. But it's, you know...'

I wave at the yellow bag. 'Is the camera for work?'

'Yeah. It's all about photos, right? The internet...'

'Sure.'

'So, like, what has this got to do with my car?'

It suddenly clicks who she reminds me of: the Road Runner. The old cartoon. The big eyes and gentle smile and total failure to judge the arseholes around her. The comparison generates so much compassion within me that I have to be honest.

'Well...I didn't exactly tell you the truth about that.'

All of a sudden her gentle smile is gone and I lurch into an excuse.

'The car was, like, a half-truth. I don't work for the council... It's like...' I shake off nervous Jason Ginaff, re-deploy cool Timothy Wentworth. 'I have a client who believes that Rudy is dangerous, and that he, my client, is in some danger.'

'Who?' Her face fills with concern.

'Not someone you know.'

She has to squeeze her eyelids shut to think.

'But...why did you lie about it?'

'I didn't lie. I mean, I only lied about that. Everything else is true. You saw my card. I'm an investigator.'

'Is this to do with Rudy's father?'

Cool Timothy Wentworth goes rigid.

'Why do you say that?'

'He died. Just recently. I thought—'

'Has he mentioned anything about it to you?'

'Anything about what?'

'About his dad. About holding a grudge.'

'No, he hasn't mentioned...'

From the hollow end of the platform comes a rumble. The big TV reads *Train now approaching* and a speaker somewhere warns us to stand clear of the tracks. At first it seems like this is what Beth shakes her head at.

'It's got to be a mistake. Rudy isn't *dangerous*.'

'I can only tell you that there's been some threatening behaviour.'

'Not Rudy. He doesn't *do* threatening behaviour.' Her eyes urge me to agree. Warm air gusts from the tunnel and wind-machines her hair. 'He's totally harmless. He's lovely.'

'Are you two an item?'

She's horrified.

'*No.*'

'Were you once?'

'No...gosh...I don't even know him that well.'

'You said he was lovely.'

'He is, but—'

'Did he admit to taking your car?'

'No...No, I didn't mention it.'

'Did you mention me? That we talked?'

'No...None of that came up. He just wants help selling his pieces and I couldn't turn him away—'

Through the tunnel comes the Upfield train. I have to shout above the noise.

'*I just think you should give me the benefit of the doubt. Until this is over.*'

She seems touched. The train squeals and stops and there aren't many people waiting to get on. Nobody gets off.

Beth sighs and yanks the door open.

'Okay.'

Having boarded she's several inches taller, looking down on me, endeared. 'I'll stay away from Rudy until I hear from you. How about that?'

'Perfect.' I feel in my stomach this new certainty that I will speak to her again, step back to leave, remember myself and blurt, 'Has Rudy mentioned anything to you about life insurance?'

She scowls. Then, questioning: 'No?'

The doors beep and close. She raises a hand and waves and drifts away amid the chuffing of the train, baffled by this last query of mine. I wave too.

25

Glen Tyan's house is a single-storey weatherboard on a cul-de-sac called Suttle Street, where Suttle Street meets Sereen Road. The irony of these names is not lost on me as I pull to the kerb.

Nothing unusual about the house at a glance. The front lawn is mowed and edged with rose bushes, thorned stems poking out through the picket fence like prisoners swiping through the bars of their jail. Left of the dwelling is a grass ribbon driveway that stretches the full length of the house, that culminates in a garage door and the spoke of a Hills Hoist just visible through the branches of a winter canopy. If that's the backyard then Tyan's property isn't just a house but a full quarter-acre block, as are the other lots on Suttle Street that have so far avoided subdivision. Some have been converted into units—yuppie dog boxes all soulless newness—while other residents take no greater advantage of the spaciousness than to park their multiple haggard sedans on their front lawns.

I'm crossing Tyan's lawn when here are the windows: massive, either side of the small verandah, allowing no amount of insight—the one-way glass Tyan mentioned. Maybe he really missed interrogation rooms after he retired. More likely he just doesn't want people to see inside.

I watch my reflection mount the concrete porch and ring the bell. The door opens at once, but only a crack.

'It's me,' I say, like it's not obvious.

The door retreats further to reveal an empty hallway. Tyan has jammed himself between the door and the wall, so as not to show himself to the street.

'Come on,' he says.

With a single step inside the cigarette smoke hits me like a panic attack: all at once, all over and hot like the house is on fire. With the dust and the sheer lack of oxygen my eyes squeeze shut and I blink against the haze, cough, weak.

Tyan closes the door, pads on bare feet to the first doorway off the hall, wears beige shorts that are best described as skimpy, along with a faded-pink T-shirt that hangs loose and merciful over his belly. I follow into a space where the light filters orange through the strange front windows: a room held permanently in sunset. There's a brightly burning gas heater and a small television and a wooden chair by the window that allows an expansive view of the street. On that chair is a threadbare cushion; surrounding it on the floor are three overflowing ashtrays and about seven used teacups, one of which has become a fourth ashtray.

I cough again, try to get as much of this air out of my lungs as I can. Then I say, 'Here's the photo.'

Tyan sits in the wooden chair at the window, doesn't just glance outside but searches like someone out there called his name.

'Right.' He holds out his hand and I bring the print to him, careful not to convey the triumph I felt at the camera store. I know Tyan well enough now: any hint of self-congratulation will be instantly condemned.

Tyan squints into the picture. The way he does that implies he might need glasses but he's not wearing any, not looking around to see where they are.

It's not a flattering picture, even if you discount Rudy's sub-photogenic head. The concentration on his face is easily interpreted as anger, portrays him as a surly child who DID not WANT his photo taken.

'Yeah, he looks like a crank,' Tyan says, drops the print to the floor and turns his squint to the window.

'We go to the police now, right?'

'Yeah...'

'Unless you prefer to stare out the window for the rest of your life.'

He ignores this, raises a finger and points.

'That's where he stopped. On the corner. The Volvo.'

I follow his finger to a red post box on the opposite kerb, marking the spot Sereen Road meets Suttle Street. It's not a thoroughfare: a man in his car watching the house would have stood out like a flashing neon bulb.

Tyan doesn't look at me as he speaks.

'Did he see you take the picture?'

'Rudy? No. But he met up with Beth Cannon.'

'She saw you?'

'Yeah. But don't worry. I told her I was investigating what happened to her car. Like, for the local council.'

No point in telling him how honest I was at the train station.

'Fuck me. She believed that?'

'I hate to say it but I'm a good liar.' While I'm full of myself, I'm like: 'And I heard Rudy on the phone. He's in the market for life insurance.'

This has the desired effect. Tyan's head snaps around. 'Hey?'

'He asked for a quote on Prime Life, which I googled. It's the name they give their product at Fortunate Australia.'

Tyan's forehead shrinks into a stack of pancakes.

'What's he want life insurance for?'

'Don't know. Said he wanted the maximum benefit. Like, insisted on it. But I don't know why he needs it. And he can hardly afford it.'

Tyan's eyes go dark. He murmurs, 'Life insurance...'

I can't deny a real buzz at how grateful he seems. 'Grateful' in that he's not interrupting me or telling me off. In my grand tradition of appearing not to care, I shrug. Even as my toes curl and my heart thumps.

'He had a tattoo on his hand, also. Looks like he might have done it himself.' I hold out the webbing between my thumb and fore-finger. 'Here. A black crown. Four points up and down...'

My finger draws the invisible picture. Tyan glares out from his rickety chair and his empty cups and his ashtrays.

'On his right hand?'

I have to think.

'Yeah.'

'Was Rudy Alamein ever in Severington?'

'Nope.'

'You're sure?'

'He doesn't have a record.'

'What about an alias?'

'I'm not sure an alias would be his thing.'

'His father died in Severington, right? Last month?'

'That's right.'

Tyan looks back to the window. This time he's not looking for anyone.

'That crown. If you looked at it upside down, what would it look like?'

'I don't know.' I rotate my hand as if the tattoo is there.

'It's not a crown, you dill. It's teeth.'

'Yeah?'

'Something they do in Severington. Blokes get the black teeth tattooed on their right hand so that people know the bloke is owned. Comes from the days when the Dingos owned half the fucking prison. Pack of bikie deadshits. They're gone, long gone, but that symbol's still used. It means he belongs to someone. As if he's property. And everyone knows it.'

'That doesn't sound cool.'

'Hey?'

'I mean, it doesn't sound pleasant.'

'Why do you talk like that?'

'Like what?'

'Like that. Like fucking…Seinfeld.'

'No, I just…' I make a face, shake my head to refocus. 'So why does Rudy have it? The teeth.'

'Maybe his old man had it.'

'So it's, like, a sympathy tattoo?'

Tyan doesn't know. We ponder the silence. Then he says:

'How did Piers Alamein die?'

'Don't know.'

A car motors past the window. Tyan watches. His eyes follow it all the way around the corner and lingers to be sure it isn't coming back. I trace a line on the carpet with my toe and ask:

'You ever feel guilty? Sending people to a place like that?'

Tyan doesn't hesitate. 'Nope.'

He hesitates now, long enough to sip his tea. But the heaving effort of his mouth and throat relay that it's something stronger than tea. 'Poor woman was killed in her own home. Still young. No other family. When you're dead you don't get a lot of justice. It's Severington or nothing.'

I'm about to rephrase my question but Tyan has slipped into contemplation, appears to be silently solving a riddle. Finally he blinks up afresh.

'I suppose you want your money?'

'Sure.'

'What was it? Two-fifty?'

'Two-fifty plus twenty-five for petrol. Plus a dollar for the print. Plus a trip to Fawkner Cemetery on Sunday.'

'I've got my hands full right now, if you can't tell. The cemetery might have to wait. How much did you say?'

'Two-seventy-six. But let's call it two-seventy-five.'

'That's big of you.' He rises delicately and waddles back to the door, says, 'Stay here.'

I stay here.

It's about half what I would have billed a typical client, given the time spent. But pointing that out would be screaming into the abyss.

A hinge squeals somewhere in the house. I wonder if I can open the window to breathe. Glancing over there I see a black handgun on the floor.

The sight of it, plus the heat…I'm giddy. I rub at my face. Now that I think about the stale air, I can't stop thinking. Am I breathing right? Is oxygen getting to my brain? I look around the room for a solution, find nothing. My eyes come back to the firearm. It wasn't there when I came in. Tyan must have taken it with him to answer the door.

My agitation pours out the moment Tyan returns.

'You're sitting around your house with a gun? Is it loaded?'

He cringes like I told an inappropriate joke. A set of bills thrusts out as he moves back to his station, surveys the outside world.

'You can't live like this.' I pocket the money. 'We *have* to tell the police.'

'Yeah.' Still it's half-hearted. Tyan's big toe blindly nudges the firearm on the floor. He nods, but his thoughts are someplace else. I want something more definite.

'Rudy Alamein is obviously deranged. He's transferred all his grief about his parents onto you. So you've got friends we can go to, right? Guys who can get the ball rolling?'

Tyan stares out the window like the star of a TV soap. I realise I'm peering out there too, searching the street for whatever.

'*Tyan.*'

He looks to me. I make a point of holding his attention and I say, 'That's what we're going to do, right?'

Tyan nods yes. Like, all things considered, we should probably do that.

Then he's like:

'I don't want to go to the police. I want him to have a go. I want him to try it.'

26

Tyan lights a cigarette.

'You hungry?'

I rub at my cheek. 'I don't understand.'

'I can make you a sandwich.' Tyan's second inhale brings on a single raucous cough, confronting like a lion's roar would be confronting if he did it right in your face and trailed off with a phlegmy hum.

'I don't understand what you mean when you say you want him to try it.'

'Catch him at it. If he comes for me. I mean, if someone's got it in for me, why should I run to the cops? I *am* a cop. Anyway...'

He drags again, lets the nicotine fuel his concern.

'Right now, we don't even have stalking. He has to do it more than once for it to be stalking, and we can't prove that. And if we could, no one gets put away for fucking stalking. He'd get off with a warning and then here I am, a sixty-year-old sitting duck.'

'Then, like, an intervention order. Something like that.'

Blue smoke rolls from his mouth. His face doesn't move, just holds on me like he can't believe what a dingus I am.

'You think he'll care about an *intervention order*? Intervention orders don't mean fuck all. They don't mean fuck all when the cunt's taking out life insurance.'

And with that, Tyan picks up his handgun and leaves the room.

He didn't tell me to stay this time so I follow. My shoes are loud against the floorboards after Tyan's pink feet. We file down a pale passageway broken up by closed wooden doors and ending in a kitchen. On the right is a formica table, braced by a strip of aluminium and scorched by a million hot mugs. Above it there's a large window facing the neighbour's house and a venetian blind crimping the daylight. Tyan moves to a refrigerator and a small green counter.

'You want a ham sandwich?' Before I can answer he hassles me: 'Sit down.'

'Sure.' I sit in one of four chairs placed around the dining table— sixties vintage, upholstered with dimpled leather. The kind that might be really valuable, might be really not. It's furniture people like Beth who decide.

'Cheese? Lettuce? Mayo?'

'Yeah…' Just these food words make my stomach rumble. 'Whatever you're having.'

Tyan pulls on the fridge door. It rocks back and forth like an excited robot and I can see that one of its front feet is missing. He's got a rolled-up newspaper wedged under there but it's not stabilising much. Inside the fridge it's pretty bare. At least three tin cans are open and uncovered, their lids poking up like thumbs. His cigarette smoulders in an ashtray beside the gun he's placed on the benchtop, within reach.

On top of the fridge stands a framed photograph of Tyan, dressed the way Australians dress in South-East Asia, his arm around a small Thai woman. Both are smiling, but her smile might be a wince because of how he's clutching her.

'I guess…' I say, easing back into the discussion. 'I guess I think that if we go to the police, then it's over. Don't you want it to be over?'

'Absolutely I do.' He finds bread in a bread bin and lays it out on plates. 'That's what I'm talking about. We bring in law enforcement and it's just the beginning. He'll have lawyers, you know? Rights. Then it all bloody drags on and the best we can hope for is we finish up right where we are now, only he knows we're onto him. But if he tries it, actually has a go at me, we've got him. Attempted murder. Maybe assault. Then he's fucked.'

A tickle of smoke in my nose—I sneeze. Tyan doesn't seem to

notice, butters bread with needless vigour, continues:

'He goes to prison, gets the bejesus scared out of him, gets counselling, and his parole conditions are way tougher than any AVO would be.' His face implores me to understand. 'That's how we end it.'

'So you're just going to sit around and wait, like, every day? Wait for him to jump out from behind a tree, or…?'

'You don't think I can take him?'

'That's not the point—'

'*Christ*, I'm not as old as all that. I was a copper, for fuck's sake. And anyway, I'm not saying we should sit and wait. Want mayonnaise?'

'Yes please.'

Tyan takes a jar of mayonnaise from the fridge, grips the lid and strains. It doesn't give. He tries again, whole body trembling, face scarlet; I feign an interest in my shoes so as not to embarrass him by watching. Perhaps he's about to ask me to have a try. But no. He places it back in the fridge.

I poke at the smoky sting in my eyes.

'So if you're not going to wait then…what?'

'Basically…' he says, unwrapping a block of cheese slices, 'we've got to find out what his plan is.'

You can see the cop in him pining for one last arrest, scratching to prove he's still got it. That's why he abandoned the mayonnaise. To hide that maybe he doesn't.

He's like, 'Know what I mean?'

What distracts me now is the air I'm breathing. The room smells like a funeral pyre. The ceiling and the upper walls are faded yellow from decades of cigarettes. Past the rickety fridge stands a second door which I assume leads to a backyard and I rise and move to it, reach for the handle—

'*Leave it!*'

I startle back.

Tyan glares, knife held in suspended animation.

'I just wanted to let in some air,' I blurt. 'The smoke…'

Tyan sucks the last moments of life from his cigarette, stabs it into the ashtray.

126

'Step aside.'

He comes to the door, turns the handle, pushes it away. It creaks into a small vestibule where the carpet is frayed and matted and smells of wet dog despite how there's no dog. Another room to the left is closed off and straight ahead a thin door with a window allows a view to an exterior court crammed with pot plants.

'Down here,' Tyan says, points at our ankles. 'See that?'

I don't at first. But as I move my head I make out a length of taut fishing line running the width of the doorway, about a foot off the ground.

'Is that…is that a trip wire?'

To my right the line is tied to a nail in the frame; to my left it runs across the entryway and into a flaky shoeshine box on the lino, wedged between the kitchen cabinet and the wall.

The lid is open.

'Have a look,' Tyan says, amused.

I edge closer, look down, can't see. Step closer.

A revolver points at my face.

I rear back. *'Jesus!'*

Tyan lols outright. It might be the first laugh I've heard from him, a long string of *hehs* like an engine that won't turn over.

'Don't worry. It's only blanks.'

He goes back to chopping canned ham.

'What's it for?'

'It's an alarm, obviously. Someone comes in while I'm sleeping, trips the wire, the gun fires.'

I'm not sure how obvious that is, quickly return to my chair.

'And I know what you're thinking.' Tyan throws me another proud smirk. 'It's a hair trigger. Fucking blow on that string and it'll discharge. Did the adjustment myself.'

'Do you have one on the front door too?'

'Nah. But mate, thirty years on the force right here. Scumbags don't break in the front door.'

I survey the room for more weapons, check between the counter and the oven, the oldest oven unit I've ever seen. Look behind me, under the seat…

'It's still pretty dangerous, isn't it? Hooking up, like, a booby-trap?'

In Tyan's hand is a salt shaker. He's about to sprinkle it on the sandwiches he's made but half-turns to me and says, 'Could have been live rounds, you know. Blank cartridges are more expensive than live rounds. But I didn't use them, did I?'

He shakes the salt.

'What about an electronic alarm? Like, a motion sensor.'

'Nah. Always going off at wrong times. Or not going off. I had a smoke alarm that kept going off. No fucking reason. This works, I know it works, that means I can sleep.'

Tyan and technology. I'd forgotten.

Finally he stops the onslaught of salt and reaches for the powdered pepper.

He's like, 'What do you think?'

'I guess, if it's just blanks...'

'No.' He comes to the table with two small plates, barely large enough to hold the sandwich each is laden with. One gets placed in front of me and Tyan sits. 'I mean, what do you think about trying to get a handle on when this prick is going to come have a crack at me?'

'He might not come here. He might ambush you at a traffic light.'

'He'll come here. That's why he's been outside. This is the place. He's getting to know it.'

Tyan picks up his lunch and sinks into it while I lower my eyes, face to face with dry white bread and wet lettuce and canned ham that smells like play-doh. The least appetising meal I've seen in a while, and I'm a mid-twenties male who lives alone.

But the appalled face on my face is not about the food.

'If you're asking what I think, I think it's crazy town. It's playing with fire.'

'He doesn't know your face, right?'

'What's that got to do with anything?'

'We've got to find out somehow.'

'You want *me* to do it?'

'Yeah, in return for, you know...whatever. I could take you to the footy.'

He hasn't finished his first bite but launches into a second. What he says next is tortured but distinct.

'But first of all…' He gestures with his soggy sandwich. 'We agree that, no matter what, we don't bring in law enforcement until I say.'

'I can't promise *that*,' I reply, righteous. 'I can't predict what he's going to—'

'Second,' Tyan continues. 'We agree on a fee upfront.'

'I don't want more of your money.'

'All right, football it is then. Who do you barrack for?'

'I want to help you, really. But I mean, finding out what Rudy's planning isn't doable. I mean, unless you want me to knock on his door and ask him, I'm all out of ideas.'

'Well, I was thinking…' Tyan puts down the sandwich and, because he's got nowhere else to do it, wipes his hands on his shorts. 'There is one thing you could do.'

'What's that?'

'You could knock on his door and ask him.'

PART III

27

The engine is running. I haven't shut it off for fear I'd sit here all night, my circumstances dancing around the car like douchebags, taunting me and pointing and making no sense.

The dead tree works tirelessly in the wind, the one I'm lighting up with my headlights. Perhaps the wind killed it, scraping and haranguing until its long silver leaves just said fuck it and died. *Every tree in Carlton has been dead for a month. You want me to feel sorry for you?*

I turn on the blinker, add that metronome to the running of the car engine, a ticking reminder that I'm supposed to leave and be somewhere. What holds me in place is that whirling-dervish question Glen Tyan cannot answer. So motoring obediently back to him, as I'd promised to do, seems at best counterproductive, at worst an outright betrayal of the question itself:

Is it wrong to feel sorry for Rudy Alamein?

When Tyan and I plotted it out over lunch, when I forced down the sandwich that he called lunch, when I researched Fortunate Insurance, when I printed the contract off their website, it never occurred to me that that was possible.

I find myself U-turning, an awkward six-pointer, aiming my headlights back at the city and checking for sure that the black teeth have been wiped clean from my skin.

Marnie Smurtch works in a pub that used to be called the Deptford before some dealer scrote got shot there and it closed down and reopened as the Cornucopia, where they give you four choices of water when they seat you—count 'em, *four*—and which, IMHO, is gapingly too cool for school. I ate there once but was out the door quick because Marnie was too busy to come and chat and the other waitstaff kind of freaked me out and I ordered the pigs trotter to seem sophisticated but I couldn't stomach much of it and also I was eating alone.

I'm hoping Marnie isn't too busy tonight.

No parks on a Friday in the city so I leave the car in a permit zone because I won't be long. It turns out I'm not even as long as that.

Rather than run the very public gauntlet of asking to speak with her among the diners and the sommeliers, I trip my way along the bluestone laneway at the rear, with its corrugated eaves and a full offering of shadowy corners for serial killers to lie in wait. The only light is a dirty bulb above the kitchen door and that's where I loiter until it's pulled opened by a teenager in an apron, cigarette almost to his mouth, startled by this sudden stranger.

'Is Marnie inside?'

The pale little face doesn't manage a word or a grunt or even eye contact but merely disappears, leaves me with the smell of grilled bacon, the sound of a woman hollering something by rote. I worry that it's Marnie's voice, that she's too busy to come to the door but then suddenly here she is, half-smiling.

The hollering continues somewhere behind her.

'Hi.' She wears a waist-high apron, quickly removes it.

'How are you?'

'I'm good. It's fucking freezing.'

'I was walking past, thought I'd drop in. How are you?'

She laughs at me. 'I'm still good. Where you headed?'

'Just home. Do you have to rush back?'

'No. I'm on break.'

This is Marnie in work attire: black pants and a black blouse and her hair pinned back with a black band. She edges out the door and closes it over in a politely futile attempt at privacy. The teenager must have found somewhere else to smoke.

'I wanted to say sorry for the other night. Rushing out on you. I don't suppose you finish up soon?'

She squashes her lips into a ball, pushes them to one side of her mouth. 'I'm here until ten.'

'You look great.' This is me building on my apology.

'You're sweet,' she says, hugging herself. Actually she looks kind of uncomfortable in that outfit, like it doesn't fit right. Like it's just a costume for a performance she's about to give.

'So why *did* you run off so quickly?'

I crush my shoulders into my ears.

'Just work. You know…The client is always right and everything.'

'You seemed scared.'

'*Scared?*'

'Yeah.'

'Of what?'

Her eyes widen, pupils shift to the far far left. 'I don't know. You said something about the police.'

'That was nothing. I was just flustered. I felt bad walking out on you.'

'Good.'

'Listen, there's something I need to ask.'

Marnie comes down off the doorstep, rests her back against the brick exterior. A wet steel chain hangs miserably skinny beside her. She keeps her arms crossed, withstanding the cold.

'Go on,' she says. Her face is flushed red with the heat of the kitchen or maybe something else and it throws me.

'It's just…I'm not quite sure how to ask it.'

'Just ask it.'

She jams her hands behind her backside, a schoolgirl waiting to be asked to the formal.

'Your father is Stanislaw Smurtch, right? He was in the council in Kerang?'

This is not what she expected. Marnie hardens, crosses her arms again.

'Yeah…'

'A couple of years ago he was charged with fraud. Like, stealing from the treasury or something? Is that right?'

'Why…why do you ask?'

'It got reported about. The *Kerang Messenger*.'

'But...why—'

'He owned a development business that didn't develop anything, I think. Or something like that. He got found out by a commission. Lost his job...'

Now it's Marnie who's thrown. She can't seem to believe I've brought this up.

'Why are you asking?'

'You wrote a bunch of Facebook posts about how they were out to get him and that *he* was the real victim. Both your parents...You swore up and down they'd done nothing wrong.'

She blanches now. Her eyes skip past me to the mouth of the laneway.

'I didn't...I didn't say that.'

'You *did*. There were dozens of posts—'

'I deleted them.'

'I *know*. That's what I'm *saying*. One day, you deleted all the posts about your father and the whole mess, and the very next day you got on a bus and moved here.'

'How do you know?'

My answer is a titter, like it should be obvious.

'I mean, you deleted the posts, but nothing's ever truly deleted, right? Anyone can look them up. All you have to do—'

'Wait...You, like, *searched* me?'

'Yeah. Two *years* ago.' I raise my hands in surrender. 'I'd just met you—'

'That's fucking *creepy*, dude...'

'Oh, what, like you never googled me?'

'What you do isn't googling.'

'Really, mostly, it is. Except, now don't be angry...' I hadn't foreseen this brutal scowl, the hurt in her eyes. 'I looked up your Telstra account.'

Her mouth hangs open. She rears back, whirls around to the kitchen door, terrified that someone might have heard. Her voice is a hiss.

'*What?*'

I lower my voice too.

'There's a Kerang number that calls you and you don't answer. Never answer. That's your mum and dad, right?'

Marnie isn't listening. 'You looked up my phone records?'

'You figured out your dad had lied. That he'd taken the money, maybe your mum helped. That was after years of not believing it and defending them, like, relentlessly. So I'm asking, what changed?'

'Oh my God.' She covers her face with her hands. 'You're a stalker. You're fucking stalking me.'

'There's no need to be upset,' I feel an urge to touch her shoulder, choose not to. 'It was so long ago that I'd forgotten. But now... now...'

I sigh. Don't have time to explain *that*.

So I say, 'Everyone knew he'd done it except you. You were the hold-out. You sang it from the hilltops how your parents had been demonised because, like, politics. But then something changed your mind and I need to know what that was. *How do you change that kind of mind?*'

Her eyes hang wide again, just like they did when I left her at Spatafina's. She pulls her chin into her chest in a classic shock-anger combination.

'This is *offensive*.'

I've planned this poorly. Confronting her on the most intense experience of her life shouldn't have been crowbarred into a fifteen-minute work break.

'I am *offended*,' she declares.

'Okay, but...' I swallow hard. 'This is important.'

'It's none of your *business*.'

'Yeah, but—'

'How long have you known?'

'Ummm...' I think for a moment. 'Like, ever since you told me your name.'

One of her hands comes free, motions with its own independent and ineffable sense of outrage.

'I can't *believe* it. That's, like...That's a *violation*. You always...'

'Come on, don't be shocked.'

'Don't be *shocked*?'

'I *have* to talk to you about this—'

'Don't be *fucking shocked*?'

'I'm sorry. I'm really sorry—'

'Go home, Steve.'

She grips herself across her apron, turns sideways to me.

'I'm sorry,' I say again because I'm a doofus.

'I need you to leave.' Righteous anger, a touch of performance to it. Settling into it. I'm not going to bring her back from that tonight.

'But I—'

'*I'm not talking to you about this.*' And she seems to realise that *she* can leave. With a violent push from the wall she re-enters the kitchen. 'Just go home.'

She doesn't slam the door closed. But she closes the door.

28

The sun rises high and unapologetic, tries to stare me down but it doesn't have the juice. Condensation has crystallised on the other cars' windshields while mine has fogged over in solidarity, scrimming the morning light even more. All I seem to do these days is sit outside people's homes.

My bed was prickly last night and the weight of me crushed my shoulder against the mattress and it ached. After determined imitations of sleep, I was awake. Of course I was. There appeared so many holes in the lies I've told that my attempt at a consolidated list of them crashed my brain. Then there were the times I told the truth. Like with Marnie.

Tyan knows the truth, but even there I lied at the outset by calling myself a journalist. More than that, I said I'd visit him after seeing Rudy yesterday. I didn't. I haven't called. I decided to come here first, to this pretty little house in Kew.

I've been here for more than an hour, waiting for a polite time to knock on the door but really I'm just waiting for my nerve to arrive. Already I've seen a man leave the house, young and strikingly neat in appearance and wearing what might have been a bow tie though the windshield fuzzed my view. He pulled invisible hair from his eyes twice in the walk to the car, reversed too quickly out the driveway and wound away along the quiet street. I count this as a point in my favour; that stooge might have turned me away and I expect I'll have enough trouble with the second, older resident.

What else kept me awake last night, apart from listening out for

Marnie to get home and doing nothing about it when she did, was a formula for stopping Rudy. For resolving the entire issue. The formula went like this:

$$\text{Rudy} + \text{proof of Piers's culpability} = \text{Tyan's safety}$$

It's not what Tyan wants—Tyan wants to relive his glory days and capture Rudy and mount his head on the wall—but I'll keep Tyan out of danger if I can prove to Rudy that his father was guilty after all. So, thinking about it last night, I got out of bed.

I get out of the car, walk through the wind with my gloves on, not hiding a fake tattoo with them this time, just cold. The scarf itches my neck as I hike the steep driveway, up two concrete steps and along the white brick veneer and curtained windows to the door. There's a button and I press it.

What I found last night, within seconds of searching the Supreme Court website, was that Rudy's power of attorney was filed by someone named Tristan Whaley.

This wasn't a raid—they store these records for people to find.

Whaley used to be a criminal lawyer and he witnessed the power of attorney in 2005, along with the transfer of title to the house in Albert Park, but that's the only place his name appears. It seems to be the only probate work he ever did. And, so far as I can tell, he had nothing to do with the Alameins prior to that, nothing to do with Piers's trial for murder. But for some reason he came to Rudy's home one day and, according to Rudy, told him his father was an innocent man.

Now he's retired. And he lives here.

From inside comes the sound of a handle turning, but I can't see much for the ninety per cent opacity of the screen door. I make out a pink-skinned shadow, a figure as tall as a bookcase. The tall man.

'Mister Whaley?'

'Yes?' the shadow says. A calming voice like he hosts children's television.

'My name is Brett Sherez. I work at the Southern Community Legal Centre. I'm really sorry to bother you, but I wanted to ask you about Piers Alamein.'

Silence. I can't see enough of that face to gauge a reaction. But then it says, 'Who?' So I suppose it doesn't have a reaction.

'Piers Alamein. You managed some matters of his estate when he was an inmate at Severington.'

More silence. Not just silence but stillness.

I jog: 'It was a long time ago.'

'Yes, I recall. But it's a Saturday morning.'

'I know,' I try to laugh it off. 'The problem is I couldn't find you at your office yesterday.'

'I'm retired.'

'Really? I'm sorry...'

'What are you after?'

'I have a client. Rudy Alamein. Do you remember him?'

'Dimly.'

'I'm gathering all the files I can on his financial matters.'

He says nothing, awaits more information.

'Aaaaaaaaaand Mister Alamein's record-keeping hasn't exactly been exhaustive.'

A snorted laugh. Perhaps he remembers Rudy better than he claims.

'I was wondering if you had any documentation relating to Mister Alamein? Or Piers Alamein.'

'I must say, for a man my age, I really do have better things to do on a weekend.' But as he speaks he unsnaps the lock.

'I know. I'm sorry. I was actually headed for my sister's place in Surrey Hills. You were on the way, so...'

The screen door swings out to reveal a handsome, kingly man in his seventies. The hair on his head is pure silver and, combined with black-rimmed glasses, gives him the weighty air of 1960s intellect. His height stoops with benevolence. Gaunt and plain vanilla caucasian.

'Do you have an authorisation?'

From inside my jacket I produce a dull fold of paper with no more than a few typed words across it. Whaley takes it, reads it.

I've seen authority forms from community legal centres; some of them don't even have letterheads, are otherwise blank sheets barely a sentence long, declaring X is endorsed to handle Y on behalf of Z. I forged a lazy signature at the bottom, replicating Rudy's on the fake insurance contract.

'All right,' says Whaley, indifferent. 'I can tell you I don't have much, but you can come in.'

The house has a Tardis aspect, expansive on the inside because there don't seem to be any interior walls. Here is a living area, colourful, oaky; beyond it a dining space and then a shiny kitchen. From the entrance I can see all the way through the glass rear to a courtyard. Along the wall to my right there's a narrow wooden staircase; rather than loop back and out of sight like the untrammelled stairs at the Alamein house, it leads up directly to an ominous red door. Whaley moves up these stairs now. I follow his loping frame and our feet clip-clop on the timber like horses. Over the banister there's a stack of blue and white boxes rising with the steps, stapled shut. They feature a baroque design on top. Bottles of wine bought in bulk.

'Can I offer you water or tea?'

'No, thank you.'

'Does the Southern Community Legal Centre do very much estate work?'

I don't know the answer, and like any question I don't know the answer to, I'm wondering if it's a trick. *Is he trying to figure me out, even as he leads me into his cave?*

'I mostly focus on immigration and family law.'

'Do you enjoy it?'

'Oh yeah.'

'I had a friend who used to manage the Bayside Legal Centre. He said he spent most of his time asking adolescents to stay off people's lawns.'

'Well that's the Bayside for you.'

Whaley pushes open the red door, enters a perfect white den. A couch, bookshelves, a wide desk with no computer, a lamp that belongs to someone wealthy, vases with fresh flowers, granite book-ends, a heater raging in the corner, a charcoal rubbing framed on one wall, a small window overlooking trees on the next. Further back stands a door to what must surely be a hopelessly tasteful ensuite.

'Have a seat.' Whaley points to the polished leather couch, studded on its seams like a child's pyjamas and just as comfortable. It creaks lovingly as I relax into it. We community lawyers don't see a lot of elegant leather couches.

A beige photocopier rests upon a black filing cabinet and Whaley opens the top drawer, looks in for just a moment, closes it again.

'No no.' He sits now behind the hardwood desk. 'My former associate always destroyed our files after the seven years had lapsed. She would have destroyed what I had on the Alamein matter.'

'They must have lapsed recently. The records were dated 2005.'

'It was earlier this year,' Whaley says with a note of condescension. His demeanour bears the lack of haste, the general lack of interest, that I've known more than one elderly lawyer to lack when addressing me. So I attempt to generate some interest.

'Rudy says you told him that Piers Alamein didn't kill his wife.'

His head jerks back like a chicken put off by unappealing feed.

'Lord above, that's not quite what happened.'

'Can I ask what did happen?'

He seems deeply put out at having to remember.

'I informed him of the possibility that his father didn't know what he was doing at the time of the crime. It's possible he was mentally dissociated and, in that sense, not morally culpable. It's a phenomenon I've come across more than once in my career. Under different circumstances it might have been grounds for an acquittal.'

'So why does he think you told him his father was flat-out innocent?'

Whaley shrugs.

'A misunderstanding, I suppose. I fail to see what relevance this has...'

'Wait a minute...' I drift gently sideways. 'I work for Rudy Alamein. *I'm* trying to understand what relevance any of this had to *you*. You rang his doorbell more or less out of the blue, from what I understand.'

'Yes, perhaps I did. But I had the courtesy to do it on a weekday.'

He smiles to disarm the comment.

'What I put to Rudy was based entirely upon a visit I'd made to

Piers Alamein at the Severington Correctional Facility.'

I tip forward; the leather couch moans: 'Oooooooh?'

'You met with Piers Alamein?'

'Yes…' He says it nonchalantly, looking to the ceiling. 'Just the once. I had a client serving quite a lengthy sentence at Severington. He told me that Alamein…Obviously I recognised the name from the media attention the case had garnered. He told me that Piers Alamein had been drafting a new will, with the aid of some contemptible prison jackleg. The rumour being that Piers had a heart condition, wasn't long for this world. He'd been abused at the hands of some of the inmates there and they had him rearranging his estate to their benefit.'

He lets that sit for a moment, then says:

'My client found it amusing. But of course I knew the real victim would be Piers's son, Rudyard. Disenfranchised as a result of this new document.'

'So you visited Piers.'

'It seemed to me the only real hope for setting aside the new will would be to prove Piers had been subject to duress at the time of execution. I didn't expect that to be difficult, provided Piers co-op-erated, so I arranged to see him in an interview room at Severington.'

'When did this happen?'

Whaley leans his right elbow on the arm of his chair and his right hand gently caresses his right ear and his head is angled to favour the hand's access: he speaks while looking at me sideways.

'Late oh-four, if I recall.'

'Did you speak for long?'

'It was a brief interview. Fifteen minutes or so.'

'What did you learn?'

He considers this for just a moment, then says calmly:

'I learned that Piers Alamein was utterly insane.'

29

'He had a tattoo on the webbing of his right hand.'

Whaley points to the familiar place. A rush of fear, but then I recall I wiped away the tattoo last night. And again for good measure this morning. Also, I'm wearing gloves.

Whaley says, 'Are you familiar with the black teeth?'

'Yes. Broadly.'

'It indicated to me that he wasn't having a good time of it inside. So I expected him to behave a little strangely. Even so, he was...'

He fixes me with eyes designed to communicate the sobriety of a situation.

'I've never seen anything like it.'

And I'm like: 'Okay.'

'I drew the conclusion that Piers hadn't changed his will under duress, but that rather he'd gone beyond the reach of common sense and had been subject to manipulation.'

'So you thought he was...mentally deficient...before he killed Cheryl Alamein? And that's why he did it?'

'No, I only said that that was a possibility. What's also possible is that prison life had done that to him.'

'So why did they keep him there? If he was crazy...'

'I'm sure they supplied him with a smorgasbord of anti-psychotics. But if every prisoner with severe mental health issues were transferred to a more appropriate facility, our jails would be next to empty.'

'During this interview, did you take notes?'

'No. I recorded it. But the tape would have been destroyed with the file.' He looks back over the top of his glasses. 'And I don't imagine it would have been of much use to *you*.'

'It's a complicated situation,' I flub. 'I want to get my hands on as much primary documentation as possible.'

'Well I'm sure all our documentation is gone.'

'Did Piers mention his family at all?'

Whaley puts both elbows on the desk, clasps his hands together. His forefingers make a steeple to his nose.

'I asked him if the new will would provide for his son. He replied that he'd left Rudy something very special. Something incredible. And I asked him what it was, and he said…'

He raises his eyebrows and holds them there, like he's holding his breath, then:

'The blessing of a short life.'

Whaley remembers this well, for all his coyness at the door. It's a story he's meditated on.

'Do you know what he meant by that?'

'I didn't know at the time. But the cognitive evaluation showed that Piers suffered from a form of cardiomyopathy called AVRC, a disease affecting the heart. And it's hereditary, from what I understand. If Rudy were a sufferer, then Piers might, in his demented way, have considered that a more generous legacy than money or property. I tried to ask about it, but our conversation drifted into the absurd.'

Rudy's face when I told him he'd go to jail. His plan to wait the thirteen months. It's not a terrible idea if he thinks he's dying anyway. But why didn't he mention it when we ran through his medical history? Does he really think there'll be a pay-out if he's kept a secret like that?

'Do you know for sure that Rudy has it? AC…'

'AVRC. No, no. That was beyond my focus.'

'But Piers definitely did.'

'According to his medical records. His was moderate to severe, which meant he could theoretically experience an attack at any time and die. But of course, that's not what did for him in the end.'

'So you know he's dead?'

'It was in the news,' he waves dismissively. 'Suffice it to say, the only actual information I gleaned from Alamein was that he lacked testamentary capacity.'

'So then you called on Rudy?'

'That's correct. My plan was to give him the lay of the land regarding his father's mental state, his position vis-à-vis a new will, and to refer him to the administration list at VCAT. But my assessment at the time—'

He cocks his head, unsure.

'You have met with Rudyard Alamein, have you not?'

'Yes, I have done so.'

'My assessment at the time was that Rudy lacked the wherewithal to follow through on my advice. And if his application were denied, if he were required to attend a hearing at the tribunal, I simply didn't believe he had the capability to put his case. So I filed the documents myself, arranged for the cognitive capacity assessment and petitioned for a statutory power of attorney.'

'Sounds complicated.'

He shrugs.

'Not really. The common law test for a lack of testamentary capacity literally includes the phrase "insane delusions", so I didn't have much difficulty there. Moreover, there wasn't exactly a glut of assets. Aside from the house, most of them had been sold off to pay his legal fees, including his apartment in…Toorak, I think it was. There was no hard-nosed opposition to our psychiatric report or our application. That's the totality of my involvement with the case.'

'You don't still have a copy of that report?'

'I'm afraid not. As I said…' He points to his filing cabinet. 'I don't even have my file notes.'

'Nothing kept electronically?'

'No,' Whaley smiles. 'I'm afraid I'm a philistine in that regard.'

Which would explain the want of a computer in here. I prepare for the golden question.

'Did Piers tell you that he murdered his wife?'

Whaley's neck straightens again. Another subtle recoil.

'No. Absolutely not. We never broached that topic. You seem to be going well and truly beyond the call of duty, Mister Sherez.'

'Why did you work for Rudy free of charge?'

I didn't mean for it to be a sucker punch, but I can tell that it is. Something flashes in Whaley's eyes and for the first time he doesn't have an immediate answer. Into the silence, I say:

'Rudy told me you did it pro bono. Which is strange, given that he had money. He wasn't a charity. Why not send him a bill?'

'*You're* obviously a clever young lawyer, Mister Sherez. Why not find a job that pays more than a CLC? Sometimes it's about more than money. Sometimes it's a matter of principle.'

'What's the principle that says you should work for free for rich people?'

'That's one way of looking at it.'

'Well how do you look at it? Who paid for the psychiatrist's report?'

A pause, then: 'I did.'

'Why?'

'It's difficult to explain. I felt sorry for him.'

And he hopes that will do the trick.

'But you saved the day. Piers lacked capacity, Rudy got the house. Why feel sorry for him?'

'You mean, aside from the fact that his mother was murdered?'

I don't answer. Whaley brings a hand to his mouth, breathes in like it's an oxygen mask, stares past me at nothing.

'All right,' he says. 'I'll show you.'

He gets up from his big leather chair but goes nowhere. Hovers, awkward, his hands fists, still thinking, staring into the floor.

'I'm going to ask you to stay put in this room and not come out for a few minutes. Until I return. Can I trust you to do that?'

'Sure.'

'It's just…personal considerations. I need you to wait here.'

'Okay.'

Whaley lingers on me to see if I mean it, doesn't seem to be satisfied, nonetheless opens the red door and shuts it again.

His feet stomp down the stairs.

30

Gravity pulls me towards the filing cabinet, but Whaley wouldn't have left me alone in here if there was anything to find. Still, I'm contemplating a quick look when my phone buzzes.

> *Hi Timothy. This is Beth Cannon. Sorry to bother*
> *you but I need to speak with you. Can I make an*
> *appointment?*

An appointment? I hadn't realised I'd seemed so professional as to seem professional.

> *My office is getting fumigated and I'm working out*
> *of my apartment. You can meet me there in an hour.*
> *5/27 Rapproche Street, Kensington.*

The first spats of rain strike the window, translucent exclamation points gathering like predators. I flick myself in the temple, hate myself for inviting her like that. How sleazy does it look, inviting her to the place where your bed is? When my phone rings I'm breathless at the chance to walk it back. But the caller ID says: *Glen Tyan.*

I turn off my phone.

Whaley returns with booming feet up the stairs, sheets of newspaper in hand. He moves to the photocopier above the cabinet. Almost invisible in the shine of his grey hair I can see cobweb entrails, sticky and fine and holding at least one tiny tiny spider-meal spun into a brown ball.

The photocopier whirrs and quacks and poops out two A4 pages.

He holds them up, examining. Through one of the sheets I see the *Daily Sun* masthead.

'I cut these pages out the day they went to print. As if I knew one day I'd be drawn into the Alamein affair.'

He offers them and I take them and he removes the originals from the photocopier, sits at his desk. We both read.

The publication date is Friday, January 23rd, 2001. The front page headline reads:

SON BREAKS SILENCE: 'DAD SHOULD ADMIT WHAT HE DID'

Most of the page is a photograph of young Rudy, moonfaced as ever, posing for the camera, sulky. The photographer surely told him, 'Look sad!' and that's exactly what he did, sitting on a couch I remember from the front room in Albert Park, the same place Rudy sat to sign my fake contract. Rudy holds up a framed photograph of Cheryl Alamein.

Whaley has reduced the full newspaper page to A4, meaning he knows how to operate a photocopier even if he hates computers. His generation, I suppose. The print is fine, difficult to read. I pull it close.

NINA CHIANCELLI
Staff reporter

THE son of a man accused of murdering his wife in their Albert Park home has told the *Daily Sun* he believes his father should confess to the brutal crime.

Speaking in the living room of the Albert Park terrace yesterday, Rudy Alamein said that the evidence against his father was overwhelming.

'Just denying it is stopping us all from moving on,' the fifteen-year-old said.

'He's not willing to admit what everyone knows. He should admit what he did.'

Rudy Alamein discovered the body of his mother, Cheryl Alamein, in her bedroom on the 7th of June, 1999.

'There was a lot of blood on the floor. I was just thinking, "Oh no"'.

Cheryl Alamein had been struck with a blunt instrument that police allege was a vase later found in a workshop used by Rudy's father, Piers Alamein.

'He doesn't want to admit the truth. They've got the proof. And he gets less jail time if he admits it.'

These blunt assertions—this certainty—doesn't sound like Rudy, but then this is eleven years ago.

The story continues on page three, which Whaley has also provided. It features another picture of Rudy, still on the couch, but this time he's seated beside a suited, moustachioed man full of sympathy and honest concern. They face the camera stoically like Batman and Robin.

I feel my eyes dilate, check the caption.

> *Strange Bedfellows: Young Rudy has formed an*
> *unlikely bond with the man who arrested his father,*
> *Detective Glen Tyan.*

The stupidity of that sentence makes me ice over with fear.

Detective Glen Tyan is Rudy's father?

But I read it again, recognise that I read it wrong, feel the adrenaline recede, leaving bafflement.

THE emotional appeal comes as prosecutors prepare for the trial of Piers Alamein, who has pleaded not guilty, due to commence next week.

Detective Glen Tyan, who led the investigation in 1999, yesterday looked in on Rudy to offer his support. He told *The Daily Sun* he was confident of a conviction.

'We believe it is a domestic incident gone bad. Relations between the parties had been strained. There was an escalation following the breakdown of the marriage which included an intervention order.'

Detective Tyan said that Rudy's best interests had been a priority throughout the investigation.

'He's a great kid. He's lost his mum, which is so hard on a boy, but he keeps his chin up. He's as tough as they come.'

Rudy told the *Daily Sun* he was grateful for the support provided by Victoria Police. He said he was considering a career in the police force.

'I asked Detective Tyan about the police and he gave me a form to do. But he said I had to finish school first.'

Rudy is set to begin Year 10 at a private school in Brighton. He fears the trial will be a distraction from his studies.

'There's a lot of people asking me questions about my dad. He should think about the effect he's having on me.'

A jury for the trial will be empanelled Monday.

By the time I've finished it's raining a brass band against the window and the roof. Whaley has finished. His plaid shirt reflects his plaid face that's watching me.

'You said you had nothing. No documents.'

'Some items I keep for sentimental reasons.'

'Why be sentimental about this?' I flash the pages in the air. Whaley draws in a long breath through his nose.

'In particular, I was moved by the callousness of the publication. These are the uninformed comments of a child, and yet they ran it like it was fresh new evidence in the crime of the century.'

I shrug. 'So what?'

The old man performs the shrug back at me.

'You asked why I felt sorry for the boy. This is why.'

'This is the reason you helped him?'

Whaley's chin jabs out as affirmation.

'We're not all bastards, are we? Lawyers, I mean.'

And he smirks. Then he says:

'I've got a very full day, so I think we'll have to adjourn this little chat.'

My eyes return to the photograph. Rudy and Tyan. Both of them somehow brighter, better illuminated than they are today. Tyan has the same face but for that brown moustache. Rudy is calm but intense. They *could* be father and son.

'May I keep this?'

'Of course.'

I'm ushered out the red door, move slowly down the stairs, understanding more than I did on the ascent. Whaley never told Rudy that Piers was innocent. That's just what Rudy tells himself out of self-loathing: he might have failed to protect his mother, but so publicly betraying his father is some next-level shit. His revenge fantasy is the music he plays in his mind to drown out the guilt.

The wine boxes below have been moved and one is set on the floor by itself. When we reach the front entrance I spot a door under the stairs: the cellar, I assume, going by the placement of the boxes. And Whaley's special hiding place, his *real* cave, going by the cobwebs in his hair.

It reminds me of Tyan, when he scurried off to get my money. These old men and their hiding spots.

'Can I give you my email address? In case you manage to find anything else.'

'I suppose so. So long as I've not given you false hope.'

A pad from the side table is handed to me, along with a biro. The address I write is: b.sherez@SouthernCLCentre3715.com.au. I pulled the name Brett Sherez out of the clear blue sky and it's a gamble that this domain doesn't exist yet. But on the off-chance Whaley can unearth something to disarm Rudy, I'll register it when I get home.

We shake hands.

'Give Rudy my regards. Though he may not remember much about me.'

'He remembers how much you did for him. He holds you in very high esteem.'

'Say hello from me.'

'I will.'

And I leave. Run back to the car, protecting the photocopies from the rain. Tristan Whaley waves from his front verandah. Lingers there as if to make sure I'm leaving.

31

It's heavy rain when I pull into the driveway so I'm not sure it's *the* green Volvo parked directly outside my flat. Then I am sure because Beth is struggling to keep her circular frame dry beneath the stairs. She waves a few meek fingers, already seeming to apologise for intruding.

'Hello. I'm sorry,' she says as I reach her.

'That's all right. Come inside.'

But as I say this I hear a door close at the top of the stairs—a familiar sound.

'Wait on.' And I usher her back under cover.

'What is it?'

'Nothing.'

I stare up at the concrete landing. No footsteps. Someone has their washing on the clothesline down here and it's getting soaked and for a moment I think it's Marnie's and she's on her way to rescue it. But these are shirts and boxer shorts—man-clothes. Then I hear the knocking.

Marnie knocking on the door of my flat.

'I'm sorry.' Beth seems to think this is her fault.

She's wrapped in a long grey coat like women in the French Resistance and a cravat pokes up through the neck. It's drenched but it's still the only colour to be seen in the dreariness of all this concrete. Her glasses are comically fogged over and her hair is flat and moulded like she just stepped out of the shower. Like when we first met.

'It's fine,' I say softly into her ear. The rain is too loud for Marnie to hear us. 'We're just being super careful.'

Beth whispers, 'Should we run to my car?'

I consider it for a moment, but fleeing with Beth would be about the most incriminating thing in the world that Marnie could catch me doing, so I shake my head, left with only admiration for this girl who doesn't know who we're hiding from, can barely see through those lenses, but she's down for whatever.

'I want to know about Rudy?' More of those harsh Australian inflections. 'He's been calling me and calling and he won't stop. He leaves messages? I know you told me not to speak with him again, but I had to. It was *weird* not calling him back.'

The stairs provide only inches of shelter and we're standing closer than I would usually be comfortable with. It doesn't seem to faze her.

'But listen,' she says. 'I found out about the life insurance.'

Another hard rap against my door above, powerful like a headache.

'You did?'

She nods, grabs my jacket sleeve and I know the wind is cold against my neck but I can't feel it.

'He said a salesman came to his house and he bought the policy.'

'Okay. Did he say anything else?'

'Only that...' her cheeks, blanched from the cold, turn scarlet. 'He said I'm the one who gets the money.'

Rudy hasn't gone twenty-four hours before telling Beth what yesterday he so keenly didn't want her to know.

'Riiiiiiight,' I say, performing a realisation. 'That's interesting.'

What is Marnie doing? Breaking into my flat? Is she at the edge of the catwalk listening in? The rain is a thousand simultaneous slaps on the corrugated roof above her so she can't possibly hear us. Even so, I peek past the clothesline along the back of the block, past the puddles in the mud and the wild grass, untended like Rudy's front yard. Not an inviting escape route.

'But he really scared me,' she says. 'On the phone. I asked him why he was doing it and he wouldn't say. He totally just...wouldn't tell me anything. So...Tim?'

'Yes?'

She sucks back her lips like she's sucking back on courage. 'I want to go to the police.'

'No—'

'You said he might be planning something bad. Is he?'

'We're going to go to the police. Believe me, every minute of the day I'm about to go to the police. But the agreement I've made is to find out as much information as I can before I do that. I'm sorry.'

'What agreement?'

'I really can't go into it. But I can tell you it'll all be over by next weekend. You just need to sit tight.'

She wipes a raindrop from her cheek that could almost be a tear. 'I'm sorry, it's just…it's got me in a tizz…'

'I know, I'm sorry.' And I snort. 'If either one of us apologises again, we should just get married.'

That makes her giggle. It is a moment, interrupted by the sound of footsteps on the stairs.

Beth must see the fear in my eyes, shrinks into the wall.

A tall figure with a golf umbrella emerges from the staircase and trudges toward the street. She's wearing about a thousand jackets, at least one with a hood that's over her head, blocking her peripheral vision. There are gloves and a scarf and her favourite red leather boots. Proper armour against the day.

The figure makes a cursory assessment of the green Volvo, if only because she doesn't recognise it, then moves off down Rapproche Street, headed for the bus stop.

I relief-smile at Beth.

'Come on upstairs.'

'No, I should go home. I just…I'm not comfortable with any of this, the insurance…I want you to know that.'

'I do know.'

'I'm supposed to go over there and photograph his furniture.'

'It's better if you don't. I'm sorry.' And in this second I *would* marry her. 'You just need to wait a week.'

She doesn't answer, mind elsewhere.

'Beth?'

'Okay,' she agrees, absent. 'I just want Rudy to be okay. I know he's kind of strange but he couldn't hurt anybody. You'll watch out for him, won't you?'

'Yeah,' I say. Like of course I will.

And I'm about to qualify that with something like, 'If I can,' when she leans up and pecks my cheek. I catch gratitude in her eyes and she probably catches lust in mine before she turns away and trots into the rain.

The Volvo starts with a splutter of old age like Tyan and his cigarettes and I can't see into the cabin to know if she's waving but I wave anyway.

32

This is Melbourne's Nuremberg rally and I'm the strange-o with his hands in his pockets, leering at the MCG from right outside it, leaning furtive against a white pole that travels a hundred metres into the sky with massive floodlights at the top and they're *on* even though it's daytime. Through my clothes I feel the cold of the metal numbing my shoulder.

I am as conspicuous as this pole.

The rain's stopped and the city is gathering, wearing their colours, eating their junk food, scolding their children. I face an actual-size bronze effigy of a man named Keith Miller and someone has decided that the pose that best captures him is one where he's falling over. Across the PA system comes an announcement that isn't a recording but which continues without interruption and is incomprehensible.

At home I googled *what to wear to the football*, and although I think I *might* be over-prepared with my two jackets and gloves and beanie and umbrella, Tyan arrives wearing just a bomber jacket and a T-shirt.

He says, 'You off skiing?'

It's good humoured.

We join the flood of pilgrims making entry into the stadium and Tyan expects me to keep up and I do, through the bag search and the turnstiles and he's already got the tickets.

'Why didn't you come last night?' he asks.

I scramble to keep close enough to reply.

'My car was having problems.'

'You could have called.'

'I knew I'd see you today.'

We lumber with the crowd towards an open stairwell, hike a marathon to the top storey and I'm winded when we get there but don't admit it. The full glory of the arena reveals itself, encompassing a patchwork quilt of shades of green and you can see how much money they spend on *grass*. Below us a cliff face of empty seats falls away and below that are people, spread thick along the lower portions and all the way around the field. Their density and their proximity is surprisingly intense. I reach for the guard rail.

Outdoors now we trudge up more stairs, reach the top of the grandstand where a giant video screen looms but up close like this it looks like the Matrix. We sit beneath it, in what is clearly the least popular part of the stadium: Tyan wants privacy.

'So how did it go?'

'Well...' I say. 'You were right. An intervention order isn't going to help.'

I recite for him my visit to the ramshackle terrace in Albert Park, Rudy's plan to murder Tyan in his bed, his expectation that he won't survive jail and his affection for Elizabeth Cannon. All the while bodies flood the field, worker bees in pink and green.

The story culminates in the black teeth. How Rudy's black teeth are everything to him.

'That's who he is,' I say, filling the silence as I wait for Tyan to pat me on the head. 'He isn't anything else.'

Hawthorn jog onto the field. I can tell by the yellow and brown muscle tops—I googled them this morning too. Tyan claps and so do I, doing my best to look on with pride. The crowd roars like someone slaughtered a Christian.

'You done good,' he says in a cowboy voice, can't seem to look at me as he says it, straightens his back. 'But what's he going to do? Ring the doorbell and hope I let him in?'

'I don't know what the plan is exactly.'

'And when? That's the big question.'

I realise I left that part out.

'Friday.'

The old man tips away, looks at me askance.

'How do you know?'

'That's the day I told him his policy would be active.'

'What?'

'He's got a policy now. Or at least he thinks he does.'

'You *sold* him insurance?'

'There wasn't a lot of choice, man. He's an intense dude.'

I take the contract from inside my jacket.

'I told him it would be processed by Friday. He wasn't happy that he has to wait. But he reckons Friday's the day.'

Tyan takes the contract from me and looks it over. The Hawthorn team tears through their banner and maybe the roaring ambience of the crowd grows by a decibel. The other team, according to the second scoreboard on the far side of the field, where the enormous lights loom over the stands like triffids, is West Coast Eagles. They prance into view and the crowd is silent for reasons I cannot determine.

And Tyan's question is: 'Did he pay for it?'

'I waived the fee. Out of solidarity. The teeth and everything. Also I don't know how to pretend to process a payment.'

'Why leave it until Friday?'

'It was the first thing that came to mind. Sort of spur of the moment...'

'Christ,' he says with a sigh. He hands back the contract.

'You still don't want to go to the police?'

'I told you, not until we've got him.'

His tone is conclusive enough that I choose not to push it. Instead I allow a moment's pause before I say:

'Did you come to the football a lot with your dad?'

A man dressed all in green stands in the middle of the field and holds a red ball aloft and the siren blarts and I have to block my ears. The crowd responds in the affirmative. The green man bounces the ball hard against the ground with both hands and two opposing players yearn for it, one of them grabs hold of it. Two others grab hold of him and someone near us yells, 'Ball!' They appear to be stating the obvious.

'My dad was an arsehole,' Tyan says, focused on the game. 'He wouldn't of taken me even if he wasn't always pissed.'

I leave space for him to say more, but he's in the spectacle now. Tribes of men seated below us drink beer from tiny plastic cups. Others arrive with more, as many as they can carry.

One of them stands and declares, '*Right*. I'm off for a slash.'

Another yells at the field, '*Who to?*'

I say to Tyan, 'I was thinking about purchasing the Jason Tyan domain name. Is that okay with you?'

'What?'

'The domain name. Like, Jason Tyan dot com. It's available, I checked.'

Tyan doesn't answer, appears to be fashioning a thought.

'Is it true they used to call you the Polygraph?'

'Where'd you hear that?' Tyan asks, suddenly interested.

'Internet.'

It's a gamble, bringing it up. Bringing up anything from Tyan's past. He could respond with a glowing smile or a bayonet to my self-esteem. For now he seems pleasantly reminded.

'Yeah. I suppose they called me a lot of things. Polygraph was one of them.'

'You could always tell if someone was lying.'

'I had a knack for it.'

'They used to call you in to help with interrogations.'

'If they had nothing else, they'd get me in. I'd give them my read and be on my way.'

'They got a lot of arrests because of you.'

'Oh, I don't know...' But he's loving this flattery. I'm loving it too. 'If I helped out, then I'm glad.'

'How did you do it? Like...'

Something dramatic is happening on the field and everyone stands up. Tyan doesn't. He looks at me with a passion for this topic.

'Well, see, something you've got to understand is, there's really no such thing as an unsolved crime. On any given case the whole fucking teams knows who it is. Five minutes in a room with the bloke and you know. All it means for something to be unsolved is that you're not swamped with evidence. These days you practically need a video recording of the crime itself to get a conviction, but that doesn't mean there's any doubt. Cops are lied to every day. Every day of our lives. We know when someone's bullshitting.'

'Is that what happened with Piers Alamein?'

'Yeah. Absolutely. One of the least gifted liars I can remember, because he wasn't a career criminal, just a fucking turd. But it didn't matter in the end because we got the goods on him.'

The red ball floats to the far side of the field and I notice five boys seated nearby, unaccompanied. Their median age is ten or twelve and one of them shouts at the game, 'Don't fucking cry, Floritt!'

'Do you remember...' I try to sound vague and entirely innocent. 'Do you remember a photograph of you and Rudy in the *Daily Sun*? It was just before Piers went on trial...'

Tyan consults his memory.

'Nope.'

'You looked young. Like a proper cop. It said the two of you had formed a bond.'

He scoffs. 'Funny bond if he wants to kill me.'

'Rudy was on the front page. Saying his dad should confess.'

'Seems he's changed his mind on that.'

When the ball bounces into the crowd the energy settles. Seagulls swoop onto the field, dip their beaks in the grass. A grating man-cackle from somewhere far off.

'My theory is that hating you is easier than accepting all the terrible shit that's happened. His dad just died, he feels guilty about betraying him. Hating you gives him something to focus on.'

'But why *me*?'

'He thinks you perjured yourself.'

'But how? And *why*? Why would I? Why would I fit someone up? I mean, *why* would I *do* it?'

Despite how Tyan doesn't appear to be talking to me, I nod in passive agreement. Doing that, I feel the telltale waft of heat in my head.

I try to act normal, say: 'I don't know.'

'What's in it for me?' he says, as if I hadn't just told him that I don't know. 'Was I supposed to profit somehow?'

My eyebrows pull my eyes open and I blink, shift in my seat. Flick at the lacker band on my wrist like there's no place like home. Despite the Arctic breeze I'm boiling up. My heart beats. Tyan continues in that strange voice.

'I'll ask him that. When he comes. I'll ask him why he thinks I could be *bothered* fixing someone up.'

I rub at my neck, nod hard, try to hide what's happening. My vision clouds. I scratch at my nose, tip forward, tip back, scratch my nose again, tip forward again.

Tyan says, 'I'll get everything straightened out. I'll have him eating out of my hand by the time I'm done.'

What am I doing here? What am I doing at the football with these *men?*

'And just when he's wondering how the fuck he got the idea that *I'd* done anything wrong, we'll prosecute him up the arse for attempted murder and he'll land in Severington just like his dad.'

Now I'm standing up, discern with my big blinking eyes the location of the stairs, slur something and lurch for the handrail and muddle my descent, try to look like I'm 'off for a slash'. The rail does most of the work, stings my hands with cold while sweat soaks my armpits.

Into the bowels of the amphitheatre. I leave behind the rumble and the war and I'm still clinging to the rail, but you know, casual. It's not exactly unpopulated, mostly more men carrying more beer, wearing more colours and shouting more profanities, but it's dark and no one's looking at me or talking to me like they're my father.

The causeway leads to an open area facing the field and the clamour of spectators is here again, but I'm behind it now. Feel the adrenaline recede. Wipe the sweat from my face with my hand and wipe my hand on my jacket and crack out a beta-blocker. I need something to wash it down.

At the bar, where the plastic cups of booze are administered to a constant stream of swaggering males, I ask for a water and pay five dollars for it, chug the pill and take a moment to let the electricity slip away, slump on a bar stool.

A brutal exclamation from the crowd. I don't turn to see what it is.

What I do turn to see is two uniformed police officers: blue, blue and more blue. Fat guns clipped to their thighs, walkie-talkies draped over their shoulders, vests that might be bullet-proof. They chat, friendly, in position at the stairwell, watching with as much fixation as the civilians around them.

What if I went over and told them everything, like how Beth wants me to? Would they care? Would they superhero the shit out of this situation? Maybe Tyan would forgive me, secretly thank me for doing away with the danger that is Rudy Alamein.

But then, what are two cops at the football going to do for me? They don't want to hear a sob story. And surely they're too young to be genuinely helpful. One of them looks about twelve. They'd tell me to call triple zero and barely take their eyes off the game.

I reclimb the stairs. The siren sounds again and I flinch. The running players stop running and dick music kicks in at once, warbling from the tannoy. Spectators get to their feet and the distant stand becomes an ants nest of people. I glance at the scoreboard to understand what's happened but it only plays a video commercial for SUVs.

When I reach Tyan, he's still seated.

'Sorry about that,' I say, manufacturing good cheer. 'Call of nature.'

'Listen,' Tyan says, readjusting himself in his tiny seat, pulling on his belly to make himself fit. He's not wondering why I left in such distress. Maybe he didn't notice. 'I've been thinking. I don't want to wait until Friday.'

'I'm not sure we have a choice.'

'No, we do,' he says. 'You have to go back. Tell him the policy is active. Tell him to come tonight.'

33

Rudy holds it tight, looks across it like it's a photograph, not a written document.

'And that's not all,' I say. 'I have news.'

Behind me the Saturday traffic is light and muted. I hover on the verandah because it hasn't occurred to Rudy to ask me inside. Probably he's not used to asking people inside. He just stands in the doorway with his prize, wearing happy pants and a pilling cotton skivvy, confounded by my visit.

Then panic: 'There's not going to be a problem with…She's going to get the money, right?'

'Oh yeah. For sure. That's what the stamp means.'

Before we left the football—ten minutes into the third quarter because Hawthorn was 'getting thrashed'—Tyan picked up a bottle cap and dipped it in the tomato sauce left over from his second meat pie, pressed it down on the front page of the signed contract, leaving a jagged circle he filled in with a set of fake initials. It looked vaguely official. Even if it stank.

Rudy sniffs, sensing something unusual, but what he smells only seems to make him prouder. A gentle finger runs across the imprint, dry now like the black teeth beneath my glove—Tyan drew those on too.

I'm like, 'That's yours to keep. Can I come in?'

He pulls on the door and I walk into the unexpected pungency of furniture polish. A bottle of it sits on the piano stool. He's preparing these items for sale. A dining chair before us gleams, arrogant.

'Anthony,' Rudy says. For a moment he's about to tell me a story about his friend Anthony; then I remember that Anthony is who I am. 'Check this out.'

The contract drops to the piano stool and Rudy squeezes himself between the random furniture, across the room to a chaise longue and a bronze lamp, two of the items he wants Beth to photograph and peddle to the high-end Melbourne furniture market. The windows are curtained, almost barricaded, and without the front door open I don't know how Rudy distinguishes night from day in this room. Even now I can barely see the object he takes from the couch.

He carries it back to me, proffers it like it's the last cup of water from the fountain of youth and I take it, thanking myself for wearing these gloves because the electricity of this thing, now that I see what it is, would be too much for my bare skin.

I'm like, 'Wow.'

'COLGATE' is printed along the handle in bright new lettering, the brush head gone, the plastic abraded to a sharp point. It totals four inches in length but I suppose you could kill someone with it if you were determined.

'Is this what your father used?'

'No, I made it.'

'I mean, did he use a toothbrush that was sharpened?'

'Yeah…Yes.'

'How long did it take you?'

He shrugs, but it's not modesty. He just doesn't know.

'Rudy, if you're going to do it in his sleep, how are you going to get into Tyan's house?'

A long pause. A baffled scowl.

'How do you know his name?'

Fuck. I can't keep these lies straight in my head.

'What?'

'How do you know his…Tyan's name?'

'I read about it. What happened to your dad. I looked it up.'

This seems to confuse him.

'Rudy, how are you going to get into Tyan's house?'

He instantly forgets his confusion, eyes gleam like they've been wiped with furniture polish.

'I know where he keeps his key. The back door.'

Another neuron fires. Tyan saying there was someone in his back-yard. He thought it was paranoia.

'You do?'

Rudy goblin-nods, unaware of how chilling that looks.

'Under the mat...doormat.'

'So you're going to let yourself in at night, and then you get him with this?'

My gloves give the toothbrush back to Rudy and I'm glad for them all over again because I haven't left any fingerprints.

'I want to talk to him first.'

'Talk?'

What is it with these two, they have so much to say to each other.

'I want him to say it. What he did.'

'What did he do?'

'He *lied*.' Rudy wails, can't believe I have to ask. 'He said my dad—'

'But what do you think actually happened? You think *Tyan* killed your mum?'

'No, but—'

'Then how else did the vase wind up in your dad's workshop? I mean, like, how else could he have found it there?'

'You...I mean—'

'They got the murder weapon, Rudy. Where did it come from if not the workshop?'

'*No*—'

He cuts himself off, mouth works but nothing comes out. He has no theory about what happened. Only that somehow his father was framed by Glen Tyan.

My hand twitches in the air to placate him.

'I'm just saying, we don't know.' This is me throwing Rudy a lifeline.

'We don't *know*,' Rudy echoes, the same tightness in his voice that was so intimidating yesterday. 'We don't...We *don't* know.'

'But if we don't know, isn't it possible that Glen Tyan didn't—'

'What's the news?'

'What?'

'You said there's...you had news. You said I'd like it.'

And he stares at me.

I make a long sighing noise, allow myself to be distracted by a creak and a thunk that could be a footstep in the upstairs bedroom. More likely it's a structural reaction to the cold that's whooshing in through the front door.

Rudy's eyes follow mine to the ceiling. More flaky paint. Long fat cracks in the plaster.

'Yeah, sometimes I hear her up there. Just, like...walking around.'

'Her?'

'Mum.'

What could also be a reaction to the cold weather is the goose flesh on my arm. But now a thought creeps into my mind, keeps on creeping once it's there.

'Rudy, when was the last time you went upstairs?'

'Don't know.'

'I don't mean specifically. Just roughly.'

'I don't think...since it happened.'

Suddenly I feel the weight of the rooms above, crushing down like they're filled with liquid. The cracks in the ceiling seem to split further even as I gaze at them.

'Has anyone been up there since it happened?'

'Just the police.'

'The police. When it happened.'

'Yeah...Glen Tyan.'

'No one since then.'

Rudy shakes his head and I stare into a void of absurdity. The absurdity of that. No one has been upstairs in thirteen years. I almost laugh. Instead, I'm like, 'Have you ever wondered why it is you're preoccupied with your father's death and not your mum's?'

Rudy squints, can't formulate a response.

'Seriously, man. I mean, if you're right, if your dad didn't do it, who did?'

'I *know* who killed my mum.'

'Who?'

'Ken Penn.'

'Who the fuck is Ken Penn?'

'He lived over...across from us.'

The name jangles in my mind. Ken Penn. A witness at Piers's trial who was never called. I remember from the transcript.

'What makes you think it was him?'

'Him and Mum were...He was in love with Mum. He *told* me.'

'They were sleeping together?'

'Ummm...'

'Which house did he live in?'

'The big red one. Across from us.'

And he points. Through the open door and the pyramid trees and across the wide road there is indeed a red-brick house, made slightly taller than the other homes by the attic that it wears like a fez.

'Does he still live there?'

'He moved out after...And *he* never had a key. So he would *have* to have...had to break in.'

'Do you know, *why* he would hurt your mother?'

'He was supposed to go to Lorne. Like, with her. But he didn't go. So they must have fought.'

'You think they fought, because he didn't go to Lorne, so he killed her?'

'*Yes. He* killed her.'

'Your father fought with your mother, too.'

'I *know.* They were fighting over *me.*'

'Did your dad ever hit your mum?'

'*No.* Never.'

'He pushed her, though. Remember?'

'Yeah, but no. I was there. He didn't. I mean, he did, but...'

'Did you ever see him strike her?'

'*No.*'

'Not her death. I mean before that. When they used to argue.'

'*He never*—'

Rudy wants to finish but doesn't know how. He never hit her

hard? His head turns away to the long hallway and the kitchen and his body follows, then just as quick he wheels back, eyes sparking with agitation.

'Are you going to say the news? What is it?'

Yeah, tell him your news, Jason. That the contract is 'enactive'. Tell him to go for Tyan tonight. Tell him it's his last day as a free man.

I shake my head at myself.

'I spoke to Tristan Whaley.'

'You...ummm...'

'That's my news. I spoke to Tristan Whaley. The tall man.'

Rudy pales.

'How...How?'

'Don't worry, I didn't give anything away. But Rudy, he says he didn't tell you Piers was innocent.'

'He *did*.'

'He only said that your dad could have been acquitted because of his mental state.'

'*No*.' Rudy turns another full circle on the spot, chasing his tail. Arms crossing his chest, planting on his hips, never resting. 'No. He said it.'

'And he gave me this.'

My hands shake but manage to bring the crumpled newspaper printout from my pocket.

Rudy takes it, his own childish face staring back at himself.

And I'm like, 'Look at that, Rudy. Look very carefully.'

He steps back along the hall like he's trying to escape from what's in his hands, head shaking too much for him to read the print so it's just the photos and the headline he's denying. This builds to an agonised *Naaaaaah* and he dashes the pages to the floor and the shiv goes with it and he grasps a pink cloth and stoops over the piano stool and polishes. All one violent action.

I'm like, 'Even *you* said he was guilty.'

He doesn't respond, just rubs at that stool, so hard he's already out of breath.

'Listen, you—'

'*No*. I never said that!'

'You *did.*'

'They *told* me to say that. They *told* me to.'

'Who told you?'

'*Her.*' He flicks an accusing finger at the paper on the floor. 'The *lady.*'

I pick up the pages, check her name. Not sure how to pronounce it.

'Nina Chian...'

'Yeah.'

'Chiancelli.'

'Yeah...'

'She told you what to say?'

'*Yes.*'

This morning, reading the article in Whaley's den. The quotes hadn't sounded like Rudy.

'But why would she do that?'

He goes to blurt an answer, doesn't have one. It comes out a fretted moan.

To upset him further would be cruel, but diffusing Rudy-the-Timebomb means applying the formula:

$$\text{Rudy} + \text{proof of Piers's culpability} = \text{Tyan's safety}$$

'Listen,' I say, can't really steady my voice. 'Your father told me. In Severington. He told me he murdered your mother.'

34

He uses all the power in his forehead to ignore me.

'He told me, Rudy.' I fumble for details that will make this sound like anything other than an improvisation. But, like yesterday, I'm hamstrung by the fact that I have no idea what I am talking about.

'We were outside on yard detail one day...And he told me it was true. Just like they'd said in court. And he made me promise not to tell anyone. But he said he had to get it off his chest.'

The mad scrubbing intensifies. Rudy turns the piano stool over, polishes the underside. Why you'd polish the underside I'm not sure. Unless you're blind because inside you're screaming.

'He said he did it. That he'd never forgive himself. I don't know for sure, but maybe that's why he took his own life—'

What interrupts me is: Rudy slaps me. He's fast, rears up quick and gets me hard on the shoulder. Makes contact and freezes in place, half-waiting for my reaction, half-shocked by his own.

'*Ow*,' I hoot. Not a reaction to the pain; a parent's reprimand to a misbehaving child.

'*You...*' Rudy manages, a tense squeal and his hand flutters before slapping again. I grab his shoulder. Teeth clench.

'*Stop that.*'

Another slap. The other hand. Suddenly it's not cold in here but hot.

'You got the *teeth*! You were his *friend*! He got you *toilet paper*!'

'Your dad was *guilty*, Rudy. He told me.'

'You're *lying!*'

'*I'm not lying*,' I say, lying. 'Look at that newspaper! You knew it was him.'

'You were his *friend*!'

I step away before he can slap me again, back towards the door. 'Your dad *killed* her, Rudy. Glen Tyan didn't do *anything*.'

What comes from his mouth starts as *No* and evolves into something monstrous, the howl of a man watching his identity get murdered. He twitches like a voodoo priest casting a spell, pumped full of the agony of thirteen years. It's the face of someone else, redder than his hair, red enough that he might be choking, but if he's choking that doesn't stop him coming at me, maybe to slap me again, maybe something worse.

My body reacts before my brain does. I bolt out the door but trip on the doormat and flail over the steps.

I am not running away. I am falling away.

At first it's not an emergency, but then my jacket catches on the iron fence and my hand can't break my fall.

Head first into the green mess and the tiles underneath. *Crack*. I don't know what it is that does the cracking. Don't think about it but stagger to my feet and run from the yard, sure that I've been stabbed with a sharpened toothbrush from behind but the way I'm running across Grand Street suggests that maybe I haven't.

Don't know if there are footsteps behind me, don't look when I reach the car. The key turns and the door locks and there's no sign of Rudy and I try to ease my blood down as I pull away but that doesn't prevent a screech of tyres and I'm gone.

A block away I check again that the car doors are locked and I do it with one eye because the other eye is closed because it has blood in it because there's a wound in my eyebrow.

And the fear comes. Or the post-fear. Angles into my lungs and stomach like Rudy stabbed me there with a syringe of something disgusting. It stays manageable until it's not and I have to clutch at my abdomen, cross my arms over and squeeze from both sides. Pull to the kerb, a weakness in my neck that makes my head fall forward. Lights across my face. The beta-blocker I took at the football bugs out. Feel for the door handle. Open it, can't lean far, yak. Tipping forward makes the streetlights move in a dance, sweat pours from my hair...

It's fully dark when I wake. The driver's door is open and I wonder if someone opened it while I slept but I remember it was me, my splash of vomit there as evidence. I take off the seatbelt and shut the door...

I wake again, or is it the same time? My right hand moves to my left eyebrow and there is liquid there and it is blood. The damage doesn't feel bad but maybe it's just numb. Maybe it is particularly deep. I need help. I need someone to help me.

I speed dial Tyan's number.

'Hello?'

But I can't speak. Or don't want to.

'Hello?' Tyan says again.

'Rudy's not coming tonight,' I say. Bile burns my throat. 'I'll see you tomorrow.'

And I end the call.

After a time I find it within myself to join the passing traffic, anonymous and lulled by the lights and the rain. There's one person I think can help. I can go up those stairs and knock on that door and she'll help me. The warmth inside, the softness of her home. She'll be puzzled and disapproving but willing. She'll take me in because we know each other. I don't have a mother to run to and she will understand and take me in and she probably would have helped me sooner if only I'd asked.

I empty myself out of the car, stumble across the bitumen and feel again at the wound, how bad it is. The glove comes back bloodied and suddenly I'm a lunatic on the run and I survey the immediate area for dangers but there are none.

Up the steps to the door and I knock.

Hear nothing from inside. Maybe she can see me through the peephole, this ragged and desperate gentleman caller with a hand to his head to hide that he's bleeding. The door opens wide and I feel the gust of warmth go through me and she smiles at first but this hardens when she sees the blood.

She says, 'Timothy?'

35

'Rudy…' I say. That's all it requires.

Because Beth is how I met Rudy, I figure the least she can do is not turn me away.

'Oh. God…'

'I had nowhere else to go.'

'Come in.'

I do come in.

'It's not too bad. I'm sorry about this. I hope you don't mind…'

'What happened?'

It probably should have occurred to me that she would ask this question. I stumble in a pointless circle, stalling as I think of what to say, a diver in the depths of my own bullshit, attempting to neutralise my buoyancy. To her it scans as helplessness.

'Here…'

And she ushers me through a warmly lit space where the TV plays mute and colourful items on shelves can't be focused on, through a door and into her bathroom the size of a closet, with a smaller closet built into the wall where this girl presumably showers. She follows and turns on the light and there's hot breath on my neck, but it pulls away as I take off the gloves and drop them to the floor.

'I went to his house,' I say, analysing the mirror. A black gash leers above my eye and my right cheek is swollen like a trackball. I don't remember getting hit there. Blood has dripped down my face, a precisely barbered sideburn.

'I went to see Rudy. Said I knew his father in jail. In Severington. I said we'd been really good friends.'

It's not all that happened but it *is* what happened. And it takes saying it out loud for me to realise how numpty it is that I tried it.

She pulls at my jacket, helps get it off. 'Gosh. Why?'

'Rudy thinks this guy, my client, got his father sent to prison. That's why Rudy's got it in for him. He says his father was innocent. So I went and told him that Piers was guilty, had confessed to me. I thought, like, if I convinced him, like...fucking problem solved.'

A wet flannel appears in her hand. She dabs at my skull, clears the sideburns.

'I think it's stopped bleeding. I'm going to put on some Dettol.' She opens a cabinet, having assumed the role of ER nurse without even a cautious pause.

The Dettol stings; I push through it.

'We have to go to the hospital,' she says. 'You need stitches or else it'll scar.'

I think about that. A scar to show Glen Tyan.

'I just need to sleep.'

Beth smiles, strange, like I might be joking. Might be delirious with fever or infection or concussion or impending death.

'Why don't you let me take you and you can decide when we get there?'

'No, but if you think I should leave, that's fine. Really. You don't need some arsehole showing up out of the—'

'I'm not kicking you out. You can sleep here if you want.'

That hot breath. I feel it on my lips.

She's like, 'Your face is a shocker. I'm getting ice.'

And Beth slips out the bathroom door and I'm feeling sleepy. As in, I am about to get down on the tiles and sleep. One hand steadies me against the basin and I lean into my reflection that's more than real now because of the thunder in my blood. Can't feel any tenderness or ache, but they're probably in the post.

'Take this.'

She's back with an icepack you use for chilling champagne. I take it but she has to tell me, 'Put it on your face, toots.'

Her hand guides mine to my cheek and holds it there.

I'm like, 'You told me Rudy couldn't hurt anybody. Those were *your* words.'

It's meant to sound playful but it comes out accusing.

'Yeah,' she says. 'He's touchy. About his parents.'

I don't know what this icepack is supposed to do. Why do people put ice on their face? I'm about to ask her when she says, 'So what does this mean?'

'What?'

'I mean, what happens now? Is there anything I can do?' Holding the ice in place keeps her close. Her chest grazes my shoulder.

'You've done a lot just now.'

'This is nothing.'

'It's more than nothing.'

'Well…' She giggles with a nervous twinge. 'It feels like nothing.'

What this feels like, I want to say, is the time I kissed Alicia Day, on the scaffolding outside the Computer Lab in O-Week. To be fair, it was the first time I'd kissed someone. To be really fair, she kissed me. And to be painfully fair, she was smashed on Jägermeister and hooked up with James Nibbit about five minutes later. But at that moment, when she held away her cigarette and snogged me in the open air, I had this exact same warmth in my stomach.

'Umm,' I say.

'Is it too cold?'

She presses harder against me, almost imperceptibly. Her breath gets hotter.

I say, 'No.'

Not many women have stood this close to me and then opted to continue doing that. It might be a trick. Or I'm delusional. Or maybe she was drinking Jägermeister before I got here.

'Why don't you come and lie down?'

She pushes five or six pillows off her bed and I flop on my back, eyes shut. By keeping them shut I might not have to *flirt* or *make a move*. But then there's the tickle of a single hair on my nose and I have to open my eyes and her face is there and it lowers onto mine.

Fuck, the smell of a mouth. The taste of a nose. A tongue, the tool she uses to scoop out thoughts from my brain. My hands find the flesh of her back, that dolphin skin, while hers hook into my collar and lever her weight onto me and I *want* to feel like she's crushing me.

All through what happens on her bed, I'm shaking like it's the Quickening. She must think I'm woefully inexperienced. That, or crazy nervous. Of which I'm both. I almost tell her I love her, but I read somewhere online that you're not supposed to do that, so I just tell her she's beautiful, over and over...

'What's this?'

I'd been drifting off, my skinny arm draped over her belly. The sheets are damp from sweat and I don't know how long it's been since we stopped what we were doing and lay back, breathless, sated, congealed in our betrayal of Rudy.

She taps at the webbing of my right hand.

I'm like, 'That's...the same tattoo Rudy's got.'

'It's smudged.'

My sweat has smudged my whole body.

'I drew it on. To try and connect with him.'

'I did the one he's got,' Beth said. 'Did you know that?'

I look at her now. The first time I've looked at her without her glasses.

'You did the black teeth on Rudy?'

'It's not like I wanted to. It was the day after he found out about his dad. That he'd passed away. He begged me and I guess, like, I have a hard time saying no. We had to YouTube how to do it.'

Exhaustion seeps up from my feet and breaks across my brain.

'Did Rudy tell you why he wanted it?'

'Not really. Just that his father had it.'

Her body lists and the lamp beside the bed clicks off. Headlights play across the ceiling, a lame kaleidoscope, meshing then rolling apart. She strokes the spot on my hand.

'You're lucky, Tim. You get to wipe yours off.'

If I were honest with her, I'd tell her how jealous I am of Rudy's tattoo. Of how he feels about it. But there's so much truth to be told, I'm not going to start there.

'My name is Jason.'

It's too dark to see her reaction.

'Jason what?'

'Jason Ginaff.'

'Why didn't you…I mean, why did you lie?'

'I don't know. I'm more comfortable when I pretend to be someone else.'

'Are you really an investigator?'

'Yes,' I say. And, I mean, basically, I am.

Her response is silence; I assume it's a stunned one.

What should I tell her next? That the man Rudy plans to hurt is my dad? That the insurance policy is a fraud?

Instead of either of those, I sleep.

36

The coldest place on Earth. The flatness of it lets the wind whip you like a slave and I'm half-tempted to steal one of the football scarves that's tied to every third or fourth headstone and wrap it around my head like a hijab. Light drizzle across the tundra, the least rain you can have and still have rain. Tyan might call this off if it gets too heavy. He stomps as he walks, wearing more layers than he's previously been capable of, matching my raincoat and boots but his gloves aren't smeared with dried blood like mine. Also, he's not wearing gloves. One hand is dug deep into a pocket, the other blanches in the open air, throttles a bouquet of carnations. I'm surprised he brought them; in fact, I'm surprised to see fresh flowers laid across the park like glitter. Even in a Melbourne winter, people make the journey to the graves of loved ones. Surely not all of them have been emotionally blackmailed into it by their estranged son.

When we met at the cemetery gate Tyan seemed actually moved by the sight of my face, the black cut over one eyebrow and the blue cheek. His voice was shaky.

'Are you okay?'

At first I was touched. Then I wondered if he was mentally comparing this beating to the one he'd administered.

'Let's do this first,' I said, too cold to linger. 'I'll tell you about it later.'

We walk apart, Tyan trailing because he doesn't know where to go. We wouldn't be likely to have a conversation in this gale if he was keeping up. From a distance we must present as wholly separate mourning parties, briefly contiguous.

Things were painfully awkward at Beth's this morning. Neither of us was used to sharing a bed, we each lay awake forever before we made our wakefulness apparent to each other. I shied away from my face in the mirror, pulled on my clothes and told her I had a 'family thing'. She suggested we meet later and maybe she was just preserving a fiction but I accepted gratefully.

Into the wind we make it past the cement tombs and the freshly dug plots and all the birdless perennials growing here because a stretch of dead trees would be just *too* appropriate, come upon her plaque: *Helen Ginaff 1958—2011. Loving Mother. Always.* I'm not sure what the *Always* is supposed to mean, except that I'll probably *Always* wish I'd written a better epitaph.

The earth is slightly sunken and the grass brighter than on other graves because it's been sown and watered more recently, but still how it scans is that fresh corpses make great fertiliser. My unconscious policy of never stepping on the grass is crashed through by Tyan when he plonks down a foot in the middle of the plot and lays his bouquet at the plaque.

Then, like it's nothing at all, he puts an arm around my shoulder.

'Fifty-three,' he says. 'Too young.'

'She was fifty-two when she died.'

'I remember her playing guitar. Did she keep that up?'

'No.'

'Finger-picking kind of guitar. It's got a name. She was great. Didn't know many songs.'

'Did you play an instrument?'

'Nah mate.'

'What songs did she play?'

'I can't remember.' There's a finality in how he says that.

'I think she'd be glad we've met.'

This isn't really true. She never seemed keen for me to meet Glen Tyan, though she knew I wanted to. After she got sick it new...

I thought she wouldn't be able to speak. Breathing like
that seemed to take all her energy, including what she
would have used for consciousness. I was watching the
clouds out the window when she murmured, 'You still...'

*I leaned in to better understand. Pressed down on the
bed to indicate that I was trying to better understand.*

'What's that, Mum?'

Her eyes were open, glaring at the dresser.

'...driving that...'

'I'm sorry, I don't...'

'...bloody thing?'

*I looked across and now I did understand. The Mitsubishi
symbol on my key ring. Scratched and faded but apparently
still identifiable from two feet.*

'Somebody has to.'

*'Not exactly...' I waited for her to continue.
'...last of...' So soft. 'V8 Intercept...cept...'*

*I smiled though she wasn't looking, didn't have the power
to turn her head.*

'It's your car, Mum. So...'

*When she'd purchased it I told her she should trade it in for
a USB stick. Now, as she liked to say, the tables had turned.*

ally came up. And then circumstances overtook us.

My comment has the predictable effect: a sigh, the arm comes off
my shoulder, but Tyan's graveside manner isn't so crude as to deny
paternity right here at this moment.

He's like, 'She was a stunning bird, I suppose you know.'

'Then why did you leave?'

I keep watching the plaque like it's the one that has the answer.

'It was hard back then. Being a cop and having a girlfriend.'

I listen. Wait for him to get it all out. How the trauma of the job
was too much to bring home to a family. How time consuming it
was to stay ahead of the criminals and their wicked schemes. How
a cop's pay was too measly for him to even throw her a few dollars
when he walked out.

But he doesn't keep going. He's *finished*. That was his explanation
and his apology and his restoration. A few clipped words in the rain.

He says, 'Were there other blokes on the scene? I mean, after me?'

'No.'

I wonder what I'd hoped to get out of this. This visit with this stooge.

I say, 'Do you remember the name Ken Penn?'

'No.'

My shoe plays with a crop of toadstools that have sprouted here.

'Rudy seems to think it was Ken Penn who killed Cheryl Alamein.'

'Well it wasn't.'

'She and Penn apparently had a thing.'

'Listen,' he says, seeing that the light is green on discussing this now. 'Are you going to tell me what happened to your face?'

I wipe the rain from my eyes.

'I told Rudy that Piers confessed to me. In prison. I told him Piers was guilty.'

'Why?'

'*Because*—' I spit the word but can't phrase the rest of it. A black hearse passes nearby. In the passenger seat a young woman checks her makeup in the visor mirror. 'Because if he accepts the truth, then this all goes away.' I huff water off my top lip.

'Then what happened?'

'This.' I point to my head. 'He freaked.'

'That's it? He attacked you for that?'

'He didn't attack me exactly. I tripped and landed on my face. But I'm fine. Don't worry about it.'

This talk of my injuries makes me want to touch them. The cut over my eye stings but the headache seems to come from the swollen cheek. It throbs, boastful.

'You shouldn't have done that,' Tyan hisses. 'Nobody asked you to do that. You'll fuck this whole thing up.'

I'm emboldened by my damaged face, like there's no way Tyan will attack me *today*. So I turn to him. Turn on him. Don't get to flex my self-righteous muscles in real life very often.

'*Somebody* has to fuck it up. Fucking this up is what we should be doing. I know you want to live out your fantasy of capturing him and getting on the TV, but you're fucking naive, man.'

More cars pass; I hope their windows are fogged enough to hide my gesturing.

'He found the key. To the back door of your house. You've got a spare key outside there somewhere? That's what he was doing in your yard the other night. When you called me. He *knows* how to get into your *house*.'

That keeps him thinking. Hands come out of his pockets, grasp each other for warmth. I continue:

'You think when he shows up on Friday night and finds you with a gun, you think that's going to *stop* him? You think he'll throw down the shiv and say, "Okay, you got me?" He's not going to sit back and let you make a fucking *citizen's arrest*. His brain is like, revenge or die trying. *That's* why we have to call the cops.'

I say that with conclusion so that Tyan knows the spiel is over. And in response, he nods. For a couple of foolish seconds I think he's on board, that I've convinced him and we will now turn to law enforcement. Undermine Rudy's plan, not help it along. He even says it out loud:

'You're right.'

He watches another sedan glide past, swish through the puddles. Blinks hard at it.

And he's like, 'We have to take him out.'

37

The vehicles convene at a distant point among the monuments. Sombre men and women emerge, stagger unhurried through the spits of rain and the wind that seems to own this place, gather where an open plot is gaping.

I can't see it but I know it's there.

'Look at your face,' Tyan jeers. 'I mean for Christ's sake…'

'This is a joke, isn't it?'

'It's the only way to keep us *both* safe.'

'What are you going to do? Go to his house and whack him?'

'Nah.' Another drawn-out vowel. He's got the temerity to be dismissive of how I've got the temerity to be dismissive of this. 'I mean when he comes for me. I've got a firearm. We're not talking about just detaining him anymore.'

A lot of grey hair crowns the mourners over there; I guess it's a burial for someone whose time had come. Someone older than Mum. Older than Rudy.

'I think we should go to the cops. I think we should go to them *right now.*'

'That's not an option.' Tyan moves closer, not to intimidate me but to better conduct a nuanced conversation. 'You said yourself an intervention order isn't going to work. That's about all he'll get, even with attempted murder. And what if he's bailed? The judge orders him not to go within a kilometre of my house. Big woops. Even if he goes away for a couple of years, do you think when he gets released he's going to waste any time before he comes after me? He's been stewing on this for years.'

I look at my mother's grave, scoff at it.

'Is this what men do without women in their lives? Just stand around, plotting to murder each other? I mean...' I laugh, pointedly. 'Are we really discussing this in a *graveyard*?'

'It's not murder. It's self-defence. It's the guarantee that I can sleep for the rest of my life with both eyes shut.'

The steam from Tyan's mouth is like the exhale from a single toke on a cigarette.

I say, 'From what I understand, he's got a heart thing. Like, a heart problem. He could drop dead any minute.'

'Only makes him more dangerous.'

'All he's going to have is a freaking toothbrush. Are you allowed to shoot him *then*?'

'What toothbrush?' He leans into my eye line. 'Have you seen it?'

'It's a tiny plastic stick. It's not self-defence if it's a stick.'

'It is if he's a real threat. If he takes me by surprise.'

'But you *know* he's *coming*.'

Tyan's eyes droop, bored with how I'm arguing. 'We don't tell anyone that I knew.'

'So you want me to lie. To the police.'

'It's a small price to pay—'

'And you think they're just going to *believe* us?'

'Why shouldn't they?'

'Because there isn't a reason that they *should*. Outside of you and me, no one knows what Rudy's planning. No one knows he hates you. He winds up dead in your house, they might not just take your word for it.'

There's Beth. But no way I'm bringing that name up right now.

'Okay,' he says, nodding with the wisdom of Yoda. 'We should talk about that. But first you need to calm down and see that this might be against the rules but it's absolutely fucking necessary.'

'It's *not*. And after what happened last night, he doesn't know what the fuck's going on with his insurance. So we don't even know if Friday's still the day. Maybe he'll just say fuck it and come tonight.'

It's raining heavier. Umbrellas come out among the mourners.

Tyan turns, starts the walk back the way we came. The visit to
Mum's grave is over.

'Then we've got to find out,' Tyan says over his shoulder. He
knows I'm following. 'And I can't fucking do it, can I? I need you.
Because otherwise all this is for nothing.' He waves at the cemetery.

'You're out of your mind. This is…This makes you no better than
Rudy.'

Tyan swivels at me with a bony finger.

'Being better than him isn't the *fucking* point. The point is not to
get *fucking* murdered in my *fucking* sleep. Can't you see that? I don't
reckon there's a future for you and me if you're like this. Sorry to be
so blunt, but it's a little chilling to think you don't care.'

'*That's* what you find chilling?'

The dirt path turns to mud, impacted and sloppy beneath our feet.
Already cars return along the blacktop, attendees harried from the
burial by the cold. In the thick of this altercation I'm still watching
in case people can tell we're arguing.

I raise my voice, bowed against the wind. 'I'm not helping to do
it. I don't care if it *does* queer things for you and me.'

The cigarettes come out now. Tyan stops to light up, thwacks
away at his plastic lighter but the elements are against him. He gives
up, waves the white stick at me.

'You should think about that.'

He continues to walk. I stay put.

'*I don't need to think about it!*'

Over his shoulder, without turning back, still holding the cigarette like he's smoking it: 'Think about *that*!'

I let him go. I'm parked in the other direction.

38

Beth is drinking cappuccino when I arrive. A chocolate moustache lines her top lip and either she knows about it, considers it hilarious, or she doesn't know. Or maybe she wants me to see how she's no less handsome for this new virility.

The Lunacy Café was her choice, so close to where she lives. Lunchtime it's crowded with Brunswick people: as I enter a young woman in full kawaii cosplay throws me a sour look from this side of the drinks fridge, one to make me shut the door against the cold, which I do, then move to Beth's table and she shows me her dimples and smiles that wide brown smile.

'Hiya, toots.'

It holds nothing of the awkwardness of this morning and it's a reminder of how not-Marnie she is, the thought of whom brings on a pang of guilt which I force down with a more powerful, somehow more acceptable, sense of shame—my father plans to kill someone.

I consider telling Beth exactly half of that, not sure I want to in such a crowded spot. Even as I sit there's someone's arse in my face, shimmying past.

'Hello.' You can't help but grin at her.

'God...' She examines the markings on *my* face. 'I can't believe we...I should have taken you to the hospital.'

The nerve-endings have come back to life. Everything's tight. My eye wants to close over.

'I'm fine.'

'Did Rudy really, like...punch you?'

'Not really,' I say. 'He slapped me.'

'That's a *slap*?'

'I was trying to get away from him. I fell and hit my head.'

'Right…'

'But it wouldn't have happened if he wasn't so aggressive. Like, way aggressive.'

She nods with an urgent understanding. I hurt myself running away.

I'm like, 'What have you been up to this morning?'

'Just waiting for you, toots. How's the fam?'

'Fine.'

'Was it like a birthday thing?' She sips more coffee and wipes her mouth, sees the chocolate on her hand and finds a serviette.

'Just a catch up with my dad.'

'Cool,' she says, her interest tapering.

'I never knew him my whole life. We've only just now been in contact.'

My lord, that feeling when you finally tell someone.

'Wow. How's *that* going?'

'Fine.'

I raise my head for a waiter. It's less that I want to eat and more that I want to change the topic. My conversation with Tyan killed my appetite, buried it and left a tasteful plaque. Which is just as well, because I can't tell which of these hipsters are waiters and which are patrons. Everyone has dreadlocks or tattoos and they all seem to have just finished having sex with each other.

'Are you okay?'

Her question catches me out.

'Why?'

'You seem weird. Did something happen with your dad?'

'No. It's a long story. Let's talk about something else.'

'Okay,' she says. 'Listen, I think you need to tell me what's going on. Like, more about, like…'

'What?'

'Like, for one thing, who is this guy? The one Rudy's got it in for?'

Toots, that is so not changing the subject.

I scan the café. Joyless gossiping twentysomethings mixed in with loners on their phones and laptops, but the dreamy ambient music is loud enough to keep most conversations private. I hold off as a dazed beard carries green juice in a jar past our table.

'His name is Glen Tyan. A retired police detective. He put Rudy's dad in prison.'

'Okay...' She scrunches her eyes, sympathetic and thoughtful.

'Once upon a time, Rudy knew his dad was guilty, told it to a newspaper, but then his father took his own life and Rudy started to think that Piers was...framed.'

I feel stupid just saying that word.

'He can't explain how or why, because there is no how or why. How and why got buried underneath this revenge thing. He just blames the guy that arrested his father. But Beth...'

I raise my fist off the table, grapple with what I'm about to say. It's time to make this particular fact clear to Rudy's number one apologist.

'Rudy wants to kill him.'

A weak twitch in her eye that makes her glasses shudder.

'No way.'

'He's going to break in and murder Tyan in his sleep. At least, that's what he was planning up until this.' I draw a circle in the air around my face. 'Since this I don't know what he's thinking.'

'He told you all that last night?'

'Sure,' I say. *Why not?* 'I pretended to have the tattoo to win his confidence. It really, like...worked.'

'You've got to tell him.' A hand flaps, frustrated. 'Glen Tyan. You've got to tell him Rudy wants to—'

'He knows.'

Her confusion seems to frustrate her and she scowls down at the table.

'He knows?'

'Yes.'

'But he won't go to the police?'

'He will on the night. He'll incapacitate Rudy and have him

arrested. He's the kind of guy who can do that.'

Only that's not the plan anymore, is it Jason?

'Why not, like, go to the police now?'

I sigh, slow. Eyebrows rise, cheeks puff.

'Tyan says they'll throw the book at him if he actually tries it. He's hoping that'll teach him a lesson.'

'God...'

She takes off her glasses and massages her head. Eyes shut, she whimpers: 'Do you think it would?'

'What?'

'Teach him a lesson.'

'Nope.'

'Why not?'

'Because I don't think he's going there to kill Glen Tyan.'

She pokes her head forward.

'But you just said—'

'He told me that's what he wants to do. Maybe he believes it himself, but...'

Without thinking I take hold of her coffee, drink from it. Just a sip to lubricate my throat.

'I think his primary intention is to make Tyan act in self-defence. That's the...the thing he's going there to do. He can't manage it himself, so he's going to force a retired cop to do it for him.'

She gently sways back, eyes gently sway back, hands rub her knees like she's staving off nausea. I'm expecting a concerted rebuttal, but instead she says, 'Yeah.'

I wait for her to say more, or at least to open her eyes.

And she's like, 'There's something I haven't told you.'

39

The ordinary atmos of coffee drinking and trip-hop rises a notch. Someone wearing an actual apron stacks milk crates in the door to the kitchen. Someone else at a table nearby complains about their communications lecturer. I rub my shoulder.

'I'm listening.'

'A few days after his father died?' She gazes at the tabletop, hands play with the waxy plant, the kind that adorns all the tables in here. 'He asked to borrow the car. I brought it round to him in the afternoon, then I came and got it back the next day.'

Someone behind the café counter, a skinny Asian girl showing her midriff in the middle of July, lets loose a great cackle of laughter. Beth waits for it to subside, edges closer.

'When I came to pick it up, he was really scattered. Like, distressed? I asked if he was all right and he said he just needed to sleep because he'd been in the car all night. I asked where he'd gone but he didn't want to say. So I just took the car and left.'

Now there comes a relentless beeping sound, begging for attention—some appliance the workers don't have sufficient time or concern to shut off.

'The thing is, though, the odometer wasn't changed,' Beth has to raise her voice. 'Not even a kilometre? It was on the half-seven when I dropped it off. It was in the same place when I picked it up.'

'So he hadn't driven anywhere.'

'*But...*'

That appliance, it's a blender. Piercing. A jigsaw piece reversing into place. Beth leans closer; her voice softer but somehow more intense.

'I gave it to him with a half tank of petrol. When I picked it up it was nearly empty.'

I try to make sense of this by peering at the air above her.

'So...you think he...'

'Yes.'

The blender goes silent. Someone has switched it off, leaving a vacuum of quiet and I almost whisper:

'That's it then. That's what this is. He can't go through with it himself, so he's made himself believe this conspiracy crap about Glen Tyan. That's why he got the insurance.'

She stiffens at that last word, turns as if to properly contemplate the mural on the café wall. A grief-filled sigh, adjusting to this new reality.

'God, it's so creepy...' Her face falls, expressionless. 'That policy makes me sick...But...you think...'

Fear comes to her eyes, verging on terror.

'What?'

'You think, if I didn't take the money, if I gave it all away...Do you think we should *stop* him going through with it?'

'You think we shouldn't?'

'What right do we have?' She leans across the table. The blue in her eyes vibrates, as if frightened by the words she speaks. 'It's the right thing to do, right? To help him, like, escape? If that's what he wants?'

'I don't—'

'I won't accept *any* of the money.' She glares, begging to be believed. 'I'll give it away. I'll give it to the shelter. But we have to think about what's best for Rudy.'

I can't assess what's best for Rudy. Don't even know the criteria. 'We have to think about what's best for us as well.'

'For us?'

'I'm not ready to just *watch* him make the last big mistake of his life. And I'm not ready yet to give up reasoning with him.'

'You *tried* that.' The strain in her eyes is extraordinary. I want to grab hold and comfort her, but not with all these people around. '*Look* what happened.'

Beth needs me to understand, even as she's drenched in the shame at what she's saying. To justify herself, she pleads:

'I *hate* to think of him living in pain.'

I do understand. If I can feel pity for Rudy Alamein, what chance does a big heart like hers have?

'What if his father *didn't* do it?' I offer this with as much optimism as I can generate. 'What if we could prove that someone else killed Cheryl Alamein and framed Piers? He'd forget all about Glen Tyan. And exonerating his father would give him something to live for.'

It's a reverse of the formula I've been applying, but it reaches the same result. Despite how unlikely we are to determine its variables.

Beth winces at my logic. But there's hopefulness in her voice when she says, 'You think someone else did it?'

'No,' I say. 'But it's possible, isn't it?'

'So…What? I mean…what do we do?'

Suddenly I'm hungry. Ravenous even. Again I search the room for a waiter. The half-stoned beard lingers by the counter, flirting with the Asian midriff. I wave and still they don't see me. Then I yell: 'Oi!'

Both of them hear me, look, move through the tables in my direction, synchronised.

I say to Beth: 'We hope the real killer's in a mood to confess.'

40

Suddenly the road is lined with eucalypts and the small-town quaint-ness of Sassafras gives way to a national park. Thick trunks drive into the forest canopy, bark hanging from their branches like spaghetti after a food fight while lichen cakes the pines and the white reflector poles and even the bus stops when we happen to pass one, lonely and forbidding among the green. There aren't many other cars. Any other cars. Maybe it's just us winding through the Dandenong Ranges. It feels like it.

Beth needs time so I'm not driving fast. Her fingers tap the tablet glass, flip from webpage to webpage. She's quiet but for the occasional coo of interest.

To our left comes a break in the trees and I look out across an expanse of tree ferns, a sea of open umbrellas. Like the umbrellas at the graveyard this morning.

To distract myself from this thought I glance at the map on my phone. We've been driving for an hour, will arrive in less than ten minutes. Beth has been engrossed in her iPad for longer than I thought she'd need. I'm about to tell her that her time is up when she stirs.

'Okay.'

'You found something?'

'I think so.'

'Are you ready?'

'Uh-huh.'

I expected her to be uncomfortable with this. The deception.

The spycraft. But she's come around to the idea and it's her presence now that drives the car as much as the petrol in the tank, my foot on the throttle. Of all the lies I've told these past days, I've not had anyone to stand there and tell them with me.

Beth taps DIAL on my phone, then SPEAKER. It doesn't take them long to answer.

'Claireborne Views Residential, Erica speaking.'

'Hello,' says Beth. She doesn't say anything else. I glance at her.

'Hello?'

Beth finds her voice.

'Hello. Ummm...I'm trying to contact Kenneth Penn?'

Not even a please. She's that tense. It prompts Erica to abandon all courtesy as well: 'Hold.'

A recording kicks in, mid-sentence. A smarmy voice like that airship in *Bladerunner*:

...the quality of a life spent among the stunning and gorgeous surrounds of one of Victoria's most scenic and beautiful—

A delicate croak cuts it off.

'Yes?'

I grab at Beth's knee, try to make the act supportive, not condescending.

She says, 'Ummm...Kenneth Penn?'

'Yes.'

'My name is Elizabeth Cannon.'

'I'm sorry?'

Her voice rises, too loud: '*Elizabeth Cannon...I'm a broker with Fredermons.*'

I gesture with a flat palm. She lowers her voice.

'I'm a broker with Fredermons. We have you listed as an authority in nineteenth-century French?'

Beth's classic upward inflection, but this time posing it as a question, asking the silence on the other end of the line for confirmation.

For my part, I've never heard of Fredermons. Beth says it's a boutique auction house with the kind of cachet that might keep Ken Penn on the line. According to the rudimentary search I did at Beth's place, he used to be the kind of collections specialist that newspapers went to for commentary, whenever there were pages to fill about exhibitions or thefts or celebrity sales. Despite her reticence, Beth's experience with antiques is the best hope we have of getting in the door.

Well, not just her expertise. Penn was born in 1931, which means he's eighty-one, which means he was twenty-five years older than Cheryl when they hooked up. So maybe a pretty face can win him over.

'What is this about?'

It's a weedy voice, like he's straining to grasp something just out of reach.

'Ummm, as I said...' Beth fumbles, leans in closer to the phone like that will help. 'I'm a broker with Fredermons.'

'Yes.'

'Ummm...' She looks to me for help but all I can do is drive encouragingly.

She reads from the iPad: 'We've come upon a germain royal soup tureen we believe dates back to Napoleon Three, and we're keen to have the item looked over. Am I correct in saying that French antiques is your area?'

The quaver in her voice probably isn't audible over the phone.

'I'm sorry, what?'

She doesn't know what to say to that; her hesitation stinks of failure, and I'm wondering if there's some way we can *break in* to the Claireborne facility. But then the voice croaks:

'My understanding is that Napoleon Three silver was all melted down. To finance wars and orgies and such.'

He makes a grotesque sound which might be chuckling and Beth pushes on the seat belt, relieving the pressure from her torso.

'I can't comment on the provenance, Mister Penn. I can only tell you that we're getting advice on authenticity with a view to putting the piece on the market.'

'If you think the piece is genuine...' comes the deathly wheeze from the phone, 'my advice is to handcuff it to your wrist and fly it to Sotheby's. No one in this country can sign it off. And no one over here's going to fucking buy it!'

Another chuckle and a long inhale. That suggestion took the wind out of him.

'Ummm…We were hoping we might visit with you to discuss it. Ummm…Today.'

Beth really pushes that seatbelt away like it's a web she's caught in.

'What's to discuss? I no longer have a client list. You understand where I am, don't you?'

'Yes, and we're just a few minutes away. We've been displaying the item for a dealer in Olinda and we thought—'

'Wait…' His voice drops past its timbre, deepens into gravel. 'You've got the item *with* you?'

She says: 'Yes?'

'*Jeeeeesus,*' Another chuckle from the string section. 'If you've got the nerve to bring it here, I'll take a look out of deference to your testicles!'

'We can be there in a few minutes.'

'You say, *we*?'

She smiles at me, confident now.

'My assistant and I.'

'All right,' he says, like *It's your funeral.* 'I'll tell them to let you through.'

Once the call has ended and I've checked that it's ended, I'm like, 'Great job. You're a natural.'

She snorts.

'I'm a fucking *liar.*'

We laugh harder than we need to. Drain the tension from the cabin.

41

'His eyes are too sensitive. He keeps the room dark. But that's a blessing.'

I don't know if she's a nurse—she has all the authority and none of the uniform. Her big beige cardigan and fantastic rump lead us from linoleum to grimy carpet, back to linoleum. Out the window the trees block whatever hilltop view this facility is supposed to command, reinforcing my suspicion that putting an aged care home in the Dandenongs is motivated less by the 'stunning and gorgeous surrounds' than by the positioning of its guests as far from Melbourne as their families' consciences permit. Beth follows close, crowding me, thrown by what happened at reception.

We were asked to wait for an available staff member, someone who would walk us through to Penn's room, so we stood politely to one side of the service window and quickly discovered that the guests were free to wander where they pleased. One of them, a bald gent with a white moustache, entered the foyer from the dining room, assessed these two visitors and hurriedly took cover behind a tall potted plant. Before long he was beckoning to me and I approached, bore a face of painful remorse that I would not be of any use to a senile old man.

'The door, Clancy,' he whispered. This required him to open his mouth wide and the spasm suggested he was choking. He had no teeth.

'I'm sorry?' I glanced around: no staff, just a scattering of ghostly women shuffling about in moccasins.

His mouth yawned wide again, trembled and he managed: *'Clancy, open the door!'*

A skeletal finger poked at the door to the carpark, where we'd entered. Beside it was a keypad and a sign that thanked you for not unlocking the door for residents.

I sighed at him, more remorse, was about to speak when a screech came from behind:

'No! Get off!'

It was Beth's voice. I knew that before I turned around.

What I saw was an eagle-faced, white-haired oldie pulling on the hem of Beth's jacket. With terrible force Beth's left hand cut through the woman's grip and she pulled herself out of range; it almost knocked Grandma to the floor and her jumper and jacket and stockings would have done nothing to prevent her skinny body from shattering into pieces. But she kept her balance, madness in her sunken eyes, turned on Beth with two raised claws that might have been attack or defence.

'Gemma!' she wailed.

'Susie!' was the whip-crack response, not from Beth but from the beige cardigan who moved through the foyer with enough dominion to paralyse the residents and compel within me a geyser of relief. She didn't look twice at Susie, simply ushered Beth and me into the corridor. Not so much as a roll of the eyes or a query as to whether we were okay. We followed in silent comprehension that visitors' identities were confused on so regular a basis that the staff no longer noticed.

Silent, that is, until we reach a closed door holding up a poster that reads: *Old Bananas are the Sweetest.* The woman stops and knocks and I'm compelled to ask:

'Why is it a blessing that he keeps the room dark?'

She doesn't wait for the knock to be answered, just turns the handle like it's her very own home.

'Let's hope you don't find out, hmmm?'

It's a tiny space, no more than a bedroom. I make out rudimentary furniture, a single bed, finally a man seated on it. Shrunken. Wears just a robe and holds a tobacco pipe in his hand. The room stinks of it. Like Tyan's house, but sweeter.

The beige cardigan coughs against the air.

'Door stays open, Ken. You know the rules.'

And off she goes, leaving us to the darkness and the smell.

'Good afternoon,' says the familiar voice, even more remarkable in person, as if he has no larynx at all but rather forms words using the rattle of his uvula against the roof of his mouth.

A lamp comes on, draped in thick silk cloth. It barely illuminates one side of the man on the bed, emphasises his desiccation, the thinness of his features and all those contours. Time has drawn a pile of lower-case *m*s on his forehead, pulled the bags under his eyes down to give them a hanging kind of sadness. The nose begins as gaunt as the rest of his face but blossoms into a bulb at its tip. Beneath the red robe there's hardly a frame to speak of.

'Sit down.'

I find a wooden chair a few steps from the door, rotate it slightly to best position myself to flee if the need arrives.

Sharing my reservations, Beth perches directly beside the door on something small and wooden. She tries to appear relaxed but fidgets with the sleeves of her jumper. We each waver, at a loss, two pupils in the headmaster's office.

'I hope my fellow geriatrics gave you no difficulty on your way in.'

'They're intense,' I say, try to appear conversational but can't stop fidgeting either.

Ken Penn's mouth barely moves as he speaks.

'I've often said that young visitors are our cherubs and our Cerberus. It confuses the softer ones.'

He sucks back on his tobacco, pleased with himself. Then studies Beth with enough overt lechery that I sense her discomfort like I would sense a desperate pounding from behind these thin unit walls.

Penn says, 'I can't help but notice a dearth of anything resembling a nineteenth-century soup tureen.' A patient observation, like people lie their way in to see him all the time. 'Unless she has it stowed away in some particularly expansive body cavity.'

'Umm...' I say. By Beth's silence I assume she no longer wishes to pretend I'm her assistant. 'Actually, we're here to see you about a different matter.'

'Oh?'

Beth suddenly bursts: 'Why does the door have to be open?'

It must be the adrenaline, the remoteness of where we are. Me, I'm *thankful* the door is open. The poor girl had no idea, when she sipped cappuccino in familiar surrounds and agreed to help me today, that our endgame was to withstand odious commentary from a pervert.

'I am sorry, dear,' Penn says. 'It is company policy. Can't have the three of us fornicating, you see. Strictly prohibited in the facility, even within the discretion of a guest's room. We Claireborne folk practise nothing if not self-denial.'

He follows this up with a lip-lick and an eyebrow-raise, so suggestive I almost laugh.

She can't look at Penn, just watches out the open door, one big anxiety emoji.

'Mister Penn,' I say. 'We're here to talk to you about Cheryl Alamein.'

A stillness descends upon the room as I try to discern Penn's reaction through the darkness. I hear a sigh. His eyes float up to a spot near the ceiling.

'Cheryl Alamein.' His voice is softer. 'Now, that is a name I've not heard in quite some years.'

I find myself scanning the lit space, the bedclothes and the small bamboo table where the lamp sits. There's a bronze clamshell ashtray and a telephone. I don't spot scissors, anything else he might weaponise.

Penn watches me in silence.

'We're wondering…' I start, only to realise I don't know how to start. 'We're wondering if you can throw any light on…what happened.'

'What happened?'

'Her death. On Grand Street.'

He seems surprised but not uncomfortable. His demeanour is that of someone gently inebriated.

Let's not rule that out.

'I have wondered,' Penn rasps, face darkening, 'if and when the day would come that someone should find me here and ask that question...'

No light in his eyes now. Perhaps they're shut.

Penn says, 'You know her husband went to prison?'

'Yes.'

He shifts his legs slightly, in such a fashion as to demonstrate that he's naked beneath the satin robe. This must be what the beige cardigan hoped we would not find out.

Beth launches to her feet.

'I'm going to wait in the car.'

She fiercely rubs the underside of her wrists against her hips.

I only say, 'What?'

'I just...' She looks nervously to Penn. 'I want to leave. Can I have the keys?'

Her face melts into such wounded despair that I can only nod, look to Penn as if she needs his permission, but Penn doesn't seem to have heard, focuses dreamily on the walls and says, 'Murdered. She was murdered. That's what happened.'

Man, the fear on Beth's face. Frightened eyes begging for safety. You can't blame her: the only thing that could have made this wax dummy more creepy was if he started talking about the murder of women. I produce the car keys and Beth snatches them from my hand.

'She was a wife of Bluebeard,' says Penn, almost to himself. 'Locked away in a castle. Too guileless to understand how guileless she was. But I taught her. I *injected* her with guile, if you take my meaning.'

When I glance back, Beth is gone.

Penn chuckles, waits to see if I will chuckle too. I don't, but I say, 'You had a relationship with Cheryl Alamein at the time of her death, is that correct?'

As I speak I stand and move to the open door, hoping for a glimpse of Beth, for an indication she's okay.

'At first she was reluctant even to remove her wedding ring. By the end she was a spring lamb, discovering the world anew. Open to all experiences.'

I peer down the corridor and she is gone. Just green–white walls and an empty whiteboard labelled *Activities*.

'I'll tell you this,' Penn says, oblivious to my thumping heart. 'I know who did it. Who murdered her. If that's what you want to know.'

I turn to him, step back into the shadow of his room, oblivious myself to my thumping heart.

'It wasn't her husband. Piers. It wasn't him.'

I edge forward. Penn can see that I'm listening.

'It was the boy. Rudyard Alamein.'

42

I feel my blood surge, try to calm it with slow steps back to the wooden chair, want to encourage Penn but my throat's too tight. He lights his pipe.

I manage, 'What makes you say that?'

Penn squeals gently through the wooden mouthpiece, gets his breath back. 'Abductive reasoning. I knew him back then. Saw in him what people here see in me.'

'What's that?'

Penn drops his lighter onto the bamboo table.

'Sin.'

And he drags back on the pipe, red coals radiating on his face.

'He understood, innately, that by doing away with moral concerns a man might become a god.'

I'm trying to develop a response to that when an outraged bird screeches past the window. I jump. Penn does not.

'The boy was a murderer *before* he killed his mother.'

I have to dwell on that, too. For a moment.

'Who did he murder?'

Thick ribbons of smoke ooze from Penn's mouth, momentarily obscuring his eyes.

'Whom.'

'I'm sorry?'

'Mister Jinx.'

Just this absurdity is enough to sink my heart. I've come to visit a man so addled by drugs or booze or just *life* that he speaks in nonsense.

He hasn't even asked my name, for fuck's sake. I'm preparing to run. Penn continues:

'Just a matter of days before Cheryl was killed. It was the Tuesday, I think. She was visiting with me. We'd spent most of the morning in the bedroom. We were like that, you know. Only emerging for food and ablutions. I came downstairs to prepare some chicken liver for lunch and there was an odour. Let me tell you, despite the full spectrum of hospitals to which I've been admitted, despite the many shameless souls I've known intimately, I've smelled nothing like it in my lifetime. Concentrated death. I believe I retched in the kitchen recess.'

A momentary tapping on the unit roof. Either the rain has restarted, then hesitated, or else the wind brought down a sprinkling of water from the treetops. I sit forward to hear better.

'At this stage, Mister Jinx had been missing for several days. I'd taken it that he'd run off with some neighbourhood jackal and was screwing her mercilessly. I was grief-stricken, but I expected him to return.'

'Mister Jinx was a pet?'

'A Maine Coon. Old, but not so old. I enticed him home again with open tins of tuna on the back stairs, to no avail. Then came that day, when I smelled that smell, and I knew.'

Smoke lingers but the pipe is out. He lays it on the bamboo table.

'We searched, Cheryl and I. We searched the ground floor, under the couch, under the stairs. I remember I even looked in the crawl-space beneath the house. We found nothing. Then Rudy came with his dog. I forget what pretence he had for visiting, but soon he was searching too. Had some laughable idea about his dog getting the scent, but of course that animal could no more track a missing cat than dance the fucking Nutcracker. It were as if the little prick was mocking me. That's when I got the idea that he knew. That this was his doing.'

I rock back on my hands.

'You think Rudy killed your cat?'

'I'm sure of it.'

'Why would he?'

'Because I made his mother moan like a grizzly bear and weep with gratitude. And did so on a regular basis. In that sense, I suppose I shouldn't have been surprised. I tried to develop a rapport with the child, oh how I tried. But he was a spiteful shit. Just a shit. Had a hatred for me that was…oedipal.'

'Did you find Mister Jinx?'

'Yes. Only by a stroke of luck. There was a pest-control fellow spraying for termites next door. I asked him for advice and he popped in and tracked the smell to my bookshelf.'

Penn edges off the bed and leans to his feet, frail, shapeless. His shoulder blades squeeze together for balance and he manages timid steps towards the bare wall and points.

'The house had built-in shelving, all the way to the ceiling. High ceilings. Filled with books, of course. We found Mister Jinx behind the encyclopaedias. The very top shelf.'

He shakes his finger at the wall.

'That little cunt broke his…' Glaring, Penn is crying. Tears backlit by the lamp. He sniffs away as much as he can. '…broke his little neck. His tail had gone rock hard and his fur had faded…the colour. Rudy dumped him there like he were human faeces. We weren't ever meant to find him. Just smell him. Smell every minute of his decomposition.'

A ragged handkerchief appears from his sleeve and he blows, uninhibited.

'I put it to him, directly. Demanded the truth. He denied it of course. Because he was nothing if not an inveterate liar, and then he ran away home. Cheryl knew it was him, she said as much. And went home that afternoon to speak with Rudy but returned that evening, said they'd fought. Rudy had confessed to hiding Mister Jinx in the bookshelf, claimed to have found him dead on the street. When she'd insisted how obvious it was that Rudy had killed him, circumstances deteriorated. She'd *fled*. My lord, the state of her. Hair a mess, face bloated. The least attractive I'd ever seen her. She said that Rudy had threatened to kill her. His own mother.'

Penn lowers his face to the floor.

'Three days later she was dead.'

He holds there like a freeze frame. A barefoot statue. The way his chin cleaves to his chest, silhouetted by the dim orange lamp, he's like a hanged man waiting to be discovered.

The corpse says, 'Cheryl Alamein was as much a blessing to me as her death was a curse. That was the beginning of the end.'

A long moan from Penn, like he's expressing grief. But actually it's the effort to seat himself back on the bed.

'Rudy says you killed his mother.'

He wipes at the bags beneath his eyes. 'Does he think I had a reason to?'

'He says you were supposed to go with her to Lorne. You didn't. You fought, things got out of hand...'

'A thin motivation, but yes, the last time Cheryl and I spoke, it was strained. Things were stressful for me at work, so I'd called to say I had to remain at the showroom. The Lorne trip was more about getting *her* out of that godforsaken house. My going was a secondary commitment. But she was disappointed. That disappointment may have been the reason she returned home when she did.'

'You were at work when she died?'

'Yes. It was busy. Clients always want the moon on a plate before a long weekend.'

'Did you tell the police about Mister Jinx?'

'Of course. I spoke to the lead detective more than once.'

'Glen Tyan?'

'Yes. Detective Glen Tyan.' Still it doesn't occur to Penn to ask me who I am. 'Great brute that he was. Very much the club-them-on-the-head-and-drag-them-behind-a-tree sort of fellow. Wasn't interested in anything *I* told him. Had his man, as the saying goes.'

'And you think Rudy pinned it on his own father? You think he's that smart?'

'No, by god. I think he's that stupid!' Penn is back to chuckling now. Cold air flows in from somewhere and he rubs his legs. 'He put the vase in his father's shop because he assumed no one would find it there. But of course they did. He didn't *intend* for Piers to get the blame.'

He tilts his head, as if listening to the rain on the roof. 'But perhaps it didn't bother him that that's what came of it.'

'Why not?'

'He didn't like his parents. They didn't like him.'

'Wait,' I say, spread my fingers and lower the points to my knees. 'Piers and Cheryl were fighting over Rudy. That's why things were so bad.'

Penn's snort is loaded with disbelief, appears to bring more tears to his eyes. 'They were fighting over who *shouldn't* have him. At least, neither of them wanted the day-to-day responsibility of *living* with him. They each sought a fresh start, you see? Their immediate family was the thorn in their respective sides, and they were going to court to determine who should be properly *unshackled.*'

Penn smiles, entertained by himself.

I say, 'Did you know there was some argument about whether you'd be called at the trial?'

'Yes. It was Piers who wouldn't have me there.'

'Why not?'

'He didn't want it announced to the world that I was shtupping his wife, most likely. And at the end of the day, they knew they couldn't hang the crime around *my* neck.'

He sighs. When he speaks again, exhaustion lightens his voice.

'It was a hard time, you know. Mister Jinx, and then Cheryl. After that, everything sort of...collapsed for me. And here I am.'

He gestures at his surroundings. A small prison cell in a forest. And what better demonstration than the beige cardigan, who appears at the door now and says, 'Group time, Ken.'

She's got a name card that I see for the first time in the light from the corridor: *Dorothy.*

Penn blinks at nothing. It seems like several seconds before the words reach him. Then he twitches, waves Dorothy away. 'Yes, yes.'

Her eyes fall on me. Something jingles in her hands.

'Your girlfriend caught a lift back.'

And she lays my car keys down on the small ornate stool where Beth had been sitting.

'Who with?' I say. But she's gone. Despite how she must have heard, she does not come back.

Penn's skinny white legs sweep out from his robe like crab claws and search sightlessly for the slippers beneath the bed.

'I'm afraid our little chat is over,' he chuckles at nothing. 'The group sessions don't do much for me, but apparently if I don't attend the other fruitcakes get the idea that they needn't either.'

'Thank you for speaking to me.'

'No need to thank me. I wish you well in…what was it again?'

'We're just inquiring about the Alamein murder.'

'Yes, yes.'

I move to the door and retrieve my keys, but before I can exit, Penn says, 'I was happy to talk, you know. I knew someone would come one day. Expected you. You needn't have pretended that your girlfriend deals in antiques.'

'She's not my girlfriend,' I say, a nod to chivalry. 'And she *does* deal in antiques. Antique furniture, at least.'

Penn snorts again. 'I find that very hard to believe.'

'Why?'

Even as he holds up a clean pair of boxer shorts, he points to my knees. I look down to see the stool.

'That's a Gerthausen, a claw-footed bath stool. It's the one thing I brought with me when I came here and it's all I've got left. If the freaks in this place knew how valuable it was, they'd murder me for it.'

I can see now, in the stain, in the curvature of the wood: it is no mere chair.

Penn climbs into his boxers, barely keeps the robe shut.

'Someone with even the vaguest interest in vintage furniture, my dear boy, would not so willingly have rested their arse on a modern Teutonic masterpiece. Even so delectable an arse as hers.'

43

'I—am—*so*—sorry.'

She underscores each word with a flat palm pushed against the air around her hips. Her other hand holds open the door.

'Don't worry about it.'

I step into the familiar living room, bright and neat. Steam rises from the kettle in the kitchen, as well as from a cup of milky tea on the dining table. Her laptop is there too; a green light indicates that it's powered on, but the display is shut.

'It's hard to explain,' she says. 'It was just like…super creepy. Don't you think?'

'How did you get back?'

'This guy was coming into the city? Um, and he worked there? He drove me all the way home.'

Of course he did. Up until a couple of hours ago, I would have done the same.

She asks, 'You made it back okay? Did you come straight here?'

'No, I went home first.' I point to her computer. 'How's business?'

'Fine.' She hugs herself. 'Slow. You want a cuppa?'

'Sure.'

She skips into the kitchen and opens a cupboard.

'So what did Ken Penn tell you?'

'All kinds of stuff,' I say. 'You know, when I was at home, I looked up the Australian Business Registry. There's no business in your name.'

'Why are you checking up on me?'

Beth turns her back, pours from the steaming kettle.

'Something to do.'

'I told you. I'm just getting started. I haven't registered anything yet.'

'Right,' I dig my hands into my pockets.

'Milk or sugar?'

'Yeah, milk, one sugar, thank you.'

She moves to the fridge. It's small, like the rest of the kitchen. A vague, yeasty smell touches my nostrils, might be the recycling bin in the corner, filled with beer bottles that have probably accumulated over months.

'Something else I found when I was home, some old-fashioned furniture for sale on eBay. Melbourne vendor. They're getting a lot of bids.'

Beth has her back to me again, pouring the milk.

'They should go through a broker. They'd get a better price.'

'Yeah,' I say. 'Does Rudy know you're selling his stuff on eBay?'

She turns to face me, holding a full mug, perplexed. All the naivety her face is capable of, like the day she first opened the door to me, is on display for potential buyers.

'What?'

But I am not in the market.

'Does he know you're clearing it all on eBay? That you're not going through a broker. That you're not this antique furniture wizard.'

'*I'm* not selling anything on eBay.'

She waits for me to agree.

'No,' I say. 'You're right. I'm just kidding around.'

Bemused, Beth places the tea on the dining table.

I say, 'The person selling this stuff is tagged Gemma-four-eight-nine. Full name Gemma Wallace.'

At this she giggles, questioningly.

'But it's funny...' I say. 'She's also selling a brand new digital SLR, identical to the one Rudy bought for you.'

'I don't understand...' And she looks as though she's really trying to.

'Your twitter password is six-three-M-five-seven-oh-N-three. That's leetspeak. And I know you know what leetspeak is.'

'How do you know my password?'

I can see her considering anger as a method of deflection.

'In leetspeak, six-three-M-five-seven-oh-N-three translates as *Gemstone*. Which might be a cute play on Gemma. Is that a coincidence?'

What's funny is, knowing personal stuff usually helps you to hack someone's password. But knowing Beth's password has helped me hack her personal stuff. And she's bug-eyed with disbelief.

'Well it *must* be—'

'What do you bet I can open that laptop and find open the eBay account for Gemma-four-eight-nine?'

Her face darkens. The time for laughing it off has passed. She drops any effort at pretence, empties the life from her eyes and adopts a look of utter boredom.

'So what?'

'So you don't have an antique furniture business. You told Rudy you did so he'd let you sell his things online. I saw him yesterday, varnishing away like a sap. Did you tell him to do that, Gemma? Is he going to see any money from the sale?'

'Of course he is.'

'Of course he is.' I can't help but bring a cynical tone. 'How much did you pay for his car?'

Her jaw cocks.

'I had to pay the registration.'

'But you got the car for free, right? And somehow he thinks you were doing him a favour?'

She says nothing.

'After I came knocking on your door on Thursday, you thought things were drying up for Rudy, wanted to get your hooks in for one last grift. *You* asked *him* to meet you in town, gave him the sob story about the damage to your car and how you weren't insured, conned an expensive camera out of him and suggested you sell his furniture.'

Beth shrugs: it's not like I'm accusing her of murder. I sip my tea, assume it isn't poisoned.

'The woman at Claireborne, the one with the hair, she recognised you. That's why you were creeped out. That's why you left, you were scared she'd give you away and that I might get the right idea. What is she, a relative?'

'*Fuck* no.'

'An old friend of the family Wallace?'

'*No*. Just…I boarded with her once. A long time ago. I barely know her.'

'She knew your real name.'

'My real name is Elizabeth.'

'Bullshit.' I put down my drink. It's difficult to be accusing with a slightly too-full mug of tea in your hands. 'If Elizabeth was your real name, I'd have found a criminal record when I looked you up.'

'Gemma used to be my name. It's not anymore. And you didn't find anything on me because I'm not from here.'

'Not from where?'

'Australia.'

'Where the fuck are you from?'

'It's not important.' She tips herself away, leans against her front door. 'I'm Australian now.'

'When did you come over?'

'Years ago. When I got here I stayed in a boarding house where Susie worked, just while I got on my feet. It didn't last long.'

'So this isn't your real voice. You're putting on an accent.'

'No. This is how I talk now. And I'm Elizabeth now. This is who I am.'

I search the room for threats. Just like I did in Ken Penn's room. Just like I always do, I suppose, when I find myself in the home of a total stranger.

'Why did you leave there? Wherever you're from.'

'It's not important.'

'Was it…Did you do something?'

'I'm not a fugitive, if that's what you're saying.'

'But you ran away.'

She doesn't care to answer, lets her head fall back against the door, a teenager suffering through another lecture from her boring parents.

'When did you get the photographs? This morning? When I was off with—'

I catch myself. *You've got secrets too, Jason.*

'—my family?'

'He called me. Wanted to know why I hadn't done the pictures yet. I didn't want to get him suspicious.'

'Of course not. Can't endanger your insurance payout, now can we.'

'Fuck you.'

'Fuck *me*? You're only friends with him for the money.'

She raises her hands in a silent, grand gesture.

'So are you. You've got a client. You're getting paid. This is another day at the office for you.'

Angry but restrained. She doesn't want the neighbours to hear. I open my arms in surrender.

'And what about sleeping with me? That was just more fluffing, to get me on side?'

Beth turns back and pouts. 'No.'

'Bullshit.'

'Don't tell me how I feel.'

'Oh, I bet it's true fucking love. So long as I'm walking Rudy to his own funeral. I'm your *dream* guy. And what about your story, how he took the Volvo to gas himself. That's all bullshit too, isn't it.'

'No...'

'Yes it is. You wanted me to think he's got a death wish. So then I'm more likely to help him along.'

'He *does*—'

'*Say it.* You made it all up.'

'*No.*' Her right hand makes a fist at her side. 'Whether or not there was insurance, I'd be helping Rudy end things as near as I could to how he wants. I'm not lying about that.'

'You're laying it on a little thick, Gemma—'

'*Even if there was no money...*'

Those blue eyes hold on me, screwing their conviction into my head.

And it does occur to me that what I'm about to do is sabotage everything. Everything. My arrangement with Tyan. My *relationship* with Tyan. All it would take is for Beth to go to Rudy and it's bombs away...

'There is no insurance,' I say, looking to each of her ears quickly, then her eyes. 'Rudy believes it, but it's all made up. I made it up.'

44

Her eyes shrink in half. Something seems to happen in her mouth.

'Bullshit.'

'That's how I met Rudy. On Friday. I was pretending to sell him insurance. And he bought it because he doesn't know any better. It's not real. It's pretend. It's what I did to get close to him.'

Her head shakes. I'm not sure if she knows it's shaking. She laughs. I've just revealed myself to be the Great Satan.

'No way. I saw it. The contract. Fortunate Insurance.'

'Printed off their website.' I point to her laptop. 'I can show you if you like.'

'Come on, there's—'

She cuts herself off, looks around the room for the third umpire, finds only white walls. *There's what?* No way Rudy would fall for that? No way *she* would fall for it?

'Didn't you notice it was stamped with tomato sauce?'

'I...' She gazes at the ceiling. 'There was a name on it. Anthony Halloway. Anthony Halloway from Fortunate Insurance.'

'Rudy thinks that's me.'

Beth reels, away from the door and into the kitchen. White hands take hold of the laminate counter and her head sinks below her shoulders.

'You're saying there's no policy.'

I want to comfort her, stop myself from wanting that.

'None at all.'

She's stuck in that hunched position.

I pick up my tea, not because I'm thirsty but because accepting her hospitality is about all I can do for her.

'You...' She trails off. Then she sighs like she's stuck on a cross-word question. Head gently wobbles.

After several seconds I take another hit of tea and then I figure she's waiting for me to leave. With one more glance to her motion-less frame, lit by the naked globe that hangs above her and her long, slow breaths, I leave and shut the door gently.

Plodding down the stairs it occurs to me that Beth knows every-thing now. After all this lying and sneaking, she is *in the loop*. Except she doesn't know about my special relationship with my client. She doesn't know just how I'm getting paid.

Outside it's as cold as I'd expected and in the shadow of the driveway it is darker. I bury my hands in my pockets and shuffle toward the gate.

The first bottle hits. On the concrete to my right.

'Fuck *yooooooo*.' A torrid shriek.

She's out on her balcony, just a shadow two storeys up and I barely recognise the voice, see she's holding a beer bottle. It winks at me in preparation.

'Fuck *yooo*. Ya lying piece a *shite*!'

She lets fly and I have to duck. It breaks into angry pieces across the concrete and scatters among the council bins. From such a height she gives these missiles phenomenal velocity.

'Ya *cunt*, ya!'

Despite the danger I have to stop, perfectly still and facing her. Not to show her my defiance, but to be sure I'm hearing her correctly.

'Ye gote a *tiny fuckin wully*,' she announces to the other flats and houses, or at least, what proportion of them can understand words screamed in such a solid Scottish brogue. 'Jason Ginaff's gote a *tiny pencil dick*!'

It's surprising. Not that she's unimpressed with me, but that she's willing to end things so bitterly.

I don't see her launch the next bottle. It crashes against the gate behind me and I flinch, cower, raise my hands because there might be more I can't see.

'Ye fuckin lying *cunt!*'

My defiance evaporates. I hurry to the gate, crushing glass beneath my shoes and I almost trip on the knob of a bottle end but I make it and lurch through the wooden shield and shut it closed even as another bottlesmash pierces the quiet and raindrops of stinking glass crackle inches from my head.

I'm safe. For good measure, I run.

45

All the way to Tyan's house, I'm managing the heartbreak. Though, to be clear, you feel this sort of thing in your stomach. Acidic and squirming like an alien pregnancy, sired by that alien voice, so jarring against a backdrop of eucalypts and southern stars. Tyan's angry words come back to me: *Who is Elizabeth Cannon?*

All the way to Tyan's house, I'm wondering what will happen. She might go to Rudy and tell him I'm a fake. Either by full-frontal confession, including how we slept together, or, more likely, by way of an elaborate fiction that few people would believe but one of those people is Rudy.

On the other hand, she doesn't want me counter-confessing: telling Rudy that she's a fraud, that she only came clean with him because the insurance is a fraud. That she seduced me, and she did that so as to nudge along Rudy's impending suicide mission.

All the way to Tyan's house, I consider telling this to Tyan. Beth is officially a wildcard now, and he'd want to know about that. But it would mean telling him I outlined our plan to a third party. He wouldn't like that. I resolve not to tell him.

It's almost ten when I pull up on Suttle Street and Tyan's Kia sedan is there in the driveway but no lights burn inside the house. Ringing the doorbell doesn't alter that and after I ring again I still get nothing. My next option is to go round the back and I stomp my feet all the way, partly because it's cold, partly so Tyan doesn't think I'm Rudy sneaking up on him.

At the end of the drive is a garage door and a stone path that breaks right between another shed and the back of the house. It ends with an arched entry to a small enclosure and I see nothing but black within. Beyond the garage is a grey lawn that demonstrates the size of Tyan's block and culminates in a garden bed I can barely make out for the darkness.

I stomp along the path to the patio, find myself among pot plants and creepers lit only by the moon and my phone. Tyan's back door glowers like a monolith, its surface a ratty kind of tin that shudders as I try the handle, then rap against it.

'Tyan!'

If Rudy has come tonight, if he felt hurried by our altercation yesterday and caught Tyan off guard and somehow overpowered him and right now Tyan is learning the true meaning of hubris, then this door would be open and unlocked, right?

Then again, no one is answering.

At first, I only lift up the doormat out of curiosity: this is where Rudy said he found a key. If he has come, if I'm too late to stop him, then it might not be here.

It's here, amid the patterns of dirt you find under doormats that haven't been moved for decades. I realise I can go inside and check that everything is okay. It's running the gauntlet, the gauntlet being a twitchy Glen Tyan with a gun. But we have to talk.

I unlock the door, hold the key with my shirt so as not to leave a print, return it to its nest under the mat and step inside yelling, 'Tyan! It's me, Jason!'

My makeshift flashlight reveals a vestibule, cobwebbed work boots and waxy sneakers. Boards creak and thunk beneath me as I make my way to the next door.

'Tyan!' I yell again, knock.

No answer.

The handle turns and I pull on the door with the flesh of my pinkie, feel the reek of cigarettes slap my face, catch sight of the sink and then a barren kitchen counter. I'm about to step through when I realise where I am.

My stomach flips. Can't help a gasp.

Bending down, pointing my phone at my feet, I see nothing. It doesn't seem to be there, which is how fine it is, because then I make out where it's tied to the nail in the doorframe.

'Better watch out,' a dry voice says from the dark.

I shudder back, frightened twice over.

'Hello?'

A long sigh in reply.

'Didn't you hear me knock?'

'Yep,' he grunts. 'Wanted to see if you'd…you'd trip it.'

I lean gently through the door and my phone reveals a thick haze of tobacco smoke and Tyan sitting at the kitchen table, grinning sleepy-eyed, a bottle of something and a glass tumbler before him.

'Come on, then.'

I step over where I think the line is and hope for the best. The green shine box is there, ominous like the home of his pet tarantula, though the weapon within supposedly only shoots blanks.

'You know, if Rudy sets this thing off on Friday, he'll just turn and run.'

'Yeah, yeah,' Tyan says, already impatient. 'I'll pack it into the corner. It's fiddly, so I haven't…haven't done it yet. Shut the door.'

'Can I turn a light on?'

'Over there, the hall switch.'

He means the switch on the other side of the room. I edge my way over and it lights up the hallway, provides a quantum of light for the kitchen.

It's whisky. The bottle on the table.

'You're just sitting in the dark, drinking?'

Another equivocating grunt.

'You know what they say. If you're thirsty then it's too late!' Tyan cackles to himself then bellows: 'Sit down!'

Tyan quickly interprets my hesitation and says, 'I'm not drunk. I'm not drunk.' He says it twice, which means he's drunk.

I pull out one of the ancient vinyl seats and lean on the table as I drop down.

'I came to tell you that I've changed my mind. I'm in. With Rudy…I mean…' I search my words. 'Taking out Rudy, like you said this morning. I agree.'

'Mmmm,' Tyan groans. It's possible he doesn't remember our conversation this morning.

'But I want to be clear...I'm only agreeing to this because it was Rudy who killed his mother, not Piers.'

Tyan groans again. 'That's bullshit.'

'Did you know he'd threatened to kill her, three days before she died?'

He doesn't respond. Maybe he's trying to remember.

'It's the only scenario that makes sense. He killed her and hid the vase in Piers's workshop and that's why you found it there.'

'He was a fucking kid—'

'Which is why you didn't suspect him.'

'Fuck me,' he says, goes to speak, belches, continues: 'Why the fuck would he be sore at me if he's the one who fucking...fucking...'

'Because he's nuts. It's how he hides from himself what really happened.'

'There's a reason they call me the Polygraph, you know.' I register his use of the present tense. 'Piers lied from the word go. Fucking... lied about everything. It was obvious. Believe me, mate...' He leans forward theatrically, head wobbling. 'I know what cunts look like when they're guilty.'

'I don't want to argue,' I say, reeling from the stink of booze. 'I'm just saying, he killed his mum. So I guess I don't feel sorry for him like I did before.'

Tyan pours himself another generous shot and declares:

'What a load of old cobblers.'

He drinks, wipes his mouth and says, 'Now listen. I want to tell you something.'

'Yeah?'

'Did you bring cigarettes?'

As if that's something I might do.

'No. Sorry.'

Tyan thinks on this.

'Fucking...' He touches his pockets like he's looking for his wallet. 'Nothing's open now, I suppose.'

'What did you want to tell me?'

Tyan hums with confusion, then appears to remember. 'Right. Yeah. I'm telling you this because...I'm just telling you.'

'Okay.'

'This is fucking ages ago.'

'Okay.'

'There was...You know Malcolm Lau?'

'No.'

'You remember him?'

'No.'

'Good. It's good you don't remember. He was a paedophile. A real fucking...Anyway, he was on the news.'

Tyan drinks again. I wonder if this is going to be a long story.

'He had a trial. In two thousand aaaaaand...' Tyan jolts his head forward, as if trying to fling the memory to the front of his brain, '...three?'

'Okay.'

'And the trial...He didn't go down. He was up on these...indecent act with a minor, these...It was fucking...He was a nonce. A disgusting bastard. You need to remember that.'

I say nothing now. Tyan doesn't need encouragement.

'And he had this scar on his belly. And the victim, who fucking got up in court, and that is fucking hard to do...This kid's fucking twelve and gets up there in front of everyone and says that the bloke who assaulted him had a scar on his belly. And then Malcolm got up in the box, and he showed the court the scar on his...here, on his stomach,' Tyan points to his appendix, jabbing himself hard with a finger. 'Here. And he *still* got off. Fucking bullshit.'

Tyan slumps on the table. In other circumstances, he would slump like this because he's exhausted. Tonight, he's just getting comfortable.

'Now I used to drink a lot. As in, a lot. *Farts* stunk of booze. And the Lau case wasn't mine, I never worked in...fucking...not sex crimes. But he got off and I was, I dunno. I was tight as fucking...of course I was...Right?'

'Sure.'

'So what would you do?'

'What would I *do*?'

'Yep.'

'If I was...drunk?'

This seems to frustrate him and he waves at the air, or maybe at me.

'I found out his home...home address. I looked it up. I got his LEAP file. I got his address.'

'Right.'

'And I went there.'

'Right.'

'And I shot him.'

46

All of a sudden we're drenched in light. I flinch and raise a hand in protection, but Tyan doesn't move. He grunts. It's only the light from a small window in the house next door, but it comes on like a Nazi spotlight compared with the darkness before.

'That's Freddie. He's got...fucking...dodgy prostrate...prostate. Cancer. Gets up a dozen times a night.'

It's a bathroom light, small and high. It allows me to properly make out the horror of Tyan's eyes. Burning red and flabby and wet. He's been crying. Not just crying, bawling hard. I don't know how he can see out of those pupils.

'He's...His name's Frederico. I call him Freddie. His dunny's actually out back, you know like an outhouse. In the cold like this he gets up and pisses in his washbasin. Shit.'

Tyan is scanning my face. It's illuminated like his own.

'I'd forgotten about that.'

He means my injuries. I'd forgotten them too.

'You were saying you shot someone.'

A small wail as he remembers.

'Yeah, now...Now, this is secret. You got to promise not to tell anyone.'

I go to say, 'I promise,' but Tyan doesn't give me the chance, just keeps on talking. My promise is assumed.

'I went over there and I was absolutely pissed. I went over to this place in Altona and I knock on the door and this cunt opened the door and I showed him my badge. I mean, I *showed* it to him. *And* I told him my name. That's…That was…That's what…was the big mistake. But I told him and I asked him if he was Malcolm Lau and he said…' Tyan scowls, trying to recall. 'He said…words to the effect of *Fuck off.*'

His expression is one of shock, like it's hard to believe that someone might resent a late-night visit from a drunk police officer.

'And he toddles off and disappears inside and *I* don't know what the fuck he's doing so I follow him…him in. And I see him. He's opening the drawer, in this desk sort of thing that's in the…inside the…Now, you imagine you're me. What do you think? What's the drawer he's opening for…in there?'

'I don't know. A phone?'

'Hey?'

'To call the police.'

'I *am* the police.'

'Yeah, but—'

'I thought he was going for a weapon, didn't I? And I drew on him and told him to raise his hands. And I said it loud and clear. And he didn't raise his hands. I mean, his hand was *in* the drawer. He just fucking…'

Tyan's eyes drop to his alcohol.

'He didn't raise his hands. So I fired. Got him in the guts and he went out like a light.'

He rotates his empty glass against the table.

'So I go over to him, to get a look at the wound, because I don't know, maybe I just fucking grazed him. But I didn't…But…'

He breaks off. More wetness in the red pits of his eyes. His voice rises in pitch: 'You can guess.'

'Guess?'

Tyan wipes his nose with his wrist.

'He didn't have the scar. The appendix…The one I told you…'

I sit back in my chair.

Tyan says, 'I had an old address. The LEAP record was wrong… the wrong address…This is…I found this out later. And the stupid bastard…It was…I mean, it was his fucking wallet. In the fucking drawer. Lung Yeung. That was his name. Why didn't he…? When I told him…'

'Was he dead?'

'Not...No. He was out, but he was breathing, blood pissing...'

'What did you do?'

The eyes widen, like that's a hell of a question. He exposes to me their full colour and convolution. The light flicks off next door: Freddie heading back to bed. In the dark I'm left with that image of Glen Tyan. Despairing and wretched.

'What I did,' he says, 'was fucking...He was fucking fucked up. I mean, I could tell. And I had this...thought.'

The bottle is mostly finished. He pours what's left into his glass. A generous portion but maybe not for him. Then he stands up, holding his drink. The chair almost tips but it doesn't.

'Someone heard the shot, right? I mean they had to. So probably there are cops...other cops...coming. They were *coming*. And this bastard was still breathing...' He points to an imaginary body on the floor. 'Has...had seen my face. Seen my badge. Fucking *knew* my name. So I'm *fucked*.'

He stumbles confidently to the centre of the room.

'But I can't fucking shoot him again, can I? If he's on the floor.'

A thumb and forefinger rise up, aimed at the imaginary innocent victim bleeding on his kitchen lino.

'I can't do a kill shot. That's fucking murder. The physical evidence...spatter...exit wound...bullet lodged in the fucking carpet. That's not self-defence. That's a fucking *execution*. I can't bullshit out any...out of that. That's fucking prison and fucking good night nurse.'

He throws his arms in the air as if to say, *What a quandary!* Still holding the pretend gun in one hand and his drink in the other.

'So what I did is...' The gun hand shakes at me to get my attention. Like he doesn't already have that. 'What I did is, in his kitchen...'

Tyan rattles open his own kitchen drawer and takes something out and I can't see at first but then the hall light catches on it, flashes a reverse silhouette right into my retina.

'Got a knife,' Tyan says, crafty. 'Like this. Put it in his hand, got his prints on it.'

He lays the knife on the floor, gets awkwardly to his knees, seemingly administering to a wounded man. With rapid movements, he points to the window.

'I shut all the blinds and the curtains. And I got his mobile and I fucking trousered that. And I locked all the doors...' He stops, as if puzzled, then switches back to his excitement: 'What...The plan was, was to climb out a fucking...window. Ditch the phone. So when the coppers got there I'd say...' Another shocking belch, but he continues without noticing. '...there was an armed man in the house. You understand?'

'Sure.' But not really.

With wordless pain Tyan gets back to his feet, limps left and right, restoring his knees.

'When the coppers got there...it's not like they'd go in the fucking door and find him and get him on a fucking gurney. It's called...' His hand flaps. 'Protocol...Something Protocol. They have to get Siege Response on the line, get them to show up, evacuate the neighbours, cut off the mobile...the fucking...coverage. Get a command centre.'

'But...if he's the only one in there—'

'*They* don't *know* that,' Tyan declares, face shining with ingenuity. 'I tell them...I was just waved down by this arsehole who fucking... tried to *cut* me. I...I tell...I fired my gun but I don't know if I got him. Don't know if he's got a *gun*. Don't *know* who else's inside. There could be hostages. There could be fucking *kids* in...in...so...right... by the time they've gone through the fucking...*Critical Incident*!' He claps his hands Eureka. '*That's* what it's fucking...Critical Incident Protocol. Once they've gone through all that...and they can't raise him on the phone...' He's laughing now. 'By the time they kick in the fucking doors, he's succumbed. And there's no one to say I'm bullshitting.'

Tyan stands with his arms out, begging me to appreciate.

'So...' I say. 'That's what happened?'

This appears to be the wrong question. Tyan scowls, drinks, peeks into the glass, drinks again to finish it.

'Nah. He was dead.'

He puts the glass on the table. All that energy abandons him. Invisible and silent. He points to the invisible and silent dead body.

'Right there on the floor. It was a cracker of an idea, but. Wish I had the chance to try and…I was going to do it. But he just…he died. He just fucking died. So I left. Fuck all to do but cut and run. So that's…'

Tyan's shoulders turn sharply and his body follows, swings over to the sink, rests with his back to me.

'Shouldn't of told you, I s'pose,' Breathing heavy, distress returning to his voice. 'But you wanted to know how come I quit the force.'

47

It's the kind of memory that *would* get you weeping in the dark, drinking a whole bottle of something, hankering to spew the awfulness out to whoever. It makes me think of the confession Piers never made. To me, in the prison yard at Severington. It's what that would have been like.

'Did they know it was you?'

When he turns back the alcohol tears are there. He's wiped some away but more glint on his cheek.

'Couldn't prove it,' he says with a calming breath. 'They knew. I mean…It was a fucking mess. He was shot with a cop gun so the sergeant had to test them…to test them all. I had to say I lost mine. Like a fucking school kid. Wrote up an incident report and everything. And they guessed what I done. How…with the wrong address. But that was it. But they knew.'

'So they fired you.'

He squirms.

'Deputy-Com got the word out I should resign. I could have fucking fought them. Fought back. They didn't want it…publicly… But I was so fucked up…'

His head lowers, watches his toes tap gently on the floor.

'His name was Lung Yeung.'

At the pronouncement of that name he's overcome with a full-throated sob. Hands grip the bench behind him and his shoulders and belly shudder with startling energy and a yawning comes from his mouth because he's feeling pain like nothing I thought he was capable of.

In between the awesome heaves he howls words I don't understand.

What do I do? Do I go to him? What are you supposed to do with a weeping father?

In the dark I can see his mouth locked wide open. The silhouette shakes and tips and the power of his suffering echoes against these old walls.

'I wish I could tell him…I fucked up…I'm sorry.'

He needs both hands to wipe at his face, manages a growl that appears to be an attempt to pull himself together.

'All my mates, they all turned their back. Fucking coppers. They love you when you're working. But once you fuck up…'

He comes at me from the sink. I startle back. But Tyan only picks up the empty bottle, doesn't see the fear.

'It's like with the poor bastards with PS…PST…' He can't say it, thinks hard. 'Fucking abandoned. Same as me. And all of a fucking sudden I'm just sitting around.' He jabs at his surroundings with the bottle.

This observation strikes a nerve. Between his teeth he says, 'And sitting around and sitting around.'

He slams the bottle into a plastic garbage bin. The shatter distorts in my ears.

'Even now,' he stares down into that different kind of wreckage. 'The way they look at me. Like at Harry's retirement the other night.'

I remember Hugh Bretzanitz, the cop I interviewed. The one who said he didn't think of Tyan as the laughing stock other cops did, but who smiled anyway when Tyan's name came up.

He rouses himself, resumes his slumped position at the sink.

'But this time. They won't even think of Lung Yeung. This time they'll be…They'll ask themselves if they could even do what I did. They'll say it was a mistake, me leaving the force. I'll shove it right up them.' His eyes come to me, drawn and sobering.

'I'm tired,' he says, and pushes himself from the sink, finds a fraught equilibrium, staggers in short steps towards the hall.

Rudy and Tyan. Both as fucked up as each other. Riddled with guilt and crazy enough to believe that killing someone will make it go away.

'We've still got a problem,' I say. My own voice is hoarse, dried up from listening. 'We don't know what Rudy is thinking. After last night, anything's possible.'

And after tonight at Beth's, anything else is, too.

'You've got to find out.'

'I can't go and see him, if that's what you think. He might flip out again. I suppose I could call him—'

His shuffling steps reach the hall, don't slow down.

'Give him a…a fucking…a peace offering. It's hard to go off on someone who gives you a…gives you something.'

'Okay. But even then—'

'And listen…What you said this morning. You're right. We need something on Rudy.'

'What?'

But he's left the room. I wait for him to come back. Give it about ten seconds. Then I ease out of my chair and follow.

The small hallway is properly lit. On the wall is a clock carved out of wood: two whittled topless Thai girls hold up the clock face, their skirts made of real straw that protrudes like the beard of a scarecrow. Three past midnight.

The bedroom screams Single Older Gentleman. Poking out of a drawer in the dresser is the corner of a magazine; I assume a dirty magazine, if they still make those. The bed is piled with old-fashioned blankets, no doona. Tyan's carcass is sprawled across them, his eyes shut.

'We need something…Something that proves what he's planning.'

'What about when he comes here…' I say this to a man who, to look at him, must be asleep. 'Won't *that* prove what he's planning?'

'Something more,' he murmurs, perhaps already dreaming. 'A fucking clincher.'

'Like what?'

He says nothing. He is still. I raise my voice.

'Like what, do you think?

Nothing. Then a breezy bagpipes snore ruffles his nose.

On the clothes horse by the dresser there's a tattered quilt that I shake out, place over him. It won't keep him warm for long but it's the most I can do short of hiring a sumo wrestler to get him under the blankets.

One last look before I go home: Tyan a sleeping child, his hair flopped away like a tiny toupee for his pillow, his mouth relaxed agog and his whiskery eyebrows twitching gently. So fragile I almost can't leave him like this.

But I do, switch off the bedroom light. Keep the hall light on. When I get home I find that someone has broken into my flat.

48

I pump the car heater too hard and with the help of my jacket I'm sweating by the time I pull into the driveway. Sweat is a pleasant change, but the moment I open the car door the moisture on my face turns to ice, freezes my brain. I climb the stairs hurriedly, stop when I see my front door is ajar, consider that for a moment, conclude that I've never left a front door ajar in my life. It's difficult to believe that someone has burgled me just as I've been drawn into my first ever murder plot. My first two murder plots.

Also, I saw the green Volvo parked on the kerb.

Is it Beth, come to trash my home in turn? Or did Rudy steal her car again, drive here with the goal of bloody revenge and I'm walking into it?

'Beth?' I say to the door.

No answer.

I tap it open with a fingernail.

The heater blares and the light I let in from outside reveals a smirk, adorable and ruthless, the kind she practises on her reflection.

'Parking your car outside kind of ruins the surprise.'

'I wasn't trying to surprise you.'

'What were you trying to do?'

'Find a comfy place to sit and wait. Obviously.'

When I trigger the light switch I find her reclined in my Herman Miller, her back to my displays, swivelling gently. Poised atop her lap is her laptop.

'You going to throw more shit at me?'

'No. I'd be too afraid to miss and accidentally improve your lounge room.'

No inkling of Scotland as she speaks.

'I'd offer you haggis, or a pint of Guinness, but I've only got tea.' With my coat off I flick the jug in the kitchen.

'Guinness is from Ireland,' I hear her say. When I return to the doorway I jut my chin at her computer.

'How goes your little daylight robbery there?'

She frowns at the screen, chooses to take my question as an unsardonic one.

'The Chesterfield will go for more than a thousand, the Zoblatini bar stools for five hundred apiece. No one's bid on the Wakeley recliner yet which makes me think there's a glut in the market.'

'Don't try and sound like a pro. Ken Penn had you pegged the moment you sat down.'

'But you didn't, did you.'

'Why are you here?'

'I want to apologise.' She closes the screen on her computer, sits straight. 'For my outburst. It was aggressive and dangerous and I'm sorry.'

'What about breaking in? You going to apologise for that?'

The kitchen whistles behind me. She smirks.

'In the business we call that a victimless crime.'

'And the money I gave you. For the dog shelter. You don't even volunteer there, do you?'

'I do. I like dogs. The closest thing I ever had to a family was a dog.'

'But you keep the money you collect.'

'A girl's got to eat.'

'Like I said, I've only got tea.'

She waits quietly until I present her with a mug: it's the one I like least—the squat one with the flower on it. Then she says, 'What I told you, about Rudy borrowing the car. What he did with it. It's all true.'

At this moment I notice, for the very first time, that my flat has only one chair. Beth might be the first guest I've ever had in here.

It's certainly the first time I've spoken with someone as *they've* sat in *my* chair. Disconcerted, I slump to the floor by the window, cross-legged, balancing my tea.

'You're saying we ought to go through with it?'

'I'm saying...' She scowls. 'I am saying we're prolonging his suffering by *not* going through with it.'

I scan for a trace of deception, catch nothing.

'There's no equity left in the house. There's nothing for you if you think he's going to leave it to you.'

'I don't care about any of that. I know you don't believe me but it's true. Whether he does it himself or someone else...it's the merciful thing to do.'

'In anyone else's book, it's not merciful. It's murder.'

We stare each other off. I lose, gaze at my mug. She's come to tell me she's on board with a killing, same as I did with Glen Tyan only an hour ago, so I shouldn't be so sceptical. And what's left for her to trick me into? Without the insurance money, there's only some old furniture she'll profit from whether Rudy lives or dies.

'What happened this morning?'

'What do you mean?'

'When you went over there. You took photos of the furniture. You saw the contract?'

'Yeah. On a chair at the front of the house. He showed me.'

Classic Rudy. He hasn't touched the thing since I left.

'Was he acting different? Weird?'

'Weirder than usual? He said he had a fight with you. I mean, with Anthony the insurance man.'

'Did he say anything else?'

She drinks some tea.

'No. He was really scattered. Biting his nails. I didn't push it.'

'Ken Penn said that Rudy killed Cheryl Alamein.'

She's about to put her mug on my desk, stops still to mock me with her eyes.

'That's not possible.'

'Why not?'

'It's not his style.'

'I agree. I agree it's not possible. I also think it's exactly what happened.'

Beth puts the mug down, tugs her cardigan across her waist.

'But there's…there's just no reason to think that.'

'By my count there's eleven reasons to think that.' My head has been buzzing with them. They're the reason I'm making tea at one in the morning. 'Twelve if we include how Ken Penn is absolutely certain.'

49

'One...' I say, drive right past her parody of someone keenly interested. 'Penn said that Rudy's parents weren't fighting over who got Rudy, they were fighting over who *didn't*. Neither of them wanted him. That gives him a motive.'

'That's not proof of anything.'

'None of this is proof of anything. I've only got a theory. Two. Wealthy, educated, middle-class parents who don't want their own child? That's rare. And what better reason could there be than that their kid is fucking batshit. I mean dangerous.'

She plants her chin on her fist, listens dolefully.

'Three. Rudy and Cheryl fought, three days before she was killed. So bad that she fled the house. Penn said Rudy threatened her. And he's brain-damaged in an old folks' home in the middle of fucking nowhere. What reason has he got to lie?'

'If you're brain-damaged you don't need a reason.'

'Four. On the day his mother died, he left school at eleven-thirty, but he didn't get home until one. Where was he all that time? If he'd gone directly home he'd have been there by about twelve-fifteen, which is Cheryl Alamein's time of death.'

'All right. But a thirteen-year-old killing someone? His *mother*?'

'Not on purpose. He lashed out, but it was enough. According to the trial transcript, there's no doubt it was a single blow to the head.'

She looks at me with the disgust of a teenager.

'You read the transcript?'

'Five. The night he stole your car he faked a robbery. Just like he did thirteen years ago. When it comes to committing crimes it's the only trick he knows. Six. If Piers did it then why did he *tell* the police that the vase was missing? And if he didn't do it, how did the vase end up in his workshop? The only other person who might have had access is Rudy.'

More disgusted scowling, this time because she's not following. I try to slow down.

'Seven. There was a hole dug in the backyard. Everyone thought that Piers was planning to bury the vase. But what if Rudy planned to put his mother in there? Bury her to hide what he'd done. No one in their right mind would have thought that would work. But a thirteen-year-old? A thirteen-year-old murderer? A thirteen-year-old *Rudy*?'

'Wait, wait, wait...' Beth holds up her palm, shakes her head, TMI. 'If Rudy did it, why is he after Glen Tyan?'

'Because at the end of the day, Glen Tyan really did jail the wrong man. By focusing on that, he blocks out his own culpability. 'Eight. Why is he so compelled to get revenge for his father, but not for his mother? Only one of them was outright murdered. He says he knows it was Ken Penn. Why not go after *him*?'

She pulls a protective knee up to her face.

'Because, like, boys and their fathers...'

'Nine. Have you ever been upstairs in Rudy's house?'

'No.'

'No one has. No one's been upstairs in that house since it happened. Not even Rudy. He doesn't want to confront it. What he did.'

She puts down her tea.

'You know what you sound like? Like you're trying to convince yourself. Like it isn't enough for you to go through with it because it's what Rudy wants. You need to convince yourself that he's, like, evil.'

'I'm not saying he's *evil*—'

'He didn't kill his own mother, Jason.'

I sigh.

'He did. He really did, Beth. It's the only—'

She stands up, suddenly exasperated.

'I need the bathroom.'

And she's gone, into the bathroom. The door closes.

I get to my feet. It seems an age since I was last standing up. Like my legs are different now. The left is entirely numb and I lean on my right, limp to the kitchen and rinse my mug.

Ten. Rudy came after me when I told him Piers had confessed, because he knew that wasn't true. If *he* killed Cheryl Alamein then I *had* to be lying. That's why he was so upset.

And then there's number eleven. He wants to die.

I hear the bathroom door creak open behind me and I dry my hands, turn to find Beth removing her glasses, wiping away tears.

'I'm sorry...' She sniffs back a sob. 'It's just...I've been alone with him, like, a thousand times.'

'Yeah,' I offer, useless. She comes to me and I put my arms around her. Everybody's crying tonight.

'You're right. It's the only way it makes sense. I feel so stupid,' she says this into my shoulder. 'Just...blind to the whole thing.'

A hard sniffle against my shirt.

She says: 'Maybe he really believes it. That someone else did it. Maybe he, like, repressed it...'

'I don't know about repressed, but yeah. I think he believes it.'

It reminds me of Paul Heaney, the fictional character I invented in the conference room of Albert Kane and Roach. The man who so effectively convinced himself that what had happened had not happened.

'Listen...I need you to go back and see Rudy.'

She pulls away from me.

'What?'

'I need to get back in with him.'

'I *can't*.'

She's terrified.

'He won't hurt you.'

'*You* go see him.'

'It has to be you.'

'*Why?*'

'Because I need five minutes. In his kitchen. I need you to get him out of the house.'

50

She leaves with a long kiss goodbye. This morning has been almost enough to make you forget how she's a con artist who yesterday showered you with glass projectiles.

Almost.

But it's at least plausible that she's sticking this out because she believes it's the right thing to do. Last night, as we sank into sleep, I even found myself foreseeing the day I introduce her to Tyan. It was Christmas or a birthday and she'd gotten over the fact that I'd kept my blood relationship with him a secret. For his part, Tyan had undergone a paternity test and subsequently fully embraced his new identity as my biological father. Beth found his gruff charm bearable and he dazzled her with war stories, PG-rated ones. We thrived, bonded by our secret...

But there's Friday to come before all that.

While I made coffee this morning I deflected further demands that I explain exactly what I needed to do in Rudy's kitchen, said only that Glen Tyan and I agreed we needed evidence of what Rudy is planning, something cut and dried for anyone who might wonder how Rudy wound up dead on Tyan's carpet—a *clincher*, as Tyan called it. To Beth I'd say no more than that. For her own good. The less she knew, the easier it would be for her to manage the police if they came knocking.

She twitched her mouth at this.

'I'm not worried. I'll act dumb. I'm good at it.'

'You've got experience lying to the police?'

She stretched her nude body on my bedclothes, pale and electrified.

'Uh-huh.'

'Back in the old country?'

'Yep. Ask me what it says on my criminal record.'

I look at her blankly. 'W—'

'Nothing. I don't have one. Despite being questioned about a thousand times. I'll smash it.'

'Hubris,' I said. 'You're overconfident.'

'We'll see.'

'What were you questioned about?'

'Petty theft.'

'What else?'

'Nothing else.'

'Bullshit. A liar like you? What about fraud?'

She picked at the sleep in her eye.

'Just a gifted amateur, I suppose.'

'What's it like?' I asked. 'Living a lie like this? Changing your name, your voice…Denying who you really are.'

'You think where I'm from is who I really am?'

I felt a distant chill and gently said, 'Okay.' I had enough to think about without mounting this baggage on top.

I said, 'The cops will come to you. They'll get Rudy's phone records.'

'What about you? You've never had to lie to the police. It's not easy.'

'My phone is registered to a different name. They wouldn't know how to track me down.'

'Hubris,' she smirked, pushed herself off the bed and skipped past me to the bathroom. 'You're overconfident.'

Now, as I listen to her scamper down the stairs and into the cold, setting out on her mission, all my confidence evaporates and I stumble to the window. It's as if I know what will happen.

Marnie comes up the driveway. She and Beth pass within a foot of each other and it's Marnie who turns and gives her a second look, watches her too-tight jeans waggle down to the street, open the door of the green Volvo, ease themselves inside. Marnie comes up the steps, oblivious to how those jeans emerged from my flat, and I launch myself into that conversation while the Volvo motors away.

'Marnie,' I say from the door.

'Hi.' She tightens her scarf around her neck. Seeing me has made her want to choke herself.

'How are you?'

'Fine.'

She never asks me how I am. It's not that she doesn't care, she just goes taut at the start of conversations.

I'm like, 'I'm sorry about the other night.'

'That's okay. Look…' She shifts her weight, settles it into one sneaker. 'I'm not happy about you, like, analysing my life. I should be able to tell you about my stuff when I'm ready.'

'I know. I'm sorry.'

'But I've been thinking, and if you want, I'll tell you about it. It's all come out since anyway.'

I have no idea what she's talking about.

She says, 'He told me. My father, I mean. I made him tell me. That's what changed my mind.'

I rewind my brain to our last conversation. In the alley behind her work.

She says, 'He said he did it for me. The dodgy deals. Wanted to leave me something. Like an inheritance, you know?'

I'm nodding along like I do know. Her parents, the embezzlers. I asked how she went from singing their innocence to abandoning them in a matter of hours.

'It was like he was telling me it was my fault. Or I mean…'

I don't know if I can handle an information dump right now, so I try to tie the conversation off.

'I'm sorry I crossed the line the way I did. I had no business digging into your life.'

She offers a modest smile, swings her purse from her shoulder and digs inside. The rustle of keys.

'We're not having a lot of luck, are we?'

'No. But that's my fault. My mind is really scattered at the moment.'

She lingers, perhaps hoping I'll ask her out again. Somewhere to make it up to her. Somewhere that isn't a pizza joint. When I don't, she pantomimes a glum shame-about-that face and makes for her door.

'Look,' I say. 'I've got the most intense workload right now. Let me get through this and then maybe we can hang out.'

'Okay,' she says, pushing her apartment door open. 'Good luck with all that work.'

I can't tell if that's sarcastic.

For the coming hours I'm at a loss. Even someone as talented as Beth isn't going to have Rudy eating out of her hand until at least midday, so I should do some work while I wait for the promised phone call. But I'd only flub it.

I could call Tyan and ask how he is. But he'll have the hangover of ten men for the next couple of days, which probably won't improve his disposition. Instead I eat toast and play around online, google Tyan's football team, the Hawthorn Hawks. Apparently they won some big game last season. What if I'd reconnected with Tyan a year ago? Would we have shared that moment? Did Tyan watch it on TV alone? Did he weep with happiness? Would we have wept together?

In the midst of these daydreams and my memories of Saturday, it occurs to me to check my Brett Sherez email address, the one I created for Tristan Whaley. I'm only killing time, so I'm surprised to find that Whaley *has* been in contact.

From: Tristan Whaley <Tristan.Whaley@auspcmail.com>
Date: Sun, July 19, 2012 at 5:31 PM AEST
Subject: Transcript
To: "Brett Sherez (b.sherez@SouthernCLCentre005.com.au)"
<b.sherez@SouthernCLCentre005.com.au >

Dear Brett

A pleasure to meet you on Saturday.

Further to our conversation, I inquired with my former office manager at Joad & Clark as to any residual documentation relating to the Alamein matter and, given things appear to be on the slow side this weekend, they happily unearthed this file from the transcription archive. Unbeknownst to me, audio files are transcribed automatically, and were as far back as 2004. In your capacity as Rudyard Alamein's legal representative, it is appropriate to forward this file to you, with the assurance that there is no further material in the possession of our office or myself in relation to this matter.

Reading over, I find myself recalling one of the more surreal interactions of my career. His comments regarding his son are particularly troubling, though it should be apparent he was not of the soundest mind. However, I speak in part of my remembrance of the interview; I wonder how much of that recollection—his fearsome anger, his unrelenting tears—is properly conveyed by this scant document.

Given the sensitive nature of the contents, I will have the original file destroyed upon your request. A destroyed-material receipt will then be forwarded to you by Joad & Clark. Please let me know how you wish to proceed.

Yours Sincerely,
Tristan Whaley

Attached is a plain text file: 20041105AlameinP001.rtf. I'm barely able to lay the mouse pointer over it to double-click. Outside it starts to rain. I start to read.

51

file 20041105AlameinP001
tape ozk0161655date deleted W-A

UNKNOWN: (*inaudible*)

W: That's all right. I'm a criminal solicitor from the firm of Joad & Clark.

A: You came here.

W: That's right. I've taken an interest in your son's wellbeing.

A: My son.

W: That's right. I'm recording this, Piers. This is a dictaphone. Is that all right?

(*5-second interval*)

W: Would you like a drink? Some water or tea?

A: I keep my fluids up.

W: Officer, we need some tea.

UNKNOWN: I'm not a fucking café, mate.

W: I saw the kettle as you brought me through. I don't suppose you know if he takes milk or sugar.

UNKNOWN: (*inaudible*)

W: One with milk and sugar and one with just milk. Please. This isn't my first time here. I'll sign a waiver if you like. It's only tea.

(*5-second interval*)

W: And excuse me. Would you get a blanket? This man is freezing.

(*5-second interval*)

A: (*inaudible*)

W: What's that?

A: (*inaudible*)

W: I can't hear you when you cover your mouth.

A: Did the dog come back?

W: Which dog is that?

A: The dog that ran away.

W: The dog that ran away.

A: Busby. The fucking dog.

W: It's all right. No no no. It's okay. Please calm down. I'm afraid I don't know about the dog.

A: The dog knew. That's why.

W: Right.

A: It's interesting, you see. Outside, dogs are good. They mean loyalty. In here, dogs are bad. If you're a dog then you're the opposite of loyal.

W: What is that? What you're playing with there.

(*5-second interval*)

W: It's all right. They're bringing a blanket.

(*5-second interval*)

W: What is that there?

A: The teeth.

W: Teeth?

A: Our idea of loyalty.

W: Right.

A: Loyalty was the first morality. Before there was law. Before there was love. Before there was God.

W: I see.

248

A: But not before there was family.

(*5-second interval*)

W: Piers, I want to determine how you're being treated.

A: It's all back to front here. They think. They think solitary confinement is a punishment.

W: You prefer not to be in the company of your fellow inmates?

(*5-second interval*)

W: Was that marking put on your hand with your consent?

A: Consent. Consent is a story you heard once.

W: Why do you say that?

A: Consent is a legal fiction.

W: What do you mean?

(*5-second interval*)

W: Piers, I've heard about your last will and testament. One that you've produced during your time here.

A: Use normal words.

W: May I ask, have you written a will while incarcerated?

A: Use normal fucking words.

W: It's all right. It's all right. I will. I'll use normal words. Please try to relax.

(*5-second interval*)

W: Thank you so much.

UNKNOWN: This one's sugar.

(*5-second interval*)

A: No.

W: Piers, you're shivering.

A: No.

W: It's all right. Just leave it with me.

(*5-second interval*)

W: Would you like yours with or without sugar?

A: (*inaudible*)

W: It's all right. He's gone now. You don't have to cover your mouth.

A: Milk.

W: Sugar?

A: Yes.

W: All right. Good. A lovely hot cup of tea. Now, you were telling me about your will. You produced it recently? In the last twelve months?

(*5-second interval*)

A: It's tainted.

W: Is it?

A: I can taste it's tainted.

W: Would you prefer we swapped? Mine isn't tainted. I've checked and it isn't.

(*5-second interval*)

W: Is that better?

(*5-second interval*)

W: Piers, does the new will include provision for your son?

A: Where is he?

W: Where is he? He lives in the house in Albert Park. You remember the house.

A: He said I should confess.

W: You mean the newspaper? Yes, I saw.

A: He said it.

W: When a newspaper smells a scoop, they're like a shark that smells blood.

A: The newspaper is not the shark.

W: You think someone else is the shark?

A: No. Sharks kill to survive. They're not assassins.

(*5-second interval*)

W: Piers, is it your intention that Rudy should be thoroughly disinherited?

(*5-second interval*)

W: They told me at the front desk that you don't permit your son to visit. Why not?

A: He has to come forward of his own accord. When he does, then ask me about forgiveness.

W: Forgiveness for what?

A: The very worst of crimes. Though perhaps it is what we demanded.

W: What did he do?

A: I choose not to say. There's a man in here who did the same thing. The same crime. His eyes are broken.

W: What did Rudy do?

A: I choose not to say. In here they call it turning dog. I won't turn dog.

(*5-second interval*)

W: Do you miss your son?

A: Do you miss your tea?

W: This is my tea.

A: No, this is yours. And you've got mine. It's got my DNA and I shunned it. Because it's tainted. But I never turned dog.

(*5-second interval*)

A: Busby knew. That's why he ran away. Perhaps he saw. He never turned dog either. Because he's a dog.

(*5-second interval*)

W: Piers, is Rudy provided for in your new will?

A: No.

W: Why not?

A: Not in the way you mean.

W: In what way?

A: I'm leaving the boy something more. Something special. A family heirloom.

W: What heirloom?

A: Something incredible.

W: What is it?

A: The blessing of a short life.

W: What does that mean?

A: Yes.

W: What do you mean?

A: Yes it has a meaning.

W: What is it?

A: African children are the same. The dead ones, I mean.

W: I see.

A: The dead ones have a meaning.

W: Right. If I arranged for a psychological evaluation for you, Mister Alamein, would you consent to that?

A: They don't know it. We all know it but we don't want to say it. They die for a rock. That's a meaning. None of us get that. I won't get that.

(*5-second interval*)

A: Just a shade of a garnet. Not a ruby.

(*5-second interval*)

W: I'm sorry, Piers. I didn't want to upset you.

A: Insects or children. Children or insects. It's biological. Reverse larval. (*inaudible*)

(*5-second interval*)

A: You think I (*inaudible*).

(*5-second interval*)

W: It's all right. Come on, now.

(*5-second interval*)

W: It's all right.

(5-second interval)

W: Perhaps I'll go.

(5-second interval)

W: It's all right. I'll go. I might come back when you're feeling better.

(5-second interval)

W: I'll come back when you're feeling better.

UNKNOWN: *(inaudible)*

end tape series ozk016

52

Around two o'clock I reach Albert Park. The weather has thawed; sunlight even broke through as I drove down Spencer Street. Upon arrival, I feel optimistic: I leave my jacket and gloves in the car.

As troubling as the Alamein transcript was in its agrammatic monotone, it confirmed what I've been hearing and saying since yesterday. Piers *knew* that Rudy had struck Cheryl and killed her—it was the only explanation for the vase in his workshop. He sat in a cell for eleven years and waited for Rudy to come forward, until one day last month when he stopped waiting.

So that's reason number thirteen: Piers said as much to Tristan Whaley.

Reason fourteen is: it explains why he didn't want Ken Penn to give evidence at the trial. Penn thought Piers was too embarrassed by his wife's involvement with the old man across the road, but actually Piers knew Penn would incriminate Rudy and he wasn't having that. His own fucked-up loyalty to his murderous son.

Fifteen. Piers changed his will. When he realised that Rudy was leaving him to rot, he decided he'd rather bequeath everything to some arsehole in prison than to the boy who killed his wife. But still he wouldn't 'turn dog'.

Beth didn't call me until my third cup of coffee and my twelfth re-read of the interview. So badly I wanted to tell her all this, but at that moment we had enough to talk about.

I reach Rudy's door and ring the bell, shift the package from one armpit to the other. Tyan said to bring a gift so I brought a gift. Not that it doesn't feel lame. Then, even as I hear footsteps beyond the door, I'm filled with panic.

The black teeth. I don't have the black teeth on my hand.

My gloves are in the car.

What with everything else, I overlooked the essential falsehood all this bullshit relies upon.

I search my body for the black texta, remember having it as I left the flat. Then I feel it poking my groin, pull it free but it comes free of my grip, somersaults into the garden.

Someone unlocks Rudy's fat oak door. It opens.

My right hand drives into my pocket.

What Rudy does first is react to my face. Like he's never seen a black eye before. It's like someone's having open-heart surgery right in front of him. He doesn't speak so much as moan.

I say back, 'Hi, Rudy.'

'I'm sorry,' he pushes out, looks to the ground. A child ordered to apologise.

'I think I look better like this. What do you think?'

Beth appears in the darkness behind him and he seems relieved.

'Anthony's here,' he pronounces.

'Hello.' She doesn't bother to stamp down a knowing smile.

'So you're Beth?'

'In the flesh.'

'Come in,' says Rudy.

The front room has been entirely reorganised, surely by Beth when she took the pictures yesterday, each furniture piece arranged in its own space like a classroom. The front blinds are open, the first time I've seen that, though the lace curtains are drawn to keep in the privacy. No contract on the piano stool. Rudy must have filed it away.

'Thank you for your phone call,' I say to Beth. 'I was worried my friendship with Rudy was finished.'

'You weren't easy to find,' she replies. 'There are lots of Anthonys who work at Fortunate Insurance.'

'It means a lot that you took the time to call my office.'

'It's really important that the two of you bury the hatchet.'

'I agree. It's really important that the two of us remain friends.'

And we both turn to Rudy, watching for a sign that our pretence holds water. It does, insofar as Rudy hasn't been listening, is busy scanning the damage to my face.

'Oh hey,' I say. 'This is for you.'

The parcel jammed under my left arm presents a problem: there follows a long moment of weirdness as I try to grip it with my left hand, to keep my right firmly shoved in my trouser pocket. Co-ordination fails me and the gift falls to the floor like a steel brick.

'Whoops!' I laugh, retrieve the package one-handed and hold it out.

Rudy grasps it and tears at it without a second thought, eyes alight like a child on Christmas morning. Inside he discovers a cream cardboard box ablaze with assurances regarding the chocolates within.

He seems baffled. 'Okay.' I'm sure he meant to say thank you. After a moment of hesitation, Rudy sets the gift down on the dustless ottoman.

'And look...' I begin. Today's fragment of insight into Piers's mind surely indicated that no one could have made friends with him while he was in jail. But it's necessary for me to maintain that I did. Or else neutralise it.

'I'm sorry for what I said. About your dad. Things were crazy in those days.'

This is supposed to remind Rudy that Piers was crazy in those days and might have said anything. But instead it reminds *me* of how Piers might have said anything. Like implying his son was a shark.

'It was so long ago that I just don't remember anything properly. I shouldn't have mentioned it to you.'

'Yep,' Rudy says back, head twitching up and down to ward off any more talk on the topic.

'I just want you to know that I'm sorry.' I look to Beth. She's grinning broadly. I am too. Hopefully Rudy will start grinning soon and then we'll all be grinning together.

'Yep,' Rudy says. His face darkens. 'Now hold out your hands.'

53

My hands in my pockets feel my testicles shrink. Rudy has sussed it. What was the giveaway? My nervousness? The stupid face on my face? Beth picks up the chocolates, places them on the floor and perches on the ottoman, an audience. *She must have told him.* That's why she's so smug. Was this her plan since yesterday? Is Rudy going to crack it again? Is she going to join in? And MyEffingGee, the look on Tyan's face when he finds out I've botched it.

All of this is in my head and I say, 'Pardon?'

Rudy is sangfroid, like he's had time to really come to terms with it, how betrayed he's been. The tiny eyes don't dance, the broken tufts of hair don't beg for sympathy.

Rudy's serious face says, 'Hold out your hands.'

'Why?'

'Just *do it!*'

I do it. Slowly draw them from my pockets and present them, palms up. Wait to be asked to turn them over. *When he does, am I going to run?*

'*I've* got something for *you!*' Rudy declares.

Out of nowhere he drops a wooden box into my waiting paws.

Beth beams on.

A chess set. Folded closed and fastened by a metal clasp. It rattles in my hands. Rudy must see the relief in my face, thinks it's joy.

'Yeah,' he guffaws. 'That's the one I played with...with my dad.'

And despite the adrenaline in my system, my certainty two seconds ago that the charade was over and I was about to be set upon by at least one demented maniac, what I'm thinking is: *Your* father's dead. How did *you* know to bring a gift?

'Oh.' My eyes flash at Beth, who appears slightly confused by my confusion.

'It's to say sorry,' she says.

'Beth told me…' Rudy says. 'About how you only just met with… up with your father.'

'Riiiiiiiiiiiight,' I perform comprehension. 'Thank you so much. I've played chess a few times, but never against a person.'

'I mean…' Rudy flusters, flaps his genuinely tattooed hand in the air to help him think. 'I mean, you can play *draughts* with him. I don't know if the chess bits are in there.'

And I'm like, 'Okay.'

'It's very thoughtful of you, Rudy.' Beth stands and clasps her hands at her waist like a governess. 'It's very thoughtful of him, isn't it?'

'Yes,' I glower at my stupid chocolates.

'I think you should say sorry, Rudy.' She gently touches his shoulder.

'*I did! I am!*' Outraged by her implication that he didn't, isn't. Then he cools, remembers *his* script, the one she wrote for him. 'I mean…' And he faces me straight on. 'I want to be friends.'

It sounds rehearsed, but still he means it.

'I want to be friends too.' I attempt to match his seriousness. 'This means a lot to me.'

Perhaps for the first time ever, Rudy holds my eyes.

'Now Rudy…' Beth's voice is so wholesome I almost laugh. She pats her handbag. 'Remember we have these DVDs to return.'

'I don't want to.'

'Remember, you said we had to.'

I say, 'I have to go anyway, Rudy. But before I do, can you and I have a word in the kitchen?'

Rudy doesn't nod or answer but rather turns straight for the hall and I follow, don't risk a glance at Beth, enter the kitchen and catch a glimpse of the refrigerator. Who knows what strain of swine flu percolates within, but on the door there's a photograph of Cheryl

Alamein—the same photo Rudy held up on the front page of the *Daily Sun* nine years ago. Beside it is pinned a flyer for a local tradesman, from back when this house had a use for tradesmen, then a lost dog poster with the Alameins' home phone number and a picture of Busby the cocker spaniel. Who abandoned Rudy in disgust, according to Piers. Who Rudy never stopped searching for, according to Beth.

I can't linger at this museum too long, usher Rudy into the pantry.

The shelves are unstocked and blotted with dirt, stencilled in by the jars and the tins and the *life* that once filled this space. At some point Rudy cleared them out, which didn't eradicate the stink of old mushrooms.

'Don't worry, you're not in trouble.' This is a reaction to the trepidation in his face. 'I just had to check. Are you still on for Friday night?'

'You mean...Glen Tyan?'

'Yeah.'

Rudy nods in big motions.

'Yep. Yeah. I'm going to do it.'

'You know it's very dangerous, what you're planning. I mean... Anything could happen.'

'Yeah.'

'I mean...It's dangerous for you.'

'I know.'

'Rudy, you could die.'

A shrug. That's all he offers. I wait, give him time to speak. To insist that he doesn't want to die. To announce that he never really planned to kill himself with Beth's car. To conclude that this is all a stupid idea and what he really wants to do with his life is parkour.

But he says nothing. Just waits for whatever else I brought him here for.

'You know...' I say, 'I used to play draughts with your dad. In the clink.'

He subjects me to another gaze of utter disbelief.

'Only we called it checkers,' I say.

'Who won?'

This is what Rudy wants to know.

'Ummm…He did. Mostly.'

'He used to beat me too.' He's visibly defeated.

'Did you ever visit Piers when he was inside?'

'No.'

'Why not?'

He shrugs and stares at the ground.

Sixteen. He never tried to visit his father.

'All right. I'll be in contact Friday, to let you know that the policy is active. Sound good?'

'Yes.'

'Okay. Right now I've got to get back to work. I'll call you Friday.'

'Okay.'

We emerge from the kitchen like two guilty toddlers. Beth stands and swings the handbag onto her shoulder.

Our march continues out the door and Rudy scrapes at his patchy hair like the DVD place is somewhere special. I put the draughts board under my arm, my right arm this time, my right hand still safe in my pocket, feel the chillsome air and use it as an excuse to hurry away, wave goodbye, give Rudy another meaningful nod, tell Beth it was nice to meet her. The pair hike off towards Montague Street and I reach my car. Get in. Even start the engine. Even drive around to the other side of the block.

Then I park, take my gloves and jacket this time, jog along Montague, see their huddled shapes moving away to what I assume is a clutch of shops. After this, after they seem to be well and truly settled into their journey, I turn back onto Grand Street, back through Rudy's front gate and push my hands in and up against the glass of the window angled to the front door. The one Beth unlocked while I was in the pantry with Rudy.

54

I've cracked the glass, can see it in the top corner now that I'm inside and locking the window. A slight crack, not enough to notice at a glance, a tiny testament to how long these frames have been shut, their function forgotten. Just lucky my hands didn't tear through and bleed on the carpet.

My footsteps on the carpet smack loud because I'm here alone and in secret, also because some segments have worn through to the plastic weave. In the kitchen I sit at the glass table after brushing off a chair which sends toenails and whatever crap showering to the floor. Above me the telephone is secured to the column and I consider it like a blank canvas.

After talking with Tyan last night I thought spoofing a caller ID was the solution, being simple enough software and I could do it from my flat. But sooner or later this will all be reviewed by the Homicide Squad, maybe even the Cyber-Crime Department, and I have to assume even they can unspool a trick like that.

Then I thought of suggesting Rudy make the call himself. I considered that for a nanosecond. Rudy would misstep, panic, mention my name or Beth's or Tyan's, and then everything would become four times more complicated, maybe impossible. If I do it, I can hang up before I say anything stupid.

The likelihood is that I'll be asked to leave a message and I run through it out loud before picking up the receiver. I found her number on the *Daily Sun* website, wonder how to say her name as I listen to the ring, resolve to use only her first name.

She answers. At least I think it's a she—a buzzy monotone like she's talking through gauze.

'Nina Chiancelli.'

'Nina,' I say. 'This is Rudy Alamein.'

Nothing from her.

'Do you remember me?'

A shuffling on her desk, like I've caught her watching porn. Then calm.

'Sure, I remember you, Rudy. How are you?'

'Okay.' I soften my voice as best I can. For all my success at lying, I've never been much of a mimic. But she's got nothing more than a memory of thirteen years ago to compare me to.

'It's been a long time,' she gruffs, too friendly. 'What…what have you been up to, darl? I was sorry to hear about your father.'

'I'm just calling,' I cup the receiver to talk even more softly. Even more like Rudy. 'Because I have something to…I want to tell you.'

'Of course.'

The background noise cuts off. She's shut her office door.

'I just wanted to say that I thought it was unfair. How you treated me.'

'Hey?'

'You put me on the newspaper, on the front page. Saying that my dad should confess.'

'Mmm–hmm…'

'I never said that. I mean, you told me to say that.'

'I'm not sure if I did, darl.'

'You told me what to say and you knew I wasn't…couldn't argue.'

'Now, that's not fair. If I helped you put into words—'

'It is fair. It *is* fair.'

'Nobody put a gun to your head, Rudy.'

'Fuck you,' I say. In those words I am more myself than Rudy. 'I was susceptible. You suscepted…suscepted me.'

'Yeah, all right…I'm sorry you feel that way.'

'But there's something else I've got to say.'

Silence now. Standing by.

'What happens on Friday night is justice. Don't...I don't want you to think it's because I'm crazy.'

'What's going to happen on Friday night?'

'You'll see.'

I let the drama of that hang in the air, then:

'Just remember that I do this of my own volition.' *Not* a Rudy word. 'I mean, like, on purpose. Not because of *drugs*. Not because I've been *tricked* into anything the way you tricked me. What happens on Friday is...is important.'

'You have to tell me more, darl. I don't know what you're on about.'

'You'll know. After Friday. A toothbrush can be...can change everything.'

I roll my eyes. Was that a step too far?

'Is this about the rumours I've heard, Rudy?'

My ear goes cold.

'What...What rumours?'

'About your mother's death.'

'What about it?'

'I heard on the grapevine that there's some kind of evidence? Relating to her murder?' She's trying to prompt me. 'Something that's yet to come to light. Or at least, the police haven't found it yet. Does that sound right to you?'

'What do you mean? Like...'

'That's all I know. It's come to me kind of obliquely, but maybe it's true. Is it true?'

Is this a bluff? An attempt to get Rudy talking?

'What kind of evidence?'

'I'm saying I don't know—'

'Does it prove that...What does it prove?'

'I don't know. I thought you might know. It's just a rumour I heard—'

'Tell me *exactly* what you heard.'

'Just that there's something out there, darl. Supposedly hidden. Why don't you and I meet up and talk—'

'Just remember what I said about Friday.'

I hang up.

My ear hurts from pushing the receiver too hard against my head.

Whatever sunshine there's been is gone for good and the wind picks up and the house groans like an old man mewling for sympathy. I drop my head in my hands to think.

What the fuck was that about? It's half impossible to know and half definitely proof that Rudy killed his mother. Did he *tell* someone years ago? Leave a bloody fingerprint behind? How does it take thirteen years to come up?

Or Piers said something. To someone inside before he died. But that wasn't *evidence*. It wasn't a *thing* yet to be *discovered*. Did Piers have proof before he went on trial? Was he hiding *more* crap in his workshop? Maybe Ken Penn has something squirrelled away in that tiny room where he lives, something that explains how certain he is of Rudy's guilt. But then why not share it with the world?

And there's Beth. She might have pried the truth out of Rudy if she ever cared what the truth was, hung onto it until whatever grift she was running required Rudy to be imprisoned.

Or maybe it's the standard Nina Chiancelli line that keeps her sources on the hook.

But among all the possibilities that swirl and shiver in the dank of the kitchen, watching me slump and glower at them, the one verging on self-evident is that it's Rudy himself. Concrete proof that he killed his mother and he keeps it under his bed because he's Rudy and he's crazy and somehow the word's got out and no one's cared enough to follow up. Because he's Rudy and he's crazy.

My eyes scan the kitchen, come to rest on the sideboard and I'm out of the chair, darting to it, pulling on the drawers and the cabinet doors: crockery mostly, silver-yellow cutlery and water jugs. One drawer is crammed with hundreds, maybe thousands of lacker bands, strung together in a single rubbery rope. A rope that could wrench me out of a million panic attacks. Rudy with thirteen years to kill.

I run out the back door and into the yard, run the path to Rudy's bungalow.

Its door is wood and frosted glass, not locked and when it opens I reel at the pong of the bedroom. My old bedroom at Mum's used to have this smell and she used to pinch her nose whenever she came in, remark with that nasal voice how she could think

A woman appeared wearing a uniform. A nurse or
an orderly. She asked Mum if she was hungry and
Mum held up her little sign that used to say 'Strewth,
Cobber!' and now said 'No'. Then she fumbled for
the other sign, the one that said 'Thank you.' But the
young nurse had already smiled at me and left.

Mum whispered something and I leaned in, 'What?'

'Single,' was her softly spoken word.

'Single?'

'Boyfriend's…run off,' she said.

'Mum, you really think—'

'She likes bad boys.'

Ah, I thought. This old punchline. When I was
fifteen I built a metronome at school and then I stuck
it in a friend's locker and left it ticking. Also, I rigged
it so the ticking sped up when the locker was opened,
and I attached a car battery to it and a whole lot
of wiring. I thought I was a comic genius. But the
whole school had to shut down and the bomb squad
came. I spent the night in youth detention.

Mum loved to remind me of this.

I was about to roll my eyes when she suddenly lurched
for breath and I gripped her hand and I could hear that
ticking, fresh in my ears. Then I was crying because
there was literally nothing else I could do.

thing better than Empty Nest Syndrome. All that's here is a single bed and a dresser that's unused. There are no clothes, hardly some belongings. After a discreet ransack I'm left with the conclusion that Rudy's stuff is upstairs.

Before going there I open a rear door to reveal a bluestone laneway, overseen by the bubbled windows of apartments crowded together, accessed to my left where it curves around the houses of Montrose

Row; to my right it's a dead end. This is where Rudy brought the Volvo, if Beth's story is true. This is where Rudy came the closest so far to joining his father in that big tapas bar in the sky. White cloud doesn't drift by but holds entirely still.

I climb the narrow stairs to a second floor the size of a living room, furnished with a single pile of junk, all the way to the ceiling, to the small skylight in its centre. Mostly clothes, that awkward smell again, items just damaged enough to be useless: a skateboard missing a wheel, a graffitied street sign, a deformed plastic Christmas tree. A mountain of shit as disorderly as Rudy's brain.

I pick through the mess like a homeless man picking through a dumpster: food-spattered curtains, cardboard boxes filled with door handles, ladder rungs without the ladder. Eventually I return a broken tiki torch and use it to rummage, saving me the anxiety of *touching* Rudy's things. At first I'm reluctant to leave any sign I've been here and I'm prudent, even careful. Then I determine it's impossible for me to leave such a sign—there's simply nothing *recognisable* in how this trash is compiled—and my actions become more forceful as I become more frustrated.

From the top of the window frame a solitary cockroach watches on, its feelers whirring, wondering who this new guy is.

With no concept of what I'm looking for, my digging becomes half-hearted. The light from the skylight is plentiful, I can see everything fine, but the mess is too dense. Rudy has never discarded a single possession, has merely set it all here as an indoor monument to lunacy.

The thing that's been eating at me ever since the phone call only now makes itself apparent, stops my searching, makes me gaze up at the skylight, then at the frosted window as if I could see out of it to the house. Then I toss the tiki torch and head downstairs, back across the garden.

Surely the most likely way for anything to remain undiscovered for thirteen years is for it to be located in a place where no human has been for thirteen years.

The house seems cooler when I come inside, the ground floor shrouded in a darkness I'd forgotten while hunting through the comparative sunshine of the bungalow. At the base of the stairs I look up, analyse each step like it might collapse beneath my feet.

The front door is shut. Rudy isn't home. It must be a long walk to the DVD store. Maybe I have time.

I start climbing.

55

A different odour. Foetid. Almost solid. I haven't even reached the twist in the stairs before I notice. A musty decay, not the fresh kind in the kitchen. The power of it itches my nose.

Around the turn is a wooden gate and the first-floor landing, barren but for the caramel carpet. Surprising how bright it is: I expected this to be the gloomiest part of the house, but Rudy seems to have reserved that for himself below.

I consider the gate. Someone has closed it and secured it with a small latch. Thirteen-year-old Rudy, knowing he'd never be back.

I undo the bolt, half-wondering if it will come off in my hands, but it snaps open easily, squeaks as I move through it, stays intact. To my right is the living room: a big couch, lots of books on shelves and a long collection of items I don't recognise until I do recognise them and they're compact discs. An old box television—not a flat-screen but an enormous CRT like a bakers oven—faces out from the sideboard along the south wall. A phase of light through the lace blind catches the silt in the air like tear gas and I put my hand to my mouth, partly to keep myself from sneezing, partly to shut my nose against the smell. Tastefully arranged on the wall are baby photos, infant Rudy wrapped in cotton, entirely indistinguishable from every other baby ever born, the hope in his eyes glimmering with irony. Lining the hall is a quality bench table, handsome wood enamel and sturdy and adorned with a single framed pic of Cheryl as a young girl, taken in the sixties going by the hairstyle and the discolouration. She appears to have been ambushed by the photographer, all naive gawk and big lashes, as unconcerned about the veil of time as newborn Rudy.

I walk through to the master bedroom.

Maybe I expected the roof to be collapsed or wild animals to be moved in, a coven of witches dancing around a cauldron. But it's just a stillness in here beneath a membrane of dust. The air doesn't seem to carry sound: I can't hear my heartbeat but I feel its frantic pump of blood in my head.

A section of carpet the size of an Xbox has been cut out and the chocolate underlay is mangled. The wall beside it features a fake fireplace in a marble frame: how they pimped out master bedrooms a hundred years ago. Piled on the mantel is all the boring real life stuff that no longer has any meaning: receipts, business cards, photos and frames left in a bundle by Cheryl under the strain of divorce, or by some zero-fucks-given investigative officer: *I'm not an interior decorator, mate.*

On the wall above it as well as on the door I see tiny spatters of black blood, circled with pencil and marked with alphanumeric codes: TM1, GH3...I tilt my head, consider them, try to decipher them, but there's no point and I have to keep moving. Past the mantel stands a chest of drawers where the fateful vase once stood. I expect to see a circular mark to indicate its position, but of course all of this dust has settled in the years since that derpy milk bottle was taken from its spot and never returned.

A couple of tasteful paintings hang on the walls and there are built-in robes and another dresser, Cheryl's, between the two windows that look out over Grand Street. It's hers because of the make-up, the jewellery box, the undergarments in the top drawer that's slightly open, that reminds me of how pointless what I'm doing is. If there was evidence up here then the police found it. Glen Tyan found it. There'd have been no hurry back then: Tyan had all the time he wanted. And he would not have spent it terrified that Rudy might discover him here.

I peer through the window, past the putrid disassembly of the balcony to the same old street, now partially obscured by pyramid trees. Flashes of colour motor by. A family packs prams and children into a people mover and one of the children is in meltdown, cherry-faced and screaming. *Don't go into the bedroom,* she cries. *There's a ghost that lives in there.*

The blood spatters and the carpet cut-out are enough to render it haunted, but the lifelessness helps too. I picture Cheryl coming home, up the stairs and in through that doorway, discovering Rudy. Did she surprise him? What was he doing? Or was she here first, flopped on the mattress and weighing up her future with the flaky Kenneth Penn when Rudy got home from school, inflamed already by a scrap in the schoolyard. He was surprised to see her, didn't react well. An unkind exchange. Another. Cheryl told him he was the brick wall between her and happiness. He triggered. She didn't know yet how dangerous he was…

Aside from the vase I can't imagine what else in this room could have mattered in those moments. The trial transcript alluded to nothing.

The smell is just the smell of closed windows, of the air after an age. Clothing, bedding, even the copper bed ornaments have turned in these conditions. Just like Rudy has. So forget the smell, Jason. Forget your crapsack dust-mite allergy and get your hands dirty.

Like in the bungalow, my search begins careful, becomes less careful as I realise how pointless it is to cover my tracks. In the wardrobes I find clothes riddled with moth holes and another box TV and a metric tonne of ladies' shoes. The men's dresser is empty but for a few damp ties. Behind tables, between clothing and under beds I look. Behind dressers, behind drawers, behind behind. No results found.

Meanwhile, I'm sneezing myself a prolapsed arsehole.

Tyan's hiding space, where he kept his money; Whaley's, where he stored his newspaper cut-outs—both of those I reckon I could uncover in a picosecond. So is Rudy more shrewd than them?

I'm about to give up on this room, head to the back of the house that overlooks the bungalow, when a last possibility sings out: the heating duct. A folded metal grille where the dresser meets the south wall, larger than the others. I lower myself to the floor.

Unscrewing it will require some kind of tool and I tap at my pockets, pull out my keys. I still have the key to Mum's room at the hospice, the key I was supposed to return. But like they get a lot of break-ins at the Belladyne Palliative Care Facility. Like they get a lot of people giving back their keys. Death is distracting.

So this thing can risk ruination. Even so, I say the words 'I'm sorry' out loud as I twist it into the screw head.

The process takes a human lifetime and my sneezing is worse and my eyes sting like the dust really *is* tear gas, but god bless whatever is keeping Rudy away so long. Finally I wrench back the grille and see now that the space in the floor is not large. A toddler could fit in there but nothing bigger. Plumes of dust come with it.

There's nothing as I look down, just scratched metal and bunnies of lint, forests of them. I poke my head in, look in both directions but it's too dark to see. Even with my phone I can't illuminate the ducts. There might be a horde of gremlins flipping me the bird, close enough to touch, and I wouldn't know.

The bedside table here is completely clear, probably Piers's side before he moved out. The other nightstand features another ancient Telecom landline that was surely out-of-date long before Rudy closed this room off to humanity. It features no LCD display, just buttons on a piece of jaundiced plastic. As well as the phone there's a lamp.

By some wizardry, the lamp still works.

With the shade off it's skinny enough to fit in the duct, a tight fit with my fat head in there as well. I manage it with a light scratch across my nose, sneeze, send up wafts of visible air. There's positively nothing in the duct as it runs to the front of the house. I haul out, reposition the lamp in the other direction and squeeze my face back in there like I'm asking for it. Like, whatever lives in here, a wild boar or a facehugger, I really *want* it to hug my face.

And I have to hump the floor to change the angle because my head is blocking the light. The plastic edge of the register cuts my neck. I strain into the guillotine. I fumble with the light. I burn my little finger and a face comes at me from the dark. A yell.

My yell. More of a scream. Loud enough for me to crack my scalp against the roof of the duct and the pain makes me scream again as

I wrench myself out and jam my wrist on the carpet and more pain stabs my arm.

Listen.

Whatever's in there, it isn't moving. It hasn't scurried away. It hasn't freaked out like I just freaked out.

It's this silence that gives me confidence. Even the most dangerous animal would react to the first disturbance in thirteen years. With the lamp held out, supplicating, I feed myself back into the floor.

It's a face. Like a mask. Empty-eyed, a jagged hole for a nose and more mushroom-brown than white. Beyond it there's more brown-white. An ivory pile. A dinosaur fossil. The bugs have been and gone. It looks back at me as if its last thought was to die in such a way as to terrify the human who found it.

What made me scream was: the moving of the lamp—it moved the shadow, created the illusion the fossil was lurching. That, and I'm a furry, furry pussy.

The long nose of the skull rests on two fang-like canines, pillars holding the jaw off the aluminium base, decayed black like an infection that only now is preparing to spread into the nose and eyes. Around the animal's neck, as if there were any doubt in my spiralling mind, hangs a silver-chain engraved with just a word: *Busby*.

And before I can so much as ask him how he got here, the front door of the house thunders closed.

56

My first thought is to climb out the bedroom window onto that birds nest of a balcony, try to catburgle myself down a drainpipe or a tree. But these windows haven't been opened since forever, so getting outside will make noise. And like I could catburgle anywhere.

What's hopeful is: Rudy won't come up here. Even if he heard my footsteps he'd blame it on ghosts. But that doesn't solve the problem of getting out of the house.

Poor naked Busby, he's got no ideas. Stripped so thoroughly it almost seems improper. *Did Rudy kill you too? Did Cheryl do it and Rudy flipped out?*

But I can have all the imaginary-dialogue-with-dead-pets I like once I'm out of the Alamein house. For now, a murderer is lurking below like an enemy sub. He stomps those unmistakable footsteps along the downstairs hallway.

I reattach the heat register as best I can, not particularly well but at least the screen is back in place and you'd have to look to see the screws are loose. Very gently I get to my feet and go to sit on the bed, but the groan of ancient springs would be too noisy. I don't want to walk anywhere in case the floorboards creak, so I just slump on the spot, ponder what to do.

The best scenario is for Rudy to go out, the front door or the back, into the world or down to the bungalow, though it seems he only spends time down there to sleep or to fine-tune his pile of nonsense. So the front door. Call him and ask him to meet somewhere. Somewhere nearby. Tell him it's important. Once he's gone,

I can slip out, meet him and make up any story I like.

I reach into my pocket. And draw out my phone.

Now, unmuffled by my jacket, delivered of its bondage, with air in its lungs and light on its touchscreen, my phone greets the world with a full-throated song of liberation.

Rudy Alamein flashes across its front. The robotic ringtone cuts through the air.

A loathsome, piercing noise meant to rouse me from whatever daydream the caller's interrupting. I shut it off in less than a second but it seems to echo through the house indefinitely, bleating off the walls and in my ears.

Rudy is calling *me*. From downstairs.

Maybe he didn't hear the ringtone. Maybe he thought it was birds or neighbours.

My ears yearn for knowledge, stretch invisible tentacles through the house, laid open and ticklish to the softest whisper.

Nothing. No speaking. Rudy isn't leaving a voice message.

A wing flap from outside. A car's locomotion far away. The hiss of ambience dialled so far up you're terrified the music will start to play.

Awareness comes to me before the sound does. In the quality of the silence. It's the silence I created as a little boy, sneaking out of bed and down to the living room to watch TV over my mother's shoulder as she lay on the couch.

The silence of someone trying to be silent.

Then it comes, the snap of a wooden step, a footfall on the carpet.

Rudy coming up the stairs.

After a vicious and silent profanity, I hobble on my softest feet to the bedroom entrance, have no time to exit. Instead I slide into the small recess between the open door and the mantel, pray that Rudy lacks the nerve to enter the cursed room where he did the terrible thing so long ago.

After a single, eternal minute, the footsteps reach the top of the stairs. A sliver of light below the door hinge invites me to see for myself, but any movement in this space might be noticed. I hold still and listen.

Nothing. No footsteps. No creaky floorboard. Rudy must be stopped on the landing.

He doesn't have the nerve, I tell myself. *I'm safe in here.*

A muscle in my lower back cramps and I shuffle to stretch it, feel the tension all the way through me. What is he doing? Has he gone back down the stairs?

My body aches, unaccustomed to this much self-imposed traction. I consciously relax my hips and shoulders...

A word. A throaty whisper, directly at me, five inches from my ear.

'Mum?'

Rudy on the other side of the door. I put a silent hand to the wall to dampen my shock, steady myself.

He's made his way along the hall without a sound and now he's practically in the room. Will he really come in after thirteen years? Just because he heard another phone ring?

Of course he will. He thinks he's going to die tonight. He's come to say goodbye.

I sense another step forward.

The offensive option: ambush Rudy with a push to the ground and sprint from the house. I'm not fast. Neither is Rudy. It would put paid to everything we've planned. Tyan would be disappointed.

But it might be the best chance I have of surviving the next few seconds.

The form steps past the door into view, edging into the room, waiting for another sign. So close I could waz on his leg. The abandoned stillness of his parents' life holds his attention. The view from the windows. The square of carpet removed. He only has to turn around and there's his ghost. Cornered.

Suddenly Rudy falls to his hands and knees, lowers his head and peers under the bed, surprising whoever's there. Which is no one. But he gives it a good long look, abrupt bird-like movements of his head.

I look to my phone. Is this an effective weapon? The screen tells me I've missed a call, gives me the option of calling them back.

I do.

In the silent moment that follows, as a cavalcade of technology lights the Beacons of Gondor and summons help for Jason Ginaff, I might really waz on the floor.

The landline by the window bursts into life, dumb and merciful, decades old but it rings as though it was freshly minted this morning.

Rudy's head jolts up.

He pushes himself to his stumbling feet and lurches around the bed. And I lurch around the door, reel into the hallway, hope the uncreaking floorboards will be as forgiving for me as they were for Rudy.

Through my phone I hear nothing. Nothing, as in the ringing has stopped. Rudy has answered. But he's not speaking, just waiting for his mother's supernatural voice to freak him out.

I end the call.

At the stairs I pull off my shoes, hope stockinged feet will make me that much quieter; fast-creep, taking as much shock in my knees as I can against the steps. Deafeningly loud to my own ears but maybe quiet enough.

With the blood thrilling in my brain I arrive downstairs, socks scratching against the sorry carpet, continue along the hall, walk against the wall where the floorboards are less likely to squeal on me, another trick I learned as a boy to fool my mum. Who knows what Rudy is doing upstairs. Still searching for the ghost? Catapulting down here to catch me in my escape?

I reach the front door and pull it open and urge it to close quietly as I step outside. But this thing doesn't do quiet, doesn't seem to manage any movement at all without a rattle and a crash. I'm saved by a passing tram with a rattle and a crash of its own that masks the sound of the door shuddering into place.

Even so, I bolt like a thief, out the front gate, glimpse nothing in the bedroom windows as I go, only stop to look over my shoulder when I reach Montague Street.

Just an empty footpath.

57

You can shoot these chickens. Shoot them or stab them. I've done that before and on purpose too, not just when I was shooting someone else. They die with a pirouette and a burst of blood and feathers and once I killed all the chickens in the marketplace because there might have been a medal for it. Like *Chicken Pwner,* +5000 XP. But there was no medal. I was just a dude killing chickens.

According to Wikipedia, Karachi is the second most populous city in the world. Oh the irony that right now it's empty but for five gnarled white stooges with bald heads and guns. My gnarled white stooge sits with a bead on the market entrance, squatting behind a bamboo cage where one of these chickens is spooked as balls: clucking and flapping and marching in and out of my sightline. It would be worth drawing attention to my position just to shoot it and shut it up.

But I've seen enough dead animals today.

The Busby discovery was less gory, more archaeological, though I have to accept that someone put him there. That duct was too narrow for him to have crawled in from someplace else, and not even the most gifted cocker spaniel is going to unscrew a heat register then screw it back. Not from underneath the floor.

Through my headset comes the inane whine of a ten-year-old Kiwi puce-farting his vowels and I mute him out, mute them all. They'll find me soon enough and when they do I'm not going to listen as they shit the bed in unison. In the previous game, *[JIVE] FaNcY_tUrD*s meleed me for jacking his care package. He called me a 'cocksucking piece of gutter meat'. His cerebral cortex would snap clean in half if he found me camping.

I can't deny that I find stillness like this gapingly relaxing. Gunshots and explosives call to me from a distance, but here I am, tucked away in secret. Just like Busby.

Something else I have to consider is the likelihood that Rudy killed Busby. And if he did it the same day he killed Cheryl then Glen Tyan's attendance, the entire crime-scene investigation, was probably completed before the body began to putrefy and smell, refrigerated by the winter cold. There would have been no reason for anyone to check the heating ducts. No one went upstairs ever again and Busby's disappearance was explained away by the front door left open.

Perhaps that's why Cheryl was killed. She came home, unexpected, caught Rudy stashing Busby in the duct. Blood on his hands from killing the dog, itself overwhelming evidence that he'd killed Mister Jinx, and Cheryl already up to her neck in his bullshit. The perfect storm.

[JIVE]FaNcY_tUrDs leaps into my sightline. I lightly machine-gun his balls and he dies where he lands. Free-For-All means you don't wait to determine if the stooge is on your team or not, you just kill him. Kill everyone. I searched for twenty minutes for a Team Deathmatch, but there's always a Free-For-All running somewhere. Kill Everyone is the default mentality.

The computer-generated corpse of *[JIVE]FaNcY_tUrDs* disappears without so much as a sound effect. That's what corpses do in this world.

How the fuck does Nina Chiancelli know about Busby? Or at least, that there's *evidence out there* which turned out to be a dead dog? Rudy didn't tell her or she wouldn't have brought it up the way she did. Maybe Rudy told someone who told Chiancelli. Beth? She's surely the only person he'd tell, all that misplaced puppy love, but what's she doing talking to a journalist? Another grift?

It takes four bullets to dispatch *FckU,Bogan_66* when he sprints into view. Even then he only dies because the last of them is a headshot. You can withstand three hits to the chest and still be functional, but one headshot and you're out of the game. Just ask Cheryl Alamein.

Chiancelli called the dog 'evidence', said it was something the police hadn't found. But why would the police care about a dead dog? What the fuck is it evidence *of*? Piers could easily have murdered Busby, so it doesn't prove anything new. What does it prove?

But the real splinter in my brain, the thing that gives me a jarring sensation when I think of it, is Rudy's behaviour after the fact. If he killed Busby, why go from shelter to shelter asking after him? For *years*. More crazy self-delusion? Is it a cover? Does he think the police are checking up on him thirteen years after the murder was solved? And if they are, does he think they're checking up on how much he misses his *pet*?

GTFO.

[JIVE]FaNcY_tUrDs must have respawned on the other side of the map but finally here he comes. First there's the telltale rattle of a flashbang, which is the telltale rattle that someone knows you're here. I'm loaded out with a tactical mask, making me impervious to flashbangs, but suddenly there are two of them, *[JIVE]FaNcY_tUrDs* and *[IMPY]Craw.fishMayo*, who turn on each other at close quarters: *[JIVE]FaNcY_tUrDs* takes a knife from *[IMPY]Craw.fishMayo*, who goes down with another lucky bullet from me. The corpses vanish and leave me with the realisation that, for the first time since yesterday, I'm allowing myself to consider that maybe Rudy didn't kill his mother.

But then who? Ken Penn, as revenge for Mister Jinx? Piers? Did he have it in for Rudy as well as Cheryl, only Rudy wasn't home so he killed the dog instead?

Whoever was responsible, why kill a pet and hide it? What did it achieve in Ken Penn's house that it had to be done again?

All three of them lurch into sight, *[JIVE]FaNcY_tUrDs* leading the way. They must have agreed to do away with the camper before they go back to murdering each other. A grenade flies by and a semtex hits my body, but before they pop I go down in a cyclone of bullets. Explosives wrench my corpse, four or five of them. These stooges really wanted me. Now I'm dead among the chickens.

What did it achieve the first time that it had to be done again?

When the killcam replays my death in slowmotion, you can see all those bullets, the detonations. And what else you see is that I don't let off a single shot, not even a spray-and-pray. I don't move in those final seconds. Because suddenly I've got a whole new idea about who killed Cheryl Alamein.

58

Beneath the button is a name, Woods, and by pressing it I pump a friendly tone into the house beyond the door. It has no peephole but a long window to my left that must be how they see who's ringing the bell. I try to appear officious and norpy with my hi-vis polar fleece and my clipboard. The clipboard is mine but I bought the polar fleece from an army disposals on my way through the city.

I woke up this morning in a kind of fugue state, the return on a night spent asleep when sleep was not possible. My curtains glowed with morning and I tried to remember what day it was, checked my phone to be sure it was only Tuesday. Not Friday. Not Friday. I sat up too quickly and stirred the codeine pill that had pooled at the base of my brain, it being my solution to last night's sleeplessness and the endless cascade of possible outcomes for what I planned to do this morning. I'm hoping eight-thirty is an acceptable time to come knocking.

A solitary chime sounds some distance off. As if someone's holding a teacup next to my ear and they're tapping on it with their fingernail. I hear it again. *Tink.* A remote worksite. It echoes off the homes and parked cars on the street, its source unclear. Too far away to be from this house.

The door opens to reveal a slim woman in a white T-shirt tucked into jeans that are fastened high on her waist. Her tan is recently sprayed on, her teeth recently whitened. My first thought is to wonder why she's done that to herself.

Before I even speak she seems to detect my judgment, winces with worry.

And I'm like, 'G'day.'

The phrase sounds wrong in my mouth and instantly I drop the rugged persona. 'I'm Craig from WestTech Electric?'

I leave it at that, as if surely I've said enough. She only stares back, still fretting.

'Sorry I'm a bit early. Got a few jobs to do along this street and I had to get started.'

'Pardon me?' A nervous laugh. 'What is this about?'

I put some panic in my eyes.

'Geez, I'm...I must have got the wrong house. I'm really sorry. I'm looking for...' I consult the clipboard. '...483 Grand Street, Albert Park?'

She's got the hips of a woman with kids and her face is slightly warped, as if childbirth was so traumatic it made her eyes bug out of her head like Quaid at the start of *Total Recall*. They wrinkle at me now, not suspicious but confused.

'That is...here. I mean, this address.'

'Are you Missus Woods?'

'Ummm...' Another nervous smile. 'Should I have been expecting you?'

Her name is Alana Woods and her electricity provider is WestTech, but that's all the information I could find last night before the codeine kicked in.

'I have a work order here...' I wave the clipboard. 'It says there could be a repair issue and I'm supposed to inspect between ten and twelve today.'

'Ummm...That's the first I've heard...'

'Your meter's working okay?'

Still that *tink tink* noise just above the traffic.

'I wouldn't know...'

'The Jebson gauge is ticking over twenty times a minute?'

I made that up. I made up the very concept of a Jebson gauge. And I choose in this moment not to feel bad for duping her.

'I...I'm not sure. It's right here.'

She pushes open the door to reveal a long hallway, tasteful pictures on the walls. A single-storey home, sparkling with fresh paint in an effort to compete with the terraces across the road and the red-brick mansion, Ken Penn's former home, that looms directly next door like the schoolyard bully. A slew of men's shirts hangs off the laundry door, a stained-glass window keeps the hallway dim and classy.

The breaker box is here at the entrance, mounted to the panelled walls. I step inside. She keeps the front door open and waits there; if I'm a psycho she can run for it.

'Just so you know,' I say, not trying to sell it anymore, just saying the lines because I spent the drive here inventing them. 'Clients with WestTech are entitled to an inspection every twelve months. You're a little overdue. Your last inspection was eighteen months back? Does that sound right?'

For a moment I'm impressed with myself. I've really got the knack of ringing people's doorbells and lying to them. You'd think I would have been caught out at some point in the last few days. Then I remember that Glen Tyan did catch me out and he pushed me into a urinal and I'm not impressed with myself anymore.

'Will this take long?'

Her hands clasp at her waist, fingers dance with embarrassment.

'About ten seconds.'

I open the box door to find a bright new board but the box itself is old so there's hope. The back of the door wears a sticker with steps on how to do a monthly safety check and a sheet of A4 held up with tape, identifying the role of each circuit on the board.

Nothing more.

I sigh. For a moment I feel a sting of tears, but that's just self-pity.

'All right,' I say. Conclusive and instantly bitter.

When Mum had our old place in Eltham treated for termites, like, a decade ago, the record of application was taped inside the door of the breaker box. We sold the house before she died but I would bet the sticker's still there. This one's been removed. The one that will tell me who it was that treated this house in 1999, who it was that helped Ken Penn find the dead Mister Jinx in his living room. The last meagerly viable suspect for the murder of Cheryl Alamein.

It's possible the box isn't as old as it looks. Or the sticker is somewhere else in the house and I don't have a chance of finding it. Or…

From a distance: *Tink*.

Before I leave, I'm going to look behind that A4 page.

Tink.

The nervous woman faces out the door, apparently talking to herself.

'What *is* that child up to?'

Tink.

But I'm not listening to her.

Tink.

I pick urgently at the tape, catch a splinter of wood under my nail but I claw harder. The paper tears and there's something here. Faded and brown. Warped and peeling.

I tear off the A4 in its entirety, don't care if she protests.

> *Treated for termite infestation: 3-4/6/1999*
> *Treatment performed by: Des Blake*
> *Treatment used: Fipronil (Terminate)*
> *Des Blake Pest Control*

It hardly seems professional. No logo, no job number or ABN. The words are scrawled in such a way that either Des Blake wrote it on a boat on the high seas, or he's someone who didn't do a lot of writing. I can't tell if I recognise the name or just want to. Des Blake. Desmond Blake.

'Okay,' I say. 'You're all good. Sorry to bother you.'

Tink.

If previously she was worried, now she seems downright panicked, but manages ordinary conversation because I think panic is her natural disposition.

'You're not going across to 486, are you?'

She wrings her hands like they're trying to strangle each other.

'486 Grand Street?' I check my imaginary work order. 'Ummm... might be. Why?'

'Just be careful.'

'Careful of what?'

'You'll see when you meet him.'

And the knowing smile she makes as she shuts the door, it's like whatever. Puh-leez. I bet she's never *talked* to Rudy, not enough to judge him on anything more than the scuttlebutt she hears from the other Grand Street busybodies.

Tink.

I'm thinking all this butthurt when I realise that the worksite sound, it's coming from Rudy's house. That's what she meant. Rudy is building something over there. A rocket to fly to the moon.

I move down the steps, pulled on a zipline to Rudy's home. Despite the lack of evidence I can tell that something's happened. Something that makes the skin on my neck tighten. I bolt across the road, narrowly avoid a speeding motorcycle. Stomp over the wilful garden. Ring the doorbell and no one comes. Ring again, wait, ring again, then again, to be sure that no one is in fact coming.

I back up, back down to the street. My phone vibrates—it's Beth, but I'm not taking calls. At the end of the row I see a laneway that I jog to and scrutinise: just a strip of wonky cobblestones between high brick walls, but it doglegs at the end—the bluestone laneway behind Rudy's bungalow. I hurry, still with my clipboard, wearing my hi-vis. What will I say if Rudy asks about them?

Around the dogleg there's an old printing factory. To my right is Montrose Row.

The noise is louder as I approach the rear of Rudy's bungalow. I can hear the belting noise, not a distant *tink* anymore but a whole-hearted *thunk*, woofing out in shock waves from beyond the wall. The door into the bungalow is ajar, itself an indication that today is not like other days.

Fumbling, I use my ballpoint pen to draw on the teeth, force myself to take my time after yesterday's disaster but my hand is shaking. The final product is not artistic, not gapingly accurate, but I'll keep it concealed beneath the clipboard.

From inside, Rudy grunts, pained.

I push the door open and step through.

59

The bedroom is austere like yesterday and Rudy isn't here but a section of brick above the window is gone. Gone as in leaving a hole like a Tetris piece and I can see clear to the house at the end of the garden. Thunks and yawps come from above, then a metallic boom that shakes the structure, all the air inside it.

I call, 'Rudy?'

Before the ceiling can fall in I scurry to the open garden door, past the stairs that are hidden beneath the junk from the first floor, past another block of missing wall above the landing. A shower of brick dust and ash swoops my path.

'*Rudy!*' I yell it this time.

Silence. I peek out and up.

His face is a coalminer's. Clothes and hair sooted grey and a perpetual mist of dust swirls around him, around the yard. The source of the dust is the second storey of the bungalow, the front portion of which, as well as most of the roof, has been demolished. Now it smoulders like London after the Blitz. A sledgehammer hangs from Rudy's hands. Rudy is the Blitz.

'Hi.' He smiles through the grime.

'What the fuck are you doing?'

'Watch!'

Rudy raises the hammer. I arch across the garden to a safe distance and watch him bring the iron weight down onto the south wall, dislodge another brick that plummets to a great pile of them rising up against the ground floor, climbing over each other to get back where they belong. He swings again, grunts, swings again and crash, another brick, his face red and intense, glowing with the accomplishment of having destroyed so much of a solid, fit-for-purpose dwelling.

His exertion triggers a coughing fit. The sledgehammer drops aimlessly to the bricks below and Rudy grins like I've caught him pulling the wings off a fly.

'I thought I'd...' He gestures at his destruction like it's a big joke. 'The roof almost collapsed on me. I mean, it *did* collapse on me. It almost killed me.'

My bafflement only makes him more excited.

'Imagine these...' he points to three thick timber beams. Before the first floor became a sundeck, they probably held up the rafters. '...and all this falling on you. Now look at me.'

Rudy pulls up the sleeves of his T-shirt, points to his face.

'Not a scratch. It's amazing.' He laughs, waits for my amazement.

I force a smile. If someone relayed that story at a cocktail party, I would be amazed. But that's not where we are. I stagger across the strewn bricks, as close to the remaining structure as I'm prepared to get, fan dust from my face.

'Why are you doing this, Rudy?'

'Listen,' he says, climbs awkwardly off the ravaged top tier of the studio and onto the bricks, still with exhilaration in his eyes as he reaches me. 'Tonight's it. The night.'

Another shiver crowds my neck.

'What do you mean?'

'I'm doing it.' He lowers his voice, self-conscious. 'I'm doing it tonight.'

'But...' Today is Tuesday. I checked. 'What about the insurance?'

Rudy grins, shakes his head, looks at his wrist where there's no watch.

'If I died right now, Beth would get a million dollars.'

'What?'

'We went yesterday. She took me. After we saw you. It was her idea. We went to this place, Tatham...Tatam Insurance, and I got this thing...provisional thing. It means I'm insured now. Starting now. So we don't have to wait for Friday.'

From the back of my mind, I hear a slow clap for Elizabeth Cannon.

Rudy senses my disbelief.

'I tried to call you. I tried to call you when I got home. But there wasn't…Something weird happened with the phone…'

'But what about our policy? My policy? It's illegal to have more than one.'

'Yeah, but your one hasn't come through, right? They told me at the place that you could just cancel it and that's all. I had to pay them the fee but…but that's okay. It's not like I need money anymore.'

'What about all the work I put in, Rudy?' This is me clutching at straws.

Rudy smarts, doesn't get my irritation.

I'm like, 'How are you going to pay the premiums?'

'Beth said she would.'

'Does she know what we're doing? What we're planning?'

Now Rudy hesitates, which means he told her. She acted surprised and supportive. And *she* told *him* there was a way for it to be over with tonight. That's what his hesitation means.

And that's why she's calling me. She wants to give me her side of the story. Smooth things over. Keep me in her corner.

'How do you know she didn't go to the police? She could be talking to them right now.'

'She wouldn't.' It's Rudy's turn to be irritated. He thought this was good news. 'She reckons Glen Tyan's got it coming. She was proud of me. She wouldn't dob me in. She…'

He's right, of course. She wouldn't do that, not now that she's actually in line for a million actual dollars. Bravo, Beth.

'Did you do a disclosure statement?'

'What?'

'A medical statement.'

'What?'

'*Did you tell them about your heart?*'

I'm not supposed to know about Rudy's heart, but at this particular moment I think I can drop that particular masquerade.

Rudy blanks. 'I don't…'

'I managed to fudge it for *my* policy, Rudy. If they find out about your heart problem, they'll withhold the coverage.'

'I don't have a...what heart problem?'

'AVRC or whatever it is. The same as your dad.'

He shakes his head, tiny titters of denial. 'My heart is normal.'

I blink back in time to my conversation with Tristan Whaley. Am I remembering this right? The interview with Piers Alamein...

'I heard that you did. That he did.' I say this meekly, my face one tight knot of confusion.

'Where did you hear that?'

My feet tremble over the bricks. The unstable ground beneath me is a brilliant metaphor.

'I don't know,' I peter out. 'I guess I'm just...'

Maybe Piers wasn't talking about a heart condition when he said he'd left Rudy 'the blessing of a short life'. Did he have some inkling, even back then, that his son couldn't go the distance? Did he look up from a game of draughts one day and think, 'This kid is just as batshit as me.'

'Today's the day, Anthony. I thought you'd be happy.'

'I am, Rudy. It's just...Don't be hasty.'

'Uh?' He picks up the hammer, cracks it gently into the rubble. 'If anything I have to make up for not...I'm not hasty enough.'

'But tonight? You don't know if Tyan will be home.'

'We'll see.'

'He's a cop. You won't be able to corner him.' This is my real life spray-and-pray.

'He's old.'

'He might have a gun.'

'I don't care.'

'Just let it sit for a couple of days. Think about it.'

'*It's all I think about.*' Rudy screams this and his voice fractures and I flinch, can't help a derpy glance at the fences around us, hope this is private. He notices, waves the hammer at the outside world.

'*They all think I'm like this total monster.*' His anguish is not what I expected. His self-awareness absolutely not what I expected. 'And I *am*. I'm not *normal*, right? And now I can cancel it all out.

So that none of it exists anymore. You see?'

His eyes squeeze shut, seem to force down what's erupting inside. The hammer thumps blindly into the bricks.

And he's like, 'This has to end.'

Beads glisten on his dusty bald head and tears blossom in his eyes again, just as ready to ambush him as they were yesterday. He grabs at his face, squeezes it between his palms, mangles his cheeks and eyes.

.   'This has to end.'

He's right. It does have to end. If only because he's got nowhere to sleep anymore. The point of demolishing this bungalow is to ensure he goes through with it. Not like last time with Beth's car. Scorched earth, applied against himself.

And Tyan will be pleased. That it's going to end tonight. The sooner he finds out, the sooner he can limber up.

'I have to go, Rudy. So...'

He sways for a moment, slumped and sullen, then climbs down off the second storey and approaches and I extend my hand.

We shake. For a moment I glimpse the two sets of black teeth. They almost touch, then don't.

'I don't like goodbye,' he says. 'Goodbyes. It was hard with Beth.'

For him it probably was.

He says, 'I know you're looking out for me. That makes you a good...good.'

'You're good too, Rudy.'

I want to tell him how stupid it was that I ever thought he could harm his own mother. But everything I can say has been said.

'See ya later, I guess.'

He turns back to his wreckage.

I stumble through the bungalow, out the door, back onto the cobblestones. As I trudge away a window opens behind me. Rudy on the first floor.

'Don't worry about me, Anthony.' The grey soot within takes its chance to escape, like a bomb just detonated. 'The roof fell on me and look, you know? Not a scratch. Nothing can hurt me today!'

60

Tyan's like, 'There you fucking are.' Forever the parody of himself. 'Come on in.'

He isn't smoking at this very moment, but you wouldn't know it from the smell. I make for the kitchen, get there and turn to face him. 'I have news.'

His hairy white legs have followed me, wearing the same skimpy shorts as always. It's warm in here and I'm glad to have shed the polar fleece. Maybe the cigarette smoke accomplishes that, but also the heater burning high on the kitchen wall, a string hanging from it like it's fishing for plastic dongles and it's caught one, not reeling it in, enjoying the moment.

'So do I,' Tyan grins. Great. Everybody has news.

He comes past me, finds his cigarettes. 'You first.'

'You said you didn't want to wait, you don't have to wait. Rudy says he's coming tonight.'

Tyan lights up, takes the stick from his mouth. Smoke oozes out of the hole it leaves.

'Tonight?'

'He and Beth went and got him a real insurance policy. Not like a bullshit one, a real one. He's covered as of today, so he's doing it tonight.'

'Thank Christ,' Tyan says. 'I thought the wait might put him off.'

'I don't think anything's going to put him off.'

More thoughtful smoke dribbles out as Tyan tips back against the kitchen bench.

'This Beth. How involved is she?'

'Rudy told her the whole plan. But she stands to make a lot of money if Rudy dies, so she'll keep quiet. She knows I'm working for you but she doesn't know that you're my...we're related. Probably related.'

'Good.'

I remember that she only hooked up with me for the angle it provided, feel that memory laugh at me then dip back under water. 'I doubt anyone would believe her if she did come forward.'

'Who have you told about me and you?'

'Nobody.'

'Not your mates?'

'I don't...no.'

'What about Facebook or something.'

'Don't use it.'

'Who have you told about Rudy?'

'Nobody.'

'Just Beth?'

'Just Beth.'

'Your phone records will say you've been in touch.'

'My phone isn't in my name. I'm a freak when it comes to privacy.'

A sideways glare as Tyan leans to ash his cigarette. When it returns to his mouth he's contemplative.

'Today's the day.'

'Apparently. So don't knock yourself on your arse like you did the other night.'

'Hey?'

'When you got pissed. What...two nights ago.'

Nothing from him but big eyes, trying to remember.

'When you told me that story. Of that dude you shot.'

'*Hey?*'

His horror is genuine.

'Yeah...' Nothing to do but keep talking. 'You were going to lock him inside and tell the police it was a siege or something. But then he died. Or something.'

If I tore my face off and revealed myself to be Lee Harvey Oswald,

Tyan would react like this. His dafuq face. Eyeballs straining, bottom lip trembling, the rest of him paralysed. The heavy drinker's no-archive directive. With a derpy scratch of my elbow I try to change topic. 'So what's your news?'

He scowls, breaks from his trance.

'Ummm…I got a phone call. This morning. From Ralph Yates. He's a senior in the Homicide Squad. Said he got a tip that Rudyard Alamein was planning something, didn't know what. But I should be careful because it sounded like the kid was nuts.'

His face fills out with a smile.

'What that means,' he explains, 'is that now, any deadly force used by me is justified because I've been *told* that Rudy is dangerous. So of course I'm going to shoot to kill.'

'Great.'

'I don't know what you did, matey. But it worked.'

'I rang a reporter at the *Daily Sun*. Nina Chiancelli. Do you know her?'

'Yeah. She's done the crime desk for fucking decades.'

'I told her I was Rudy, said that something was going to happen. Didn't mention you.'

He nods, assessing. 'Sounds like we're laughing.'

'But I said it'd be Friday. Not tonight.'

The same nod. 'Who cares? It'll only matter that he's wacko.'

'Your mate…He's not going to, like, put surveillance on Rudy or anything?'

Tyan's use of cigarette smoke is a gift. It communicates without words. This time it snorts out his nose.

'What, you reckon they're made of fucking money? He knows I can handle myself.'

The hand with the cigarette comes at me and I flinch. But the hand rests on my shoulder.

'Listen. You did a good job. Anybody else your age would have shanked it.'

I don't notice the smoke that's wafting up my nose.

Tyan's like, 'I'm trying to tell you that I'm…'

But he draws his arm away and drags on the cigarette. 'What's that?'

'What?'

'That.'

He points to my elbow. I look and see the chessboard there. It was still in the car from yesterday and I came in with it.

'That's, um…That's a gift for you.'

I offer it.

'It's a chessboard. Or a draughts board. It doesn't have the chess pieces.'

Tyan drags again, says nothing.

'It used to belong to Rudy. It's old.'

His big man hands take the set, hold it up for appraisal. 'Expensive, is it?'

'I guess. I don't know. I thought we could play some time.'

Tyan unsnaps the gold lock and looks inside at the red felt and the marble pieces. 'Nice,' he says, closes it. Inspection over.

I say, 'Don't leave it out for Rudy to see tonight.'

'Why not?' He seems to genuinely wonder.

'Because…' And I realise he's right. There's no reason why not.

'So I've been thinking,' Tyan says, putting the box on the kitchen table. 'Maybe we should do that test. The DNA…the paternity test. So that it's official and everything.'

'Yeah, no…That'd be great.'

'I don't really know how to do it…'

'That's okay. I'll look it up.'

'And if Friday night is free now, how about we go for dinner? I'll pay.'

Friday. It feels like years away.

'That sounds great.'

He holds out his hand and we shake. Just like I did with Rudy half an hour ago.

'Good luck,' I say. I think that's also what I said to Rudy.

'You'll never have to draw that silly thing there again.'

He's talking about the fake tattoo.

I'm like, 'Can you call me tonight? I mean…Just to tell me it's over.'

He nods his sage nod. 'All right. Yeah.'

'Okay. Good luck.' I try to find something else to offer but it's not there.

Tyan walks me to the porch and I leave with an awkward wave. From the gate I look back and see him disappear behind a closing door.

61

By the time of Beth's second call today, I've found a clipping that mentions a young Desmond Jeremy Carne, the name he was born with. It's on the State Library website, from their archive of the *Truth*.

The heater pukes its warmth in my face but somehow I'm still cold. Clouds outside gather like a gathering storm, but don't they always look like that? The light from my displays is a soft sideways snow.

I do not answer the phone. I hope she's fretting that she won't get to me in time. Hope she's pacing that tiny living room, waiting for the call back that's never going to come.

> ## YOUNG WIDOW HAS HER DUCKS IN A ROW
>
> *12 March, 1975*
>
> JEFFREY MARCHAND
> *Society Writer*
>
> POULTRY baron Henry James Blake, 50, announced on Tuesday his engagement to Lydia Anne Carne, 29, confirming rumours that have had tongues wagging ever since the pair were photographed together on Oaks Day last November.
>
> Despite the 21-year age gap, close friends of Blake—a millionaire by way of his syndicated Gippsland farming—told the *Truth* the pair were 'simply perfect for one another.'
>
> Mrs Carne became a mother when she was

only 16, and her first marriage, to Franklyn Carne, took place, it would appear, to the sound of a shotgun ratcheting a shell.

However, Franklyn Carne was killed in a machinery mishap in 1973.

Since that tragedy, Mrs Carne has employed herself as a seamstress while also raising her son, Desmond Jeremy Carne, 13, who is said to remain deeply affected by his father's death.

Mrs Carne has been at her wits' end to provide young Desmond with a father and financial security. It seems that fortune has now smiled on them both. And a very broad smile it is.

Mr Blake first met Mrs Carne when she was engaged to produce a First Communion gown for his son, Gary, also 13.

It would seem that romance lingered not long upon the vine, but blossomed and was harvested in quick succession. The pair shared regular picnics together with their sons (and Gary's pet dog, Conan!), soon to be step-brothers and to share the name of Blake.

It is said the boys are becoming fast friends.

While there has been much tut-tutting in response to the announcement, given Mrs Carne's Anglican upbringing, this writer heartfully congratulates the pair. Gone are the days when sanctimonious wowsers should be permitted to come between a man and a woman very much in love. Heaven forbid they come between a nubile young woman and such a poultry amount of money (pun intended!).

It is worth noting, however, that the bride-to-be and young Desmond were baptised in St Patrick's Cathedral in a hastily arranged service in February, attended by Blake and close relatives. That should put anxious minds to rest.

A wedding day has yet to be announced.

Superimposed behind the words is a photo of Henry and Lydia, their faces clean white in the overexposed style of the day. He is smiling, hair thinning, tall and dripping with wealth. She does not smile, her hair held aloft in the form of a miniature beehive, but peers back at the camera like she knows what the accompanying text implies.

There's no picture of Desmond.

After another hour's searching, it's clear that Desmond Jeremy Blake is one more numpty with no existence on social media. Just like Tyan and Rudy. All the players in this comedy seem to have missed the digital revolution. It's like they never *left* 1999.

So I have to scrounge.

By the time of Beth's third call, I've found tax summaries. His primary occupation at the time of Cheryl's murder was 'pest extermination'. He gave his address as a Mornington caravan park.

Desmond had a son of his own in 1985, with a woman named Maria Talumbi. They named him Franklyn after his late father. Des and Maria were never married and from what I can tell they never lived together. That they *met* at some point is about all I can discern.

His income tax is regular and neat and he never paid money to Maria or his son. It's not clear he had any contact with them at all. They were listed as dependents when he applied for a small-business grant in 1998, but that appears to have been a lie. And he didn't get the grant.

Then, in 2000, there's this.

LIFE SENTENCE FOR GRANNY MURDER
June 21, 2000

NINA CHIANCELLI
Crime Reporter

A Mornington man has been sentenced to life imprisonment for smothering to death his 53-year-old mother in her Ivanhoe mansion last year.

Desmond Jeremy Blake, 37, pleaded guilty to the charge of murder but otherwise made no comment to investigators. His motivation for the crime remains unknown.

On June 15th 1999, police were dispatched to the Ivanhoe address after Blake telephoned emergency services and said his mother, Lydia Blake, was not breathing.

Paramedics found the front door unlocked

and treated her at the scene. She died en route to Royal Melbourne Hospital.

Desmond then attended the home of his stepbrother, Gary Blake, 38.

Gary, his wife Katrina and their 5-year-old son were shocked when Desmond entered the house carrying a cotton sack at around 3 o'clock that afternoon.

Inside the sack were animal remains.

Gary told the court that Desmond believed the remains were that of a family pet that had been missing for more than twenty years.

He told Gary that he'd killed the dog in 1975, and had dug up the body 'just to see the look on his face.'

Desmond also told them that he'd suffocated his mother. He didn't know if she was alive or dead.

Police were called and Desmond made no attempt to resist arrest.

Lydia Blake was twice widowed. Her first husband died in a workplace accident in 1973, her second husband succumbed to emphysema in 1989.

She was known for her charity work and her commitment to children's health.

Gary Blake, speaking to reporters outside court after the sentence was handed down, spoke fondly of his stepmother.

'She was always raising money for something.

'The whole bottom floor of the house is lined with certificates and letters from people thanking her for her work.'

Desmond Blake was estranged from his family in the years leading up to the crime.

'Des was always the bloke who didn't fit in. He moved out when he was a teen and we only saw him on and off.

'He told us he was working. But who knows what he was up to all that time?'

So a week after Cheryl Alamein is murdered, Desmond Jeremy Blake kills his own mother for no discernible reason and goes to

Severington for life. The end. Despite a load of google dorks on Desmond Blake, Gary Blake and Lydia Blake, there's nothing more to the story. Blake never explained what his motive was.

But then, at the precise moment of Beth's fourth call, I find this postscript on Blake's LEAP file: he was moved to a prison hospice in Fairfield last year. The treatment he received, is probably still receiving, appears only as 'severe psoriatic arthritis' and 'SCLC extensive stage'.

Words that mean very little to me.

What I might do next is squeeze my way into the Adult Parole Board database, wallow in that glut of information. But an exploit like that is a monumental timesuck and isn't going to answer the biggest question of all.

By the time of Beth's fifth call, I'm in Mum's old Mitsubishi Magna, heading east.

62

There's an entrance off the street that's as sad as I imagined. The concertina wire around the carpark appears to serve no purpose but to reinforce that this is indeed a correctional facility. Inside, the absence of windows serves likewise. Young faces of security personnel meet me at the archway of a metal detector, but even as I step through they don't appear to notice me. Like *I'm* the ghost, despite their translucent skin and walled eyes.

My mother died in a place like this. Except that the inmates could come and go as they pleased, if they were capable of it. Most of them weren't so I suppose it probably felt like a correctional facility. The same stench of sweat, bleach and microwaved soup as I walk the long corridor. No posters about the strength to be found in hope or the miracle of each day; the echoey beige walls are nothing more than functional and the beige lino is somehow less colourful for the coloured lines that lead you where you want to go, chipped and faded and entirely worn away in parts. At the end of this walk is the visitation wing where weak green light struggles out from the fluorescent tubes with a buzzy moan. Another uniformed stooge at the reception desk tries to look busy, but if his job is to preside over an overwhelming sense of hopelessness I can't imagine what more there is to be done. Saddest of all is the set of bench chairs and the shiny spots on the wall behind them, the paint worn away by a thousand heads tilted back to ponder the reality of a loved one dying in jail. But for now, at least, no one else is here.

The uniform seems to roll his eyes as I approach the desk. Not *another* visitor in the visitation wing.

I'm like, 'Good afternoon.' Try to be cheerful.

He says nothing. Beyond him there's a set of heavy double doors with enough steel around its frame to indicate a magnetic lock. On the reception desk are three displays, two of which feature live vision of what's going on behind those doors, broken up into nine segments apiece with running timecode. Most of the segments show hospital beds, people in them.

'I was just wondering how I can arrange to see Desmond Blake?'

The uniform doesn't look at me, presses keys on his keyboard.

'Visiting times don't start for another fifteen minutes.'

He's got a lisp, I think. But it might just be how little effort he's putting into speaking with me.

'So I can see him in fifteen minutes?'

'There's a stipulation on Desmond Blake.'

And he looks back flatly, like that settles it.

'What does that mean?'

A digital bell rings somewhere. The man analyses his displays and his hand moves under the desk. One of the heavy doors swings open and a female officer exits, another cool blue uniform. She walks past, purposeful, back the way I came. As the door falls shut I glimpse an empty bed and a curtain in a bleak hospital space. Less like a hospital, more like a dorm.

The uniform says, 'No one can see him without written permission.'

'Written permission from who?'

The man sighs. This means clicking a button on his keyboard and it's awful for him.

'Franklyn Blake,' he reads. Desmond's son.

'How do I get in touch with him?'

'Can't give you that info.'

'Then how can I get permission?'

He shrugs with a dour face, like that question's a doozy but it's not his problem.

'You can tell me I need permission, but not how to get it. So you're, like, the Riddler?'

The man says nothing, seems to wait for me to go away. For less than a second I consider blindsiding him, triggering the doors from under the desk. But who am I kidding?

'Is there a manager I can talk to?'

'Only me, mate.'

I sigh in search of a remedy. If Franklyn Blake came to visit today, maybe he'd let me in to speak with Desmond. I can wait. And sooner or later this blue-clad power trip has to be relieved. Maybe by someone more helpful.

The bench chairs are empty because no one else has shown up early, but as I slump into one a slow trickle commences, emerging from the wide corridor, registering at the desk. They look like people who would leave stains of misery on the walls. None considers this a pleasant Tuesday outing. Some are more stoic than others.

A woman sits next to me and immediately breaks wind. She's about as old as people get, but apparently she's come to visit *someone else* who's dying. What a maudlin row of pain we make, me and her and the Sudanese man next.

My mother died in a place like this. Only it had fewer security guards and more windows, some with flowers on the sill. But the spirit of death was ubiquitous there, too. Is it the smell of the place, or your state of mind?

Facing me is a Japanese woman with a rugged–up kawaii

> *A gentle tug on my sleeve. I wouldn't have known what it meant on any other day but I leaned in close, put my ear to her lips because that's the only way I would hear. She said, 'Jason.' Like she wanted me to know that she knew who she was talking to. She said, 'Don't go.' I told her I wouldn't. She whispered again and I couldn't understand, thought to go to the door and beckon a nurse, someone who could maybe translate. But I just nodded like a dingus and told her I was here.*

by in a pusher. They remind me of the family I saw at the court a week ago. Dads disappear—the lucky ones get to witness their child's first steps—then Mum unpacks the stroller and just gets on with it.

I'm flicking too hard at the lacker band. Turn to my phone for a distraction.

Severe psoriatic arthritis means that Blake's skin is inflamed and topped with silvery scales like he's turning into The Fly. I have to prepare myself for that. Along with it comes permanent, disabling joint pain, especially in the fingers and toes, as well as a 'loss of skeletal architecture'. Which also sounds like The Fly.

'SCLC extensive stage' is more straightforward: small cell lung cancer, the aggressive kind of lung cancer. Extensive stage means it's spread somewhere like the lymph nodes. It's inoperable, the survival rate is minuscule and most people don't make it twelve months past diagnosis. Chemotherapy is rarely effective, probably isn't an option if Blake is losing skeletal—

'You looking for me?' A man is seated beside me on the bench, has slumped there without me noticing.

I try to speak but my throat catches and I don't manage any words before he clarifies: 'I'm Frank.'

He's my age, wears a dusty jacket and jeans, messy hair the way some men choose not to care, a beard that's also unkempt but which seems at least to be deliberate. A crucifix hangs around his neck, matches the silver in his eyes.

He shakes my hand with a dry, callused paw. Frank works for a living; a tradesman or labourer with time off to visit his dying dad. I wonder if he tells his boss what kind of hospice this is.

'Frank. My name is...'

I realise I don't have a cover story. All this time to kill and I didn't come up with one.

'Um...My name is Jason Ginaff.'

63

The blood thuds up the back of my neck and brute forces my brain, so hard and quick that my skull impacts the spot on the wall so many heads have impacted before. Franklyn looks me over like a farmer looks over a broken-down tractor, his lip hoisted in a sneer not of disdain but merely bafflement.

'Um...' I say. He can see me thwacking away at the lacker band around my wrist but that's not going to stop me doing it. 'I wanted to visit your...Desmond Blake.'

'Right.'

Nothing from him except that sneer.

'I need to see him today...It's important.'

'How come?'

'Cheryl Alamein.'

Franklyn's eyes freeze over and at first it seems that he *must* recognise that name. His body goes rigid and he grasps at the back of his chair. Then I realise what it is that's freaking him out.

'You were in Severington?'

I should have remembered to wash the black teeth off. For now I cover them with my left hand, keep flicking the rubber band and my heart shoots another warning shot across my brain.

'No,' I say. 'Just...it's a long story.'

'Yeah. I've been hearing a few of those lately.'

Flinty eyes in a sun-damaged face. I peer back and they don't falter.

'So...like...what? What have you been...heard?'

That Des killed his mother. He would have heard that. But the toughness in his voice, the shaking of his head…It's like he doesn't want to be impugned by what I've come to say.

'Listen, I just met the guy, okay? Two weeks back the chaplain here calls me up out of friggin' nowhere, says my dad's in here and didn't have long.' He raises his hands in surrender. 'So I just met the guy. I don't know anything. I just come along and, you know…This is all new.'

'Did he tell you about Cheryl Alamein?'

'I don't…' He's confused by how to answer. A long sigh. 'I don't know what he told me.'

The band snaps loud against my wrist. He seems to decide not to wonder about it. Meanwhile I'm pulling air into my lungs by the metric fuckload, fighting the urge to flee.

'Um…He's awake? He…He can talk?'

'Not really anymore.'

'Can I see him?'

But Franklyn is already winding up. His sneer turns apologetic. 'I'm sorry. I don't think people should be, like…'

'But…Can I…'

'He can't really talk anymore. That's why there's this stipulation thing. The psoriasis is everywhere now. I mean, it's spread and it's infected. It's all over his body. I mean, you don't want to know. And he can't even really open his mouth.'

With no sound at all, the lacker band breaks. The absence of the snapping sensation or any registration on the pain scale sends another pump of blood upstairs and I think I'm going to faint, blink hard

One hand swung wildly to her side, enough to be on purpose, and I saw she was pointing in the most feeble way to the wooden cabinet bedside her bed. My flowers were there, chrysanthemums like she liked, as well as her purse. Something I hadn't rummaged around in since I stole from it as a teenager. It was the only thing she could have been pointing to and I opened it. Did she want to give me money? But no. Inside was the scrap of white card, the one where I compared my love for her to some stooge in a movie.

ipe the green flashbangs from my eyes. I shake my head, tip back and forth but it doesn't clear. With my lids squeezed shut and while I'm poking them with my fingers I realise Franklyn's still talking.

'...A test. Like, friggin' biblical.' A bitter laugh, water in his eyes. 'You grow up hating the guy because he's not around. Then all of a sudden here he is, and you have to watch him die in more pain than you thought was possible.'

I'm guessing he doesn't have a lot of people to pour this out to. He's taking the opportunity, despite how obvious it must be that he's chosen the wrong person.

'Father McLeod says it's not a sin to wish him a quick death. He said it's okay to pray for mercy. Whatever the mercy is.'

'But...How long?'

'Oncologist reckons days. But he'll suffer like this for as long as he has to.'

I'm pinching my eyes so I can't tell what this is supposed to mean. Can't see whatever has come over Franklyn now. It's in his voice when he says:

'He's got a lot to do penance for.'

I manage to blink my eyes open despite how my brain is an ocean and I'm drowning in it.

'Apart from his mother?'

Franklyn stares at the lino.

'Sounds like you know.'

'*Cheryl Alamein*,' I say again. I have to grind it through my teeth because it's hard to breathe.

'It'll all come out. Once he passes.'

'What? *What* will?'

The broken band that held to my skin by way of static

She clutched it in her hand which had no strength but which could still destroy that flimsy slip of card it was so old. With a titanic effort she hoisted her arm onto her chest and held the clenched fist against her heart. Her eyes rolled back then settled dimly. Then another gesture for me to come close. I obeyed and really stuck my ear in her mouth and she said, 'Love you.'

*I was crying all over again and I turned to face
her so she could see that I was.*

I said, 'Of course you do. You're my mum.'

*'No,' she shook her head, mad sidelong twists.
I leaned in again.*

'I love you because of who you are.'

tricity loses its grip on my wrist hair and falls to the floor.

'He wrote it all down,' Franklyn says. 'When it happened. He wrote it down and gave it to his lawyer.'

'Wrote *what* down?'

'Sorry, mate.' He plants his hands on his knees and stands up, moans like an old man. 'Even if I knew the details, I'm not allowed to tell. And he can't now. He's done all the confessing he'll ever do.'

'Listen...' I can somehow *feel* the green lights in my eyes. 'Listen. I know...I mean...'

'This lawyer bloke, he goes to the cops once Dad passes. And that's, like, any day now. That's the deal they made. Dad wrote down what happened. The bloke's keeping it till Dad dies.'

'But *why*?' I say. 'Why did he do it?'

My eyes close tight against the heat in my head and I don't see his reaction.

He says, 'I don't friggin' know.' His voice is further away. He's walking away.

'Just...Just...' I lean out, almost fall off the chair. Heads turn. I call out to Franklyn, just a blur in my vision. 'How did the vase... How did the vase get in the workshop?'

'What?'

'The vase. How was...How did it get into the...

*A nurse entered, ignored me and rushed to my mother's bed.
Something brought him here, a silent alarm that triggered at
his station but not in this room. Another entered and I saw
Mum's eyes were wide like she was searching me for a response
to what she said but when they unlocked the wheels on her bed
and guided her out I realised it wasn't me she was searching.*

*The moment she was gone and I was alone in that
room, there came a startling discomfort. Not something*

I'd ever felt, like a rebellion of the blood in my veins.
It crashed over me with such a monumental suddenness
I had to sit on the tiles. Was I hyperventilating? Was
there too much blood in my head? Too little?

I squirmed away on that hospice floor, tried to stay
upright. Sweat poured out of my hair and soaked
me down to my shoes. I pulled at my clothes until
that wasn't enough and I lay flat and I might not
have lost consciousness, or maybe I did...

The thing about that first panic is that I'd invited it.
Like a vampire, it knocked on the door and I saw who
it was and I let them in. I chose to feel this. To be
overwhelmed. Because that would reflect my feelings for
the woman dead in the next room.

mean...How did it get into Piers's workshop?'

It's entirely obvious to Franklyn that he's in conversation with a freak. He says, 'Sorry,' and turns and walks away. At the reception desk he points to the security door and says something breathy, wants to be let in. With a long stare at me, the officer obliges, hits the button and the door opens wide.

I peer after him at what I can glimpse...

Is it a man hunched in a cot? His face so flaky and ravaged with disease that it's impossible to determine his age? Is he sitting up, awaiting his son, a red bandana around his head, making the nurses laugh with his handwritten placards? Or is he setting out a game of draughts with trembling, palsied digits, the black teeth still visible through the crusty scales on his right hand?

Maybe. I'm not sure. The door shuts. Franklyn is gone.

The wind strikes my face like a punishment when I reach the outdoors. I run to the car and get inside and for a minute my hands are too cold to turn the ignition. Though also, they're too shaky. I need brain clarity, take a moment to breathe. Tell myself I'm not going to pass out. Watch gang-gangs screech in circles overhead.

I follow Heidelberg Road past Fairfield Park and over the train tracks into Clifton Hill. Then I turn right onto Alexandra Parade.

I realise that I've pulled over. I'm in Carlton again. There's a Big Thirst bottle shop dominating Rathdowne, one of the ones the size of a submarine hangar. Automatic doors open and close, sober pedestrians come and go and I watch. The engine is running.

A car horn from somewhere. The ticking of a Don't Walk light.

And what I think is this:

I'm going to buy some wine.

PART IV

just like ~~the~~ ~~the~~ black teeth &
my hand ~~I am~~ ~~today~~ looking
at them ~~while I write~~
this afternoon.

64

Her phone is closed so probably she thinks she's going to surprise me, sitting at my terminals, backlit by the streetlights and silent. I trigger the lights, put the wine on the kitchen counter, my keys and gloves too and without looking I say, 'Hello, Gemma,' because I am a gaping chadwick. No response while I fire up the heater so now I look. Her eyes are half-closed in a way I'd never seen until she turned out to be somebody else. Now she seems to do it all the time. That pointy tongue wets her lips to speak but then she doesn't.

'You want a wine?'

Licks her lips again.

'Yep.'

I break the seal on the bottle, don't sniff at the vapours, just pour straight into tumblers from the dish rack and take them over.

'You keep coming in here uninvited I'm going to call the police.'

She drinks thirstily. Doesn't seem to taste it.

'You're no more likely to call the police on me than me on you.'

I offer a mock toast and drink. Like paint. Maybe I was supposed to let it breathe. My thought is to sit on the floor again but it seems wise to keep a distance; I stroll back to the counter and lean there. 'I saw Rudy this morning.'

'I thought as much.' She kills her wine, puts the glass on the carpet. 'When you didn't answer your phone.'

'You wouldn't have liked what I had to say.'

'I only got him the policy he wanted, that you were keeping from him.'

'The one that's going to make you rich? How generous of you.'

'I'm, like, the one positive presence in Rudy's life. I think I deserve it.'

'I didn't see your car outside. Where did you park?'

'Took the bus.' She adjusts herself in the chair and crosses her black denim legs. 'Rudy borrowed the Volvo.'

'For tonight?'

'Yeah.'

This all started with Rudy taking that car to Tyan's. Perhaps it's fitting that that is how it's going to end.

'Was it a teary goodbye?'

Her jaw clenches with too much resentment to bother lying.

'You would have been proud of me.'

'He told me how moved you were. What a supportive friend. Must have been a cracking performance.'

'If it hadn't been, your pool would have pretty soon dried up.'

I can't argue with that. So I say, 'Let's not argue.'

Then I say: 'Tyan will call me when it's over.'

By way of assent she picks up her glass and waggles it at me. I refill it, turn pointedly to my phone and she does the same. We sit for an age, try to maintain our interest in the screaming triviality of everything that isn't about tonight. I expected to come home and google DNA places but can't summon the concentration, just swipe through clickbait slideshows of upcoming movies and adorable TV actors, not even seeing these pictures. I wonder what Rudy is doing right now. Is he still alive?

What else I intended to do when I got home is drink a bone-crushing quantity of alcohol, but that desire has been snuffed by Beth's presence and instead of finishing the bottle I tap myself a glass of water. She takes the opportunity to close her phone and I feel her eyes as they wait for me to feel her eyes, so I drink and flick my slideshow, whatever it is.

She says, 'Jason.'

Don't look up.

'I'm not the arsehole you think I am.'

Keep flicking.

'I know I've been a little tight with the truth. But you know everything about me now. I've got nothing else up my sleeve.'

'I know nothing about you.'

'You know more than anyone.'

I shut my phone.

'Okay. Where are you from?'

'Glasgow.'

'Why did you leave?'

'Fresh start.'

'Why Australia?'

'The warm weather.'

'Warm weather? It's three degrees outside.'

'Fuck…' she scoffs, shakes her head. 'You think you know cold? If you don't have to dig yourself out of your home each morning, you don't know cold.'

'Your parents still alive?'

'I expect so.'

'Do they know you're over here?'

'Nope.'

'So for all they know, you're like…'

'I'm not losing sleep over it.'

She pulls on one knee, tucks that foot beneath her buttocks. The other knee she hugs to her chest, all the while balancing her glass on her fingertips.

I'm like, 'When are you going back?'

'I'm not.'

'But it's your home.'

'This is my home.'

I smile at that.

'Yeah, but…And I mean, and I've got some experience with this, with…' I cough to clear my throat. '…my father, finding him and meeting him. No matter how much you resent them, the day is going to come when you want to be around these people. People you share a bond with.'

'What bond?'

'Blood.'

'*Pfffft.*' Her mouth farts at me. 'That's all bullshit.'

'What is?'

'Blood relations. Who gives a fuck. I'm not going to love someone because we're related.'

'It's not about love. It's about belonging with them.'

'Same difference. If I felt I *belonged* with my parents, which I fucking don't, it'd be because they raised me. Their *idea* of raising me, at least. Not because of some blood bullshit. That's the fucking aristocracy, mate. That's *last century.*'

'Okay,' I shrug. 'But the whole world disagrees with you.'

'Excuse me while I don't give a fuck.'

I'm happy to leave the conversation there, safe in my sense of quiet righteousness. Which is just as well, because before either of us can speak again there comes a gentle thump thump thump.

Someone is knocking on the door of my flat.

65

My first thought is irrational—it's Rudy. Beth is thinking it too. But Rudy is busy tonight, so I breathe. Is he killed already? Is this the police? If so, I see no point in faking like I'm not home. The lights are on.

Which is what she says when I open the door.

'Your lights were on so I thought I'd—'

These aren't the clothes she wears to work. These are fancy. Marnie is going out, looking as classed-up as I can remember. A clot of mascara in her left lash only accentuates the vitality of the rest of her and when I see it I have to close my eyes because it appears to be a critical moment in an epic story I will never be a part of. I open my eyes when she cuts herself off.

She's seen Beth.

And I say, 'Hi!'

'I'm sorry,' Marnie says, my epic story unfolding for her now. She shakes her head at us in apology, denial, disappointment, rejection, all rolled together into one meatloaf emotion.

'No, don't worry…Heading out?'

I can feel in my kneecaps how obvious it is that I've slept with the girl behind me.

'Yeah, yeah.' She flushes, her eyes flare. 'With friends.'

I'm not a former police officer known as the Polygraph, but I can tell she's lying. Her levels of earnestness don't gel with how I've been busted. Like, ED-209 busted. She's dressed like this to come see me, to take yesterday's apology and use it to found something. And

I nod, encouraging, like I think it's just *great* how she's heading out with friends, too caught up in my own shitfuckery to offer anything further. Then, into the tense silence comes a loud slurp of wine. I don't turn around, don't want to acknowledge that Beth is there. I step outside and close the door, feel the cold that Beth says is nothing.

Marnie squirms, tugs her sleeves with her fingertips.

'I just wanted to say that I'm sorry. About yesterday. I was in a hurry. I hope I wasn't rude...'

'No, no. It's fine. I said, you know...'

'I know...'

'I just wanted to tell you I was sorry about, you know...'

'Yeah.'

'I think I kind of resented you.'

This breaks the circuit. Marnie straightens slightly.

I'm like: 'I never knew my dad and my mum's gone. When I googled you...there you were, not talking to your parents. I think I just resented you for it. That's why I was such a dickhole.'

'Shit. I'm sorry.'

'You don't need to say that.'

She snaps out of the seriousness.

'So, this...' She fans our groins. 'This is all fine?'

'Copacetic.'

'You're sure?'

'Yeah!'

'Great!'

She takes a step back.

'Let's get a pizza soon.'

'For sure.'

Her red hair and nice clothes turn to the stairs.

'Wait,' I say. 'Can I ask you something?'

She looks back and bites her lower lip.

I'm like, 'You said you got your father to tell you the truth. About what he'd done.'

'Yeah...'

'How did you do that?'

'You mean...'

318

'I mean…like…how did you do that?'

She sighs: the long stretch of steam catches in the light from the stairs. She appears to be caught between our reconciliation and her ongoing reluctance to even think about the past.

'I told him that Mum had confessed it all to me. I told him she'd broken down and it had all come out. She hadn't, but I said she had. I really sold it. And he cried. And then he came clean.'

'So you—'

'I bullshat him. To make him tell.'

And she lingers at the stairs, like I might have more to ask. When I don't, she offers up a glum smile and a glum shrug. 'I never told anyone that before.'

My response is useless. Just a nod.

'See ya, Stevey.'

And then she and that clot of mascara, the blemish that proves the rule, are gone.

Beth waits for me to close the door before she says, 'What was *that*?'

'My neighbour.'

'Are the two of you…*particularly* neighbourly?'

'No,' I scowl, though being particularly neighbourly with Marnie Smurtch was once a dream of mine, an *intention* even, only days ago. Each one of those days now feels like the rise and fall of a civilisation. For that time when Marnie and I were just two weirdos with a yen for one another and zero self-esteem, I actually feel nostalgic.

What if I'd run to her arms that night instead of Beth's? Me with my blood and my bruises and my victimhood. If she'd been the one to dab Dettol in my eye and fold me into her bed, I would have told her everything, like I did with Beth. I would have told her my real name. I might have gone further and told her that Glen Tyan is my dad. And she would have reciprocated: the secrets of Kerang, the ones she'd never shared, the whole story, being her contribution to our midnight indoor truth picnic. And she would have taken me to the police the next day and I'd have told them everything too and right now we'd be laughing about it, getting over it, moving on.

Instead I'm here, waiting for confirmation that someone is dead.

'If you're going to talk...' I rub at my face, sidle back to the kitchen, now my preferred base from which to engage Beth. 'Use your real voice. Your real accent. When you sound Australian I just think you're lying.'

She sucks her teeth. 'I told you. This is my real voice.'

'I mean, believe me, I'd welcome a distraction.' I pour myself another wine, wish I were drunk. 'But every word you say reminds me what a liar you are, which renders moot literally everything that comes out of your mouth.'

'Whatever,' she says, with those new sleepy eyes but that same old voice. 'I'm happy to not talk.'

And we don't.

I fold my arms and rest my head there, don't know how long for. It's not sleep I disappear into but thoughts as fathomless as sleep. When I blink myself upright, Beth *is* asleep, legs splayed out like she's baring to me her black denim genitals, and I think I might ask her to go home. But she won't go and we'll fight and I don't want to talk to her, let alone wake her up to talk to her, let alone wake her up to fight with her.

The time on my phone is after eleven.

I will it to ring. Telepathically tell it to ring. And right then, it rings.

Beth jolts awake, instantly wide-eyed.

I clear my throat.

'Hello?'

For a moment it's just breathing. Then the unmistakable squeak:

'Anthony?'

'Rudy?'

Beth straightens, as baffled as me.

I'm like, 'Where are you?'

'Um, I'm right...I'm outside your place.'

66

None of my windows faces the street, but I wave Beth away from them anyway. Into the phone I say, 'Why?'

'I don't know.'

'Have you been to Tyan's?'

'No.'

'Do you want to come inside?'

Beth slaps my arm. And no, I have no idea how we will explain why she's here. But cagey is not an option.

Rudy says, 'Um...I think I'm better in the car.'

'All right. Hold on. I'm coming out.'

I end the call and reach for my jacket.

'What's happening?'

'I don't know. He's outside.'

'Why?'

'Maybe he changed his mind.'

I fumble with my gloves and get them on, pull on my scarf. 'Stay here and keep the lights off.'

When I turn them off Beth sighs, but she doesn't have time to protest because I'm out the door, scurrying downstairs, hugging myself. My nose throbs against the cold and something seems to hiss at me but it's only the wind.

There's the Volvo. Parked on the far side of the mailboxes.

What I notice when I open the passenger door is that Rudy is sweating. And here's me, I can see my breath. That face though. All of it trembling white and his eyes big like I'm here to save the day.

He's chosen his very best hairshirt jumper with orange stains for tonight's occasion and there's still concrete dust in his hair and down his neck. What I see next is the thing cradled in Rudy's lap, an artifact he made himself and which is priceless.

The shiv. The murder-weapon elect.

I sit into the passenger seat and shut the door. My first time in the cursed pistachio Volvo. It's roomy. The dashboard is baked black and the upholstery old-fashioned, velvety. Even without the engine running it's a sauna. I rub at my nose, encourage a thaw.

'Second thoughts?'

Rudy looks at what he's holding, might be trying to remember what it's for. I follow his eyes to the weapon. It would barely put a dent in Glen Tyan.

'Rudy, how do you know where I live?'

Did he follow me home one night like he followed Tyan? Did I *tell* him at some point?

He doesn't seem to have heard.

I'm like, 'So what's happening?'

'I don't know,' he shrugs. 'I'm not scared.'

'I know, matey. I know you're not scared.'

He only stares at the toothbrush. Happy, I suppose, to have something down there to look at.

'Maybe you should go home. You'll still be covered tomorrow. Insurance, I mean. And Glen Tyan will still be living in the same house.'

'I think I should stay in the car,' Rudy repeats, eyeballs quivering.

'Okay. You want me to drive you home?'

Before he can answer, and who will ever know what his answer might have been, he sees something in the rearview, swivels to see out the back windshield but it's misted over.

I say, 'What?'

Rudy winds down his window fast like he can't breathe, reveals a black and frozen street.

'It's…'

Beth smiles into the cabin, wrapped up in a puffy asexual jacket, the innocence in her eyes restored.

322

'Hiya! What are you guys doing?'

'Anthony lives here,' Rudy excitedly points to my flat.

'Wow,' says Beth, gawking at me, at the coincidence. 'I had no idea. I was just visiting a friend and now I'm heading up to the shops.'

Rudy says, 'Really?'

He can't possibly fall for this. But he can, because it's her.

'Is everything okay?'

'Nah, everything's good.'

'Can I get in? It's freezing.'

She opens the back passenger door and sidles inside. 'Good and warm in here.'

'Yeah,' says Rudy, overjoyed she's experiencing this warmth with us.

'Rudy was just saying...' I turn to give her a pointed face. '...that maybe tonight isn't the right night.'

'I didn't say that,' Rudy corrects.

'But you need time to think, though, right?'

He wants to refute this too, to save face in front of Beth, but also he wants a reason to go home. He consults with the shiv in case it knows what to do.

'Is that true, Rudy?' She's the stern teacher again.

'I don't know.' And he's the recalcitrant student.

'Perhaps the best thing to do is to go there and see how you feel then.'

'Can you come?' he asks, his eyes pleading.

'Sure,' Beth says. 'Sure, Rudy. I can come.'

'You too,' Rudy looks at me. The man strangely silent in the passenger seat. Who right now is shaken by how much he and Rudy have in common.

'We can't come. Someone might see us.'

'The windows are fogged,' Beth says, helpfully. 'No one can see in.'

'Someone might see your licence plate.'

'They were going to see that anyway.'

She peers back with those innocent eyes, not dropping her act. Rudy considers it resolved.

'And also…' He's back to analysing his toothbrush, the death it foretells. 'I'm not good at driving right now.'

Beth says, 'I can drive.'

She seems remarkably cheerful given where she's offered to drive *to*, but Rudy doesn't pick up on behavioural anomalies, even when he isn't on his way to a home invasion. He and Beth swap seats and without any more talk the engine turns over and the heater roars and the stereo comes alive.

A gentle, almost beatless track. Bongos and a man singing.

I know this song. 'In the Air Tonight'. It's like a funeral march. So loud that the speakers distort on the heavier notes.

We motor east through the fluid streets and when the song ends it starts again. The CD player in this car still works and it's programmed to repeat. I let it play. I do not adjust the volume.

67

We pull over a block short of Suttle Street. Phil Collins has felt it coming in the air tonight about a thousand times since we left Kensington, while tonight's air itself hasn't offered much more than a frigid wind and a moon that glows behind the clouds like it's ashamed. We're silent: Rudy slumped in his seat, toying with that thing that isn't a toy. Beth has been following my minimal directions and praying like fuck, I suppose, that Rudy doesn't pike. For my part, I've been preparing for when Rudy asks me how I know where Tyan lives. But also, I know he won't ask.

I tell him, 'You can walk it from here, I reckon.'

His face is one of such wide-eyed expectancy it's like he's waiting for me to tell him where we are. Then he grins.

'It's like you're my mum and dad.'

My response is a snort and a nod. I guess it does seem that way. Mum behind the wheel, Dad giving directions, baby-Rudy warm in the backseat on a freezing winter's night, watching out the window as the moon follows them home. Maybe it brought back memories.

'Which is which?' I ask. A joke that Rudy doesn't get. But he chuckles because chuckling is how you forget what you've come to do.

'The thing is, we're not your mum and dad, are we, Rudy?' This is Beth, talking into the rearview. *We're not far off*, I say to myself. Rudy's parents didn't want him. They saw him as a burden and raced to abandon him. Now here we are, just as treacherous, ushering him to his doom.

Beth says, 'Your mum and dad are dead.'

Not even that can kill off Rudy's desperate grin. Stay on the lollercoaster. Don't let it stop.

I'm like, 'I'm not sure I could pull off high heels, Rudy. What do you think?'

Rudy guffaws with the back of his throat, mouth wider than it needs to be. Beth turns to him, bassfaced.

'Are you ready?'

In return she receives a wide smile like he doesn't know what she means but he's too polite to inquire.

'Rudy?'

Big shrug. 'I don't know.'

'Anthony can walk you to the door if you like.'

He's just as surprised as I am.

'Yeah. That's…That'll be good.'

'I can't do that.'

'We'll be quick.'

'Just to the door, Anthony.' She beams.

'If I get spotted then I'm screwed.' I try to communicate using just my tone of voice that if I'm spotted then she, too, is screwed.

She matches my tone.

'It's. Dark.'

'Pleeeeeeeeease,' squeals Rudy, like we're talking about an ice-cream from the ice-cream truck.

'Please, Anthony,' says Beth. She stares me down. 'For Rudy.'

I can barely see out these windows, but what I can see is quiet and suburban and deserted. A weeknight in workaday country.

'No,' I say to her, sharply, then rotate to the effervescent child in the back seat. 'It's not too late to back out, Rudy. If that's what you want.'

'Mmmm,' Beth confirms, to my surprise. She rotates too. 'It's okay if you want to give up.'

Rudy lowers his head and he's silent. Then he appears to laugh at nothing. Then another big shrug.

Beth is thoughtful.

'I guess the question is, what does your father mean to you?'

I stop nodding along. The boy chuckles again, a titter quelled by the steel in Beth's eyes.

'For some people, they don't care about things like that. Family. Some people don't care about the blood in their veins. Maybe it's not important to you, Rudy.'

'It *is*.'

'Well, that's what you need to ask yourself. Do you feel that bond? Do you have that sense of *belonging*?'

She doesn't have to look at me for me to know she's mocking my words. And while I know that, I'm listening as keenly as Rudy.

'Does it mean something to you? If it does, then I don't know if you have a choice. Are you your father's son?'

Now she nods, like she wants a response.

'Yes,' Rudy says, meekly.

'You can't just say it, Rudy. You have to do it. Or else, hey… Maybe Glen Tyan isn't such a bad—'

'*No*,' he interrupts. Absolutely sure of that one thing.

'Then it sounds like you know what to do.'

Rudy swallows using all the muscles in his neck. He turns to the car door and peers at it like he's been given his punishment and he's to administer it himself. Then in a quick scurry he mumbles, 'Okay bye,' and gets out.

The door slams shut and his figure lingers there through the frost of the window. In this private silence I want to say something. Can't think of what.

She speaks, only softly, only after it's apparent that this is the end.

'Luiks like ah am th'arsehole ye think ah am.'

I don't know what to say to that, either. So I'm like, 'You should go. I'll catch the train.'

She looks at me, almost worried for me.

I say, 'Better the car's not seen.'

And I'm out the door too. The Volvo pulls away and Rudy and I watch it go. I wonder if *I* have some inspirational words for Rudy.

Nothing.

I just lead the way.

68

We trudge the cold path onto Suttle Street and the house looms ahead like the structure itself holds a shiv behind its back. We are siblings, Rudy and I. Twin sons of the orphanage. On approach to repair our orphan pasts.

My gloves and scarf keep me warm enough but Rudy's only insulation is his jumper and tracksuit pants. He's shivering, though maybe not from the cold. I walk ahead and he comes on with his bald head bowed and I decide now that Rudy won't get another word of encouragement from me. If he can't do it, if he can't so much as get inside the house without a push, then that, I believe, is a suitable line to draw. Tyan will just have to live with it. If that's what happens, then what happens next is I take Rudy home.

This resolution is put to the test when we reach Tyan's gate. I wait for Rudy to turn the handle, don't gesture or speak, just wait. Rudy seems to recognise that this is a threshold moment and his moon-face shines hot, wants me to tell him what to do; considers me, it seems, more than the house or the gate. But he reaches out, gently depresses the metal lever and we pad to the driveway. It's too dark to spot our reflection in the police glass and that's enough to convince me that it's too dark, now that we're off the street, to be spotted by sleepwalking neighbours.

Along the crumbled drive I turn back every few steps to be sure Rudy is there. He is, sharpened toothbrush at the ready, glaring at every black window because the terrace on Grand Street doesn't have windows like this, and also because of who's inside. The rose bushes appear especially thorny in the dark and while I try to keep my footsteps as quiet as possible I know that Tyan can hear them, is listening out for them.

Can he tell that there are two of us?

We pass the garage, move away from the patio entrance, partly because I don't want to demonstrate that I know my way around, also because it's actually the smart approach. The lawn is quieter, darker, a less likely direction—Rudy has to arrive in the belief that we are ninja. But then, on the far side of the weatherboard shed, painted a colour I can't determine for all the darkness but which is flaking off in handfuls of hard dandruff, Rudy's pattering steps come to a stop and I turn to see why.

He says, not whispering, 'Anthony?'

I do whisper. 'Yeah?'

'What's, like...?'

'Oh,' I hush, looking around at nothing to see. 'I just...I'm not sure where...Is this the way?'

'I mean...' Rudy lowers his voice now, steps closer. 'Like, what's actually...?'

'What?'

He looks down at his toothbrush. 'Yesterday...I found a pen in front of my house. And like, there was a crack in the glass in the window.'

I shrug, big so Rudy can see it. 'Yeah?'

'Also,' he continues, 'I got phoned by Fortunate Insurance today. They asked if I wanted to buy the policy. And I said I already had, and they checked and said I hadn't.'

'Right...'

'Also, I heard your phone. Yesterday. Upstairs. At my house. Is that...did it?'

Despite what this means—that I've failed and that I've failed Glen Tyan—what I'm thinking is, *Good for you, Rudy.* Finally a note of suspicion as the entire world conspires against you.

'Glen Tyan is waiting. He's got a gun. He knows you're coming.'

All that planning and commitment. Done away with in a whisper.

'How…? How?' The question is all-encompassing. Rudy's teeth chatter in the cold.

'I told him.'

His eyes bat. He tries to understand. He bites his lip as he tries. Bunches the skin around his eyes.

'Why?'

What I say next I don't whisper because I want Rudy to hear.

'He's my dad.'

And in response the full moon springs from its hiding place and glows all over Rudy, who steps back, cocks his head a fraction of a degree but otherwise registers nothing.

'But…'

'And my name's not Anthony. It's Jason. Jason Tyan.'

'Ummm…' Still blank-faced, imitating the moon.

'And I don't sell insurance. And I was never in Severington. I never met your dad.'

'You're his…your father?'

'Yes.'

'But he…'

'I know.'

'He *lied*—'

'He thought Piers was a killer—'

'He *wasn't*.'

'I know.'

Cloud sucks up the moonlight again and Rudy's face dissolves into darkness. In a moment my eyes will adjust, but all I see now is a black figure stuck against a grey lawn.

'So what do we do?'

After a silence, he says:

'Let's go.'

'You mean, let's go home?'

'Nuh. No. Let's go.'

'Inside?'

'Yeah.'

'You're sure?'

'Yeah.'

'All right. That's okay. But you have to know, if we go in there…'
Steam from my mouth gathers around my head and seems to hang.
'He's got a gun.'

'I know.'

'There's only one way this can end.'

'That's okay. I know. It's okay.'

Beth was right. Her stories about Rudy. It's what he's come here
for. I nod, grasp his shoulder. All the pain of his existence buzzes
through my hand and we are resolved.

'Okay then, matey. Let's go.'

He doesn't hesitate, leads us to the rear patio, seeing better than
me. He raises the doormat and takes out the key. The hanging pots
squeak gently like a horde of frightened mice.

Rudy whispers, 'Can you open it?'

He offers the key. I shake my head.

'I'm sorry, matey.'

He waits, still. I can't hear him breathe, can't see his face, can feel
his apprehension but that might be my own.

He jabs the door with the key, hands shaking, looking for the
lock. It opens silently. I can smell the oil Tyan must have applied to
the hinges to keep them quiet.

Rudy doesn't go in. So I take his hand, the one that isn't holding
a weapon, and I say, 'When you're ready.'

69

The vestibule is just as dark as everything outside and we probably should have brought flashlights. More than anything it's sonar we use to navigate: the sound of our breathing tells us where we are, the creak of the floorboards relays our progress. I wanted Rudy to lead the way, but it's me, really, who finds the kitchen door.

'There's another door here.' This is a whisper into what I think is Rudy's ear.

He squeezes my hand.

'I can't open it, Rudy.'

Silence, then the sound of fingernails licking the wood veneer, then the bass thunk of a spring catch released.

This door is oiled too. I only know that Rudy has opened it by the cold air that sweeps across my face, this interior colder than the winter outside, like it's been refrigerated for hours. More like years.

A tug on my hand. Rudy steps into the kitchen. No tripwire, no gunfire. Just old sneakers on linoleum. It seems the blinds are open but it makes no difference to the darkness. I try to follow, try to blink away the dark, try to make out the figure of Tyan hiding under the table or in the hollow by the stove. From behind me comes another gust of air, this time it's the door that swings shut slowly on its spring.

Tyan must have heard footsteps on the driveway, must have been impatient when Rudy didn't instantly show himself and he must be ready to pounce. But I don't know. He might be standing two feet away, tracking us with night-vision goggles.

Before I can further think on it, the hallway lights up. Rudy squeals.

Tyan, silhouetted in the kitchen door by the dim orange bulb behind him.

'What the fuck are you doing here?'

He wears jocks and a singlet. How a real man dresses for a killing. Legs so pale they glow in the dark. I can just make out his face, his look of perplexity, almost hurt.

'He wouldn't come alone.'

Rudy shudders with a guttural moan, steadies himself and clutches the toothbrush to his chest like it will save him.

'He knows,' I say. 'He knows what's happening.'

Rudy's big eyes, pinned on Tyan's belly button.

'I know...' He moans it.

Hovering there is Tyan's right hand, something black and glimmering. The sharpened toothbrush falls to the lino. Rudy doesn't notice. He's too busy hyperventilating.

What I notice is the draughts board. It's under the fridge, jammed beneath one corner in place of the newspaper. Deep in this tension, that's what draws my eye. Tyan has used the board to stabilise his refrigerator. I wonder if he said 'I'm sorry' out loud when he did it.

'How does he know?' Tyan doesn't take his eyes off Rudy. 'You told him?'

'He just kind of...figured it out.'

'Stop fucking holding hands, would you?'

Rudy's hand has felt so natural in mine that I'd forgotten it was there. Instantly I release it and it hangs in the air like an astronaut cut loose. Then Rudy plants it on the kitchen sink, keeps himself standing.

'You can't be here,' Tyan says, flicking the gun at me. 'Go over the back fence. Don't make noise.'

'Okay.'

I move a few steps to the table, cling to it for balance.

'*Go on, then.*'

'Okay.'

I do not move.

'I know…' grinds out Rudy again.

Tyan makes a disgruntled face at me, rotates slightly to address the other weirdo.

'If you know…then you know.'

He adds, by way of consolation, 'I'm not going to give you some big speech.'

Already Rudy is nodding.

'But the fact is, I'm sixty years old. You think I'm going to sleep with one eye open the rest of my life?'

And then, without warning, a kind of compassion comes to him. 'I'm sorry about this.'

Although Rudy nods, face screwed into a toddler's tantrum, he is reversing. His back hits the door, presses against it.

I feel a heavy pain in my chest, realise I'm holding my breath.

Tyan's speech, the one he wasn't going to give, continues.

'You remember the day I come there? To your house? And the bloke took our picture for the paper? We talked. You knew I wasn't a bad sort of a bloke. And now here you are. It can't go on, mate. It has to end.'

'I know…' Rudy manages to raise his eyes. When he says it again it's found spit and anger. 'I *know*.'

'Fuck you. What do you know, hey?' Tyan, working himself up. 'What do you *know*? Your father killed Cheryl Alamein. He killed your mum.'

'No…'

'You told the fucking paper—'

'I *didn't*—' Rudy yells at the floor. Voice cracks. Both hands pinned to the door like a prisoner.

'But now your life's turned to shit and you need someone to blame. Why not muggins here? Poor bastard just doing his job. And so here you fucking are.'

My stomach is in spasm, searching for air.

'*No*,' Rudy cries. So certain despite his ignorance. 'You *lied*. You *lied* about it. You said it was my dad and he *didn't*!'

'Pick that up.' Tyan gestures at the toothbrush on the lino.

So slowly, in spite of his tears and that mouth drawn open by invisible hooks, Rudy bends down and grasps the shiv. It takes three attempts.

To this phenomenal sight, Tyan says, 'You're a fucking joke.'

He raises the black glimmer, levels it. Arm straight like a gallows.

'Nargh…' Rudy moans. 'You *did* lie.'

Blood bashes my eyeballs.

Tyan: 'I did my *fucking job.*'

'You *lied.*'

'*Fuck you.*'

'*He didn't.*'

'He *did.*'

'*Tell him.*'

They each snap their heads to me.

I gulp a tonnage of air. Those words were the cork that stopped the bottle and now my head swims and I suck in the full atmosphere of the room, don't notice the acrid taste now, clutch the table edge, blink yellow flashes in the dark.

'Tell him,' I say again before anyone can change the subject.

'What?'

'You have to tell him.' Dry mouth. I swallow. 'After that, you can…whatever. But you have to do this first. You have to say it. You thought Piers was lying.'

'He *was* fucking lying.'

'The Polygraph…' I push fists into my abdomen. 'You thought he was lying so you fixed him up.'

Tyan, in jocks and a singlet, looks at me like *I'm* ridiculous. 'You've swallowed his bullshit, have you?'

'Look at him.' I gesture at Rudy's cramped, melting figure, face frozen in that butoh agony. 'He can't hurt you—'

'You *did* it,' is all that Rudy whimpers.

'*Piers Alamein killed his wife.*' Tyan shouts it at both of us. A ligature to tie off the discussion. And it's there, in that adamance, that I see a crack.

Rudy doesn't. He slides down the kitchen door, mimicking the tears that slide down his face. His backside reaches the lino, knees wrap up to his chin.

'You thought he did,' I look to my own grip on the kitchen table as I speak. 'You thought he'd kept the vase he used, but you couldn't find it. So you bought a second one.'

'Fuck off...'

'You knew where to buy it. And you cleaned it with the same detergent they had at the house. That's why there were no fingerprints.'

I'm not sure, but Tyan seems to roll his eyes.

'Then you got Cheryl Alamein's blood on it. And you took it to the workshop. And you pretended to find it.'

'Don't be bloody stupid.'

'But you got it wrong...'

'Fuck this for—'

'You thought he'd confess, but he didn't. So it went to trial and you didn't care because Piers Alamein was guilty. You were the Polygraph. You could always tell if someone was lying.'

'This is bullshit.'

'You got it wrong. If he was weird with you it's because he thought Rudy had something to do with it. But it wasn't Piers.'

'Then who *was* it?' The incredulity is back.

'Ken Penn!' Rudy yells this from the floor.

'No,' I say. 'Not Ken Penn. A man named Des Blake. He broke in, Cheryl surprised him and he hit her with the vase.'

'Fuck you.'

'He's in a hospice in Fairfield.'

Tyan blinks back thoughts. He wasn't expecting actual proof.

I'm like, 'He's dying and he left a confession. A signed statement that he killed Cheryl Alamein.'

Tyan's gallows arm goes slack, the one that had followed Rudy on his slide to the lino. Still he holds it out there like he's offering it to us. His head retreats two inches on the axis of his neck.

'Come on,' He grins, indignation stifling his voice. 'You're making this up—'

'I'm not.'

'Anthony?' Rudy's face is scrunched skin, eyes in there somewhere. I don't try to remind him of my real name. Instead I say to Tyan:

'It all goes public once Blake dies. Any day now.'

'Why are you saying this?' Tyan *really* wants to know. I thought Rudy was Paul Heaney, that he'd somehow convinced himself the past hadn't happened. But here is Tyan, seeing me as if for the first time, righteous and wounded. 'Why…?'

'Because it's true. Because you fixed up an innocent man. And he went crazy. And so did his son. That's what happened.'

'*That's not true.*'

'You just have to admit it.'

Tyan's thoughts seem to cave inwards. But only for an instant before he straightens that arm again, points at Rudy's head. Rudy flinches, grabs at nothing.

'Stand up,' Tyan says to him.

'Tell him,' I say.

Rudy is such a mess down there beside the shine box, his arm flapping useless and his head beating against the door, that I don't know if his brain would receive the information if Tyan *did* tell him.

'*Stand up,*' Tyan's voice is sludge.

Rudy hears that. His pencil arms push to the floor and he gets to his feet. Ready. Shrunken and terrified and willing.

I say, 'He deserves to know the truth first.'

'It's *bullshit*,' Tyan roars, inhales hard through his teeth and burns at me. And I soften my voice.

'Tell him the truth, Dad.'

That's what I say to end it. That's the capper. Call the man Dad and see what happens. Tyan's grip loosens, the revolver lowers an inch and drifts. He goes to speak but doesn't. He peers at the figure of Rudy, somehow both cowed and stoic, then back at me and then at nothing, beaten in a game that has gone on so long.

The gun lowers another inch and he wants to speak again. That face, though. I know that face. I know the face that comes before a confession. Tyan knows it.

He whispers: 'I had to.'

Rudy and I extend to him. Like, imperceptibly. The way flowers extend to the sun.

What comes next—within a second of realising that I've done it, that Tyan is capitulating, that he isn't going to shoot Rudy Alamein—is a gunshot.

Two gunshots, actually.

70

Prostate cancer is a terrible disease. The tumour squeezes your urethra so you never really feel relieved, kind of always have to go. Every moment of your life gets planned around your access to a toilet. You're up six or seven times a night. You worry whenever you leave the house.

It's a terrible disease so you can't blame the guy. What, he should have held it in so that we could all live happily ever after? He should have stayed in bed so we could somehow cathartically dispel all our bad ju-ju? He should have undergone a stabbing pain in his guts tonight so that none of *us* had to? Freddie probably doesn't even know the light from his bathroom window, the one that throws across the fence and into Tyan's kitchen, is like daylight compared to the darkness that preceded it.

What happens now takes place at such speed that only a Thruware botlog can capture it.

20120714 23:49:28:66 Freddie feels the stinging in his groin for the first time tonight.
20120714 23:50:36:03 Freddie gets out of bed. He has no idea what's going down in the house next door. Even if he heard anything, even if he bothered to look, all he'd see is that the lights are off in Tyan's kitchen.
20120714 23:50:42:89 Freddie switches on his toilet light.
20120714 23:50:42:90 The stupid light lights up Tyan's kitchen.
20120714 23:50:42:95 Rudy, who already thought he was about to die, shrieks and recoils.
20120714 23:50:43:01 This recoil includes a kick into the shine box that's still in place beside the door. The pistol inside is still loaded, still on a hair trigger.
20120714 23:50:43:02 The pistol discharges.
20120714 23:50:43:04 We all jerk at the noise and the flash. Tyan jerks back.
20120714 23:50:43:05 Tyan's firearm, the one he's holding in his hand, discharges.
20120714 23:50:43:06 Exploit resolved, retrieval j98::%lo07, link#1…

A ringing comes from somewhere but that might just be my ears. Movies don't prepare you for how loud guns are—so loud it feels like *I've* been shot. My instinct is to look where Tyan's gun had been pointing: the refrigerator where he keeps his food and any jars he's too weak to open. The ringing doesn't come from there, might be from behind me. I look around. Behind me is just the stove.

Tyan stumbles forward. A step. He triggers the kitchen fluoro. The room blazes. I want to step towards the fridge as well, want to know what that ringing noise is but I can't step forward. Something holds me back. Something behind me has a grip and it's keeping me in place. I rotate to see what it is and on the stove there's a steel saucepan. It is empty and it is ringing. A tiny lunk of black metal lodged in its side.

Tyan gapes at me.

'Fuck.'

I want to look at Rudy for some hint of what has happened but I can't. Something is preventing me from turning. What is that? Why is that saucepan *ringing* and *how* is it that loud?

To find the rope that has lassoed me I wave my hands around my waist like a hopeless nightclub dancer. Tyan responds with an appropriate, 'Oh fuck, Jason.'

No rope that I can find. What I feel is how slippery my belt is. I dab at my stomach, feel the wet even through the leather of my gloves.

'Oh, wait…'

I collapse and the moment the back of my head hits the lino the ringing stops and I hear my own screaming. A monotonal complement to the voice in my head: *this is happening this is happening this is happening this is happening this is happening.*

Any expectation that I could get shot and then bitterly prop myself against the wall and ask for a cigarette is properly laid to rest now when I defecate slightly.

A thumping noise from Rudy, like he's punching the door and I can hear him moan. Is Tyan hurting him? I can see only the piercing fluoro tube on the ceiling, press down on my stomach because that's what you're supposed to do with wounds.

Tyan is there. He hasn't moved. Stands by the light switch, gazing at me like he's just realised for the first time he has a son.

'Fuck,' I slur. 'You shot...'

Tyan steps closer. Eyes as big as eggs. Points aggressively at the fridge.

'It bounced...I didn't...The bullet bounced.'

When I cough I feel fluid in the crack of my arse.

'Don't hurt Rudy.'

'*What?*'

'Don't shoot Rudy.'

I cough again, feel the fluid suction against the floor.

'*Rudy,*' I shout. '*Rudy, man...You gotta go...*'

Tyan's sweaty face, its grey whiskers and chapped lips, it turns to look at where Rudy must still be cowering against the door.

Tyan blinks.

'Rudy's dead.'

'Don't shoot him...Please don't shoot him.'

'I'm not going to shoot him. He's dead.'

Tyan steps out of my eye line, leaving only the light on the ceiling.

'Don't shoot him,' I rasp.

Tyan's voice from somewhere. A soft voice. Equable.

'I won't. Don't worry, matey.'

The effort it takes to roll and look there at the door, a place only inches away but which feels like football fields, prompts a sleepy wave to crash on me and suck me under water then let me back up. The pain in my stomach has numbed like a burn.

Tyan stands over Rudy and he blocks my view but I can see feet and some legs and they're not moving. Two of Tyan's fingers press against Rudy's neck and he draws them away at a speed that indicates how much of a pulse they found.

'You said...' I have to summon my voice like an angry parent. 'You said they weren't real bullets...'

'They're not.' His disapproval of Rudy returns to his voice, disapproving this time of his mortality. 'There's no wound. He just died.'

Tyan shifts and there's Rudy's face. A child sent to the electric chair. An angel so surprised by something that he expired. One leg bent awkwardly beneath him because his personal comfort is no longer at stake.

'Fuck,' I say again with a weird sob.

Tyan murmurs, 'I don't know what happened...'

And I figure Rudy doesn't know either. Piers Alamein's AVRC. His heart condition. Risen again in his son. His last gift to Rudy in a long line of shitty gifts. The Alamein curse claiming one more oblivious victim.

'Ambulance?' I say. I really do phrase it like a question. Tyan was a cop; for all I know he's got a quick-solve for heart conditions and bullet wounds and people dying on your kitchen floor.

'Don't worry,' he says. 'Someone heard the shots.'

I roll on my back and cry out at the wet slapping sound that depicts just how much blood there is beneath me.

'Where is it?'

'What?'

Tyan raises the gun, but really he's just pointing angrily at me the way he would with a finger.

'The confession. Blake's confession. *Where is it?*'

'It's *not*...' I blurt. 'It's not...'

'What?'

'It's not...'

Tyan steps closer. Now he really shakes that gun like he's going to shoot me. On purpose this time.

'It's not *what*?'

'It's not real. I just said that. I bullshat you...To make you tell.'

Marnie's final words. Risen again in me.

At that, Tyan grabs at his hairline like this is too much information.

'I *knew* it. You *fucking stupid*...'

He whirls away in disgust, considers the room. The corpse against the door. Holds his hand to his head to help him think.

'Okay. You'd come to visit. We were sitting in the kitchen. And then he came in.'

I say, 'No.' But Tyan doesn't hear.

'You'd never met him. He didn't know you. He came in, and I had this…' He holds up the black firearm, so shiny it could be wet. 'I warned him but he said he was here to kill me.'

And I say, 'No, Dad.'

'We saw the toothbrush. It looked like a knife. He ran at me—'

'*I'm not lying anymore.*' My guts are in my throat.

'What?'

'I'm gonna tell.' I try to repeat it but don't have the strength.

'Tell them what?'

'*Fuck you.*'

'But…'

And he gapes at me. Gun limp. All the regret of life in his face. I'm turning dog.

Slowly this time he turns away, considers the room again as if he's just found himself here and doesn't recognise it. The muscles in his forehead twitch, widen his eyes in bursts.

'I gonna tell them,' I manage. But there's no need because he gets it.

'You know what that means?' Tyan says, fretful. 'You know what has to happen next?'

I want to be cool when I say this, but I'm mugging at the brightness of that fucking fluorescent oblong on the ceiling. Still, my voice is nice and hoarse.

'What happens next doesn't matter.'

71

He gazes at my wound, or at least, where my gloved hands are piled over my wound, weakly stemming the flow. And he's sad, like I'm already dead and he's grieving. Like there's nothing to be done.

Then he moves into the hallway, out of sight.

I shut my eyes. All I can see is the blood in my eyelids because of the kitchen light. I guess it's nice to know there's still blood in there somewhere.

Tyan returns. He's got a new-looking tracksuit on and the gun in his hand is different. It's silver while the black one is tucked under his arm. He seems to unfold the silver gun and a series of droppings fall into his waiting palm. Then he puts the black one down on the counter along with the bullets and puts his keys there as well and he comes at me with the silver gun.

I know he's not going to shoot me. I mean, I know that.

Down on his knees now like he's going to say a prayer over me. I feel compelled to demonstrate for him that I am in fact still alive.

'Fuck...' I say.

'You stupid bastard,' Tyan wheezes. 'You stupid, stupid bastard.'

He pats at my pockets, pulls out my phone with two delicate fingers, then he lifts my lifeless right hand, blood-smeared and dripping, yanks on the glove to get it off.

It's a father's-discipline face. A this-is-going-to-hurt-me-more-than-you face.

'I'm sorry, matey.'

The glove comes away with a gross thwacking sound and he drops it like a soggy condom to the floor. Then he presses the revolver into my hand, inches my finger over the trigger. The hand and the gun fall to the floor.

'You stupid bastard. I was going to do the test…the DNA test…'

'Why bother?' My voice is a slithery grunt. 'I know who you are.'

He stands, backs away, moves to the sink and washes his hands. Washes *my* blood off *his* hands.

It takes every muscle in my body to raise the weapon so that, when Tyan turns back and sees, it's pointed at him. But it's hardly pointed at anything. It's swaying like I'm drunk.

If this thing was loaded, I'd miss.

Still, it stops Tyan dead. His shoulders collapse and his stomach appears to expand, like he gives in. He scrutinises this bloodied harmless fool on his kitchen floor, waiting for it to happen.

And I pull the trigger. And the trigger goes click. And the hammer goes click. And that's all it does.

But it appears to trigger something in Tyan. His face curls into an outrageous grimace and his eyes bind shut and a sob bursts through his tautened mouth and he looks away to hide himself. Like my gun has shot him through with raw emotion.

His pudgy frame lurches to Rudy's corpse, stops short of it and leans across. He locks the door, lowing in long draughts through his nose. A funny way of crying, a cow in labour. I've never heard anything like it. Something wholly new, a musical note undiscovered until now. You'd think he was the one who'd been shot by his own father.

I whisper, 'Hey…'

I try to speak but can't. I try to shout at him but likewise.

Tyan moves past me with a purpose, keeping a wide berth of something I can't see but which I assume is a river of my blood. At the sink he drops my phone and opens a drawer and brings out a kitchen knife and he's weeping now like slowmotion laughter: *heee…heee…heee…*

He smashes the phone with the butt-end of the knife, runs water over it, twists it in his fat hands to be sure.

From somewhere now we both hear the sound of a police siren.

'Hey, Polygraph,' I say again.

He drops the pieces in the pocket of his tracksuit and looks to me, already disappointed in what I'm going to say.

I say, 'Come here.'

He steps closer, wipes tears from his face.

And I'm like, 'There's something else I've lied about.'

The curl in his lip makes me lol. The confusion in his eyes is a blessing.

'What is it?'

'Can't you guess?'

'Tell me.'

I only laugh because that's literally all I can do.

The siren closes in and Tyan looks to the sound, then back to me. His time is up. He takes the black gun from the bench and I see the tears shine on his face. When he looks at me for maybe the last time ever, I see red in his eyes. A shoulder-shudder. Tyan surveys the room for some kind of option but there's none. If there's any place in the world that isn't going to help you when your life is at a crossroads, it's this dismal kitchen. With another squeal, a child whimpering, he steps through to the hallway and he's gone. The door clicks shut, deadlocked.

The police siren is piercing now, and now it stops. Here's me, actually pleased to hear the party van outside. The irony. Tyan's keys are there on the counter, so no one's getting in without an axe or a brick through the window.

But first they'll evacuate the neighbours. That poor bastard next door with his bladder. Where's he going to pee while he's standing outside in his underwear?

I flick at the weapon, try to loosen my grip. My finger is caught against the trigger and I have to shake like it's molasses, not a revolver. Finally it gets free and skids across the floor. Not that it matters. My prints are on it. Which was the point.

The pain of staring into that light is too much and I turn my head away but all I'm looking at then is Rudy slumped in the corner, as witless now as ever.

Rudy's insurance won't pay out if he was on the verge of death when he bought it, like being dead now would suggest he was. I don't know much about the insurance business, not as much as I once pretended to, but it seems obvious to say that Elizabeth Cannon will get nothing.

Which means she'll be disappointed. Doubly disappointed if I don't survive because she won't get to kill me herself.

I can't look at Rudy anymore so I turn back to the light, surprisingly calm. The shock or the blood loss has generated some chemical in my brain like diazepam.

Nothing from outside. Tyan will be there, telling his tale. He'll have gotten rid of the bullets and the pieces of my phone.

The only option is to wait. This is the sandwich Tyan has made for me. But it's nice to think there's nothing *else* I should be doing. Responsibilities fall away when you're shot in the guts. I only have to wait for Tyan's plan to fail, for the paramedics to rush in and sew me up, or else for the other thing. The permalogoff. The big AFK.

Another wave of exhaustion hits and I close my eyes and hang on while it subsides. No strength in my arms now, nothing applying the necessary *compression* but for all I know I'm not bleeding anymore. Maybe it's only a scratch and now it's clotted and healing and this *paralysis* is just in my head. The fluoro glows so bright that I struggle and manage to raise a hand to block it out, and in that cool darkness the lassitude takes hold and I think this is literally as relaxed as I've ever been.

When I open my eyes I see the teeth.

Scratched there into the webbing of the hand that protects me from the light. But somehow the light is breaking through my flesh and it peeks out the edges of the teeth like there's a fire burning in my veins and the teeth only darken, crystal-clear silhouettes so defined they're three-dimensional, raised from my skin, embossed there and floating. My relaxation deepens and I sink into the linoleum and still the black teeth hold me, glowing, tongues of flame dancing beyond them like this is the sun itself and I am adrift, simultaneously underground and in orbit. I let my hand drop and the light burns into my eyelids and through them and through my brain and through the floor and down to the very core of the earth, pinning me in stasis for the wait on our deliverance.

PART V

They should ~~just~~ have the death penalty ~~for~~ people & like me.

72

The doorbell. It echoed through the house, held its volume as if time had stopped and none of what lay ahead would ever happen. So analogue, the man thought. It made you wish for a satellite to crash down through the roof and thrust these people into the modern age.

The door was opened by a young male who wore a jumper over a collared shirt. His face was tanned, his shiny hair flat like a lego man. Beyond him the expanse of the house was deserted but for the small dog in the backyard, visible through the living room and the spotless kitchen and the rear glass door. No further humans.

By his relaxed stare he was not surprised to find a courier on his doorstep in a hi-vis polar fleece, carrying a heavy cardboard box with a clipboard balanced on top.

'How are you today?' the courier said. 'My name's Benjamin. Package for you.'

The man sighed as though Benjamin's presence until now had been fine but these words presented an insurmountable problem. 'I think you had better leave it there and we will bring it in ourselves.'

He pinned an invisible lock of hair behind one ear, cocked his head to read the brand name on the box. His brow furrowed.

Benjamin said, 'The other bloke usually has me bring it to the cellar door. Just there under the stairs. I'm happy to.'

But familiarity with the house was not enough to put the resident at ease.

'I'm sorry,' he said with the tone of voice he probably used to discipline that tiny dog. 'Just leave it there and he'll come—'

'Now, I'm not going to hurt you, but I'm coming in.'

Benjamin placed the box down on the verandah tiles and pulled from the back of his trousers a crowbar. He pushed against the door.

The small man's neck-flesh wobbled. He was confounded at first, then Benjamin stepped into the doorway and the man fled the ground floor, heaved himself up the long staircase screaming indiscernible words, didn't stop to see that Benjamin wasn't following, that he'd tossed aside his clipboard; that he had, in fact, wiped his feet.

Benjamin's assumption that the cellar would be locked was correct. He jammed the crowbar into the crease in the staircase and barrowed his weight against it. With a third shove came a crack of timber and paint but it was the lock that gave, levering the door out and revealing a black unlit nothingness.

He found the light switch and flicked it.

It was the size of a disabled toilet, walled with cobwebbed racks and wine bottles, the ceiling slanted with the angle of the stairs.

Commotion from up there. Benjamin slipped in and shut the door.

The wine racks revealed nothing more than wine and racks. By edging out random bottles he found only the red brick of the walls behind, had to clap the dust from his hands. A ratty Persian rug covered the floor, ornate but apparently tasteless enough to belong out of sight. He peeled it back and saw a beetle run for cover, other dead insects noosed to the rug's belly, the sunken edges of the central floor tile.

Footsteps again on the stairs above. Not the panicked mallet steps of before but cautious ones in softer shoes. Inches from Benjamin's head the ceiling creaked. He was shaking but he hardly needed the crowbar to jemmy up the tile. It rose loose.

Packed into the cavity was a black garbage bag, slightly damp, enormous in comparison with its contents but heavy, folded around on itself so that Benjamin had to twirl it like a circus clown before he could reach in and grasp.

Papers. A will by Piers Alamein. Other important-seeming documents as well as newspaper. A *Daily Sun* front page featuring Rudy

Alamein. These he dropped to the floor and drove his hand back inside.

The footsteps arrived at the last stair and stopped.

The chiming rattle of keys.

Benjamin fingered more papers and finally a crease of plastic around something solid, graspable. He drew it out and the weight of the bag dissolved. It fell to the floor, leaving in his grip another bag, transparent. Inside were two more, snap-locked shut.

One held a document of four or five pages. Handwritten. The words unreadable through the plastic layers.

The other enveloped a thick and detailed artifact. The one he'd dreaded and hoped he'd find.

More rattling. The door shook. It seemed Benjamin hadn't ruined the lock by forcing it. Warm air swirled around him as it opened but he could barely raise his eyes from the plastic, smeared it with his glove, checking and re-checking he was holding what he held.

A tall man, gaunt and grey, spoke from the doorway.

'I thought it might be you.'

He would have to bend down to get through the door but he didn't try. Only stood out there in the afternoon light of the living room and loathed this intruder.

'Desmond Blake was your client,' Benjamin said.

The tall man's eyes sparkled with surprise, which he tried to hide.

'Who told you?' His voice was dry and he coughed for lubrication. Before he could continue Benjamin throttled the plastic wrappings, shook them in the air.

'He told you he killed Cheryl Alamein. He gave you proof.'

'Who told you about Desmond Blake?'

A cry from the top of the stairs: 'Tristan, the police are on their way!' A clear and careful voice, designed to be understood by the man in the cellar. Tristan didn't seem to hear.

'Who are you?' He asked, temperate. 'Not, I suspect, a community lawyer.'

Benjamin's shoulders shivered. He had no desire to speak quietly.

'Rudy's father sat in prison for *eleven* years. He went nuts. He *killed himself*. And you had this and you did nothing.'

'My agreement with Desmond Blake was that I would take the relevant evidence to the police after his death.'

'A fucking *agreement*? Piers Alamein is *dead*.'

The rage was overwhelming. He'd invited it to be, but now that it was he had to steady himself with a hand against the wine rack, heart drumming like an army.

Tristan said, 'Distasteful though it may be to you, whoever you are, solicitors have a responsibility to act in their client's interest. We swear an oath to do so.'

'*Fuck* you.'

'Please…' He raised a delicate hand. 'Put those items down.'

Benjamin held the bag like a dangerous animal was captured within. Such weight.

'It was Blake who told you Piers was changing his will.'

The tall man crossed his arms. You could see the instant he resolved to keep Benjamin talking, keep him here until the police arrived.

'Blake was in Severington. For matricide. Having Piers Alamein on the same floor was an infinite source of amusement for him. In conference I received regular updates about Piers's deterioration, the black teeth, the new will…'

'That's why you helped Rudy. Because you knew. It had nothing to do with some bullshit in the newspaper. You went to Rudy and you *told* him his father was innocent.'

'It was a moment of weakness.'

'There's a reporter at the *Daily Sun* who knows about this.' Benjamin shook the bag again. 'Did you tell *her* in a moment of weakness?'

'I never spoke to the press. But colleagues…It was difficult, being the only one who knew.'

'So difficult you did nothing about it.'

'On the contrary, I had the will annulled.'

'The fucking *will*? You had *this*. You had *everything*.'

'Everything but an ethically acceptable means of betraying my client.'

He drew his face even longer, could see the disbelief in Benjamin's.

Behind his horn-rimmed glasses his eyes twitched.

'It's not as though I didn't beg him to come forward. Someone must have fabricated the evidence against Piers Alamein and if that came out then Blake would look like a hero. That's what I told him, anyway. But he felt he had enemies enough. Then he received a rather dispiriting diagnosis and I persuaded him to write that statement. It took him all afternoon, because of his arthritis. But he got there. That's something, isn't it?'

'And then you hid it in your cellar.'

'On the proviso that I withhold it until the event of his death. And believe me, he took some convincing to agree just to that.'

'Step aside. I'm leaving.'

Tristan shifted his weight.

'I can't let you leave with those items.'

Benjamin raised the crowbar. Not menacing with it, just to be sure Tristan saw it.

'You think I won't hurt you? After what you've done?'

'Look here,' he said, raised his hands. 'Desmond Blake is dying. It's a matter of days. The truth will come out then. You won't be the only person calling for my blood when that happens.'

Benjamin repeated: 'Step aside.'

And he flung himself up the cellar steps.

In a single flinch the old man lurched away. A hand grabbed for Benjamin, for the plastic bundled in his grip, but it was mostly symbolic. The comic, sickened face watched Benjamin make for the door.

'Where are you going with them?'

Benjamin stopped. Turned, pointed the crowbar. Felt the dumbness of the steel through his gloves.

'*You* don't get to demand answers from *me*.'

'I think I do. In my own home—'

'Fuck, your nerve.' Despite taking a stand here at the door, Benjamin couldn't help a quick glance at the leafy street. Idyllic. You wouldn't believe a police car was rushing to get here. 'What would it take for someone like you to feel guilty?'

'You think this was *my* decision?' Tristan lingered there, wrinkles around his mouth growing deeper and longer even as Benjamin watched. 'It's *demanded* of me. You *commit* to your *client*.'

At the top of the stairs, standing this side of the big red door, was the other man, Tristan's partner. The terror on his face, his fear of Benjamin, was enough to indicate he didn't understand. Tristan had kept this secret to himself.

'You *met* Piers Alamein.' Benjamin's lips trembled. 'You saw what had happened to him.' And now, when he spoke, his eyeballs stung. 'You've seen what's happened to Rudy.'

Tristan dipped his head as if a script was taped to the floor and he had to check the line.

'You have to understand,' his arms held each other at the elbow. 'When you make this kind of commitment to a person, the whole point is...what happens next doesn't matter.'

And his face: he wanted Benjamin to understand. But Benjamin only walked away. Felt the cold air wrap around his head, as tight as his grip on the plastic bag. No sign of police cars. No further protest from Tristan and Co. No demand that he come back. No snide remark about the cheap plonk he'd left in a box on the doorstep, one bottle missing. Just a thirteen-year silence bidding him farewell.

While he drove home the day was dimming the lights, secret fingers of evening across the firmament. He opened the car window and the wind was more than cold, it was pain. It helped, to feel that. Focus there.

Benjamin did not make for the refuge of his front door, rather jogged on for warmth, came to Hobsons Road, passed the service station and the supplements store and the barber, his shoulders bunched, one hand happy and warm in his trouser pocket, the other jealously, achingly hugging the crinkled package to his chest.

It was his second visit to this nameless park in the twelve months he'd lived so close, the first being out of curiosity as well as the belief that a walk along the river would be a regular means of getting outdoors without having to interact with people. But it had remained, he thought as he moved through the boom gate and on towards the picnic tables, too much of a risk.

He stuck to the bike track that traced the river, didn't know the name of the river either. Maybe it didn't have a name. On its bank was a large shed and a sign offering group kayaking but the shed was locked, its roof and driveway overblown with black bracken and leaves. Not even with the protective membrane of a kayak would anyone touch that water in July.

On he went in the half-light. A momentary gaze at the clouds and his gloved fingers gripped the plastic and tore at it, opened it to reveal further layers. These he tore as well and drew from its insides the document, scrawled in something like a child's hand. He peered over it like just an impression would be enough. There were as many mistakes as words, crossed out with such vehemence they looked like scorch marks on the yellowing paper.

Beneath the Joad & Clark letterhead was a single word— AFFIDAVIT—and beneath that:

> I, Desmond Blake, the undersigned, of the Severington Correctional Facility, hereby make oath and state:

Then, in malformed, almost illegible writing:

> *I killed Cheryl Alamein on June 6, 1999.*

Benjamin jumped with a vocal shock: a cyclist had suddenly overtaken him. She gave no indication that she'd heard his exclamation and was soon around the bend. A shudder of blood hollowed out his stomach and he was beset with a nauseous reluctance to continue reading. There was, after all, no point.

> *I find myself speechless to some extent today. Mr Whaly said for me to write here about the incedient and I know it was about as serius as a crime could be I dont point that out in the sence you probely expected but I was refering to hitting her with the bottle. She died.*
>
> *Her husband was inprisoned for it and it's obvius I am many things but I am not a lier it was not him. I dont know why he got inprisoned except that I know sometimes inncocent people are inprisoned because our Justice system is not without it's falts and this is something that I think is wrong.*
>
> *The doctor has told me that I probely going to die of cancer of the lungs and so it's like Pauline Handson because if you are reading this it means that I am dead! I don't want to take this terible burdon to my grave such that I will not mince my words.*

Benjamin's feet carried him past the weeds and the grass and the grass that looked like weeds. The undulating path led along a row of conifers and he sniffed in the air the sheer unfamiliarity of this place. Parks and rivers. Wind and all the rest of winter.

> *My real father died when I was 11 and Henry Blake became my father but he was not he was actualy my step father but I had to be given his name I had no say in stopping it. Before him and Lydia my mother got maried we had to become Roman Catholic and I am glad we did but I was very confused at the time ha ha!*
>
> *When I was thirteen I killed my step brothers dog Conan but at that moment in the past he was not my step brother yet but he was almost. Gary was a bully and I think that bullying is wrong I put up with alot may I repeat alot of darision from Gary literaly. Conan (Labrador) would help him and do things for him and it made me very angry.*
>
> *I killed Conan with a rock while Gary at school and it distrubed me to the stage of peril I knew I should own up I would of told Gary because to see the look on his face but mother Lydia cort me and she simply could not contane her terror and and she had me berry Conan. I had to promisse to not tell anyone and she give me her new bible and made me promisse on it or else everything would go into catastrophy.*
>
> *After they got maried I got sent to Assumption and I was there then got expeled. I got work as trapper and a pest ex-terminator I didnt see my family.*

Each segment took a stutter of re-reads to properly comprehend. Benjamin rose the crest of a hill and found the mouth of a foot-bridge overstriding the silent water, a shortcut from Kensington to Footscray. In this openness the world felt smaller; perhaps a trick of the light. Again he turned the page, more sorting than reading, took his first step onto the bridge.

> *In 1999 I was working across from Cheryl Alamein and there was a cat and I told it too rack off it kept being a common newsance and I hit it with the shovell and put then the animal in the backlane.*
>
> *Cheryl Alamein and a man asked me to find the cat and I thouhgt it was in the lane but it was not. The cat was in the book-shelv and the boy was there with a cockaspaniel. Cockaspaniels are dumb dogs. The boy was who put the cat on the book-shelv his*

mum was really angry. You can not control flameable situations and I left.

When I finished the job I saw cockaspaniel going to the toilet on the mans car. He had a BMW and the dog went to the toilet on the tire and I was veryt angry and deeprest I dont like animals especialy that do things for bullys.

The wind caught the paper, tried to drag it from Benjamin's hands and over the handrail. The vase in its translucent sheath swung like a pendulum and poked his groin when he came to a stop at the centre of the bridge. It was stuck to its plastic wrapper, the blood on it had done that, was surprisingly adhesive. Funny how it's glue in your veins, Benjamin thought, whatever else you'd call it.

I went to the house because Cheryl Alamein said she was going to going away it was raining. I went there to kill the dog and I was going to berry it in the backyard but my flyer was on the frigde and I put the dog in the vent so she could call me like the cat and I would be there when the boy saw the dead dog with the knowing fact that it was me because Gary never knew it was me and so I put the dog in the vent.

Benjamin turned the page, harried by the cold gale.

Then Cheryl Alamein came home and I was very angry. I promised my mother that NO BODY would know what I did and I if Cheryl Alamein knew about me and this dog then they would know about Conan in all rastional probability. I tried to hide but she was looking for some one and she found me I was very angry and deeprest branding the vase and I promised such that I hit her on the head her life was taken. I know I could of left behind foot prints on the floor because of the rain but I burned my shoes I did not want to burn the vase I dont know why even tho I should of.

The sun was low and setting without splendour, sneaking away, hoping no one would notice. He turned up the collar on his jacket. Another cyclist ticked past. He felt he must look strange: shivering exposed on a bridge and shrinking from the cold, not demonstrating enough sense to go home. His knuckles ached from how tightly he held these items. Rain on his face. No, only water blown off the river, flashing onto the footbridge, onto Benjamin's clothes.

*For many days I was upset for what I had done. I am not a murderer.
I do not know what I was thinking? I have created a Jeckel and
Hide kind of caracter. They should have the death pennalty for
people like me. For a deturment and concepts such as this. I have
always excepted death but now I long for it. I was very discomforted
and angry I went to mother Lydia and told her. It was just like
the time I told her about the dog she was very horifide. But she
said I had to go to the police I said I couldnt because of Conan
and she said that does not matter and I was angry because I had
promissed and I had kept it and she said it wasnt inportent this only
increesed my instincts. I was very angry and then thats why I'm
inprisoned.*

*I am very sorry I hurt Cheryl Alamein. I love Australia and
I realise now it was wrong. I should not of promissed Lydia it was
because of her that I did it. I was in eror but GOD knows I tried to
do the right thing a clean conshious is the softest pillow. It's funny if
you think about it the people we do things for I am just like Conan
like that.*

*I dug up Conan and went to Gary's house and showed him
and he was very horifide and the dog bones had black teeth just like
the black teeth on my hand I am looking at them while I write this
affidavid.*

Signed by Desmond Blake and witnessed by Tristan Whaley, Senior
Partner at Joad & Clark, stamped with the word *Affidavit* as well as
an office address and a phone number.

The river rolled on below him. Anything that fell from this
bridge would be gone in an instant, borne away to wherever this
water went. Anything dropped from here would be irretrievable.

In a single motion Benjamin tore the document in half, then
in half again. After that the pieces became less symmetrical, each
one shredded to a geometric oddity. A hundred faded scraps in his
leather hands and while they prepared for allahu akbar one lone wolf
pre-empted the ceremonial moment and lifted off, not down but
up and away and Benjamin clasped the rest of them at his throat to
watch it swoop and dive-bomb the water. Despite the rolling of the
river it floated atop, held its position, caught in the tractor beam of
him, but the current was too strong and it slipped away under the
bridge. He lurched to the opposite rail, watched it drift easily toward

the highway overpass, had to blink to hold his gaze until it was indiscernible in the dusk.

With elbows on the rail he looked down through the mess in his hands and past it to the water, watched his fingers slowly splay, release puffs of white that drove, tumbling, hurriedly to the water. None stopped to float in his line of vision. They were instantly merely something he remembered holding in his hands.

The vase dropped directly. Didn't spin or tumble or flutter out of sight. It thunked into the water with all the conspicuousness of a murder weapon. In a moment it too was in the past.

Pulling his jacket tight he turned back across the bridge the way he'd come. It was difficult to see now as the daylight was giving out, even so that basic shapes were not differentiated. He navigated past the conifers and the picnic tables and the trash can, where he disposed of the plastic bags, spotted no one else brave enough to ride or walk through the park this evening. The desolation reminded him of the city on Christmas Day, an emptiness he'd often revelled in. But tonight he rushed home.

At his car he retrieved the bottle of wine he'd taken from the box at the lawyer's house. This he would use to put the moment at the river behind him. To convince himself that that which had happened had not happened. He trudged up the drive but stopped. Light in his window. Not a lamp or an overhead but a cool glow. A phone. Someone had broken in.

She might have left the door ajar again but he dug in his pocket for his key anyway and his hand got stuck because it was gloved. He removed the hand from his pocket and the glove from his hand, tucked the wine beneath an elbow and caught a glimpse of the black drawing on the webbing of his thumb and forefinger. As he climbed the steps he removed his other glove, licked a finger and rubbed at the black teeth, made circles that formed grey stains that he could just make out in the dark. By the time he reached the top of the stairs, the dull bulb that burned there, the symbol was wiped away.

He could taste the ink on his tongue. Free of gloves, free of drawings, his right hand turned the key in the lock and he stepped inside.